Praise for Peter Spiegelman's

DEATH'S LITTLE HELPERS

"With *Death's Little Helpers*, Peter Spiegelman cements his growing reputation as one of the finest of the new generation reworking the PI genre. Spiegelman is that rare novelist who knows what he wants to say, and he knows how to say it, which makes for an absorbing, suspenseful and thoughtful book."   —David Liss, author of
A Spectacle of Corruption and *A Conspiracy of Paper*

"Plenty of artful twists and turns. . . . Forecast[s] a flourishing career in crime for [the] series."   —*Newsday*

"An engaging, sometimes tender and ultimately explosive story. . . . [Spiegelman writes] with great power and effect."
—*The Huntsville Times*

"A thrilling read with lots of heart."   —*The Observer* (London)

"Peter Spiegelman has an equal intimacy with the workings of an investment bank and those of the human heart, and he can paint them with equally nuanced colors. A fine book by a fine writer."
—S. J. Rozan, author of *Absent Friends* and *Winter and Night*

"A taut, toothy thriller with one of the genre's most promising new protagonists."   —*Ruminator Review*

"*Death's Little Helpers* meets, and exceeds, the expectations created by *Black Maps*. In the short space of two books, Spiegelman has made a place for himself on the A-list of writers of noir fiction. Highly recommended."   —Bookreporter.com

"Engrossing and finely rendered narrative. . . . *Death's Little Helpers* is as emotionally rich and delightfully complex as its predecessor."
—*January Magazine*

PETER SPIEGELMAN

DEATH'S LITTLE HELPERS

Peter Spiegelman is a veteran of more than twenty years in the financial services and software industries and has worked with leading financial institutions in major markets around the globe. Mr. Spiegelman is the author of *Black Maps*, which won the 2004 Shamus Award for Best First Novel. He lives in Connecticut.

His Web site is www.peterspiegelman.com.

ALSO BY PETER SPIEGELMAN

Black Maps

DEATH'S
LITTLE
HELPERS

DEATH'S LITTLE HELPERS

PETER SPIEGELMAN

Vintage Crime/Black Lizard
VINTAGE BOOKS
A DIVISION OF RANDOM HOUSE, INC.
NEW YORK

FIRST VINTAGE CRIME/BLACK LIZARD EDITION, JUNE 2006

The Library of Congress has cataloged the Knopf edition as follows:
Spiegelman, Peter.
Death's little helpers / by Peter Spiegelman. —1st ed.
p. cm.
1. Private investigators—New York (State)—New York—Fiction.
2. Television personalities—Fiction. 3. Investment advisors—Fiction.
4. New York (N.Y.)—Fiction. 5. Missing persons—Fiction. I. Title.
PS3619.P543D43 2005
813'.6—dc22
2004061541

Vintage ISBN-10: 1-4000-3360-8
Vintage ISBN-13: 978-1-4000-3360-7

Book design by Virginia Tan

www.vintagebooks.com

Printed in the United States of America
10 9 8 7 6 5 4 3 2 1

For Adam, Ben, and David

ACKNOWLEDGMENTS

Thanks are again owed to many people for their help while I was writing this. To my early readers—Nina Spiegelman (who shares with the Nina of this story only her name), Barbara Wang, Joe Toto, and Jan Taradash—for their time, honest opinions, and invaluable encouragement. To Jay Butterman and Stewart Rothman, for technical advice, local color, and directions to Surrogate's Court (any errors in the nuts and bolts are mine, and mine alone). To Denise Marcil and her team at the Denise Marcil Literary Agency, for their unfailing support. To Sonny Mehta, for making this a better book. And to Alice Wang, for everything.

DEATH'S LITTLE HELPERS

1

"As a husband, he was a lying, selfish prick," Nina Sachs said, and lit yet another cigarette. Her silver lighter caught the late-April sun as it came through the big windows. She flicked a strand of auburn hair away from her face and blew a plume of smoke at the high ceiling. "And as a father, he's no better. But he's our meal ticket, Billy's and mine, and if something's happened to him—if the cash is going to stop—I want to know about it sooner, not later."

Nina Sachs was a few inches over five feet tall, and wiry. Her short straight hair was pulled into a blunt ponytail, away from a pale elfin face that was full of motion. Grins and frowns and ironic twists flickered by, and I saw a lot of her teeth, which were uneven but not unattractive. Her hands were quick and so were her hazel eyes. Nina Sachs was close to forty, but despite the chain-smoking she looked ten years younger.

"What makes you think something's happened to him?" I asked.

She crossed her legs and uncrossed them and regarded her small bare feet and her toenails, which were painted apple green. She crossed her legs once more and finally tucked them beneath her. She fiddled with one of her silver earrings and picked with a thumbnail at a fleck of paint on her black yoga pants. She took another hit off the Benson & Hedges.

"I've got a picture of him somewhere," she said, and uncurled herself from the green leather sofa. She crossed the loft with quick steps, opened the center drawer of an ebony desk, and began rummaging.

I didn't need a photograph to recognize her ex-husband. Though he hadn't been on television much lately, anyone who watched the cable business channels over the past few years had seen plenty of Gregory Danes. Still, I let her go on searching. I was happy for the distance. Between the smoking and the fidgeting, she was making me edgy.

"What makes you think something's happened?" I asked again. She pulled the desk drawer out and dumped its contents on the desktop. She sifted through the pile, her back to me as she spoke.

"Five weeks ago—right before he was supposed to pick up Billy for the weekend—he called to say he couldn't make it. He was all pissy about something and said he was taking time off—going away someplace—and had to postpone." A box of paper clips slid off the heap and scattered on the floor. Nina cursed and kept searching.

"He's canceled last-minute plenty of times, so I wasn't shocked. I said *Fine, whatever,* and we rescheduled for three weeks later. So three weeks comes, and we're here waiting for him to get Billy, and he's a no-show. No call, no message—no word at all. I tried his place, but there was no answer. I left messages on his machine and got nothing back." She turned to look at me and took another long drag on her cigarette. "That was nearly two weeks ago. Since then, I've tried his cell phone, his office, left more messages . . . and heard nothing." She ran her fingers across the base of her throat. "Maybe he just doesn't want to come back, or maybe . . . I don't know what. That's why I'm talking to you."

"What did they say at his office?" I asked.

Nina snorted. "At Pace-Loyette? They didn't say shit. All they gave me was a runaround and a weird vibe." Some envelopes and matchbooks joined the paper clips on the floor. She stared at them.

"Weird how?"

Nina turned back to the desk and started picking through the heap again. "My lawyer told me you were a cop before this PI thing," she said.

"I was a sheriff's deputy—an investigator—upstate. What kind of weird vibe did you get from Pace-Loyette?"

Nina Sachs laughed. "Deputy John March, huh? Get out of Dodge by sundown and all that?"

"Just like that. Weird how, Nina?"

"It was . . . I don't know . . . weird. I called his direct number—figuring I'd get his voice mail or his secretary—and instead I get bounced to some woman named Mayhew, in Corporate Communications, she says, who tells me Mr. Danes is away and I can leave a message with her. When she found out who I was, she got all freaked and transferred me to some legal guy. He started asking questions and finally it dawned on me: They don't know where Greg is either." Her cigarette was down nearly to the filter. She squinted at it and stubbed it out in a small metal bowl on the desk.

"He didn't say anything to you about where he was going?"

Nina shook her head and fished her cigarettes and lighter from a pants pocket. "He doesn't tell me shit like that."

"He ever do anything like this before—just take off?"

Nina shrugged. "I guess so."

I waited for more but it didn't come. "Care to elaborate?"

"There were a couple of times. Once, right after we were separated, he split for maybe ten days. And after the divorce was final he did it again, for two weeks. And I guess there was a third time a few years back—not long after the SEC people first called him in—he took off for a week or so."

"And each of those times he just up and left—with no notice and no word to anyone?"

"He didn't say jackshit to me, I know that, and he didn't call either. He just went away for a while, and then he came back."

"So what's different about this?"

She shrugged once more. "Maybe nothing, but . . . he's never been away this long before. And before, he called to cancel with the kid—he's never just been a no-show." Nina turned to the desk again and started pushing the mess around. "How'd you get from upstate to down here?" she asked.

I sighed. I'd been through all this two days ago, when her lawyer, Maggie Lind, had phoned me to set up this meet. But what the hell.

"I'm from down here. I came back when I was done with being a cop."

"How come you're not a cop anymore?" she asked. "You get into trouble?"

"I quit."

"I knew it was around here," she said. She padded across the floor, trailing smoke, and handed me a photograph. She perched again at the end of the sofa.

It was a Polaroid, ridged and faded, and it showed Nina and Danes side by side at a glass-topped table, under a big striped umbrella. There were palm trees and leafy plantings and part of a swimming pool in the background. Danes was dressed in canvas pants and a guayabera, and Nina wore a gauzy caftan over a wet tank suit. Her hair was longer and her face was fuller and less interesting—more conventionally and forgettably pretty.

Danes looked much as he did on television, the same wayward straw-colored hair, the same regular, somehow unfinished features, the same shadowed eyes and thin lips and vaguely mocking smile: the same overall impression of precocity and arrogance. His hand was on Nina's shoulder and she didn't seem to mind, and I figured the photo was at least ten years old—taken before the divorce, before Danes had become the head of equity research at Pace-Loyette and ubiquitous on the business channels, before his long slide down. I looked at Nina.

"How about his friends or family?" I asked. "Have you been in touch with them?"

"I wouldn't know who to try," she said. "He didn't have a lot of friends back when we were married, and I bet he has less now. And I sure as hell don't know any of them.

"And as far as family goes, Billy and me are pretty much it. Greg's old man died when he was five. His mother remarried, but she and the step-father died just after Greg got out of B-school. He's got a creepy half brother somewhere in Jersey, but I don't know when Greg last spoke to him." She smiled and blew out some smoke. "Pathetic, isn't it?"

"You said he sounded *pissy* the last time you spoke. Any idea what about?"

She shook her head again. "We don't exactly confide in each other, you know? We don't have that kind of relationship."

"What kind of relationship do you have?" I asked.

Nina got no farther than a smirk when a cell phone chirped. She cursed and tracked the sound to the kitchen, beneath some sections of the *Times* that were spread on the counter. She bent her head and spoke in low tones. I got up and stretched.

Windows covered one wall of the loft, from floor to ceiling. The metal-framed glass was thick and clouded, and some of the panes opened on a pivot. I pushed on one, and a small breeze came in. Sachs's place was in Brooklyn, on the third floor of an old factory building off Water Street, tucked between the Brooklyn and the Manhattan bridges and near enough to the Brooklyn–Queens Expressway that I could hear the rush and rumble of traffic. The outside air was warm, tinged with exhaust and soot and the sour, salty smell of the harbor and the East River. Even so, it was better than the heavy cloud of cigarette smoke and paint and old food that hung inside. I took a deep breath and looked down at the cobbled streets. They were quiet on a Monday morning. The loading docks across the way were empty.

Once upon a time, I'd roamed this neighborhood on a regular basis. It was twenty years ago, and I was in the eighth grade and hanging with a kid named Jimmy Farrelly. Jimmy lived in Brooklyn Heights, in a brownstone near the Promenade, and we'd ride the subway from Manhattan after school and walk to the river from the Clark Street stop. If the neighborhood had a name back then we didn't know it, and if any artists lived there we didn't care. We were drawn by the derelict factories and abandoned warehouses, by the rotting piers and the lattice of stone and ironwork overhead, and by a consuming interest in smoking dope, drinking beer, and learning, from Jimmy's neighbor Rita and her friend Angela, the finer points of French-kissing.

A lot of artists had moved to the area since those days, looking to homestead after being priced out of places like SoHo and TriBeCa and the East Village. The developers had followed them, and then came the realtors—who bestowed a name on our old playground: DUMBO, for Down Under the Manhattan Bridge Overpass. With the name had come immaculate art galleries, like the one downstairs, sleek coffee bars, like the one across the street, and designer grocery stores, like the one around the corner. The march of progress.

If she hadn't been an early homesteader, then Nina had paid a fortune for her place. She had an entire floor—an easy 4,000 square feet—with good light and a swatch of downtown Manhattan skyline in sight, if you craned your neck. The walls were unadorned brick, faded to a warm rose color, and the floors were cement, finished and sealed so that they were smooth and wet-looking. The high ceilings were hung with new ductwork.

The loft was divided into four distinct areas. At one end, behind white Sheetrock walls, were bedrooms and a bath. Next to these was an open kitchen, with pale wood cabinets, steel counters, and an armor-clad oven. Tatami mats defined the living area, which was dominated by a sleek L-shaped leather sofa, some matching chairs, a green glass coffee table, and tall freestanding shelves. The other end of the loft, walled off by unpainted Sheetrock and a white fabric scrim, was Nina's studio.

The space was impressive and also a mess. Besides the small havoc Nina had created around the desk, there was a collapsed stack of dog-eared art journals near the sofa and another on one of the chairs. There was an empty bottle of merlot on the coffee table, with two sticky-looking glasses beside it. Two more bottles were on the kitchen counter, along with the remains of several meals. The sink was full of dirty dishes, and everywhere the ashtrays were brimming. A mess—but a grown-up one.

I walked slowly around the living room, and nowhere did I see traces of Billy. There were no schoolbooks or comic books, no video games or back-packs, no sneakers or skateboards. And while there was clothing strewn about, on the backs of chairs, on countertops, and crumpled at the base of an overloaded coatrack, none of it seemed to belong to a twelve-year-old boy.

Nina was still muttering into the phone, and I drew back the white cur-tain and stepped into her studio. It was a larger space than the living room, and more sparsely equipped. A big drafting table and two elaborate easels stood in the center of the room. Three metal trolleys were parked nearby, laden with brushes, tubes of paint, solvents, palettes, and other tools of her trade. There was a steel utility sink along the opposite wall, and to one side of it some metal shelves and more supplies. A gilt-framed mirror—eight feet high at least—leaned against the wall on the other side. A commercial fan and two reflecting lights stood in one corner, near a scruffy armchair and a pint-sized stereo.

By comparison with the rest of the place, Nina's studio was immacu-late. The supplies on the shelves and trolleys were organized and tidy. The floor was bare and clean. The sink was empty but for a half-dozen brushes drying in a precise row at its edge.

Some pencil sketches were taped to the Sheetrock on my right: two of a female nude draped in an armchair, a third of the same figure kneeling, with head inclined, and two more of something that looked like the Flat-iron Building, set on a bluff over a churning sea. They were nicely done, with a sure delicate touch. There was a canvas on one of the easels, and I walked around to take a look.

I'd done a little online homework before my meeting with Nina and knew she had enjoyed some success as an artist. She'd had exhibitions in New York and Boston and London that were—insofar as I could decrypt the reviews—well received. Her work had been acquired by some notable private and corporate collections, and recently she'd been picked up by museums in Chicago and Dallas and LA. But I'd not actually seen any of her paintings, and I didn't know what to expect.

It was striking. The canvas was about three feet high by two feet wide, and the painting was in oil, with blues and grays predominant. I recognized the subjects from the sketches on the wall. The triangular building was at the right of the picture, set back, and the angry sea swirled in the foreground and to the left. The bowed kneeling figure appeared in a window, halfway up the side of the building.

But the final renderings were very different from the sketches. On canvas, the building was taller but more delicate and somehow resembled an ocean liner. The sea was more muscular and aggressive, and it merged without horizon into an empty, icy sky. The sea took on another aspect as well, of a roiling complex of city streets into which the building might at once sink and crumble. The kneeling figure was different too, more sinuous and sexual, and something—in the set of her shoulders or the angle of her head or the fall of her hair—left you certain she was crying.

Nor could the sketches hint at what Nina did with color and light. Her ocean was as threatening as a funnel cloud, and her sky as desolate as winter twilight. The yellow corona around the kneeling figure was as bleak and forlorn as a bare lightbulb.

"You find what you were looking for? Or you want to go through my underwear drawer too." I hadn't heard Nina come in. She was standing by the drafting table, her cell phone in one hand, a smoldering cigarette in the other. She was stiff and angry.

"This is nice," I said, gesturing toward the painting.

"Great. Swell. Next time, wait for an invitation. I'll be off the phone in a second—now get the fuck out of here." She did not wait for a reply but returned quickly to the kitchen and her conversation.

"I'll say it again: I don't do the installation shit. You got questions, talk to Nes, not me, okay?" Nina watched me as I walked into the living room. I stood by the windows. "I don't know—I'm not the answering service, either. Call the gallery and leave a message."

She snapped the phone shut and tossed it on the counter. She took a drag and looked at me through the smoke.

"You're a nosy bastard, aren't you?"

"It's part of what you're paying for," I said. "But maybe we should rethink that." Nina stared at me for a while, and then the tightness went out of her jaw.

"Okay, I was a little raggy. Sorry. All right?"

I looked at her for a couple of beats and nodded. Nina smiled. She came back into the living room and sat on the sofa.

"Armed truce," she said. She saw my puzzlement and smirked. "You asked me before what kind of relationship I've got with Greg, so I'm telling you: It's an armed truce."

"Meaning what?"

"Meaning we deal with each other when we have to but neither of us likes it. You know what I think of him; well, he feels pretty much the same way about me. He doesn't like the way I live or the people I hang out with. He doesn't like me. But we deal with each other anyway—for the kid."

"You have joint custody?"

Nina took another drag and cast about for an ashtray. "Basically," she said.

"What does that mean?"

Nina scowled and looked like she was going to bite, but she shook it off. "We have an informal kind of deal. Technically, I've got custody and he's entitled to monthly visitation. But we arrange things between us and he ends up seeing Billy more than that—when he doesn't cancel."

"He pay child support?" Nina nodded. "Alimony?" Another nod. "Everything current?"

"Until about a week ago, when the check didn't show."

"If he's in violation of your settlement agreements, you can take that to court. They might even help you find him."

Nina's mouth puckered and she shook her head. "You sound like my lawyer, for chrissakes. But trust me, court battles are definitely *not* the way to deal with Greg."

I nodded and thought for a while. "You said he doesn't have many friends. How about enemies? Does he have any of those?"

She laughed out loud. "Only a zillion or so. Being as fair as I can, John, I got to say that Greg is just not a likable guy. Smart, yes—even funny, in a nasty sort of way—but not likable. And besides the people who know him and don't like him, there are all those people who followed his stock advice. I don't expect they're too happy with Greg either."

Nina had a point, and I laughed a little too.

"Maggie told me you had good references," she said. I nodded. "She said she didn't know you personally but everyone she talked to gave you high marks for smart and persistent." I didn't disagree. Nina went on. "I hired a PI once before, you know, in the divorce. He was about twice your age and twice your size, and I had to talk real slow around him and use small words."

"What did he do for you?"

"Pictures, credit card receipts—the usual divorce stuff. He did his job."

"So why didn't you call him for this?"

"Because I didn't trust him as far as I could throw him. Plus, his liver's probably given out by now." She stubbed out her cigarette and looked at me. "So how about it—are you going to do this for me?"

I looked back at her. "Why haven't you talked to the cops?"

"The cops?" Nina Sachs looked appalled. "Why the hell would I do that?"

"Because they have a whole bunch of people who have nothing to do but work missing persons cases, and they have resources and access that I don't. If you really think something bad has happened to Greg, the cops are the way to go."

Nina shook her head vigorously and dug in her pocket for another smoke. "No fucking way. Cops—that's all I need. You know what Greg would say if I brought them into his business, snooping around? As torqued up as he is about his reputation? Jesus—he'd go ballistic."

I held up a hand. "You may not have much choice in the matter. His employers could file a report—if they haven't already—or a friend or neighbor could. Or the press might get hold of it. On a slow news day, they'd love a story like this.

"If something *has* happened to him, he might be grateful that you called the cavalry. Either that or he'll be beyond caring. And so what if he gets pissed at you for calling the cops; what do you care? You don't seem to like the guy much anyway."

Nina fired up another cigarette and shook her head some more. "I may not like him, but I've got to deal with him, for chrissakes. He'd make my life miserable over something like that—mine and Billy's both—trust me. If the cops get into this, let it be on account of somebody else, not me." Nina looked at me, waiting for an argument, but I wasn't going to give her one.

While I'd meant what I said about the police, I also knew what they were likely to tell Nina, or anyone else who filed a report: that there was nothing illegal in a grown man going missing, and nothing particularly unusual about it either; it happened every day, all across the country, and only rarely was foul play involved. They would take down the facts, and, as the guy had a history of disappearing for weeks at a time and there seemed no reason to suspect wrongdoing, the case would join a lot of others on a very big pile. There were many things the cops could do that I couldn't—at least not as easily, or legally—but there was something I could do that they wouldn't: make finding Gregory Danes my highest priority.

"So, how about it?" Nina asked again. "You going to do this or what?" I looked at her and nodded, and she gave me a quick, crooked smile.

I had a few background questions for Nina and she answered them and I was about to wrap up when we heard a key in the lock. The front door swung open and a dark-haired woman and a boy came in.

The woman was five-ten and supple, with cat-black hair precisely cut to shoulder length. It was parted on the side and fell in a glossy wing across her forehead. She had a long face, olive skin, and large almond eyes that were dark and vigilant. Her nose was straight and strong, and there were lines around her wide mouth and in the gap between her brows. I put her age south of forty, but not far south. I thought she might be Latin or Asian or both.

She wore a green silk suit with a simple cut and a thick gold chain on her neck. She fingered the chain absently as she looked around the apartment. She smiled at Nina, and the somber traces went out of her face. The smile disappeared when she looked at me.

The boy, I knew, must be Billy. He was small—five foot zero—and slight. His hair was very short and auburn, like his mother's, and he had her thin face too, though not her pallor. His eyes were watery blue and smudged-looking like his father's, and his mouth was thin-lipped. But there was none of Gregory Danes's mocking superiority in his son's face, at least not yet. Instead there was petulance and anger.

He wore sneakers that looked like bowling shoes and baggy jeans and a navy-blue parka, too heavy for a warm spring day. He shrugged it off and left it where it fell. Underneath, he wore a black T-shirt, too large for him, with part of a song lyric printed in white across the chest. *Like sittin' on pins and needles / Things fall apart, it's scientific.*

It was unattributed, but I recognized it: Talking Heads, "Wild, Wild Life." Everything old is new again. Billy's gaze skated across his mother and me and never paused. He headed for the kitchen, his skinny freckled arms stiff.

Nina stood and looked at the dark woman, who closed the door and returned a heavy key ring to her green leather handbag.

"The doctor see him?" Nina asked.

The dark woman glanced at me and nodded. "She saw him and said he is fine. She said he had no fever; it may be a virus that is going around." The woman's voice had a nice timbre, and her English was quick and exact but heavily accented. Spanish. "He is fine to go to school—even this afternoon if he likes." Her dark eyes flicked toward the kitchen.

"He doesn't like," Billy said, in a reedy voice. His head was buried in the refrigerator. The dark woman raised an eloquent brow. Nina jammed her cigarette into an ashtray. Billy leaned on the open door of the fridge and stared inside. Nina put an awkward hand in his short hair.

"C'mon, honey, Nes will fix you something—or we can order in—and then I'll run you over to school. You don't want to miss another day."

Billy twisted away from her, his shoulders hunched. "I don't want anything and I'm not going to school," he whined. "I still feel like shit." He took a last disgusted look in the refrigerator and disappeared into the bedrooms. Nina closed the refrigerator door and looked after him. The dark woman sighed heavily.

"He is just—," she began, but Nina cut her off.

"Don't say it, Nes. I know what he's *just*—he's just a moody son of a bitch." She shook her head and followed after Billy. I heard doors opening and closing and tight, muffled voices.

I turned to the dark woman, who was looking around the room. She stared at the mess on the ebony desk and pursed her lips. She put her green bag down and took off her suit jacket and somehow found a spot for it on the coatrack. Her ivory blouse was sleeveless and her arms were sinewy. She sniffed the air and wrinkled her nose. She flicked a wall switch; somewhere a big fan whirred and air began to move and freshen in the loft.

She picked up the desk drawer, slid it halfway into the desk, and swept the pile on the desktop inside. She knelt and scooped up the paper clips and envelopes and matchbooks, tossed them into the drawer, and closed it. Then she turned to the coatrack.

Her movements were quick and efficient and practiced. Clothes were plucked from the floor and the furniture and folded or hung. Journals were stacked on a shelf. Tables were cleared, counters were cleaned, and dishes scraped, rinsed, and put in the dishwasher. Her heels made hard sounds as she moved about the loft. She spoke not a word and paid me less attention than the furniture.

With her advent and Billy's, I felt as if I'd suddenly become audience to a piece of theater—something contemporary and far-off-Broadway—staged not so much for my benefit as for that of the actors themselves. My business with Nina was done for the moment and I could simply have left, but I didn't. I was curious; I wanted to see it play out. I got up and gathered a few full ashtrays and carried them into the kitchen. The dark woman was at the sink and looked at me.

"Garbage?" I asked.

She looked at me some more and finally pointed. "Under there," she said.

I emptied the ashtrays in the trash and went out to get some more. When I returned, the dark woman was drying her hands on a dish towel.

"I was rude. I apologize. It was a very hectic morning." She put out a hand. "I am Ines Icasa. You are the detective, no?" Ines—Nes.

"John March," I said.

Her grip was firm. "Come, sit," she said, and I followed her into the living room. She retrieved her purse and we sat on the sofa. She took a gold lighter and a blue package of Gitanes from her bag and dug in the package for a cigarette. It was empty.

"*Mierda,*" she said softly, and crumpled the pack. There was a fresh box of B&Hs on the coffee table, and Ines slit it open with a sharp well-tended thumbnail. She drew out a cigarette, tamped it down, pinched off the filter, and fired up the ragged end.

"You have settled things with Nina? You will look for Gregory?" I looked at Ines but said nothing. She didn't seem to mind. She ran a hand through her hair and over her neck, and I saw a scar on her smooth right arm, on the inside, just below the elbow. It was wide and shiny and flat.

"It is enormous trouble to go through," she said. She exhaled a great cloud and watched the draft carry it away. "As busy as she is—she should not waste her energies." Ines turned her vigilant eyes on me. "But this is not your concern, I know," she said.

A door opened and closed and Nina Sachs stood in the kitchen. She leaned against the counter and rubbed her forehead with the heel of her palm and sighed. Ines went into the kitchen and stood very close to her and spoke softly. After a while, Nina bowed her head and rested it against Ines's breast. Ines stroked her hair and neck, and Nina ran her fingers up Ines's bare arm, from elbow to shoulder and back again. Then she leaned away slightly and turned her face up and they kissed.

They kissed slowly and for a long time, and when they finished they stood entwined, looking at me. Ines was without expression; Nina wore a smile that was strangely like her husband's.

"You still here?" she said. "I thought we were done."

I nodded. "I'll call in a couple of days," I said. "Sooner, if I learn anything." They turned away from me and back to their soft conversation. I let myself out.

2

Flesh & Blood was a new place just off Union Square that specialized in red meat and game birds and nostalgia for the bull market. It occupied what was once a firehouse, and the hundred-year-old building's elaborate plaster and tile and brass work had been lovingly restored and augmented with dark wood paneling and crystal chandeliers and a bar across the back that looked like J. P. Morgan's yacht. It was a small place, but its designers had successfully achieved the cavernous feel and stupefying din of much larger spots. The wine list ran to several volumes, as did the list of single malts and cocktails. The waitresses—and there were only waitresses—were uniformly young and attractive, and clad in short black skirts and white shirts with plunging necklines. If not for city ordinances to the contrary, they would certainly have had cigarette girls in spike heels and fishnets working the tables and firing up the customers' stogies. It was not my usual sort of place, but Tom Neary was a slave to food fashion, and I owed him more than a few favors—the latest one being this job for Nina Sachs.

He was at the restaurant when I arrived, standing near the hostess's podium and making the hostess slightly nervous. Not that Neary was particularly threatening—in fact, with his short dark hair, clean-cut good looks, and horn-rimmed glasses, he could pass for a grown-up Eagle Scout.

And he wasn't saying anything, or doing much at all besides studying the platters that the waitresses hoisted by. But at six-foot-four and 250 pounds, he had a tendency to loom.

Neary wore a dark suit, a white shirt, and a striped tie—the same G-man look he'd sported when I first met him, back when he was with the Bureau's resident agency in Utica, and I was a sheriff's investigator in Burr County. Nowadays, though, the clothes were more expensively cut. Gone from the Feds over three years, Neary had a big-deal job with Brill Associates, a big-deal corporate security and investigations firm. The division he ran covered the whole East Coast, and his clients included some of the largest banks and brokerages around.

Neary was more comfortable in the private sector than he had been at the Bureau; his masters at Brill let him run on a much looser lead, so long as revenues kept growing. And now that he was firmly ensconced in management himself, a little of the edge had come off his reflexive distrust of authority. And, of course, the money was a whole lot better. Neary used to worry about the moral gray areas of private security work—his Jesuit schooling, he said—but he seemed to navigate those waters well enough, and I didn't know if he still gave it much thought.

There were plenty of things I didn't know about Neary. I wasn't a guy he invited over for Sunday barbecues or a guy he sent family photo cards to at Christmastime. But he and I had traded favors for years now, and I knew the important stuff—that he was smart and tough and could think on his feet. That he knew the difference between what was right and what was expedient. That I could trust him.

Neary offered me a massive hand and we shook. The hostess looked relieved and led us to a table near the back. Neary hung his suit jacket on the chair, loosened his tie, and unfurled a white cloth napkin on his lap. A blond waitress recited the menu to us, and he listened closely and nodded slowly as she spoke. She took our drink orders and left, and I took a closer look at him.

Success was taking its toll. Behind the glasses, his brown eyes were bleary, and the skin beneath them was pouched and dark. There were new lines around his mouth and new gray in his hair. His big shoulders were slumped and rounded. He yawned and stretched out his arms and rolled his neck. I spoke over the clamor.

"Too much work?" I asked.

"Too much work, not enough hours. Too many meetings, too much talking—" There was a muted chime from under the table, and Neary pulled something hardly larger than a deck of cards from his belt. It was black and had a tiny screen and keyboard on the front.

"E-mail," he said. "Like a fucking electronic dog leash." But he read it. He shook his head and put the deck back on his belt. The waitress returned with a bread basket and our drinks: ginger ale for Neary, cranberry juice for me. She left with our lunch orders. Neary swallowed some ginger ale and rubbed his eyes. "You take the job?" he asked.

"About an hour ago. Thanks . . . I think."

"You're not sure?"

"You ever meet Nina Sachs?" I asked.

He shook his head. "I've known Maggie Lind for a while, and done some work for her and her clients, but not Nina Sachs. Why?"

I shrugged. "A difficult personality."

"I thought that was the definition of *client*," Neary said. He reached across the table for a roll.

"Why did Brill pass on this?" I asked. "Was it too small for you guys?"

"Small was part of it," he said. "But we had a conflict of interest, too. Brill is on the short list to take over security services for Pace-Loyette."

I thought about that for a while. "Nina Sachs told me that Pace had more questions than answers about where Danes might be."

Neary nodded, eyeing an elk steak that passed our table, gleaming and smoking. "If we win this beauty contest, I expect that finding him will be one of the first things Pace management asks us to do. If you've already located him by then, all the better."

Wheels within wheels. I smiled. "Why are they so interested?"

"Danes isn't just another office grunt," Neary said.

"I know, he's their wunderkind stock analyst—or he was until a few years ago, when he crashed and burned along with the rest of them. Now I guess he's like all the other ex-superstars, the pile of dog shit on the kitchen table that everyone's trying to ignore."

Neary smiled. "His management is afraid he might be an exploding pile of dog shit." I raised an eyebrow and Neary continued. "You see the articles in the *Journal,* on pending enforcement activity?" I shook my head. "I thought you followed this stuff," he said, smiling. "I thought it was in your blood."

"I'm in recovery for it. What's the *Journal* say?"

"They've been running a series on what the next wave of Fed actions might be. Speculation is that the SEC and the Justice Department are look-ing at the small boutique firms—the niche players—and that they're set to land hard on anyone who didn't come to Jesus when they had the chance a couple of years back."

"And Pace falls into that category?"

"Yep. They've got a nice little franchise, providing investment-banking services to tech companies. They're a one-stop shop: doing M and A, underwriting, lending, syndications, and research. A lot of folks think they never really fessed up, back when the analyst shit first hit the fan—which could make them a prime candidate for some Fed attention this go-round. Pace management has consistently denied any wrongdoing—big surprise—but it's no secret that they're nervous."

"Danes is a part of their worries?"

"He's been their chief analyst for a long time. He'd inevitably be at the center of any investigation into whether or not Pace tailored their stock recommendations to curry favor with their investment banking clients—or potential clients. A firm in that position has to do some fancy dancing with a guy in Danes's spot. A guy like that is under a lot of pressure. He could be . . . unpredictable. He could do damage. So they've got some tough calls to make."

"Like what, whether they can serve him up to the Feds before he cuts a deal of his own?"

Neary laughed. "They haven't been quite that blunt about it with me," he said. He drained his ginger ale and waved to the waitress for another. "But they *are* worried about what Danes might be up to."

"Is that just corporate paranoia, or has Danes given them reason?"

"The last time they saw the guy, he was storming out of his office after a twenty-minute shouting match with the head of the legal department, and he was muttering something about forwarding his e-mail to the SEC. The next thing they know, he's on vacation. It got them a little nervous."

"Very dramatic," I said.

"But not out of character," Neary said. "Not for him. You know much about the guy?"

"Not too much. I've seen him on the tube—though not lately. Today I heard he's an asshole, unreliable, a bad father, a liar, and friendless—the usual stuff you get from the ex. But I realize that might not be the whole story."

Neary made a *maybe, maybe not* shrug and started to speak, but he was interrupted by our waitress, bearing lunch. Neary's buffalo steak ran with blood and juices and threatened to overwhelm his plate. My duck sandwich on sourdough was a bit smaller—but just a bit. She laid platters of carrots, steamed spinach, and spicy onion rings in the middle of the table. I took a bite of my sandwich. Neary cut himself a piece of steak and chewed it with his eyes closed. He sighed and nodded to himself. Finally, he came back to earth.

"I never met the guy, but I got an off-the-record earful from some folks at Pace. According to them, Danes is a massive pain in the ass: an egomaniac, a bully, and half a nut job to boot—maybe more than half." He paused to savor another hunk of buffalo. Color was returning to his face, and his eyes had lost some of their muddy look.

"When the market was up and he was on TV every other day, he was a real prima donna. He roared around the office like a bull in a china shop, terrorizing everyone who crossed his path—including senior management."

"Nice hobby, but maybe not wise."

"Apparently he wasn't too worried. He fancied himself the greatest thing since sliced bread—or the smartest thing, anyway—and he had the press to back him up. He barely tolerated the less gifted—which, according to him, covered pretty much the rest of the world. And they tell me he reserved a special contempt for the Pace-Loyette management committee, his bosses. Thought they were bureaucrats, second-raters, et cetera, and he made no secret of his feelings."

"No one ever took him out to the woodshed for an ass-whipping?"

Neary shook his head. "I guess the committee tried to get him to chill a couple of times, but in those days—when the market was riding high, and Danes was their analyst poster boy—he had them by the balls, and he knew it."

"He sounds more like a head trader than an analyst," I said.

Neary nodded. "Except back then he made more than any trader at Pace." He picked an onion ring off the platter.

"I take it he toned down his act when the market tanked."

"A good guess—but wrong. The Pace people tell me that, if anything, he's gotten worse. Going from hero to goat overnight was a real kick in the head for him—which is maybe understandable. I mean, one day he's everybody's favorite market expert, and the next nobody takes his calls. That's got to hurt."

Neary shook his head and helped himself to more onion rings.

"Once he got over the initial shock, he demanded that his management get out there and defend his good name—circle the wagons, call out the marines, that sort of thing. That went over like a lead balloon, of course.

Pace-Loyette just wanted it all to go away. Their tactic was to say as little as possible, and they suggested to Danes that he do the same. That apparently made him crazy—or crazier. He's gone from arrogant and contemptuous to openly hostile and paranoid. He claims management is setting him up as a fall guy."

I worked on my sandwich for a while and thought, while Neary put an end to his buffalo. "If he's so hostile and so nuts, why hasn't Pace gotten rid of him?"

Neary put his flatware at parade rest and took up his napkin. "If not for this SEC threat, and the investor grievances still floating around, they would have. As it is, they're reluctant to force him out—and all but guarantee that he becomes a hostile witness in any action. They need to keep up at least the pretense of a united front."

"Then why not do what other firms have done? Make a deal with the guy. Agree on a sum in exchange for a nice quiet resignation."

"From what I hear, the issue with Danes is ego, not money. He wants his rep restored; he wants vindication. He's got no interest in going gentle anywhere."

"So he's still got them by the balls."

"It seems to be a talent of his."

I finished my sandwich and the waitress came by to clear the table. We passed on dessert but said yes to coffee.

"How good is the *Journal*'s information?" I asked. "How likely is it that the Feds will target Pace?"

Neary snorted and shook his head. "How the hell should I know? I'm only slightly more welcome than you are down at One Saint A's these days—which means not at all. And I've been getting the cold shoulder at the Woolworth Building too."

One St. Andrews Plaza is downtown, near the courts and City Hall, and it's where you find the office of the U.S. Attorney for the Southern District of New York. Neary and I had had dealings with that office late last year, as part of a case he'd helped me with, and the ill will we had left in our wake apparently extended a block or so west, to 233 Broadway—the Woolworth Building—and the regional offices of the Securities and Exchange Commission.

"Tell me these guys have nothing better to do than nurse their grudges," I said.

Neary gave a rueful laugh. "Don't kid yourself. We got special training in that, down at Quantico."

"Still, I find it hard to believe all your sources are dry."

Neary shrugged. "I've got some friends of friends who tell me that Pace is just one of several firms the SEC is looking at. Apparently, no decision's been made on who or when."

"Have they been talking to Danes?"

"Not that I've heard." The waitress refilled our cups and Neary's belt chimed again. He pulled the wireless out, peered into the tiny screen, and read. He shook his head and sighed.

"Fuck it, John. How about we give up the investigation shit and go halves on an eatery someplace. Maybe a bistro in Murray Hill or a tapas bar in the East Village. It couldn't be more aggravation than this." He drank some coffee. I smiled.

"Has Pace filed a missing persons?" I asked him.

Neary ran a big hand through his hair. "Not yet. So far they've convinced themselves it's not their responsibility. And it's not like they're in a big hurry to have him back. Besides, they don't relish police attention or the kind of publicity that goes with it."

He reached into an inner pocket of his suit jacket.

"A present for you," he said. It was a small paperbound book with yellow covers. On a gray square on the front were the letters *PLS* in black capitals. "Pace-Loyette phone directory. I marked the names that might interest you." I looked at Neary. He looked back.

"You're awfully helpful today," I said. "And you know a lot of Pace-Loyette gossip, considering they're not a client yet." Neary smiled enigmatically and drank more coffee.

"I like to look before I leap," he said. Wheels within wheels.

It was late afternoon by the time we picked our way across Union Square toward the subway station. The crowd was light at the farmers' market in the square, and the vendors were restocking for the evening rush. The yeasty fragrance of baked goods, the scent of cut flowers, and the earthy smells of produce and potted plants masked the less appealing city odors. The sky was full of high thin clouds and pink light. We walked slowly, looking through the stalls as we passed. Neary's wireless chimed a few times along the way, but he ignored it. We crossed 14th Street and stopped outside the station and shook hands.

"You still seeing that neighbor of yours—what was her name?" Neary asked. The question took me by surprise.

"Jane. Her name is Jane," I said.

He nodded. "You look . . . better." His belt chimed again and almost simultaneously his cell phone trilled. He shook his head. "Fuck this," he said, and disappeared into the subway.

It was a short walk home, and I went back through the farmers' market. I stopped at a flower stall for some tulips for Jane.

Winter had taken hold early—well before Christmas—and it had held on tight till April Fools'. Nearly every week had brought a storm, and in between the blizzards and the frozen rain there had been long stretches of head-cracking cold and breathtaking wind. It seemed that I'd been running through ice and sleet and blackened city snow forever. So these last few weeks had been a gift.

Overnight, the plow shavings and dirty rinds of ice had vanished from the curbsides and intersections, and a drenching rain three weeks ago—the day we'd changed the clocks—had sluiced away the sand and salt and flotsam that remained. Feathery blossoms had appeared on the trees, faintly at first, like tentative green sketch marks, and then with more color and conviction. Grass was coming in on the dirt patches in the parks. Even now, the sidewalks and buildings had a scrubbed, surprised look—like a drunk, waking up sober and in his own bed for the first time in a long time. I picked up my pace.

I turned west on 20th Street, and ran between Peter Cooper Village and Stuyvesant Town. I headed south at First Avenue, and west again at 17th Street, past some Beth Israel Hospital buildings and over to Stuyvesant Square. I had five miles behind me. I checked my watch. It was after seven and there was still some light in the sky. I felt loose and limber, and my breathing was easy. I was good to go for another two. I dodged around a pair of dog walkers on Rutherford Place and went west on 15th Street. Thoughts jumped and skittered in my head as I ran, like a ball over a roulette wheel.

Nina Sachs was an edgy, prickly woman, and she emanated a tension that seemed to permeate her household. It was there in her son—in the painful twist of his shoulders as he shrank from his mother's touch and in his thin, angry voice. And it was there in Ines Icasa, too—in her quick movements about the apartment and in her face that was like a smooth dark-eyed mask.

There was something about Nina's story that didn't sit quite right.

Maybe it was her reluctance to call the police—and risk upsetting the ex-husband she so obviously disdained—that didn't make sense. I'd seen enough of divorced couples, though, to know that sense only rarely entered into things—and particularly not when kids were involved. And I'd had few clients whose stories hadn't raised at least an eyebrow.

I turned north onto Irving Place. The street was quiet and yellow light came from the windows of the town houses and old brick apartment buildings. The block was lined with spindly trees, studded with white blossoms. A gust of wind sent some drifting, like fat snowflakes, as I passed. My thoughts turned to Jane Lu.

We'd met last November, when Jane moved into the loft apartment above mine, and fate—in the form of my younger sister, Lauren—had made our meeting inevitable. Lauren owns the apartment I live in, and she works at the dot-com that Jane has been nursing back to health for the last year. Lauren also takes a touching, if sometimes invasive, interest in the state of my social life. But in this case I had no complaints. My attraction to Jane was immediate and powerful and like nothing I'd felt in a long time.

Jane and I were lovers by New Year's, and in the brief hours that we weren't working—in the odds and ends of late nights and early mornings and rare weekends off—we fell into a sort of intimacy. We slept together and ate together, and we walked the city and talked at length about work and politics and the sad, sorry state of the world. It wasn't a lot of time as the clock told it, but in the years since my wife had died it was more time than I'd spent with anyone besides myself. It was also a precarious thing.

By tacit agreement, we kept our relationship balanced in the present tense—with few references to our pasts and none at all to any prospects beyond the most immediate. And when anything threatened that equilibrium, we would retreat to the familiar security of our jobs. I'd had some practice at this, and so had Jane.

Jane didn't often withdraw, though she had ample reason to be wary. In fact, she had ample reason not to touch me with a ten-foot pole. Not long after we'd met, Jane was swept up—and almost swept away—in the violent currents of one of my cases, the same one that had run me afoul of the Feds downtown. Her injuries had been slight, but only by a hairsbreadth, and she'd seen firsthand the ugliness that could erupt in my life, that was a part of it. Jane herself never mentioned the violence, and I never asked, but she knew how close she had come—closer than inches—and she knew how my wife had died. I came to the top of Irving Place, and looped twice around Gramercy Park. The sky was reddening, and purple shadows lay on the square.

It would be four years in August—four years since Anne was murdered, the final victim of a man I'd suspected in a long string of killings. Four years since my own arrogance and stupidity had put her in harm's way. I'd stopped being a cop—or much of anything else—right after the funeral, though it was another few months before I got sober enough to resign. After that, I was alone with a ravenous, angry grief that I'd been certain would swallow me whole.

As it happened, it didn't—at least, not entirely. It left some scraps behind, bits and pieces, some threads and a few shards, and from them I pasted together a life—a half-life, my sister Lauren would say—of work and running and solitude. It was sparse, but it was manageable. It was what I had and what I knew, and I wasn't sure that I could handle much more.

I turned north on Lexington Avenue and ran faster.

It was nearly seven-thirty by the time I got back to 16th Street. The arched windows that run across the front of the converted factory building that I live in were dark. I took the elevator to the fourth floor and flicked on some lights. My place isn't half the size of Nina's, but it's big enough, with high ceilings, bleached wood floors, and a wall of tall windows. There's an open kitchen in cherry and granite at one end, and a bedroom area and bathroom at the other, and in between a few pieces of comfortable furniture, mostly in leather and dark woods.

I drank water from a bottle in the refrigerator. Then I stretched for ten minutes and peeled off my running clothes and stepped into the shower. When I stepped out again I smelled curry and cilantro and coconut milk, and I heard faint guitars. I wrapped a towel around my waist and walked out of the bathroom.

Jane waved at me across the loft. She was sitting at the head of my long oak table, a cell phone at her ear, a pen in her hand, and a thick sheaf of documents in front of her. Farther down the table was dinner—chicken satay, pad thai, vegetables simmered in curry and coconut milk, and crab rolls—all from the Thai place around the corner. Caetano Veloso was singing soft Portuguese from the stereo. I picked a crab roll from its white cardboard box and took a bite.

"Shit," Jane said into the phone. "We sent them the audit papers three weeks ago, Roger. They're only getting to them now? What lazy bastards." She was wearing a white MIT T-shirt and snug blue jeans. Her small feet were bare, and there were two black loafers under her chair. Her left leg was tucked beneath her, and she brushed the ball of her right foot lightly against the floor.

Jane was about five-foot-four and slim, with a shapely layer of muscle on her arms and legs and on her flat belly. Her cropped jet-black hair was damp just now, and I figured she'd stopped upstairs to shower and change. She listened to Roger talk and said "uh-huh" and jotted notes in the margins of a page, and there was an intent look on her heart-shaped face. Her small mouth was pursed, and the pout in her bottom lip was more pronounced. Her fine brows were furrowed as she scanned the pages. She looked much younger than her thirty-four years.

Jane made some final notes and put aside the document. Roger spoke, and she drummed her short glossy nails on the tabletop. She took up another document and flicked through the sheets.

"I'm on page seven of the memorandum of understanding, third paragraph. You with me?" She waited. "They screwed up the revenue targets for year two.... Yeah, all four quarters." Roger talked some more, and Jane looked at me and rolled her eyes. She made a *one minute* gesture. "And the same thing with the head-count projections on the next page. You see that? ... All right, I've got to eat now. I'll call you when I'm back in the office." She laughed. "Yes, I actually eat, Roger." She closed her phone and sighed heavily. She looked me up and down.

"Nice outfit," she said, smiling.

I smiled back. "Glad you like it. How's your deal going?"

"*Lurching* is the word that comes to mind. Par for the course with law firms and investment banks, I guess; lots of well-credentialed people billing lots of time while avoiding much actual work. Pass me those noodles, will you?" I handed Jane a container and a pair of chopsticks. She ate from the box. I sat down next to her with the container of crab rolls.

Jane is a CEO-for-hire, a kind of über-consultant called in by the boards of companies in deep trouble to save their sinking ships—or at least to get a good price for the scrap. Her gigs are strictly short-term, two years or less, and she demands—and gets—a piece of the action for her efforts. Jane was brought into the dot-com about a year ago, by the venture capital firm that held a majority stake in the company. Her mandate was to get the business back on its feet, make it profitable, and find a buyer, and through a combination of scary intelligence, relentless energy, and icy political savvy wrapped in irresistible charm, she was three-for-three. For the last six weeks, she'd spent most of her time on closing the deal.

"You're really going back in?"

"I have to. They're reviewing our contracts tomorrow, and I've got people getting ready. They'll need help."

"So it's going to happen?"

Jane picked a crab roll from my container. "It'll happen. It may age me by ten years—but it'll happen. It's a great fit for the buyers, a great price for us, and the best thing for the company. It's a win all the way around. Slide those veggies down here."

I did, and helped myself to a skewer of chicken satay. "Are they still asking you to stay on?"

Jane winced and shook her head. "It's just a crush," she said. "They'll get over it." She got up and gathered her papers and stacked them on the kitchen counter. She saw the tulips there. "These are pretty."

"They're for you," I said.

Jane smiled. She opened a cabinet beneath the counter and came up with shears and a blue glass vase. She slit the wrapping on the tulips and snipped an inch from the bottom of the stems. Her movements were quick and sure. She ran water in the vase and put the tulips in.

"Nothing they can do to make it worth your while?" I asked.

"Nope. The buyers are okay, but it's still a big company and way too much of a boys' club. There's no way I'd sign up for that again."

After B-school, Jane had done time at a prestigious investment bank and at a big management consulting firm, and both experiences had filled her with a fierce resolve to be always self-employed.

"Besides," she said, "it's been a long year. I've got another few weeks on this deal, and all I want afterward is to ride into the sunset." Jane looked up at me. "Have you thought any more about riding along?" she asked, and the air seemed to thicken between us.

In the brief reprieves she granted herself from the office and the culmination of her deal, Jane had been planning a very long vacation, and she'd invited me to join her. Guidebooks and travel magazines had been turning up in my apartment for weeks now, and we'd been tiptoeing at the edges of this conversation for almost as long. Each time we did, it was a cautious tug-of-war, a wary testing of resistance and balance over suddenly unstable terrain. And each time left us both a little edgy.

"Sure," I said.

She cocked an eyebrow. "Sure, you've thought about it, or sure, you're coming?"

"I've thought about it. I'm still thinking about it."

"Thinking that it's a good idea?"

"That it's a good idea, but . . ."

Jane looked down at the flowers. "But what?"

"But I took a job today, and I don't know if it'll be a long one. I have to see how it plays out."

Jane pursed her lips and nodded minutely. She stared at the tulips and spent a while rearranging them in the vase. "I guess your trip to Brooklyn went well," she said eventually.

"Well enough," I said, and I told her about my meeting with Nina Sachs and my lunch with Tom Neary. She listened carefully and shook her head when I was through.

"If it was anyone else, I'd say maybe he'd run off to hide his face in shame. But as it's Danes, my bet is that some investors bought him a room at the Jimmy Hoffa Hilton." There was a wry twist to her mouth and I was relieved to see it.

I laughed. "Do you know the guy?"

"Just from the stuff in the papers—about Piedmont—and from when he was on *Market Minds* all the time. I remember the bratty know-it-all attitude. I was actually referring to the whole analyst species." She opened the fridge and took out a bottle of seltzer. She brought it and two glasses back to the table.

"You have it in for them on general principle, or do you have a more specific grudge?"

Jane filled the glasses. She drank from hers and stretched her legs out. "Both, I guess." I raised my eyebrows, and Jane continued. "I never had illusions about analyst independence. I knew who paid their bonuses and who they were beholden to—and it certainly wasn't the investing public. I mean, the notion of getting an objective opinion about a company, or an unbiased recommendation about its stock, from somebody who's essentially a paid pitchman for that company—it's ridiculous. And even if they weren't thoroughly compromised, what are their opinions worth anyway? They're like weathermen. Being right has never been a big part of the job description." Jane took another drink. She put her right heel on the edge of her seat and rested her arm on her knee. She flexed her toes, and the tendons were taut along the top of her foot.

"I thought the reforms changed things," I said.

Jane shook her head and gave me a sympathetic, *silly-boy* look. "That's the party line, I suppose—that the reforms got rid of a layer of conflict by separating the analysts from the investment bankers and separating analyst pay from banking fees. But so what? It's still the same guys at the top of these firms, deciding who gets paid and how much. If investment banking is important to them, and if they think a certain analyst has helped win business, they're going to make sure he gets paid for it. Senior management knows it, the investment bankers know it, and so do the analysts—they just try to be a little less brazen these days."

She drank some seltzer and shook her head some more.

"And sure, firms are very careful now about saying so if they do business with a company that their analysts are touting. But telling people about conflicts of interest doesn't make the conflicts go away. A cynical person might even argue that all this disclosure just gives the firms more cover for the next time around."

Jane was relaxed, and her compact body was at ease in the chair, but she nonetheless projected a latent, supple energy—like a coiled spring or a watchful cat. It was in her every fluid motion, and it was even in her voice, in the chords of certainty and confidence of her pleasant contralto. She flexed her fingers, and I watched the muscles shift smoothly in her wrists and forearms.

"And what's your personal gripe?" I asked.

She puckered her lips, as if she'd tasted something sour. "I guess I don't like being bullied," she said.

I thought about that for a while. "It's hard to imagine anyone trying."

Jane gave a humorless laugh. "You'd be surprised," she said. She drained her seltzer, and I poured another glass. "It was a few years ago, when I was running that little biotech in Cambridge. They'd had some problems—with low production yields and a couple of nasty lawsuits—but we'd sorted those out and the worst was behind us, and we were shopping for a new credit facility. We were talking seriously to three big lenders when, one day, I got a call from an analyst—one of the few who covered the company.

"I knew him, of course. He was from a big regional firm, and I'd talk to him a couple of times a quarter at least. He was one of those frat-boy-gone-fat types, but he'd always been friendly and reasonably straightforward. That day, it took him a while to get to the point.

"He started asking about our hunt for new credit, which I had just talked about to a bunch of investors and analysts—including him—two weeks before. I thought he was looking for some inside dope, and I started to explain that I wasn't going to tell him anything I hadn't told the group, but he cut me off. That wasn't what he wanted to talk about, he said, and he started telling me how there were other motivated lenders out there besides the ones we had on our short list. By that point, I was feeling like we were in some very weird territory, but I still had no idea what the guy wanted. Finally, he got to it.

"He asked if I was aware that his firm was in the lending business too. I said that I was, but that I thought we were getting into an inappropriate area. I tried to end the conversation, but he pretty much ignored me. He said he wasn't sure I'd considered the *big picture,* and maybe it was because I was a short-timer—just an interim CEO—that I was ignoring a firm that had always been very supportive of my company. He said that if I kept on ignoring his firm, that support could evaporate. I asked him if by *support* he meant his coverage of the company—his research reports—and he said he'd always known I was a bright girl."

"*Bright girl?*" I said.

Jane laughed. "I was stunned—as much by his heavy-handedness as anything else."

"What did you do?"

"I thanked him for his advice and hung up, and then I called the vice chairman of his firm. I told him what had happened and pointed out that—just for appearances' sake—he might want his boy to ease off a little. A few days later the firm announced that our analyst had been promoted and transferred, and they assigned a new paunchy frat boy to cover us. He was dumber than the first guy but quieter. End of story."

"Except that you carry a grudge."

"I have a long memory."

"Duly noted."

"I always knew you were a bright boy." She smiled and glanced down at her watch.

"You've got to get back to the office," I said. "I'll put on some clothes and walk you over." I went into the bedroom and Jane was behind me. She tossed her T-shirt on the bed and stood, backlit, in the doorway. Shadows fell across her small round breasts. Her nipples were dark and hard.

"Not just yet," she said softly, and she came across the room and pulled away my towel. Her hands were soft and warm on my body, and so was her mouth. She pushed me down on the bed and wriggled out of the rest of her clothes and lay next to me. Heat came off her in waves. It carried the milky scent of her soap and the faint spice of her perfume, and beneath them both, the tang of her. I breathed deeply, and my heart hammered against my ribs.

I kissed her and her tongue played slowly in my mouth. I caught the flavors of mint and curry and cilantro. I slid my hands down her back and sides and along her thighs. She shuddered and rolled against me. I kissed her breasts and her belly, and spread her legs and tasted her.

She said something unintelligible and buried her fingers in my hair and moved her smooth legs against my shoulders. She pressed herself against me, quivering, again and again, and suddenly she twisted out from under me.

"Not yet," she whispered. She pushed me over on my back and hooked her leg across my hips and slid on top of me. She took me in her hands and slowly fit herself around me and we lay there, barely breathing. And then she began to move.

I came out of the oblivion that had taken me, lying sideways across the bed. Jane was beside me, her dark head on my chest, an arm and a leg flung across me. The room was full of her scent and the heat of her body. In the dim light, I watched the slow rise and fall of her back, the faint flutter of her eyelids, and the tiny random movements of her bow-shaped mouth. I ran my finger lightly along her hairline, just above her right temple, and felt the small ripples there, invisible to the eye—the wake of the bullet that had grazed her last year. Jane opened her eyes and looked at me for a long while before she spoke.

"No harm done," she said softly. I wanted to believe it.

3

Find the real estate. Find the cars. Look for criminal records and civil suits. Get the phone bills. Check the hospitals. Check the morgues. Every missing persons case is different, but every one begins the same way. It's like the opening gambit in a game of chess, and if your missing person isn't actually in hiding—or isn't any good at it—play can often stop soon after. I spent much of the morning making these moves, and thanks to the marvels of technology and the wonders of outsourcing, I could do it all without leaving home.

I put a Charlie Haden disc on the stereo, filled a mug with coffee, powered up my laptop, and fed Gregory Danes's name and Social Security number to several of my favorite online search services. For a price, they would make mincemeat of his privacy.

Nina Sachs had already given me the address of Danes's Upper East Side apartment and his home, office, and cell phone numbers, and she'd told me about the big black BMW he sometimes drove on weekend jaunts, and all of that was helpful. But what I was really interested in were the things she couldn't tell me about—like any other phone numbers listed in Danes's name, for example, or any other cars or houses he might own. The search services could find those for me, and a whole lot more. Plane registries, boat registries, criminal convictions, voter registrations, bankruptcies—the vast universe of public records was at their disposal. One service would even find any court cases that Danes had been involved in, and another would scan the SEC's databases for any complaints or arbitration claims made against him. They weren't infallible, but they were a good place to start, and a lot faster than doing the legwork myself. And they were legal. Buying his phone bills was another, murkier story.

Telephone bills are not public records, and the online services that deal in them sometimes vanish from the Web without warning, often to reopen—under new names and at new sites—a few days later. Their legality is questionable but not their usefulness, not to someone like me, and I submitted Danes's home phone and cell numbers to one of them.

Not all the preliminary work could be done online; for certain things, I had to pick up the phone. Simone Gautier is an elegant Haitian woman who runs a small detective agency in Forest Hills. She does mostly personal injury and divorce work, but for a reasonable fee Simone will send one of her many day players out to cruise the hospitals and morgues. We agreed to start in the five boroughs and we agreed on a price. I e-mailed Danes's description to her and faxed her a photograph.

Results would take some time—hours for the search services, days for Simone, and more days for the phone bills—but Danes's trail on the public search engines was enough to keep me busy in the meanwhile.

Danes had been more or less invisible lately, at least as far as the media was concerned, but before the bubble burst—and immediately afterward—he had been a very public guy indeed. In the perpetual now of the Internet, his fame lived on. I started clicking on links.

Danes's biography on the Pace-Loyette corporate Web site was terse to the point of mean. It gave his date and place of birth (July 23, 1962, Maplewood, New Jersey), and told of his undergraduate (BS, Cornell) and graduate (MBA, University of Chicago) education, and stated that he'd joined Pace as an analyst in the late eighties. And that was it; there wasn't even a picture. I kept clicking.

A long derelict investment advice site, *iLoveYourMoney.com,* carried a head shot and a more expansive version of his biography, probably copied in happier times from the Pace-Loyette site. This edition included a laundry list of Danes's professional affiliations and the accolades he'd received over the years from the industry and the business press: Tech Analyst of the

Year, Top Tech Stock Picker, Most Influential Tech Analyst, New Economy Avatar of the Year . . . it went on and on.

A more current site, *RobberBaronsRedux.com,* carried the same bio on a page entitled "Top Pimps." This account, however, was ironically and brutally annotated, and adorned with a large photo of Danes, digitally enhanced with mustache, goatee, glasses, and devil's horns. Childish, yes, but I laughed.

I clicked away, and the arc of Danes's career emerged from a fog of data. He'd started as a computer hardware analyst, initially at a big broker-dealer and then at Pace-Loyette, and never distinguished himself from the legion of other analysts tilling the same soil.

That all changed when he was reassigned to cover what was then a relatively new market sector: computer-networking equipment. The first company he analyzed was a little-known manufacturer of network routers called Biscayne Bay Technologies. When he called Biscayne management's projection of earnings "cautious to the point of wimpy" and predicted that the company's share price would triple in six months, reaction ranged from incredulity to ridicule. In fact, it took five months and Biscayne's shares quadrupled. It was the first in a string of home-run calls.

Danes was the right guy in the right place and time. He saw the coming commercialization of the Internet and understood its implications, both for the tech companies that were making it possible and for companies that could sell their goods and services there. And he had the courage of his convictions. He followed Biscayne Bay with similarly astonishing—and accurate—predictions on Ambient Reasoning, Surfside Search, ColdKarma.com, and a half-dozen other companies. By the late nineties, Danes had made his bones many times over. He was The Man in the tech sector, and his word was enough to move share prices. More importantly, it was enough to ensure a successful IPO.

Danes logged a lot of miles in the late nineties on road trip after road trip with Pace-Loyette investment bankers, pitching the prospects of one tech company after another that Pace was about to take public. A few of those firms would grow into real businesses, with actual products and profits, but most would not, and many were no more than cocktail-napkin doodles, tarted up with PowerPoint. But the Danes imprimatur pulled a lot of weight with investors who, if they didn't always buy his hype, at least understood the buoyant effect it could have on a newly issued stock.

When the new millennium came, the market, like so much else, turned to lead. And though he had predicted the boom, Danes hadn't foreseen the bust—or maybe he'd believed that his say-so alone would be enough to prevent it. While share prices plummeted, Danes and a handful of other analysts maintained their crazed enthusiasms, until many of their favorites became penny stocks or vanished altogether.

If the collapse of the market was a surprise to Danes, its aftermath was a whack in the head with a two-by-four. The hopeless tangle of quid pro quos and conflicting interests that bound together investment banks, their corporate clients, and the people who ran those corporations were open secrets on Wall Street. But when the particulars of these arrangements—the bartering of favorable stock ratings, personal loans, and shares of hot IPOs for lucrative investment banking engagements—were dragged out for the public-at-large to see, the public-at-large got sorely pissed off. While analysts hadn't built the trough or gorged themselves at it as deeply as some, they were wide and obvious targets—and so often painted with convenient bull's-eyes. The brightest one on Danes's backside was Piedmont Science and its affable chairman, Denton Ainsley.

Piedmont Science was a software company, a supplier of billing systems to medical and dental practices. It was an undistinguished firm in its early years, with a share price that barely supported its NASDAQ listing and no coverage at all from stock analysts. When its president died in his sleep, it seemed as if the company might soon follow suit. Enter Denton Ainsley.

Ainsley was the star of a dozen infomercials that hawked the wares of Dentco, the consumer products company he had founded. Ainsley was lean and handsome, in a silver-haired, leathery sort of way, and his rugged wrangler persona was immensely popular with TV viewers in search of laundry soap and floor wax. They liked his cowboy hat and easy humor and imagined they heard something genuine in his broad Texas twang. No one seemed to question how a man raised in Connecticut had come by such an accent.

Friends on the Piedmont board had opened the door for Ainsley, and his disarming personality—and the sizable chunk of Piedmont shares that he purchased—secured his position as CEO. But Ainsley had more than just charm and money to recommend him; he actually had an idea—a vision of Piedmont's future.

Ainsley saw that Piedmont's marketplace was badly fragmented, with many small suppliers and no dominant player. He recognized that the market was ripe for consolidation and that, with the right financing, Piedmont could grow by acquiring its competitors, moving their clients to Piedmont's products, and squeezing out costs. And there was another, more radical, aspect to his plan. Ainsley understood the growing reach of the Internet and saw in it an opportunity for Piedmont to transform itself—to become a provider not of billing software but of billing services. He saw, in short, an opportunity to get Piedmont out of the software business and into the outsourcing game. This was what had caught Gregory Danes's eye.

Three months after Ainsley's installation as CEO, Danes became the first analyst to cover Piedmont. He was unequivocal in his support for the company's strategies and beyond bullish on its future value. His declarations attracted more research coverage to Piedmont, and more investors, and the company's shares jumped.

None of this was lost on Denton Ainsley, who proceeded to cultivate close ties with the analyst and his firm. He invited Danes to speak at several of Piedmont's lavish corporate retreats, solicited his views on takeover targets, and made him guest of honor at one of his celebrity-laden charity pig roasts. As for Pace-Loyette, Ainsley tapped the firm as Piedmont's investment banker on all acquisitions and named it lead underwriter on the company's secondary stock offering. Pace also became Ainsley's personal banker, extending him hefty loans, collateralized by hefty chunks of ever-more-valuable Piedmont stock.

For a while, while the market climbed, all was well. Piedmont's growth strategy proceeded apace, subscriptions to its new outsourcing service sold faster than planned, and the company's stock became a must-have for anyone who wanted to invest in the Internet. Pace-Loyette collected its fat banking fees, Danes's reputation shone ever brighter—as did his outlook on Piedmont shares—and Denton Ainsley undertook elaborate renovations to his newly purchased Napa Valley château. And no one paid much heed to talk of accounting irregularities and falsified sales figures at Ainsley's old company, Dentco, or to questions about Piedmont's subscriber numbers, or to complaints that its software just plain did not work.

When people did take notice, the unraveling was fast and violent. The SEC announced its inquiry into Dentco one Monday early in the new millennium; the following day came its notice of an inquiry into Piedmont. Wednesday saw a class action suit by a group of Piedmont customers; on Thursday the Justice Department declared its interest in interviewing Piedmont board members. On Friday, the first shareholder lawsuit was filed.

On Saturday, Denton Ainsley's bright Italian car was fished from a pond on his Napa estate, and Ainsley's body was fished from the car. *Suicide by Ferrari* was the unofficial finding of one cop on the scene—an opinion bolstered the next day, when the coroner established Ainsley's astonishing blood-alcohol levels.

The forensic accountants took a bit longer on the autopsy of Piedmont Science, but when they were through their report revealed massive fraud, hidden debt, and systematic looting of the company's coffers—all orchestrated from the very top. By which time the company had largely decomposed.

Piedmont had little in the way of assets, and its executives and directors relatively shallow pockets, and it wasn't long before irate customers, investors, and regulators turned their torches and pitchforks on Piedmont's bankers. At the time, their claims were novel: Pace-Loyette and Gregory Danes were either fools or criminals, negligent incompetents if they were unaware of Piedmont's true financial condition, despite extensive dealings with the company, or co-conspirators in Ainsley's fraud if they knew but didn't tell. And either way, they were horribly conflicted: Pace's interest in keeping Piedmont as a client, and in keeping Piedmont's shares inflated, led it—and Danes—to distort research reports and to mislead investors.

Though they made for fun reading, the allegations were difficult to prove. There was no trail of memos or smirking e-mail to indicate that anyone at Pace-Loyette had known of the fraud, or to suggest that Danes had not believed his own research reports. And there was the fact, besides, that Pace had lost a large pile of dough on its loans to Ainsley. But the absence of a smoking gun hadn't deterred the lawyers, and it hadn't saved Gregory Danes's reputation. Pundits, politicians, and op-ed columnists feasted on the Piedmont affair—and on Danes—for many months, until a host of larger and more garish frauds came along.

The search engines returned links to interviews that Danes had given over the years, and I skimmed through a few of them. There was something almost quaint in his rosy pronouncements—on e-commerce, broadband, data mining, and a dozen other jargon-soaked topics. It was like reading about eight-track tapes or bongs. I read farther down the list of links and stopped at something called *LindaObsession.com*. I clicked, not knowing what to expect.

It was a disturbing and aptly named site. A page entitled "Our Mission" summed it up:

We are here to appreciate and adore the most beautiful and intelligent and most totally HOT host/reporter/superstar/diva on television today (OR EVER!)—the Amazing, Incredible, Spectacular LINDA SOVITCH! We Are Totally Linda!!!

Linda Sovitch was the blond glossy host of *Market Minds,* the Business News Network show that offered analysis of the day's market action and features on investing, the economy, and politics. In recent years, Sovitch had also become the glamorous face of BNN itself. Gregory Danes had been a frequent guest on *Market Minds,* practically a fixture there since the show's debut in the late nineties, and this was why *LindaObsession* had come up in my search.

Along with the fevered deconstruction of Linda Sovitch's physical charms—the cornflower eyes, the ash-blond hair, the delicate nostrils and bee-stung lips and swelling bosom—and the meticulous parsing of what seemed her every utterance, there were stills and video clips from the *Market Minds* show. In among these was Gregory Danes.

There was Danes on the show's premier segment, and when the Dow hit 10,000. There he was when Cisco surpassed GE in market capitalization. And there was Danes on the first anniversary show and on every subsequent one—except for the last few. I clicked on a video clip.

It was fuzzy and jumpy but watchable nonetheless. The topic was the significance of adding Microsoft and Intel to the Dow Jones Industrial Average. Sovitch was smiling and flirty and pitching softballs; Danes was arrogant and preening and knocking the hide off them. But there was a twitchy, adolescent quality about him too, which came through even on the murky video—like the class wiseass who's suddenly found himself captain of the football team. Even so, his message was simple and clear: It's a whole new world, and there's no place to go but up. For sure, Greg.

Most of the references that turned up in my search were several years old, and they were all business. There were no references to him in the social pages, and—apart from Ainsley's posh barbecue—no reported sightings of him at any of Wall Street's many charity events. Even the few magazine profiles of him mentioned nothing more personal than his fondness for classical music.

The only exception was a mention of Danes in a 1998 article from a Newark, New Jersey, newspaper. It was a short piece, reporting on an administrative action by the SEC against a tiny Jersey City firm and a broker there named Richard Gilpin, for a slew of violations that seemed to stop just short of outright fraud. Gilpin, the article noted, was the younger brother of "prominent Wall Street analyst Gregory Danes." The reporter was almost right; according to Nina Sachs, Richard Gilpin was Danes's creepy half brother. Gilpin was on my list of people to talk to, assuming I could find him, and I took down the details.

I went to the kitchen and warmed my coffee in the microwave and looked out the window as I drank it. The sky was a soft, even gray, and the gulls, wheeling slowly over the building across the street, were nearly lost against it. I had a lot of windows opened, and a small breeze wandered in with the street noise.

I thought about Danes and the traces he had left behind on the Web—his footprints across the big stage of Wall Street—and I thought about the other actors recently brought to heel. I recalled the televised hearings and the faces, pale under their golf-course tans. Some had been annoyed at being called to testify and others had been downright angry, and a few, perhaps, had been something close to scared, but regardless of demeanor they seemed to share a common sense of astonishment that questions had been asked at all.

Thoughts of arrogance and money and Wall Street led me, inevitably, to my family. Money is the family business—on my mother's side, at least—and it has been ever since my great-grandfather founded the merchant bank of Klein & Sons. One of my uncles runs the bank these days, with help from my eldest brother, Ned. My other brother, David, and my older sister, Liz, work there too, along with the rest of my uncles and countless cousins. Not every Klein offspring has gone into banking, though. My baby sister hasn't, and through the years there'd been heretics who'd wandered off into medicine, law, and academia. But there'd never been a cop or a PI before—not until me.

This was not a source of particular family pride, but I was used to that. By the time I'd found a career—or it had found me—I'd already amassed twenty-two years' worth of underachievement and unfulfilled expectations. Even now I could hear my mother's chilly tones: *You surprise me, John, only in the particulars of your choices, not in the degree of their foolishness.* She's gone now—both my parents are—but her sentiment lingers like a ghost around my family.

Not that I'd never toed the family line. I had, albeit sporadically. In college, I was a business major for about ten minutes, and for several summers I'd interned on the trading floor of a big broker-dealer. I'd gotten coffee, answered phones, run pricing models, reconfirmed trades, and tended my hangovers there, and I'd listened quietly, over long expensive lunches, while people barely older than I tried to sell me on a future with the firm. It didn't take. The avarice, egotism, and self-delusion I'd seen there approached caricature, and when the dismay wore off, Wall Street had bored me to tears.

Several times in recent years clients and cases had led me back there and afforded me a darker but more interesting view of the place. In seven years as a cop I'd seen what greed and arrogance could do when they were mixed with desperation and opportunity; that was old news. What was different on Wall Street was the stakes that people played for, the variety of their games, and the particular mix of brains and vanity they brought with them to the table. I took a deep breath and let it out slowly.

I topped off my coffee, found the Pace-Loyette phone directory that Neary had given me, and turned to the listings for Gregory Danes's department, Equity Research.

Research wasn't a big group at Pace-Loyette—fewer than thirty analysts in all—but it didn't need to be. Pace-Loyette wasn't a big firm, and they didn't cover every sector of the market; technology was the specialty of the house. Danes's name appeared at the top of the page, with the title Director of Research. Immediately beneath his name was his assistant's, Giselle Thomas. Neary had put a check alongside it. Below her, also with a check by her name, was Irene Pratt, Assistant Director of Research. Halfway down the page, another name was marked: Anthony Frye, Telecommunications Research. Leafing through the rest of the directory, I found only one other name with a check beside it: Dennis Turpin. According to the directory, Turpin was head of the legal department—the chief in-house counsel. Turpin, Neary had told me, was the guy who had had the shouting match with Danes, right before Danes's sudden vacation. I carried my coffee to the table and picked up the phone.

Giselle Thomas answered on the first ring. Her voice was mature and musical and Caribbean. I asked for Danes and there was a little sigh at the other end of the line.

"Who's calling, please?" I gave her my name. "Mr. Danes isn't in, Mr. March. Is there someone else? Irene Pratt, maybe?"

"When is the last time Mr. Danes *was* in, Ms. Thomas?"

She paused. "I need to refer you to Ms. Mayhew, in Corporate Communications, sir."

"Does *she* know when you last heard from Mr. Danes? Does *she* know where you think I might find him?"

Giselle Thomas laughed. It was liquid and pleasant. "Well, Mr. March, I can't say exactly what Ms. Mayhew knows, but I expect it's many things. And she'll be pleased to tell you, I'm sure. Shall I transfer you?"

"I understand the company has its rules, Ms. Thomas, and I appreciate that you've got to follow them, but it's not Ms. Mayhew who can help me, it's you. You know Mr. Danes. You've worked with him for—how long has it been? If you'd rather not talk at the office, I'd be happy to meet you someplace. Just name the spot."

She laughed some more. "You sound like a nice fellow, Mr. March, you do. And it's nice that you want to talk to me. But that just isn't going to happen. Now, would you like me to put you through to Nancy Mayhew?" I declined politely and rang off.

I tried Irene Pratt's number next, but it was answered immediately by a computer voice that asked me to leave a message. Giselle Thomas had made it sound like Pratt was in the office, so I hung up and waited five minutes and tried again. The result was the same. I skipped down to Anthony Frye.

Frye's line also went straight to voice mail, but the voice on the recording was a woman's and the message was brief. Anthony Frye was no longer employed by Pace-Loyette, and any inquiries should be made to Irene Pratt. I made a note to find a home number for him and tried Pratt's line once more. This time I got through.

"Research, Pratt," she said quickly. I introduced myself and asked her if she knew how I might get in touch with Gregory Danes.

"And this is in reference to what?" she said. Her voice was high and nasal, and she had a faint Long Island accent. She sounded impatient, and I heard pages turning at her end.

"This is in reference to the fact that I'd like to know where he is."

"Greg is on leave. If you want to know anything else, you've got to talk to Nancy Mayhew in Communications."

"Have you heard anything from him in the last five weeks, Ms. Pratt? Has anyone there?"

"You're with who, March?"

"I'm an investigator, and I'm trying to locate Gregory Danes."

"You're with the police?" she said. I had her full attention now.

"I'm a private investigator. Have you heard from him, Ms. Pratt?" She was quiet for a while, and when she answered she spoke softly and more slowly.

"I'm sorry, but . . . I really can't help you. Let me give you Nancy Mayhew's number." She read it to me and said good-bye.

I sighed and worked the kinks from my neck. All roads seemed to lead to Nancy Mayhew. I punched her number.

Nancy Mayhew and I got on first-name terms right away. She was crisp and smart and friendly, and she laughed like an aunt of mine from Oyster Bay. And besides the business about Danes being on leave, she told me not a single thing.

"Did he actually tell someone there that he was going on leave, Nancy?"

"I'm afraid I just can't say, John."

"Can't or won't?"

She laughed. "I'm sorry, John."

"Can you say when you last spoke with Danes? Was it any time in the last five weeks?"

She laughed again and didn't bother with an answer. "Perhaps you can tell *me*, John—who is it that you're working for?"

It was my turn to chuckle, after which I hung up.

Through the open windows the breeze had picked up, and there was a bite to it now. Rain was coming. My coffee was cold again, but I drank it anyway and watched some clouds slide by. Three people with nothing to say. I called Dennis Turpin.

An assistant answered, took my name, and asked me to hold. I didn't hold long.

"I know who you are, March, and I know what you've been up to," Turpin said, when he came on the line. He had a faint New England accent and an irritated, scolding tone. "You've harassed three of my people today with your questions, and we don't appreciate that around here."

I was surprised that Turpin knew about my other calls so quickly; Neary was right about Danes having his management spooked. And I was surprised by Turpin's choice of words. *Harassed?* I wasn't even warmed up yet. And *my people?* That was a rather pompous construction for a mere in-house lawyer.

"I'm not trying to harass anyone. I'd simply like to get in touch with Gregory Danes."

"And I believe you've been told—more than once—that Danes is on leave. But you don't seem satisfied with that answer."

"That answer is fine, as far as it goes. It just happens not to go very far. Do you expect Danes back anytime soon? Has anyone there actually spoken to him since he's been away, or gotten messages from him, or e-mail? How about a postcard?"

Turpin made a puffing noise. "You have no standing," he snapped. "We're not obliged to put up with this." He went silent then, and I got the distinct impression he was counting to ten. He sighed loudly.

"Maybe you want to answer some questions yourself, March—like who you're working for on this. Maybe we could do a little horse-trading." Turpin was trying for conciliatory, even friendly, but it came out sounding sneaky. Still, his offer was my best bet for getting into Pace-Loyette, at least for now.

"I need to talk to my client first," I said.

Turpin snorted. "You do that," he said, "and you come see me, tomorrow at one—assuming you've got something to trade." He rang off.

I put the phone down and wondered what Nina Sachs would have to say about my meeting with Turpin. Giving him her name seemed like a small thing to me, considering that the folks at Pace-Loyette already knew that Nina was trying to locate her husband, but I wasn't sure she'd see it the same way. I punched her number and Ines Icasa answered. She spoke quietly, and told me in her precise accented English that Nina was not available. She asked if I'd like to leave a message. I declined.

I stood and stretched. I was stiff from too much phone time and jumpy from too much coffee and I needed a run to work it all out. And then I needed to go uptown, to Danes's apartment building. But before that, I had two more dots to connect.

I slid my laptop over and opened a file I'd saved two days ago. In it were the links I'd found when I'd been studying up on Nina Sachs. They consisted mainly of reviews of her shows and announcements of significant sales of her work. I scanned a few of them. In the last three years, Nina had had a half-dozen shows at a SoHo gallery called I-2 Galeria de Arte. I put the gallery name in a search engine.

According to its Web site, I-2 Galeria de Arte had been around for a dozen years and dealt in a wide variety of contemporary art: painting, sculpture, even video. It specialized in works by women and by Latin American artists, and it maintained three exhibition spaces: in SoHo, in Brooklyn, and upstate on the Hudson River in Kinderhook. I looked at the gallery's Brooklyn address. It was the same as Nina Sachs's. I looked at the picture of the gallery's owner. It was Ines Icasa.

4

Gregory Danes's brick and dressed-stone apartment building squatted prosperously on 79th Street, between Lexington and Third avenues. I stood with Christopher beneath its green awning, out of the rain. Christopher was my height—just over six feet—and skinny, and he looked twenty-something going on sixty. His narrow face was pale and pocked with acne scars, and his bony fingers were cigarette-stained. His gray doorman's uniform hung off him like skin sloughing from a snake, and his thick hair struggled beneath his uniform cap.

Christopher was happy to take my money and happy to talk to me in return, but he was nervous just then. His small eyes flitted around and he looked through the glass doors behind me, into the building's lobby. He stiffened, locked a polite smile onto his face, and barely moved his jaw when he spoke.

"Here's that motherfucking super; that fucking guy hates my guts. Does nothing but give me the evil eye all day. Do me a favor, man, take a walk around the block. Give it ten and come back. He'll be gone then and we can talk." I looked past him and nodded and headed west on 79th Street. The rain made a gentle patting sound on my umbrella.

I walked up Lex and looked into the small handsome shops that lined the street. They were full of delicate wicked-looking shoes, and stationery made from butterfly wings, and French baby clothes that were hand-stitched by blue-eyed virgins. The window displays were intricately wrought and exhibited the merchandise with fetishistic devotion, and they all made me think of Joseph Cornell. I crossed Lex at 83rd Street and went west toward Park Avenue. I meandered slowly down Park, past big old buildings of the sort Danes's building aspired to be, and went east again on 75th. And then I headed back.

Christopher gave me a relaxed nod as he pulled open the heavy door. The lobby was wide and deep, with a vaulted ceiling and Persian rugs on the polished stone floors, and it was empty but for us. We stood in a vestibule near the entrance and Christopher's eyes scanned the sidewalk out front. I slipped him a twenty and he made it vanish.

"That prick should be out for twenty minutes at least," he said. "What do you want to know?"

"You work here long?" I asked.

"About a year, part-time. I fill in for the regulars when they're on vacation or out sick. I end up pulling eight, maybe ten, shifts a month."

"All daytime shifts?"

Christopher snorted. "I wish. Usually they shuffle the duty so I work the overnights—midnight to six." I nodded.

"How'd you get lucky with daylight hours today?"

Christopher gave a wry smile. "Super-Prick is short-staffed the next few weeks; he had no choice."

"You know the tenants at all?"

He shook his head. "Not really. Working the late shift I don't see much of them, plus a lot of them are real assholes—wouldn't piss on 'em if they were on fire." A bronze elevator door slid open at the back of the lobby. A fiftyish woman in a Burberry trench coat got out, trailed by a dachshund in matching outerwear. She glanced at the empty concierge station and sniffed. She eyed Christopher and sniffed more loudly. She looked at me. My hair was shorter, my clothes fit better, and I had no acne scars, but she was unimpressed. Christopher said hello and held the door and she sniffed once more as she went through.

"See what I mean?" he said. I nodded sympathetically and pulled out a photo of Danes.

"You know him?"

Christopher looked at the picture and looked at me. His small eyes got smaller. "Danes, right?"

I nodded. "Seen him around?"

He shook his head slowly. "Not for a while—I don't remember when the last time was. I told this to the other guys."

I looked at Christopher and took a deep breath. I slipped the photo back into my pocket. "What other guys?" I asked quietly.

Christopher shuffled his feet and looked away from me. His eyes were nervous when they finally came back to mine. "I guess you're not with them, huh?" he said.

"What other guys, Christopher?"

"The two guys who asked about Danes before."

"When before?"

He shrugged. "Ten days ago, maybe."

"What did they ask?"

Christopher ran his eyes around the lobby. "The same as you. They showed me a picture, asked if I'd seen him around and when I'd seen him last. Asked if I knew his friends in the building."

"And you told them . . . ?"

"Same as I told you. I haven't seen the guy, and I don't know shit about the tenants."

I nodded. "Who were they?" Christopher shook his head and looked confused. "Were they cops? Were they lawyers?"

"Not lawyers . . . not cops, either. They were private, like you."

"These guys have names?"

Another headshake. "Not that I remember." I stared at him, and he ran a stained hand over the back of his neck and said nothing.

"You remember what they looked like?" I asked.

"They just looked like . . . two guys."

I sighed. "Were they short, tall, black, white?"

He shrugged. "I don't know. They were . . . medium. They were white, the both of them, and I think they had brown hair. They were about the same height—maybe six feet, maybe a little shorter."

I shook my head. "Did they say anything about calling if you happened to see Danes?" I asked. "Did they give you a phone number?"

Christopher tugged at his ear and rubbed the back of his neck again and looked around the lobby. "No, bro, they didn't say anything about that. They just asked their questions and split."

I looked at him some more. I was fairly sure that Christopher was not being entirely truthful with me. I was fairly sure, in fact, that he was lying through his teeth. But I still needed him, and there wasn't a whole lot I could do about it. "And you haven't heard from them since?" I asked.

"Nope," Christopher said, and looked at his watch. He craned his neck to check the sidewalk, east and west. "Not to rush you or anything, but that prick'll be back soon."

"Sure," I said. "We're just about done. Anybody working here who knows the tenants well?"

"The guy I'm subbing for today: Paul Gargosian. He's been here since they opened the place, and he knows everybody. He's an okay guy, too— you grease him and he'll talk to you."

"When's he back?"

"Couple weeks."

"Know his number, or where he lives?"

"In the Bronx someplace—I don't know." Christopher looked at his watch again, more nervous now. "I don't want to rush you, but . . . "

I nodded. "No problem, Christopher, you've been a big help. How much to get into Danes's apartment?"

Christopher looked at me and winced. "Shit, bro, you don't want much, do you?" He shook his head and tugged on an ear. "That could be my job, for chrissakes." I nodded and let him keep talking and thinking about it. "Oh, Christ, what the fuck are you going to do in there?"

"I'm just trying to find the guy, Christopher. I'm not interested in taking his stuff."

"Shit . . . it'd need to be at least a hundred—no, two hundred." I nodded.

"Two hundred's fine," I said. "When?" Christopher was looking paler.

"It's got to be next week—Monday afternoon. Super-Prick will be out then." I wasn't happy with a six-day wait, but I didn't have a lot of options. I nodded. Christopher checked the sidewalk again. "You've got to split."

"Just one more question," I said. "Where do the tenants garage their cars?"

"I know two places people use," he said, and gave me their names. "Now get out of here, man." I went.

The parking garages Christopher told me about were each within four blocks of the building, but in opposite directions. I went north and got lucky.

It was off Third Avenue, tucked between two worn apartment buildings, and its entrance was a narrow oil-stained ramp leading down. I found a small quiet man named Rafe in a glass booth at the bottom of the ramp. His hair was black and wavy and his dark eyes were set deeply in a weathered intelligent face. He recognized Danes's picture and identified him as "black '04 BMW Seven-fifty." He told me the car wasn't in and hadn't been for a while, and for twenty bucks he looked through a stack of wrinkled papers and gave me its plate number and the date and time it had last gone out. It was five weeks ago, the day after Nina Sachs had last spoken with Danes, at nine-twenty in the morning. I asked Rafe where the nearest gas stations were. He told me, and I thanked him. I turned to leave and then turned back.

"Has anyone else come asking about this?" I said.

A look of calculation passed quickly across Rafe's face and he nodded at me. "One guy, a week and a half back."

"What did he ask about?"

"About the car and the customer—like you—and I told him the same things. I got twenty-five out of him, though."

I fished a ten from my pocket. "You remember what he looked like?"

Rafe tucked the bill away. "White guy, in his thirties maybe, skinny, about five-ten, with dark hair and a mustache."

"He give you a name or show some ID?" He shook his head. "He give you a number to call, in case Danes showed up?"

"He tried to. I told him no thanks. It's one thing taking cash and answering questions, but being a spy is something else."

I nodded. "Has he been back since?"

"Nope," Rafe said, and then the phone rang in the glass booth and he picked it up and started talking. I made my way back up the ramp.

The closest of the gas stations was north, near an on-ramp to the FDR Drive. I was still feeling loose from my run and the rain was still soft, and I walked uptown and wondered all the way about who else was searching for Gregory Danes.

The station was on the corner, and a steady stream of cars pulled in and out, veering dangerously across many lanes of traffic as they did. It was not quiet. Besides the pumps there were two greasy repair bays with car lifts and a cramped store that sold cigarettes, lottery tickets, and soda. Jammed between the bays and the store was a filthy glassed-in office. It smelled of gasoline and cigars and dirty socks. I waited at a chest-high plywood counter for Frank to get off the phone.

Frank was black, about sixty and mostly bald, and he looked like he'd spent much of his life moving heavy things around. He was just under six feet, with a massive chest and shoulders and no neck to speak of. He wore a gray uniform shirt with an open collar, his name on the pocket, and the sleeves rolled up over beefy forearms. He hung up the phone and ran a hand over his broad, tired face.

"Let me see that again," he said. I gave him the picture of Danes, and he fished a pair of half-glasses out of his pocket and peered at it. After a while he shrugged.

"He drives a black BMW Seven-fifty, if that helps," I said. "An '04."

"I don't know . . . maybe. He's not one of my regulars—not one of my weekly guys—but I've seen him before."

"You remember when the last time was?" He shook his head. "Were you here five weeks ago, around nine-thirty in the morning?"

Frank snorted. "Buddy, I own this place. If I'm not asleep, I'm here. But I don't remember if he was in or not."

"Would any of your guys remember?"

Frank laughed. "I'd be surprised but go ahead, knock yourself out." Frank was right.

It was after five when I got home. My apartment was full of gray light and my head was full of questions. There was a phone message from Jane, telling me she had a dinner with the buyers that night, and another, from my brother Ned, reminding me of my nephew's birthday party that weekend and telling me to expect some e-mail: three résumés and a schedule of interviews.

Klein & Sons was in the market for a security director. Ned had tried to sell me on the job and wasn't happy when I'd run in the opposite direction. In a momentary spasm of familial conciliation, I'd offered to interview the candidates on his short list. It was one of those good deeds that had certain punishment written all over it.

I checked my e-mail and found the résumés there. I also found reports from the search services. I poured myself a cranberry juice and sat down to read them, wondering if they'd shed any light on where Gregory Danes had driven to when he'd driven off the map.

5

Richard Gilpin was calling himself Gilford Richards these days, at least at the esteemed investment firm of Morgan & Lynch of Fort Lee, New Jersey. His voice was deep and ripe with sincerity, but he went quiet when I used the name Gilpin and hung up when I said I was calling about his half brother, Gregory Danes.

Finding Gilpin hadn't been hard; he was in the book, at an address somewhere in Englewood. I'd called that number and an answering machine there told me I'd reached the residence of Gilford Richards. I'd plugged Gilford Richards into a search engine and come up with Morgan & Lynch's cheesy Web site. According to the site, Morgan & Lynch was a Cayman Islands company that operated half a dozen hedge funds— microcap stock and foreign equity funds mainly. They claimed steady growth in assets under management, and remarkable returns, and they made elaborate and incoherent statements about the mathematical models used to manage their investments. The whole thing reeked of Ponzi.

No one named Morgan or Lynch seemed to be associated with the firm, but Gilford Richards was listed as one of its principals. Richards's CV was impressive but curiously failed to mention his earlier incarnation as Gilpin or his run-ins with the SEC. An oversight, no doubt. After five attempts, I gave up trying to reach him again, and resigned myself to a trip to Fort Lee. But not today.

Today, Dennis Turpin was on my calendar. I'd called Nina Sachs last night, to get approval to disclose her name to Turpin. It was a surprisingly painless experience. And from what I'd heard on the phone, the whole gestalt at Sachs's place had taken a definite uptick.

Nina had answered. Her voice was light and her mood was expansive. There was music in the background, and Billy was laughing and calling to Ines.

"Come on, Nes, I put on that Miami shit you like." He sang "Turn the Beat Around," badly.

I told Nina about my talk with Turpin and about his offer to trade information, and she didn't think long before agreeing.

"Hey, what the hell—they already know I'm looking for Greg." She thought longer about my conversations with Christopher, the doorman, and Rafe, the garage attendant.

"It wasn't the cops?" she asked after a while. She was quieter and worried.

"It doesn't sound like them."

"So, who then?"

"I was hoping you might have an idea."

"Fuck, no. People from work, maybe?"

"Could be," I had said. "Maybe I'll find out tomorrow."

I had some time until my afternoon meeting with Turpin—time enough for lunch and more phone calls. I punched Simone Gautier's number.

She had no word for me yet on the hospitals and morgues, but that's not why I was calling. I gave her Danes's plate numbers and a description of his BMW and agreed on a fee to have her check out the long-term parking lots at Newark and LaGuardia and JFK. I'd already searched for Danes's car in the NYPD's online database of impounded vehicles and come up empty, and I didn't hold out great hope for the long-term lots—Danes struck me as the type to use a car service for his airport trips—but I'd feel stupid if I missed something so obvious.

My next call was to Paul Gargosian, the vacationing doorman from Danes's building. I'd found him in the book, too—the only Gargosian with an address on City Island, in the Bronx. Mrs. Paul Gargosian answered. She had a heavy Brooklyn accent, and she was friendly and forthcoming.

"Paulie's away, hon, down in Sarasota the next couple weeks, with his brother, Jerry. They're out on Jerry's boat most of the time, and I don't know when he's going to call. You want to leave a number, maybe he'll get back to you." I gave her my number and thanked her.

Then I went to the kitchen, made two peanut butter and jelly sandwiches on wheat bread, and poured a tall glass of milk. I sat at my long table and opened up my laptop, picking up where I'd left off last night, reading the reports from the search services.

They held no easy answers. The apartment on 79th Street was Danes's only real property; there was no weekend place in the Hamptons and no winter home in Florida; there was no summer cottage in Maine. He'd bought the apartment almost four years ago, and at the same time sold a place on 90th Street, in Carnegie Hill. He'd been in that place since the divorce, when he and Nina had agreed to sell the co-op they'd owned on Monroe Place, in Brooklyn Heights. And there was only the Beemer to look for; no other vehicles were registered to Danes, not in the fifty states anyway. There was, however, a long list of court cases and arbitration claims.

The search services had provided me with docket numbers, and now I was plowing through online court records and the SEC database for the details of each case. I hadn't realized there were so many of them. Nor had I realized that, in addition to charging Pace-Loyette with wrongdoing, some made claims against Danes specifically. A lawyer named Toby Kahn represented Danes in the suits, and I spoke to his voice mail and asked him to call. It was slow going, and I hadn't gotten through many cases when it was time for my meeting at Pace-Loyette. I added water to Jane's tulips and headed out the door.

Pace-Loyette's headquarters occupied eight floors of a tower at 52nd Street and Sixth Avenue, a block up from Radio City. The main reception area was on the twentieth floor and was done up like Mies van der Rohe's rumpus room. The furniture was black leather, chromed steel, and sharp angles, the marble floors were bare and whiter than eggshells, and the walls were mostly glass.

The reception desk was a glass and steel sliver, nearly invisible edge on, and so was the receptionist. She was tall and thin and bloodless, with platinum hair and big gray eyes. Her dress was steel-colored silk, and she spoke softly and in a monotone. She bade me sit, and played her fingers across the keys of a slim phone and whispered into the handset. She put down the phone and looked at me and nodded, but the look and the nod were empty of meaning. In a while a young woman came to get me. She was small and nervous-looking.

I followed her onto the elevator, and off again on the twenty-fourth floor. We went to the left, past a waiting area with blocky leather chairs and glass end tables, and through a pair of glass doors. Everything beyond the doors—the carpet, the cubicle walls, the filing cabinets and furniture—was shades of gray. The cubicles were full of people talking on telephones and peering at computers. Their low voices merged into an ambient murmur, punctuated only by the soft tapping of keys. The young woman led me down a hallway to a door with Turpin's name on it. She knocked sharply and pushed it open and I went in.

It was a corner office, square, with big windows and nice light and views west and north. I saw the CBS building across 52nd Street and a chunk of the Hilton across Sixth Avenue. The walls were white and the floors were covered in thick beige carpet. The furniture was office modern: warm woods and brushed steel, earth tones and soothing patterns. There was a tan sofa to my right, and two matching chairs arranged around a low table. An L-shaped desk dominated the other end of the room, with a leather throne and a long credenza behind it and a pair of chairs out front. There was a woman in one of the chairs, who looked up when I came in. There was a man on the throne, who did not.

The woman was a well-maintained forty. She wore a black suit and a white blouse, with a green silk scarf at her neck. Her hair was a glossy auburn, with just enough gray to make it plausible, and there were freckles sprayed across her cheeks. Laugh lines bracketed her mouth and brown eyes, but just then she wasn't laughing.

From behind his desk, Turpin ignored me elaborately. He was fiftyish and small, but fit-looking. His pin-striped jacket lay smoothly on his shoulders and around his bright white shirt. His gray hair was short and parted neatly on the right, and his brows were dark, perfectly clipped lines above nearly black eyes. His face was clean-shaven, and his skin fit so tightly over the muscle and bone underneath that it gave him a slightly simian look—like a very tidy chimp. He perused the monitor before him and laughed to himself now and then, ostensibly at something he saw there. No one said anything.

The woman looked at me and gave nothing away. Turpin gazed more intently at his screen and laughed more loudly. I figured the performance might go on for a while, so I took a seat next to the woman and looked at Turpin's bric-a-brac.

There was a framed photo on the credenza behind him, of himself in the cockpit of a sailboat with three people I took to be his wife and kids. The wife had lank blond hair, a sour mouth, and a seasick look. The kids looked teenaged and sullen.

Next to the photograph, in a neat row, were a dozen Lucite tombstones commemorating M and A deals that had been presided over by the law firm of Hazelton, Brown & Cluett. I hadn't heard of any of the companies involved, but I knew Hazelton as a white-shoe securities law firm. The deals were a decade old, and Dennis Turpin had been the firm's officiating partner on each one.

It was at best a step sideways—and arguably a step down—to go from partner at a firm like Hazelton to head of legal at Pace-Loyette, and I wondered what had happened to Turpin's career. Maybe his billings had dried up when the mergers and acquisitions market tanked, and his partners had forced him out. Or maybe they'd just gotten tired of his overacting.

Down from the tombstones was an elaborate pewter beer stein, decorated with two enamel seals, one the Justice Department's, the other the FBI's. Next to it was another framed photo: Turpin in black tie standing with the U.S. Attorney for the Southern District of New York. Alongside that was a coffee mug with the Marine Corps insignia on it. *Semper fi.* Great. Turpin gave a last little laugh and swiveled in his chair to face me.

He looked at me and sighed and looked around the room theatrically, as if he'd been expecting someone else.

"That's it?" he asked. "Just you?" I didn't say anything. "No representation? No counsel?" His voice was flinty, and the New England accent more pronounced. "Friends of mine downtown told me you always travel with a lawyer. They said it was a good thing, too."

He studied my face for surprise but I just raised an eyebrow. Turpin shrugged.

"Jan Carmody from Harris, Coldwater, our outside counsel," Turpin said, gesturing with his head toward the woman. He looked at me some more. "You know, I worked a deal with your brother Ed a few years back," Turpin said. "A management buyout that Klein funded."

He looked for surprise again, but again there was none. Wall Street is in many ways a small town and my family is not unknown there, so I'd long ago lost interest in the game of who knows whom. But I was amused that Turpin had referred to my brother as Ed. While Edwin is his given name, no one who knows my brother even casually calls him anything but Ned. Turpin looked at Jan Carmody.

"You know Ed March, over at Klein, don't you, Jan?"

She nodded and smiled thinly. "I know Ned," she said. Turpin didn't notice her correction, or pretended not to. That amused me too.

"And we know you too," Turpin said. "We know you fancy yourself some kind of cowboy, and we know what a high-handed pain in the ass you can be. So let's get something straight from the outset: We have no intention of putting up with your bullshit here." Turpin pointed at me, and the scolding tone I'd heard on the phone came back to his voice. "You keep harassing my people, you mess with the conduct of our business, and I'll have your license—and your goddamned trust fund—in my pocket before I'm through." Turpin gave me a hard look. Jan Carmody stuck with empty.

I smiled at them. "Unless I'm mistaken, you asked me here today, and I thought it was to have a grown-up conversation, not to sit through a piece of bad theater." Carmody stiffened. Turpin began to color and drew a breath to speak, but I continued. "I understood what you said yesterday, and I still understand it today, though I hardly think a few phone calls qualify as harassment. My only interest is in finding Gregory Danes. If you want to talk about that, fine. Otherwise, I'll let you get back to work." Turpin's lips were pressed together and his face was dark. Jan Carmody cleared her throat, and she and Turpin exchanged glances. She spoke.

"The point Dennis is making, Mr. March, is that Pace-Loyette takes its responsibilities to its shareholders and clients and employees very seriously. And it will react seriously to anything that impedes its ability to serve those constituents." It was impressive lawyer-speak—a gentle threat, a claim to the moral high ground, but oblique and ultimately elusive in its meaning. And Jan Carmody delivered it well: polite, reasonable, and serious, and without a hint of Turpin's posturing. I nodded at her.

"About Danes . . . ?" I said. Carmody looked at Turpin, who'd come off the boil.

"I assume you got your client's say-so to talk to us," Turpin said. I nodded. "And? Who are you working for?"

I smiled. "Before we get to that, I need some assurance that I'll get my questions answered."

Turpin leaned forward in his chair. He pointed again. "That depends on your questions, doesn't it? Don't think you're getting a goddamn blank check here."

"I don't. But I want to know that you're willing to talk about certain things—like when you last saw Danes, or when anyone here last spoke with him, or what his mood was—that sort of thing."

Carmody answered. "And in turn, Mr. March, you're authorized to tell us what?"

"I can tell you who I'm working for and what I've found so far." Carmody and Turpin looked at each other and reached some sort of agreement. Turpin nodded.

"All right," he said, "you first." I told them who had hired me and what I knew so far. It was a short story and they were silent when I finished, as if they were waiting for something more.

"That's it?" Turpin said. "That's what you've got? There's nothing there I didn't already know." I shrugged. He knitted his thick brows. "How do I know you're not feeding me a line of crap, anyway? You have proof you're not working for someone else?"

"Who else would I be working for?"

"How the hell should I know? There are plenty of plaintiffs out there."

Jan Carmody interrupted with a cough. "We have Ms. Sachs's number. Why don't we call and verify." She slipped a cell phone from her pocket and stepped out of the room. She was gone less than five minutes, during which time Turpin and I sat silently, looking at nothing. Carmody nodded at Turpin when she returned; he looked at me. My turn.

"Has anyone at Pace heard from him since the day he stormed out of here?" I asked him.

He leaned forward and his color began to rise again. "Who the hell says he *stormed* anywhere?" he growled. "Who've you been talking to?"

I looked at Carmody. She sighed.

"As far as we know, Danes has not been in touch with anyone at the firm since he left," she said. Turpin smacked his palm on the desktop.

"What the hell are you doing, Jan? Why should we tell him a goddamn thing if he's not willing to play ball?"

Carmody looked at him. "He *is* playing ball, Dennis. He's held up his end of the bargain. Now he's asking his questions and doing a little fishing in the process. There's nothing wrong with that. And there's nothing that says we have to take the bait, either."

Her voice was calm and level, and I smiled at her. While Turpin might have been—and maybe still was—a high-powered securities lawyer, it was clear he hadn't spent much time in court. And it was just as clear that Carmody had.

Turpin's mouth got tight and his nostrils flared, and I could see him talking himself down.

"So this business of his being on leave . . . ?" I asked.

"Technically, he *is* on leave," Carmody said. "That's the status he was placed on when he didn't return from vacation." Turpin shot her an annoyed look, but it passed.

"When did he tell you he was taking vacation?"

Turpin answered this time. "The last day he was in the office—or that night. He left a voice mail with his number two in research, saying he was taking three weeks. She got it the next morning."

"He say anything about where he was going?" Turpin shook his head. "And he hadn't mentioned this vacation to anyone beforehand?" Another no. "That didn't worry anybody?"

"I thought a vacation was a good idea," Turpin said. "He had a lot on his mind."

"Like lawsuits and arbitration claims?" I asked. "Like the SEC?"

"That's something we're *not* going to talk about today, Mr. March," Carmody said. I nodded.

"Anybody he's particularly friendly with here at the office?" I asked. They looked puzzled.

"Not that I know of," Turpin said.

"Have you been looking for him?" I asked.

"We've made some calls," Turpin said.

I nodded. "Calls to whom?"

Turpin stiffened visibly and looked at Carmody.

"We've spoken with his lawyer, Toby Kahn," she said. "He hasn't heard anything from Danes since he left. On the other hand, he wasn't expecting to. The cases are moving to settlement, and there's nothing happening now that requires Danes's input."

"And that's the extent of your search—calling his lawyer?"

Turpin's face darkened. "What the hell would you have us do?" he said.

I shrugged. "You're not worried about him at all?"

"We'd like to know if he plans on coming back," he huffed. "We'd like to—"

Carmody cut him off. "Do you have reason to worry about him, Mr. March?" she asked me. "If so, you should take your concerns to the police. That's what we would do."

"But you haven't yet?"

She shook her head. "As Dennis said, we've made some calls. But we haven't found out any more than you have, and nothing that would lead us to bring in the police."

Turpin checked his watch. "I think you've hit your limit here, March," he said.

"Just one more thing. What *were* you and he fighting about the day he walked out of here?" Turpin may have had a short fuse but he wasn't completely stupid, and this time he managed a respectable lie.

"I don't know who you've been talking to, but whoever it is they're not reliable. Gregory Danes is a smart guy, with firm opinions that he defends vigorously. I can respect that—I'm that way myself. Sometimes Greg knocks heads with people—and so do I. Occasionally, we've knocked heads with each other. Voices get raised, doors get slammed. It happens in business; sometimes it's even healthy. *Creative tension,* they call it." His smile was crooked and disturbing.

"And what were the two of you creatively tense about that day?"

Turpin's face got tight, but Jan Carmody spoke before he could. "I think Dennis was right when he suggested we wrap this up, Mr. March. Thanks for your time today." She didn't wait for a response but pulled a date book from the briefcase at her feet and began leafing through it. Turpin was perfectly still. His thick brows were knit together, and he stared at me as if I'd stolen his last banana. I left.

I waited alone for the elevator, and it arrived empty. I knew from the directory Neary had given me that Danes's department, Research, was on 22. I rode down two floors.

The reception area was unattended when I passed through, and for no good reason I turned left. The color scheme on this floor was slate blue and white. Otherwise, it was nearly identical to 24: cubicles and thick carpet, telephones and computers, bent heads and hushed tones. The people in the cubicles paid me no heed as I walked by.

I turned a corner and came to another acre of blue and white cubicles, bordered by offices and conference rooms. But in this neighborhood, instead of bland corporate art on the walls, there were long chrome racks stocked with Pace-Loyette research reports. The cubicles here were larger and equipped with more imposing computers, sometimes several of them, and the stacks of paper and periodicals rose higher. There was a big glass room along the rear wall, outfitted like a library. I figured this was Research. Although it was well past lunchtime, there were few people about. If any of them noticed me, they didn't seem to care. I went looking for the biggest office.

It was on a corner, and Danes's name was outside. Nearby was a large low-walled cubicle with Giselle Thomas's name on it. It was empty. I looked around and saw no one. I tried the door. It was locked.

"Can I help you?" It was a woman's voice and nothing like helpful. I turned around. She was tall and very thin, and she was standing near Giselle Thomas's cubicle, holding an armful of journals. She wore khaki pants and a beige button-down shirt and a wary expression on her pinched face.

"Irene Pratt's office?" I said.

She scowled. Her eyes went to Danes's nameplate and came back to me. "Well, this clearly isn't it." She looked me up and down and decided I passed some sort of muster. "Irene is back that way and around the corner." She gestured with her head. I thanked her and walked off. I glanced back as I was rounding the corner and saw her talking to a tall black woman. They were looking in my direction. Shit.

My pulse quickened. It was just a matter of time now; I needed to pick up the pace. Irene Pratt's office was where the skinny woman said it would be, and the door was open. Her assistant's cubicle was empty. I looked into the doorway.

Pratt's office was similar to Turpin's, but with more evidence of actual work being done in it. There was more technology on her desk—three big flat-panel screens—and more paper, too—wobbly stacks of spreadsheets, prospectuses, research reports, and trade rags—and no room for knick-knacks. Pratt was at her desk, talking into a telephone headset and scanning one of her monitors, when I stepped in. She looked up.

Disheveled chestnut hair fell past her shoulders and framed her pale oval face. Round wire-framed glasses sat askew on her short straight nose; the eyes behind them were large and dark and intelligent. Her mouth was small and skeptical and partially obscured by the headset microphone. Her pink blouse had a square neck and a coffee stain down the front. If not for the headset and the speed at which she spoke, it would've been easy to imagine Irene Pratt as an academic—a Beowulf scholar, perhaps, or an expert in medieval textiles—something dusty and far from the world of commerce. A fragment of her conversation dispelled the thought.

"I'm telling you, they're full of shit. They're shading the costs, and their pension assumptions are solidly fucked." The high nasal voice was as I remembered it.

Irene Pratt tilted her head and looked at me. There was no alarm in her gaze and not much curiosity, just a mild annoyance. She nodded as she listened through the headset and turned back to her monitor. She started speaking again but I never heard what she said.

"Excuse me, sir, can we help you?" It was a stern, skeptical voice—a cop voice—from the hallway behind me. They were faster than I expected. I felt an adrenal surge and turned.

There were two of them, both well over six feet, in ill-fitting blue blazers, sagging gray pants, and thick cop shoes. They wore equipment belts under their jackets, a radio on the left hip, a telescoping baton on the right; the cuffs and mace were probably in back. The older one was broad and balding and sleepy looking. The younger one had a blond crew cut and a thick face and big hands he couldn't keep still. The cop voice belonged to the older one.

"Could you step over here, sir, and show us some ID?" he said. He gestured to his younger partner to flank me, but their rhythm was disrupted by Dennis Turpin, rounding the corner with a full head of steam. Standing up, he was no more than five-foot-six, and his rolling bandy-legged gait and long arms accentuated his chimplike qualities.

"I knew it!" he said. He was huffing and somehow pleased. "I knew I couldn't trust you. What the hell do you think you're doing here? Did you think I wasn't serious when I told you to stay away? Did you think I was just blowing smoke?" He jabbed his finger in my chest. I smiled down at him.

"That's the problem with playacting—too much of it and people don't know when you're blowing smoke and when you're not. Like that nonsense about *creative tension.* What was I supposed to make of that?" I stopped smiling. "And please keep your hands off me." Turpin sputtered and glanced at his security guards and at the people who stood staring from their cubicles. The balding guard still had his sleepy look, but his brow was furrowed, as if he'd forgotten something. The younger one looked eager.

"You'll see how serious I am when I have these men toss you out of here, and I have you up on trespass charges."

"Trespass?" I smiled again. "I took a wrong turn on my way out, and when I found myself in the Research department I thought I'd drop in on Ms. Pratt. That's pretty thin grounds for trespassing, Turpin—especially when I came here at your invitation." I looked back at Pratt's office. She was watching from her doorway, but her expression was hard to read. Turpin sputtered some more. He shook his head fiercely and poked me in the chest again.

"Throw this bastard out on his ass," he said. The older guard started to speak, but the young guy couldn't hold his water any longer. His voice was nervous and excited and surprisingly high-pitched. Probably the steroids.

"You heard the man, shithead, you're gone," he said.

"No, Jimmy—," the balding guard said, but it was too late; Jimmy had already gripped my arm, just above the elbow, and was reaching for my wrist to complete the come-along hold. I took a step forward and Jimmy followed, off balance and leaning into me. I took a quarter pivot and drove my free elbow into his ribs. He gasped and loosened his grip, and I pivoted again, jerked my other elbow loose, and popped it into his nose. His head snapped back and his hands flew up and I spun away, adrenaline dancing through my arms and legs.

"Fuck!" he yelped. Blood trickled between his fingers. "My fucking nose!" Turpin looked—open-mouthed—from Jimmy to me and back again.

"Jesus," he said. The older guard shook his head ruefully. Jimmy wiped his nose with the back of his hand and winced. He stared at the blood and then at me, and his eyes got small.

"Bastard," he hissed, and he reached for his baton. The older guy put a hand on Jimmy's wrist and stopped him in his tracks.

"Okay, Jimmy," he said softly, and he looked at me. His eyes were hard and shiny, like blue marbles, and there was nothing sleepy left in them. "This fellow is just leaving, and he's doing it quietly and right away. And he knows, if he does that, then nobody has to lay hands on nobody anymore. Isn't that right, sir?" I nodded slowly, and something relaxed in the old guy's shoulders. He tensed up again when Turpin spoke.

"He's not going anywhere, goddammit. He assaulted this man, and we're holding him for the police." Turpin rocked from one foot to the other and the older guy shook his head.

I took another deep breath and managed a small laugh. "That's your story. Mine is that you incited this guy to attack me and I defended myself. I'm happy to stick around and let the cops and the press sort it out; I'm happy to leave, too. It's your choice."

Turpin's face was an odd mauve color, and his lips all but disappeared. The balding guard looked at him sadly, but Turpin didn't notice. He just stood there—red-faced, silent, and shaking with anger. I looked over at Pratt's office. She was still in the doorway, watching, and her expression was still a mystery. After a moment, I headed for the elevator.

6

I slouched in the back of the cab and cursed myself all the way to 34th Street. Mixing it up with Turpin and his security thug had been stupid and pointless, and I was angry with myself for doing it. He was a posturing little martinet and I didn't like being poked, but that was no excuse—nor was the fact that he'd been so easy to bait. Screwing around with him hadn't bought me anything, and it could have landed me in some time-wasting trouble.

The rest of the way home, I thought about the little I'd learned at Pace-Loyette. As Nina Sachs had gathered, Pace management had no better idea of Danes's whereabouts than she did, but they were definitely interested—enough to have made some discreet phone calls, anyway, and to have had a meeting with me. But I didn't think their curiosity—or worry—had led them to dispatch any errand boys uptown to grease palms and ask questions. And it hadn't been sufficient to get them to call the cops. Or maybe, as Neary had suggested, the imperative to keep a low profile trumped all. Which left them little else to do with the question of Gregory Danes, it seemed, than to wrap some lawyers around it.

It was after three when the taxi dropped me at home. The building was quiet except for my footsteps. I opened windows and soft air worked its way around my apartment. It stirred a faint surprising trace of Jane's scent and I wondered what she was doing just then. I poured a glass of water and let my messages play. Lauren's voice came over the speaker.

"Just reminding you about Ned's, on Saturday. Keith and I will be there at two. See ya." I'd seen more of my family in the past few months than I had in years—at brunches, birthdays, an anniversary, and even a second cousin's bar mitzvah. But the rapprochement was a tentative one for all concerned, and Lauren and her husband, Keith, had decided that I should be chaperoned at these events lest I cut and run, or worse. They'd appointed themselves to the job.

After Lauren came the hushed schoolmarm tones of Mrs. Konigsberg, my brother's assistant. She was about three hundred years old and, before my brother, she had worked for my uncles and my grandfather at Klein & Sons. Besides ancient, Mrs. K was precise, rigid, and entirely humorless, and she couldn't have disapproved of me more if she'd been my own mother.

"Mr. March, this is Ida Konigsberg calling from Klein and Sons," she said, as if I might not recognize her voice or her name or might think she'd changed employers after all these centuries. "I'm confirming your meeting tomorrow afternoon, at two o'clock, here at our offices." She recited the address and I laughed out loud, fully expecting her to follow with directions. "You'll be interviewing Mr. Geoffrey Tyne, whose curriculum vitae you should already have received. The interview will take place in Mr. Ned March's conference room, next to his office on the seventh floor. Mr. March would like to meet with you afterward for about fifteen minutes, to discuss your impressions of Mr. Tyne. Please call me to confirm." I didn't dare do otherwise.

Mrs. K's call ended in a discreet click, and then Jane's voice was there. There was noise on the line and other voices in the background.

"I'm with the lawyers again, and it looks like I'll be here late." I heard the rueful smile in her voice. "Leave a message, tell me what you're up to. Maybe we can have dinner, if you don't mind waiting." I heard someone call her name. "Got to jump. Call me."

I'd learned that, to Jane, *late* could mean anything from nine till after midnight, and I called to tell her voice mail that tonight I couldn't wait. Tonight I'd be working. I'd made two failed attempts to speak with Irene Pratt; the third time, I figured, would be the charm. I opened up my laptop and started my browser.

There were three Irene Pratts in the metropolitan area, but only one in

Manhattan—on the Upper West Side. I dialed her number, and an answering machine picked up. I recognized the quick talk and the Long Island accent. I didn't leave a message. I couldn't count on finding Pratt at home for at least a couple of hours, so I heated some coffee and returned to the court records databases and my list of the complaints against Danes and Pace-Loyette.

The list of the aggrieved was long and varied—from pension funds in the Midwest to coupon clippers in the Sun Belt and day traders on both coasts—and their allegations ranged from plain old negligence and conflict of interest to elaborate conspiracy and fraud. Most, though not all, involved Piedmont Science. Some of the claims had been resolved, settled out of sight for undisclosed sums and with all concerned silenced by nondisclosure agreements, and some were still pending, drifting slowly through a limbo of depositions and discoveries, but none of them had yet made it to an actual judgment.

Mixed in with the investor suits were others, unrelated to Danes's job as an analyst. There was a six-year-old action—ultimately dismissed—against Danes and every other shareholder in his old 90th Street co-op, brought by a bicycle messenger who'd sprained his ankle in the building's lobby. And there was an eight-year-old claim, brought by Danes, which involved chipped granite countertops, a broken sink, and an unrepentant contractor. It had dried up after five months. At the bottom of my list was the ten-year-old case of *Sachs v. Danes,* the divorce proceedings. Seeing it there reminded me that I owed Nina a progress report, and I called her before I headed uptown. She answered on the eighth ring, and she was distracted and barely civil.

"I'm working, for chrissakes," she muttered, and I heard her lighter snap. "You can come over tonight if you want to talk." I told her I would.

Irene Pratt lived in the upper seventies, on a leafy street of brownstones between Columbus and Amsterdam avenues. It was nearly six when I got there, and the narrow sidewalks were crowded with people walking dogs and toting groceries and heading for expensive workouts. Pratt's building was a Romanesque town house of rough, tobacco-colored stone. It was five stories tall, with narrow arched windows, a cavernous entryway, and lots of decorative masonry. There was a video intercom system at the door. Judging from the buttons, there was only one apartment per floor. Pratt was on the third. I buzzed and waited and nothing happened. It was still early and I wasn't surprised. I walked down the street.

There was a bar on the corner of Columbus, with small tables out front. I found one with a clear view of Pratt's building and ordered a ginger ale. I stretched out my legs and worked my way through a bowl of cashews while the soft air grew dark. Noise and smoke and the smell of liquor thickened around me, and with them—suddenly—came a strong and acrid nostalgia.

It could have been the light that set it off—the ripening purple sky and the swelling shadows, the sense of recklessness and promise that seemed to fall with evening—or it could have been the jumble of voices—laughing, flirting, boasting and arch, eager to please, studiously bored, and all a little slurred. It could have been the tiny buzz of danger as the customers grew louder and less cautious, or the possibility of violence—however remote— that rode with every jostling arm and elbow. It could have been the anonymous feel of being alone in the midst of a raucous crowd that did it, or my own incipient restlessness, scratching in my head like a low-grade fever. Whatever the cues, the memories—of other bars and other evenings, years ago—were powerful and close enough to taste. Columbus Avenue was a world away from Burr County, and from the dives I'd haunted in the months after Anne's death. But the jagged, angry feeling that was always with me then was abruptly back again, lodged in my chest like a hunk of broken glass.

Back then it was broken glass and a head full of static, a furious buzzing that I could never silence but could only distract. And every night, for four blurry months, I did just that, trading grief and guilt for motion, for drink and drugs, for violence and sex. I crashed along the back roads with my headlights dark and a chemical fire in my brain, and I made the rounds of places like the Rind and Buddy's Fox and every other bucket of blood in the county. When I paused it was only to pass out, and when I came to I was often bruised and battered, or else I was sprawled alongside women whose names I never knew and who were never pleased to see me in the light of day. After a while, I took my act to the neighboring counties, to spare my colleagues the bother and embarrassment of cleaning up after me. It was only luck that no one got killed.

I swallowed some ginger ale, and for an instant it tasted smoky and bitter and my throat closed up. These were long-absent feelings, but they were more than familiar. They dwelled someplace below conscious recall and were bound in me like muscle memory. Like riding a bike. And they scared the hell out of me.

A shudder ran through me and I looked up the street and saw Irene Pratt, walking east from Amsterdam. She had a purse and a big leather tote bag on her shoulder and a plastic grocery sack in her hand, and her gait was awkward. Her head was down, but I recognized the thick chestnut hair and the pink blouse.

I watched her fumble for her keys and disappear inside. I gave her twenty minutes—time enough to sort the mail, put the groceries away, check messages, change clothes; then I took out my cell phone and punched her number. When she answered, I spoke fast.

"Ms. Pratt, this is John March. We spoke yesterday morning, and I stopped by your office this afternoon—"

She cut me off. "Jesus Christ, what the hell are you calling me at home for? What do you want from me?"

"I want to talk about Gregory Danes, Ms. Pratt. I'm trying to find him, and I thought maybe you could help."

She heaved an exasperated sigh. "I told you, we can't—"

It was my turn to cut her off. "I know what your orders are, Ms. Pratt. I'm at the bar on the corner, sitting at a table outside. I'll be here for another half hour if you want to talk." I clicked off.

It took her forty-five minutes, and her steps were tentative. She'd changed into jeans and sneakers and a blue T-shirt from an electronics trade show in Las Vegas. She was small-breasted and slender, and her arms were soft looking. There was a gold watch on her wrist and a plastic clip holding back her heavy hair. She stood near my table and looked down at me.

"You're still here," she said. There was a dark shine to her eyes and more color in her face. A light perfume wafted toward me, something with lilac. I nodded.

"Sit," I said, but she didn't.

"What do you want from me?"

"I told you, I'm trying to find your boss. And I'm trying to find someone who cares enough that he's missing to help me out. I thought that might be you." Pratt squinted at me but did not speak. "Sit," I said again. I pulled out the metal chair next to mine. "I'll buy you a drink."

She rested her hand on the back of the chair and shook her head. "Why do you say *missing*?"

"I don't know what else to call it. The guy's gone away—no one knows where—and he hasn't come back when he said he would. And no one has heard from him since the day he left. What do you call it?"

Pratt bit her lower lip. "There's nothing I can tell you. I don't know where he is, and the last I heard from him was his voice mail, telling me he was taking time off."

A waitress orbited the table; I caught her eye and she came closer. "Another ginger ale for me, and . . ." The waitress and I looked at Irene Pratt, who looked irritated, and then resigned.

"I don't know . . . a Bud, I guess." The waitress went away, and Pratt looked down at me.

"Sit," I said. Pratt pulled the chair out and sat at its edge. "Nuts?" I offered her the bowl. She ignored them.

"I don't know where the hell he is," she said softly. She played with the clasp of her gold watch. Her hands were small, and her nails were clipped short and unvarnished.

"How long have you worked with him?" She looked up at me and I noticed the lines around her eyes and mouth. I put her age at thirty-five.

"What's that got to do with anything?" she said.

"It has to do with how well you know him, which has to do with how much help you might be to me."

Pratt wrinkled her brow and the waitress came. I drank some ginger ale. Pratt drank her Bud from the bottle.

"I've worked for him since I got out of B-school—almost a dozen years," she said. "And I guess I know him as well as anybody—better, maybe."

"You knew him when he was married?"

She smiled sourly and nodded. "And during the divorce," she said.

"You know his wife?"

Another sour smile. "The Brooklyn Frida Kahlo? I met her once or twice, before the bullets started flying." She drank some more Bud and picked a nut from the bowl.

"Their breakup was ugly?"

Pratt laughed. "Like you wouldn't believe." She took another drink and shook her head. "I'm amazed they got through it without somebody being dead. 'Course, I'm amazed they got together in the first place, or ever had a kid." Another drink and more head shaking. "I don't know why people do it." I wasn't sure what *it* was exactly, but I didn't ask. Her beer was gone, and I waved to the waitress for another.

"He fool around?"

She frowned. "Is that why you want to talk to me? You think we had something going?"

The thought had occurred to me, but I didn't say so. The waitress brought another beer, another ginger ale, and a fresh bowl of nuts. Pratt took a swallow.

"Well, that's bullshit," she said. "*Old* bullshit, too. Jesus, I'd have to be crazy. . . . His wife tried to make something out of that in the divorce, but it didn't fly. And she had plenty more to sink her teeth into."

"Meaning he did fool around?" Pratt nodded. "A lot?" Another nod. "With anyone in particular?"

"Back then? With no one in particular, and everyone he could." She drank some more Bud and looked at the bottle and then at me. "Not that Greg was some kind of sex machine. In fact, I always thought there was something . . . I don't know . . . kind of neutral about him—sexually, I mean." Pratt picked another nut from the bowl. "But what the hell do I know? I guess what I'm saying is I think the fooling around was more an ego thing than a sex thing for him."

I nodded. It usually is. Pratt hitched her chair closer to the table and put her bottle on the tabletop. It was nearly empty.

"Was the divorce rough on him?"

"Oh, yeah, it was a big ego bruise. Losing the kid, and a big pile of dough, and his wife—to another *woman*—he was a goddamn mess."

Pratt sat back and crossed her ankle over her knee. A strand of hair had worked itself loose from her clip and fell across her cheek, and her eyes were unfocused behind their glasses. She looked young and bookish in the fading light. She had hold of a thread now, and I didn't want her to lose it.

"Was he as bad then as he has been lately?" I asked.

She shook her head slowly. "No . . . that was different. That was just one thing—just one part of his life, I guess. And even though it pissed him off something fierce, the rest of his life—the work—was going fine. Better than fine. Now it's all turned to shit."

"I guess it's been a rough few years for everyone in your department," I said. I pushed the nut bowl toward her. She took a handful and looked over my shoulder at the crowds—heavier now—that passed along the sidewalks. The bar was packed, and the voices and the music and the traffic sounds ran together in a blur of white noise. The sun was all but gone, and sodium lamps and neon tinted the faces around us. Pratt killed the Bud, placed the bottle carefully on the table, and looked at me.

"A nightmare," she said softly. "You wouldn't—"

The words caught in her throat and she looked down and swallowed a couple of times. Our waitress spun by, and I motioned for another round. Pratt looked up at me.

"For a while there, you couldn't escape the stories—in the papers, on TV, all over the Web—it was fucking open season on stock analysts." A bitter smile crossed her face and faded to a grimace. "If you read enough of them, you'd think all we did was sit around and dream up lies to tell the widows and orphans—when we weren't busy sucking up to CEOs and cashing our bonus checks, that is. They died down finally, the stories and the bad jokes, but it's a different world now. The department's not even half the size it used to be, and the pay . . ." Pratt shook her head and picked up her empty beer bottle and put it down again.

"Did they get those stories wrong?" I asked quietly.

"The press?" Pratt's face was sour, and so was her voice. "They always get it at least half wrong."

I had no argument with her there and I nodded. Pratt continued.

"I've been an analyst for nearly twelve years. Besides my MBA, I've got a BS in computer science and a master's in electrical engineering. I've covered semiconductors, consumer electronics, the video game industry, and—modesty aside—I probably know as much about the companies I follow as the CEOs who run them.

"My average workday is fourteen hours—wall-to-wall, six days a week. And you know what I do when I get home at night, after I feed my fish and call my mom? I read: annual reports, quarterlies, mid-quarter updates, economic analyses, purchasing statistics, and you wouldn't believe what else. I read the science journals for original research and the trade rags for gossip. I read about who's hot and who's not, whose project is over budget and whose got canceled and who just jumped from one ship to another. And of course, I read all the product profiles—the head-to-head comparisons, the top-ten lists, the focus groups . . ." Her voice wavered, and she coughed and shook her head. "I read reviews of video games, and hang out in fucking chat rooms—just to hear what the goddamn fourteen-year-olds think.

"And when I'm not reading, I'm crunching numbers—earnings projections, cost estimates, market share, financing costs, interest rate scenarios, cash flows. . . . Jesus. It's made me half blind."

Our drinks came. Pratt took a long swallow and seemed to steady.

"You like those violins?" she asked. She laughed bitterly. "I'm not a fool, and I'm not looking for sympathy. I know plenty of people work hard, and hardly any of them get paid like I do. But my point is, I never phoned it in—not once. My point is . . ." She took another drink and put her bottle down. Her hands were wet with condensation, and she stared at them for a long moment and wiped them on her jeans. "I don't know what the hell my point is."

"You said the press got it only halfway right."

Pratt sighed and shook her head. "My mom has never had a clue what I do for a living—just no idea at all. She used to ask about it the first few years I was in the business, and I used to try to explain, but it went in one ear and out the other, and after a while she quit asking. But you know what she said to me at the height of the frenzy, when those stories were running practically every day? She said, *You just start writing what you think about those companies, honey, and don't let anyone make you say anything different. You just start telling the truth—no one can blame you for that.* Can you believe it? My own mother—and she assumes it's all some kind of scam. She assumes that I've been lying.

"The press went on and on about *conflict of interest* and *lack of independence* like they'd discovered a new planet or something. Like it was a big secret that securities firms do business with the companies their analysts cover—like we were trying to hide something. Jesus, if that was a secret, it was the worst-kept one of all time."

"I think it *was* news to some investors. And I think the horse-trading part of it—swapping *buy* recommendations and God knows what else for investment banking business—was a little hard for anyone to swallow."

Pratt's face reddened and her dark eyes shone. "Hey, I'm not saying there weren't abuses. And if somebody decides the rule book was no good and we need a whole new edition, that's fine by me. I lived by the old version and I'll live by the new version too. But don't turn me into a criminal retroactively, for chrissakes—just for playing the game the same way everyone else did." Pratt wiped something from beneath her eye and drank some more beer.

"And just for the record, you know the last time I said, *What the fuck, what's a couple of cents EPS one way or the other*—the last time I thought about how much business one of my companies does with Pace and what kind of recommendation might win us some more—the last time I put out an opinion I didn't believe in one hundred and ten percent? Never. Not once. Not fucking ever."

She took another long pull and smiled crookedly.

"Mom doesn't talk about my work anymore," Pratt said. "Now all she wants to know is when I'm getting married." Another strand of hair fell into Pratt's face, and she pushed it behind her ear. She took a deep breath and let it out slowly. "What the hell does this have to do with Greg, anyway?" she said. A truck rumbled by, and the air was burnt in its wake. I looked at Pratt, but she wouldn't meet my eyes.

"Does he feel the same way you do about all this? Does he feel as . . . let down?"

She took her glasses off and cleaned them on her T-shirt. Her face looked bare and confused without them. She put them back on and shook her head.

"It's worse for him. Until all this shit, Greg bought into the whole star-analyst thing; he believed his own press. For years he lived on a steady diet of money and TV and people saying yes to anything he wanted, and putting up with all his crazy bullshit in the office. It's like eating nothing but chocolate. And then overnight we went from being the village wise men to being the village idiots—or worse.

"It was hard on everybody, but Greg most of all. He'd been into it the most, and I guess he needed it the most. So when it all stopped, when people stopped calling . . ." Pratt ran her finger along the edge of the Bud label and began picking at it with a fingernail.

"I heard he went nuts."

"From who?" she said, but she waved away her own question. "Fuck, it doesn't matter. You heard right. He was off the wall for a while—obsessed with his reputation, convinced he was going to be left holding the bag for Piedmont and every other thing, while everyone else made out like bandits—really paranoid. He's finally settled down to merely impossible." Pratt drained her third Bud, and waved the empty at the waitress. Her glasses slipped down her nose and she pushed them up with her thumb.

"Why do you put up with it?" I asked her.

Her laugh was loud and girlish. "Beats me," she said. She looked at me, waiting for a response. When none came, she shook her head. "You never heard that joke—about what the masochist said, when someone asked why she hung around with the sadist? *Beats me.*"

She laughed some more, and the waitress delivered another round. Pratt sipped at her fourth beer and found the chain of her thoughts again.

"If you don't know him, he comes off like an asshole—vindictive, arrogant, nuts. But that's not really Greg—not all of him, anyway. Like the arrogance. Some of that is just his sense of humor—he's really sarcastic. And some of it is just . . . he's like a kid who's always got to be the smartest one in class and makes sure everybody knows it.

"A lot of his press was for real, though. What he can pull from a balance sheet is amazing, and the information he keeps in his head . . . You want to know the average revenue per employee of the top three database software companies or how much debt each one is carrying, just ask Greg. He's faster than the Internet. I learned more from him the first month I was at Pace than I did in two years at NYU.

"And it isn't just having the numbers handy. There's as much art as science in this kind of analysis, and when it comes to the big picture—the macroeconomics, the forces and trends that can change whole industries—Greg sees things way before anybody else. He sees the shape of things to come."

I swirled ice in my glass and looked at Pratt. "How did he end up on the wrong side of so many calls, then?"

She shrugged. "I don't really know. Maybe he got a little too fond of one of his own theories, or maybe he didn't pay enough attention to new data; maybe he was a little slow to reevaluate certain companies—I don't know. Like I said, it's as much art as science, and you don't always get it right; no one does. At the end of the day, Greg was less wrong than a lot of people. The guy is a fucking genius, March."

I nodded. "Genius isn't always easy to be around."

Pratt smiled ruefully. "You got that right," she said. "But Greg can surprise you. He can be . . . nice. You don't expect it from him, but he can be incredibly generous and loyal."

I looked at her and raised an eyebrow. Pratt shook her head, and her hair tumbled free of the clip and fell around her shoulders. She didn't seem to mind.

"I'd been at Pace a year and a half when my mom got sick. Breast cancer—very aggressive. It's just the two of us, and she's out on the Island, and I didn't know what the fuck to do. I go into Greg's office one morning and tell him about it—and that I might need some time off—and he just looks at me and nods and basically doesn't say shit. Great, I think, real supportive. One more thing to worry about.

"That afternoon, he calls me back in his office. He hands me a slip of paper with an address and a time on it. Tells me my mom has an appointment the next day at Sloan-Kettering with the top breast cancer guy, and he's made arrangements with Bobby Loyette about us using the corporate apartment if my mom needs to stay in the city for treatments.

"I was blown away. I just sat there, not knowing what to say. Greg didn't seem to expect me to say anything. Hell, he barely looked at me the whole time he was telling me this stuff. I sat there, and he sent some e-mails, and after a while we started talking about Intel's valuation." Pratt picked up the bottle again and looked at it, but put it down without drinking.

"He's fucked up, like a lot of people are." She paused and stared at me. I wasn't going to argue with her. "But he's a decent guy too." Pratt leaned back and worked her fingers through her thick hair. Her clip fell to the ground and she stooped to get it. She steadied herself on the table on the way up and laughed. "Christ, four beers on an empty stomach. You got me shitfaced."

I nodded. "You want dinner? My treat."

She looked at me and straightened her glasses. "And then what, you going to take advantage of me?"

I shook my head and laughed. "No more than I have already." I signaled the waitress, who brought two menus.

"Why not? You married or something?" Pratt blushed even as she asked the question.

I smiled. "Or something."

She nodded and looked over the menu.

The waitress came again and Pratt ordered a burger and a Coke; I had the vegetarian chili. Pratt was quiet, and I thought that embarrassment and worry might be setting in. I didn't want her dwelling on it.

"I heard he had a lively meeting with Turpin the day he left," I said.

Pratt smiled. "*Lively*—that's a nice term for it. Any more lively, and we would've called the cops."

"Any idea what it was about?"

"The same old thing, I'm sure: the lawsuits. That's what Greg and Tampon always argue about."

"Tampon?"

Pratt colored again. "That's what Greg calls him. It's kind of caught on."

"I can imagine. What about the lawsuits do they argue over?"

"Fight or flight, Greg calls it: fight it out in court or settle. Greg is all about fighting."

"And Turpin wants to settle?"

Pratt nodded. "That's what they brought him in to do."

"Who are *they*?"

"Management. They brought Tampon in five, six months ago—*to clear the air,* they said—so we could focus on other things. Apparently that meant settle the cases quickly, quietly, and as cheaply as possible."

"Greg disagrees with that strategy?"

Pratt snorted. "It makes him crazy. He says they aren't giving him an opportunity to clear his name and that they're selling him out. Greg is not the most trusting guy in the world to begin with, and this plays right into his paranoia."

"I gather he doesn't have that market cornered, though."

Pratt gave me a quizzical look. "You mean Turpin?"

I nodded. "If his attitude is anything to go by, Pace management seems pretty nervous about Danes."

"Between the arguments and the rumors about another look-see from the regulators—and now with Greg being gone—yeah, I guess they're tense."

"Should they be?"

"About Greg turning on them or something?" I nodded, and Pratt's brow furrowed. "I'd like to say no, but the truth is—I don't know. Greg *is* paranoid, and he never, *ever* leaves his ass uncovered. He's definitely not a guy I would play musical chairs with—not without a lot of padding. But . . . I don't know."

The waitress brought our food. Pratt took a desperate swallow of her Coke and a bite of her burger. Juice ran down her chin, and I handed her a napkin. I took a spoonful of vegetable chili. It tasted like old succotash, soaked in Tabasco. I pushed it aside.

"You've said Greg can be difficult"—Pratt snorted—"is there anyone he was particularly difficult with? Anyone holding a grudge?"

She shook her head. "He's difficult with everyone." She chewed some more of her burger. "But someone holding a grudge? Nobody jumps out, unless you count the people suing him."

"Who else is he close to, besides you?"

Pratt wiped her hands on her napkin and pulled her hair back and was quiet for a while. She shook her head slowly.

"I don't really know. I know he loves his kid—Billy—as much as he loves anybody. He may not know what to make of him half the time, but he loves him. Besides that?" She shrugged.

"No other family?"

"There's the ex, if she counts. They still talk—about the kid, mostly— and she still pisses him off. And I think he has a brother or stepbrother who got himself in trouble a few years back—somewhere out in Jersey, I think. A reporter picked up on it, and it was five minutes of embarrassment for Greg."

"How about his friends?"

"There's some guy he goes to hear music with, up in the country some-place. I don't know his name, though." She thought some more and hesitated. "And . . . there was Sovitch."

"Linda Sovitch? From *Market Minds*?" Pratt nodded. "They're friends?"

"They used to be—when Greg was on the show all the time. I'm not sure how friendly they are now; he wasn't happy when the guest spots dried up. But I know Greg had lunch with her—right before his last session with Tampon."

I finished my ginger ale and crunched on an ice cube and thought. "Did he ever talk about leaving?" I asked.

"Leaving Pace? We talked about it a lot—especially lately—about go-ing out on our own, setting up a research company. One of the things that drove him nuts about settling the lawsuits was he thought it would screw that up—screw up his reputation and his earning power. Screw them up more, I guess."

"You would do it—go into business with him?"

She nodded vigorously. "For an equity stake? You bet I would. Nothing like that is coming my way at Pace."

"You're not in line for Greg's job if he walks?"

Pratt made a derisive sound. "Are you kidding? I'm fine to keep the seat warm while Greg's away, but when it comes time to fill his spot perma-nently, they'll bring a name in from outside—assuming they want to keep a research department at all. If Greg leaves, I've got to make plans, one way or another." She fiddled with the pile of slaw on her plate and looked at me. She wasn't as light-headed now, and worry was coming back into her eyes. I didn't have long.

"Do you remember what he said in his voice mail—when he told you he was taking vacation?"

She nodded. "I remember. It wasn't a long message—something like *I'm out of here for three weeks—starting now. Tell whoever you're supposed to tell. Good luck.*"

"That's it? He didn't say anything else?" She shook her head. "Any thoughts about his timing—about why he left when he did?"

She pursed her lips and ran a hand absently through her hair. "I know he was pissed off about a lot of things—the lawsuits, all the bad press, Tampon—and he had been for a while. I guess it all just got to him that day. Tampon was the last straw." Pratt worried her lower lip and checked and rechecked her watch. She glanced down the block, toward her apartment building.

"Has anyone besides me come looking for Danes? Has anyone else called or come to see you?"

"As far as visitors go, you're it, but people call for Greg all the time. If it's business they talk to me or one of the other analysts; otherwise we refer them to Nancy Mayhew."

"He ever do anything like this before—just take unscheduled vacation time?"

Pratt nodded. "Two or three times, I guess, but then he called after a few days and told us when he'd be back."

"But he hasn't called this time, and he hasn't come back. Any idea why?"

Pratt got quiet and looked away, at the street beyond my shoulder. She pursed her lips and shook her head. "I don't know," she said softly. "I just don't know."

"Are you worried about him?"

Pratt's eyes were large and dark behind her glasses. She looked at me for a long time and nodded.

7

It was a long run—two miles up, six miles around, and two miles back home—and I was right in the middle of it, at the north end of Central Park, on the steep climb up one side of Great Hill. It was five-fifteen, just past dawn, and the thin clouds that had brought showers overnight had begun to fray. The pavement was still wet and traffic was light: a few cabs, a few black cars, an aggressive peloton of racing bikes, and some other solitary runners, cocooned in thoughts and breath. I leaned into the hill and tried not to gasp. My own thoughts turned to Nina Sachs and her family.

It had been close to ten last night when I'd walked from Clark Street down Old Fulton to Water Street. Brooklyn was cooler, and the breeze off the river had sent a chill through me. Lights were burning in Sachs's loft and also at street level, in the I-2 Galeria de Arte, Brooklyn branch. I stood at the big glass door and looked inside.

It was a huge space, as large as Sachs's loft, with bleached wood floors and a wall of sidewalk-to-ceiling windows. The other walls were white, and a dense constellation of lights hung from the ceiling. Also hanging—from ceiling-mounted tracks—was a platoon of room dividers, movable walls of various widths presently arranged to divide the gallery into three exhibition bays. In the foreground, about ten yards inside the door, was a long mahogany counter, chest high and elaborately paneled.

There were people in the gallery, a skinny young woman with bleached hair, camo pants, and a T-shirt that let her midriff peek through, and an even skinnier young man with shiny blue bellbottoms and a steel ball through his nose. They were sealing and hauling wooden crates with impressive speed and skill. There were two opened wine bottles on the long counter, and three glasses, and an ashtray with a smoldering cigarette. I heard music through the glass—something thudding and techno.

Ines Icasa came through a door at the back of the gallery. Her hair was pulled back and she paused in mid-stride when she saw me. She was perfectly still for a moment, and then she moved again, walking to the counter, plucking her cigarette from the ashtray, and waving me in.

I pushed open the heavy door. The music got louder and I felt the bass in my gut. I smelled tobacco and sawdust and wood polish. The skinny people looked up from their crates and eyed me speculatively. Ines called me over.

"¿Qué tal? Just passing through the neighborhood, detective, or are you shopping for some art?" I smiled. Ines took a deep hit off her cigarette and reached for a wineglass. She poured some red wine, showed me the bottle, and raised her nice eyebrows. I shook my head. Ines frowned melodramatically and poured herself some more. I heard a noise from the end of the counter, and a foot, wearing something like a bowling shoe, slid into view. I walked over and looked down. It was Billy.

He was sitting on the floor on a huge paisley pillow, his back against the end of the counter. There were earphones on his head that snaked off to a sleek MP3 player hooked to his belt, and there was a spiral notebook and a thick text—*Trigonometry: An Introduction*—open in his lap. He raised his head and looked at me, blankly at first and then with recognition, but without discernable interest. He had a pencil in his teeth and a bottle of Sprite at his side. He was wearing baggy pants and a T-shirt again, but he'd swapped the Talking Heads lyric for a blowup of a Dr. Strange comic book cover. I raised a hand in greeting. Billy looked at me for a while and nodded minutely. I pointed at his shirt.

"Master of the Mystic Arts," I said. "One of my favorites—though he's no Batman, of course."

Billy winced theatrically and let the pencil fall into his lap. "Batman's a pussy," he said softly, and turned again to his book.

I laughed. "I'll let him know you said that."

"He is working, detective, and he is very focused," Ines said. She put a hand on my arm and led me back down the counter. "Are you sure I cannot get you something? Something stronger than wine, perhaps." I shook my head. There was a moist sheen to the smooth skin of her face, and her big almond eyes were gleaming.

"Trig's advanced for a twelve-year-old, isn't it?" I asked. "It seems to me I studied it in high school."

Ines smiled proudly and nodded. "Guillermo has always been many years advanced in maths. He takes most of his classes in the upper school." She glanced at the skinny man and woman, who had gone back to sliding wooden crates around. "We are packing up the last of an exhibition," Ines said. "*Iguacu,* we called it—the work of five painters from the Paraná region of Brazil. They are very talented, and the show was well received."

"I'm sorry I missed it."

"I will add you to our mailing list. You will never have to miss another." She drank some more wine. Her glass was nearly empty.

"Nina upstairs?" I asked.

"She is expecting you," Ines said.

"Then I'd better not keep her waiting." Ines nodded, and I started for the door. Halfway there I stopped and turned back to her. "You have any thoughts on where he might be?" Ines looked at me. She shook her head slowly and blew out a cloud of smoke.

Upstairs, Nina Sachs was still working. I'd rung twice and waited several minutes for her to answer. She wore a paint-splattered T-shirt and jeans, and she was barefoot. She had a smoke in one hand and a paintbrush in the other and her hazel eyes were jumpy, but she'd smiled when she opened the door.

"Back here," she said, and walked quickly across the loft to her studio. The place was a mess again, as if Ines had never cleaned it, and the smell was back. I followed Nina's smoke trail to her easel. Her little stereo was pounding out The Subdudes.

"Pull up a chair." She pointed to the beat-up armchair in the corner. "I'm doing busywork now, so I can talk." I turned the stereo down a notch and dragged the chair closer and sat. Nina paced back and forth before her canvas, and occasionally daubed at it, and sang along with The Subdudes as I spoke. She never interrupted and she never glanced in my direction. I told her about my trip to Pace-Loyette and my discussion with Irene Pratt, and about the long list of lawsuits and arbitration claims that Danes was involved in. When I was through, she stepped away from the easel, lit another cigarette, and leaned her hips against the utility sink.

"So, basically, you haven't found out anything." She said it matter-of-factly.

"I haven't found out much. But we know that the people at Pace are worried—"

"I knew that before," Sachs interrupted.

I nodded. "We know that someone else is looking for him—"

"But not who it is."

"And we know that Irene Pratt is genuinely concerned about him. As far as I can tell, she's one of the people closest to him, and she has no clue of where he went or why he hasn't returned."

Nina laughed nastily. "What did you think of Pratt? She's like a frustrated librarian, isn't she? Or the nun who secretly lusts for the priest."

"You think she and Danes had a thing?"

Nina shook her head and chuckled. "She's not his type. She's smart enough, but Greg likes a jagged little pill—he likes them edgy. Pratt's too much of a schoolgirl. But she was interested, God only knows why. No accounting for taste, I guess."

"I guess not," I said. "Though you must have thought he had something going for him—once upon a time."

She snorted. "Sure I did—back when I was fresh out of art school and fighting with my parents over the dump I was living in and the shithole where I waited tables. Back then I thought Greg was a hoot. He was smart and he knew it, and he had no time for people who weren't. And unlike most of the wannabe bohemians I hung with back then, he actually liked what he was doing, he made good money doing it, and he planned to make a lot more. Plus, he was fucking funny, too. He'd say anything to anybody, and he didn't give a damn who he pissed off. He was a real poke in the eye back then, and so was I. Maybe I still am."

Nina looked at her high ceiling and blew out a long cord of smoke.

"'Course, all that gets old fast when you live with it every day and he decides he's smarter than you are and you're just there to fetch and carry while he's out conquering the universe." She ran a hand through her hair and crossed her arms and looked at me. A fleck of ash floated past her ear. "You really *are* a nosy bastard."

I shrugged. "Like I said, it's part of what you're paying for."

She rubbed her chin with the back of her hand and puffed on her cigarette. "Yeah, well . . . what else do I get? What's next?"

"Next Monday I get into his apartment. That should tell us something. Between now and then, I keep an eye out for whoever else might be looking for Danes, and I try to talk to Linda Sovitch."

"Isn't that risky?" Sachs said. "Talking to her is kind of . . . public."

"Sure. She gets wind that he's missing—and for how long—and it could be all over cable the same night. And there's not much I can do to finesse it. But he did have lunch with her on the day he walked out of the office, and according to Pratt she was one of his few friends, so it's hard to ignore her. Besides, some press coverage might not be a bad thing. If he's near a TV, it might flush him out. And maybe he won't find out who broke the story—or how."

Sachs looked skeptical. "He'd be so pissed—"

"Assuming he's in a position to be." She squinted at me. "I want you to think about the police, Nina," I said.

"No fucking way. I told you, I'd never hear the end of it."

"Nina, his employers are worried, the closest thing to a friend of his that I've been able to find is worried, even *I'm* worried—and I've never met the guy. You should be worried too."

She looked at me and sucked on her cigarette and shook her head slowly. "Okay, okay, talk to Sovitch—but be discreet, for chrissakes. Give me some time to think about the cops." I wasn't sure how much discretion was possible, but I had nodded anyway and left.

The grade eased as I neared the top of Great Hill, and I backed off my pace a little. My heart was pounding and my breathing was fast and shallow. I lengthened my stride and inhaled slowly and deeply. A well-muscled woman in Rollerblades, spandex, and a helmet like a shark fin passed me going in the opposite direction. She was pushing off smoothly, her face lit with anticipation of the downhill glide.

By the time I reached the Loch and the 100th Street entrance, I no longer felt as if my heart would explode. The North Meadow was to my left. They were laying sod there, and I could smell the mulch and the wet earth and the grass. The sky was lighter now, and sunlight touched the crenellated line of buildings along Central Park West.

I passed the 97th Street transverse and wondered if Irene Pratt was awake yet. She'd been only slightly wobbly when I'd dropped her at her door last night, but she'd been awash in an anxious silence. Today she would have a bad case of regrets.

My heart rate was steady as I came to the Reservoir. I shook out my arms and breathed deeply, and my thoughts shifted again—this time to Jane.

It was near midnight when I'd gotten back from Brooklyn, and my head had been full of Nina and Billy and Ines. There'd been lights in Jane's windows, but I hadn't gone to her apartment. I went to mine, instead, and poured a glass of water and stood in the kitchen. There was a travel magazine on the counter, open to an article about Venice. I turned the pages as I drank and looked at pictures of the Piazza San Marco and the Ponte di Rialto and the exquisite windows of exquisite shops near the Ponte dell'Accademia. I wondered what it would be like to go there with Jane, and walk with her on the bridges, and sit with her in the cafés into the wee hours. And then—from nowhere—I thought of my Proustian moment on Columbus Avenue, and my wondering turned to how long we might stay in Venice, and whether it was a runner's town, and how I would get in my miles with all that water and all those crowds. A surge of annoyance rushed up my spine and I pushed the magazine away.

I went into the living room and pulled a book from the shelf and sat with it in my lap and didn't read. I listened for half an hour to Jane's kickboxing workout—the *thump-thump-whump* of her beating crap out of the heavy bag that hangs in a corner of her loft—and when the pummeling stopped I listened to my telephone ring. I sat for a while after it went quiet, and then I peeled off my clothes and got into bed. I lay there, watching the play of lights across the ceiling, listening to the rain, until about four-thirty, when I'd pulled on my running clothes.

I still didn't know why I hadn't called her or answered her call, or why it had taken so long for my irritation to subside, or why there was a trace of fear in its wake. I didn't know why I couldn't sleep.

I was covered in a skin of sweat, and my joints were loose and springy now. A lot of oxygen was bubbling around in my brain. The Museum of Natural History was on my right, bathed in yellow light. I shortened my stride and picked up the pace.

It was nearly six when I got home, and nearly seven by the time I'd stretched and showered and shaved. I came out of the bedroom and there was a note under the front door. The stationery was heavy ivory-colored stock and the printing was angular and precise, like an architect's. It was from Jane.

Dinner? Call me.

I put the card on the kitchen counter, by the tulips that were shedding their petals. I flicked the coffee machine on and spooned yogurt into a bowl with a sliced apple and some granola. And then I thought about how I might get in touch with Linda Sovitch.

Sovitch was a star of sorts, the most recognizable of BNN's talking heads and the host of its most successful show. As such, she would be attended by a cadre of PAs, flacks, and other assorted minders, wrapped around her like the skin of an onion and paid to keep riffraff like me at arm's length. If I wanted to wait a few days, I could root around for some friend of a friend of a friend who might know one of Sovitch's gatekeepers and might arrange a proper introduction. But I didn't want to wait a few days. I wanted to talk to Sovitch soon, and that required something more direct. I called Tom Neary.

"You know anybody who deals in celebrity cell numbers?" I asked.

"And hello to you too. Somebody have a little too much coffee today?"

"Somebody hasn't had nearly enough. Surely a fancy outfit like Brill must have a few gray-market contacts for stuff like this."

"Surely we do. And they're so useful we don't waste them on free agents like you."

"I'm not asking you to waste anything, I just want a number."

"Whose?"

"Linda Sovitch's."

"From TV?"

"Is there another?"

"I'll see what I can do," Neary said. "I hear you had a nice visit with Dennis Turpin, by the way."

"It had a certain entertainment value," I said, "but I'm not sure how useful it was. I did have an interesting chat with Danes's doorman, though." I told Neary about it, and he was quiet for a while, thinking.

"Not cops," he said finally.

"And not Turpin's people, either—at least, not according to him. And I assume you'd tell me if they were yours."

"They're not mine," he said.

"Then whose are they?"

"I don't know," Neary said. "Not without more coffee, anyway. I'll call if I get a brainstorm, or if I can find Sovitch's number."

While I waited, I read through Geoffrey Tyne's CV, in anticipation of interviewing him that afternoon. As I'd gathered from his name, Tyne was a Brit, though he'd spent much of his twenty-five-year career overseas. His background was in the right ballpark: university, some military service, a stint with a big UK security consulting firm, doing "personal security"—bodyguard—work before graduating to the corporate side of the shop. And then came a succession of jobs abroad, mainly with banks, in capacities of branch or country or regional security director. But he hadn't stayed at any of the companies longer than a few years, and he'd never managed to secure a top spot. I was wondering why when the phone rang.

It wasn't Neary. It was Gregory Danes's lawyer, Toby Kahn, returning my call. He was on a cell phone, on his way to court. His voice was deep and local, and his rushed words were half swallowed by a bad connection.

"You're who?" he asked, and I explained it to him again.

"I get paid to handle securities cases for Greg, and that's it," Kahn said. "I'm not qualified to do family law, and I get no brownie points for mixing it up with his ex-wife or her hired hand—which I guess is what you are. I got to go inside now—sorry I can't . . ." His words grew fainter and the static grew louder, and then the line was dead. I put the phone down.

When it rang again, Neary was on the other end. He had no ideas about who else might be looking for Danes, but he did have a telephone number for me.

"It's supposed to be her supersecret, private, family-and-close-friends-only number, so use it wisely."

Linda Sovitch's supersecret, private, family-and-close-friends-only number was answered by her supersecret, private, family-and-close-friends-only personal assistant, a single-minded young man named Brent.

"How the hell did you get this number?" he demanded.

I suppressed the urge to say something about a bathroom wall. "I'm a PI, Brent, I do this kind of thing for a living. And if I can get a little time with Linda to talk about a case, I'll happily go away."

"How the hell did you get this number?" We went on like this for a while. Finally, my patience ran dry.

"Just tell her I need to talk about Gregory Danes, okay? It won't take more than a half hour of her life, and we can do it at a time and place of her choosing."

"How the hell did you get—"

"Tell her, Brent." I hung up.

I wasn't sure when, or if, I'd hear back from Brent—much less from Sovitch—and I had a few hours until my interview with Geoffrey Tyne. I opened my laptop to research the last items on my list of Danes lawsuits. I turned on the television for background noise. It was tuned to BNN, and after twenty minutes of half-bright market commentary, Linda Sovitch came on the screen.

It was a short blurb, no more than fifteen seconds, pitching that night's segment of *Market Minds*. Sovitch's hair hung in a graceful blond bell, framing her face and long neck. Her flawless understated makeup accentuated the blue of her eyes, the curve of her high cheeks, and the fullness of her mouth. She was babbling something about her scheduled guests when my phone rang. It was Brent.

"You know the Manifesto Diner?" I didn't. "It's on Eleventh Avenue, between Fifty-third and Fifty-fourth. She'll meet you there this afternoon at three-thirty—exactly—and you'll have exactly fifteen minutes." He hung up. It had been easier than I thought.

I changed channels and went back to my laptop and the lawsuits. I stayed there for about an hour, and then I changed into a navy suit, white shirt, and tie and caught a subway downtown. But my mind was not on the interview with Geoffrey Tyne, or even on my meeting with Linda Sovitch. Instead, I was thinking about the last of the court records that I'd read and about making another trip to Brooklyn later that night.

The offices of Klein & Sons are downtown, just off Hanover Square, a short walk from the Exchange, a slightly longer one from the Fed, and a stone's throw from the two cramped rooms my great-grandfather had leased when he founded the firm one hundred years ago. Though it was early afternoon, the narrow street was already in shadow.

The Klein building is a minor Deco masterpiece, with elaborate chevron designs in green and gold around its base and a tower clad in stylized bronze fronds. The lobby is a vaulted cave of polished black stone, inlaid with gilded zigzags. Being there set my teeth on edge.

I didn't visit the office much as a kid. I was bored and cranky whenever I went, and I annoyed my uncles and was in turn annoyed by them. My father, I suspect, shared many of my feelings about the place and rarely invited me down. And as an adult, I visited even less. So besides my relatives, there were few people there who recognized me. My name was a different matter.

The guards were deferential and apologetic as they waited for word from above to let me pass. And the pale young man who escorted me through the hushed teak-paneled maze of the seventh floor—the managing partners' floor—was overawed and tongue-tied. Only the sturdy Hispanic woman who led me through the double doors of the conference room and offered me coffee was unimpressed. I said yes to the coffee, and she left me alone.

It was a long high-ceilinged room, with doors at one end and a white marble fireplace at the other. The walls were mahogany panels below the chair rail and plaster above. The ceiling was heavy with molding. Two brass chandeliers hung gleaming above the mahogany oval of the conference table and were flawlessly reflected in its flawless surface. Sixteen green leather chairs surrounded the table, and a pair of matching leather sofas ran along one wall, beneath four tall windows. Along the opposite wall were the photographs.

They were portraits of individuals and groups, expensively mounted and gilt-framed—Klein & Sons partners down through the ages. For the first few decades, it was all blood family: Morton Klein, his younger brother Meyer, and their male offspring. As the firm grew and the Klein daughters married, sons-in-law began to appear in the pictures, and by the forties there were a couple of unrelated partners. By the sixties—Klein being rather ahead of its time—it was possible to spot some nonwhite faces in the crowd and even a few women. And the recent photos were of as diverse a group of executives as one could find anywhere on the Street. But evolution has its limits. Klein progeny and their spouses have always held the topmost spots and a controlling interest in the firm.

I walked along the wall until I found my father. He appeared only in the group portraits and only in the back—a pale distracted-looking figure, tall, with straight black hair, a widow's peak, and an angular sharp-featured face—looks my sister Lauren and I had inherited, down to the green eyes. For a dozen years he'd occupied a spot my grandfather had made for him at Klein, and then one day he didn't. He never explained why he stopped going to the office, and his in-laws never pressed.

The doors opened and the Hispanic woman returned, carrying a silver tray with a china coffee service on it. Behind her was a gray switch of wood, wearing a blue Chanel knockoff and patent-leather flats: Mrs. Konigsberg. Her cold eyes inspected the coffee service, shifted to me, and narrowed.

Her hair was battleship gray and lay in flat curls against her head. Her precise features were close on her face, and her skin was paper-white. The shoulders beneath her suit jacket were thin as wires, and her tiny hands were veined and spotted like dry leaves. She didn't weigh more than a hundred pounds, and it had been many years since she'd been five feet tall. She perched half-glasses on her nose and approached.

"Good afternoon, Mr. March. Nice to see you again." Her voice wasn't quite a whisper, but it somehow encouraged restraint.

"Always a pleasure, Mrs. Konigsberg." She examined me and the picture I'd been looking at. Her mouth became a sliver of disdain and she made a tiny clicking noise.

"Well, then . . . Mr. Tyne is on his way up. Is there anything else you require?"

"No, thank you, Mrs. Konigsberg."

She nodded. "Then I'll just show him in." And she did.

I haven't gone on many job interviews—not the résumé, what's-your-greatest-strength, where-do-you-want-to-be-in-five-years kind. Maybe half a dozen apathetic attempts all told while I was in college, maybe fewer. But despite my limited experience and my apathy, there was one bit of wisdom I did acquire about the process: the one about not showing up drunk. Not obviously drunk, anyway. Not extravagantly drunk. Not slurring-your-words, bumping-into-furniture, spilling-coffee, cackling-wildly, pissing-down-your-leg drunk. Not throwing-up-on-your-shoes drunk. Geoffrey Tyne had missed this lesson.

My first clue was the look on Mrs. K's face as she ushered him into the room—as if someone had simultaneously goosed her and lifted her wallet. Tyne was a medium-sized doughy guy in his fifties, with shiny hair that looked twenty years younger than the rest of him. His face was heavy and flushed, and his small eyes jumped around beneath unkempt brows. His nose was shot with broken capillaries, and his mouth was full of gray teeth. He brushed the lapels of his suit jacket and tugged at his shirt cuffs, and Mrs. K backed away quickly.

My second clue came when he wrapped a moist hand around mine, breathed a gin cloud at my face, called me Mr. Marx, and commented that I didn't look Jewish. It went downhill from there.

Tyne sat long enough to spill my coffee and tip the sugar bowl; then he rose, to career around the room and babble. From what I could follow, his rantings had mainly to do with his assignments overseas—which, as he made it sound, had taken place sometime during the reign of Victoria, in locales he described as *the back of beyond* and *the Fourth effing World*. They were peppered with phrases like *our little brown brothers*, and they went on for a long twenty minutes. For his grand finale, Tyne turned a khaki color, ran trembling hands down his face, and puked on his brogues. Then he collapsed on one of the sofas. I'm not sure when he wet his pants.

I checked his pulse and loosened his tie and made sure that his airway was clear. Then I left quietly. I never asked a single question. Ned was in his office.

As offices of the second-in-command go, his was a modest affair, barely a thousand square feet. It was half-paneled in mahogany, like the conference room, and the upper walls were painted a pale yellow. To my left was a miniature version of the conference room table, with seating for six, and to my right, a living room: sofa and chairs upholstered in yellow silk, spindly end tables, brass lamps, and a few English landscapes on the walls. The long wall to my right was floor-to-ceiling shelves. One section, I knew, hid the door to a washroom, and another opened into a kitchenette. The desk was at the far end of the room by the big windows, a carved black reef in an ocean of yellow carpet. There was a console table beside it, covered with silver-framed photographs. Ned was on the phone when I came in. He turned around and a smile lit his square face.

Like most of my siblings, Ned favors the Kleins in his looks: wavy ginger hair, ruddy complexion, small blunt features. He's approaching forty-five, though the running of Klein & Sons has put more miles than that on him. Behind his reading glasses, his pale eyes were lined and tired-looking, and there were new creases on his forehead and at the corners of his mouth. His stocky build had edged a little closer to fat. He put his hand over the telephone mouthpiece.

"Five minutes," he whispered. He smoothed his tie down on his bright white shirt and made an affirmative noise into the phone. I wandered to the console table and looked at his photos.

It was not a collection of vanity shots, no pictures of Ned gripping and grinning with the great and near-great; that's not his style. Rather, it was family. The largest photo showed a smiling woman sitting erect in a Napoleon armchair, with two small boys standing beside her. The woman was blond, blue-eyed, and hollow-cheeked, with the sort of finely crafted good looks you see a lot of on the Upper East Side, the sort that could be anything from thirty-five to fifty and are unmistakably rich. Her slender hands rested comfortably—rings gleaming—in her small lap, and her smile was cool and practiced: Ned's wife, Janine.

The boys at her side were grade-school age and had full round-featured faces and thick ginger hair—plastered down for the occasion.

They were dressed identically in blue blazers and white shirts, and with identically hideous madras ties around their necks. Their smiles were artificial and inert, but their eyes were full of wild scheming. Derek was the older one; his brother was Alec. I knew the look in my nephews' eyes well, and I smiled to myself. I was willing to bet the photo session hadn't lasted long after that shot.

Not all the pictures were posed. There were snapshots of the boys playing soccer in Central Park, of Janine on a chestnut mare, and of the boys with both parents atop a ski slope somewhere, leaning on their poles and squinting in the glare. And not all the photos were of Ned's brood. There was a nice shot of Lauren and her husband, Keith, outside the laboratory building at Rockefeller University where Keith does arcane things with DNA. They stood against a brick wall, and orange leaves fell all around them. Next to that was a picture of my older sister, Liz, seated at the trading desk she runs for Klein & Sons. She was talking on the telephone, surrounded by monitors and keyboards and stacks of paper. Her thick blond hair was pulled back in a ponytail, her dark brows were drawn together, and she scowled menacingly at whoever was behind the camera. Beside her picture was another posed portrait, a man and a woman standing at the foot of a curving marble staircase. The man was slender and had the same wavy, gingery hair as Ned but more of it. His pointy features were crowded together on a narrow face that seemed on the verge of some rebuke. The woman beside him was skinny and pale, with odd wiry hair, and dark overlarge eyes full of tension and envy. My older brother David and Stephanie, his wife. I worked my jaw around, to loosen it.

At the end of the table were two pictures I hadn't seen in a long while. The smaller one was in color, though the color had faded over time. It was taken on a beach and showed a tanned fair-haired young man and a dark-haired boy pulling a dinghy out of the surf. The man was stocky and the boy was skinny and pale, and white foam swirled around their knees. The man was laughing, and muscles stood out in his arms and legs as he hauled on a dripping line; the boy gave the camera a surly stare as he tugged— halfheartedly, I recalled—at his own rope. Ned was barely twenty-four then, fresh from B-school and just starting work at Klein & Sons. I was no older than Billy Danes. I put the photo down and picked up the one next to it.

It was black-and-white and brittle-looking under the glass. It was of a man and woman, and they were very young. They were outdoors, walking hand-in-hand down stone steps that I knew were not far from here. The woman was small and compactly built and wore a light-colored skirt and a white sleeveless blouse. Her thick fair hair was bound behind her with a scarf. The man was tall and trim, and he wore dark trousers and a white shirt with rolled-up sleeves. He had black hair, combed straight back, and his widow's peak was pronounced. The woman's face was full and pretty and there was nothing cold or reproachful in it. The man's face was pale and angular and not at all remote. In fact, they were both smiling and their eyes were lit with . . . I've never been sure what. Happiness? Anticipation? The thrill of having kicked over all the traces? Whatever it was, they made it look glamorous and sexy and somehow conspiratorial, like they'd just swiped the Hope Diamond and were making their getaway in broad day-light. Actually, they were heading for a friend's car, a ride to the airport, and a plane to Rome. And the job they had just pulled wasn't a jewel heist but a City Hall wedding that neither of their families would learn about for sev-eral days to come. Her name was Elaine, his was Philip. My parents.

I heard Ned say good-bye and hang up the phone.

"It's a great picture, isn't it?" he said. "Janine found it a couple of weeks ago, tucked away in a drawer somewhere. You remember it?"

"I remember."

"I didn't. They look happy there, don't they?" I nodded and put the picture down. Ned came around the desk, gripped my shoulder, and looked me over. He had to look up a few inches to do it. "You finished with Tyne already?" he said. "That was quick."

"He was very forthcoming," I said.

Ned smiled and ran a hand through his hair. "That's great. Well, have a drink and give me your read." He went to the wall of shelves and pushed on something and a wet bar was revealed. He fixed a cranberry and club soda for me and poured a ginger ale for himself. He carried the glasses over and looked at me expectantly.

"Mostly I think that all his other interviews were scheduled before lunch," I said. Ned looked puzzled, and I told him my story. His expression went from disbelief, to alarm, to disgust and settled finally in astonished amusement. He shook his head.

"You think he's still in there?" he asked.

"I'm sure Mrs. K has had him carted away by now."

"To sleep it off with the fishes, no doubt." Ned laughed, and looked ten years younger when he did. "You sure you won't reconsider, Johnny?

It's really a pretty good job, you know." I held up my hands and shook my head.

"Mrs. K would never approve," I said. Ned smiled and nodded and rose to refill his glass. He started to say something, but his phone chimed and Mrs. K's disembodied voice filled the room.

"Your three o'clock is early, Mr. March. They're in the lobby."

Ned grimaced. "Shit," he said softly. The lines deepened around his small mouth and he looked ten years older again. "Sorry to waste your time with this Tyne guy. I'll make sure the other two are vetted better than he was." I nodded. "We appreciate your help with this, Johnny—it's great working with you on it." I nodded again. "See you Saturday, right?"

"Saturday," I said, and left.

The conference room doors were open and I looked inside. It was empty and, but for the faint bouquet of an air freshener, you'd never know that Tyne had been there. I passed Mrs. K's desk on my way out. She made another clicking noise and eyed me warily.

8

I took a window seat at the Manifesto Diner, looking out on Eleventh Avenue and the trucks that rumbled by, northbound and south. Directly across the street was a block of low brick tenements with an adult video store, a locksmith, and a plumbing supply shop at sidewalk level. Diagonally across, to the south, was a corner of DeWitt Clinton Park. I saw some flowerless rosebushes and a pair of shirtless handball players bounding around on a concrete court. I'd ditched my jacket and tie, but I was still overdressed for the Manifesto and for the neighborhood.

Eleventh Avenue between 53rd and 54th streets is the north end of Clinton—or Hell's Kitchen, as it used to be known. The neighborhood has a sordid and much romanticized past, full of grog houses, luckless sailors, and ravening street gangs. Its present is more prosaic. These days, Clinton is in the later stages of a remorseless gentrification, its old tenement buildings and factories giving way to residential high-rises and dramatic eateries, its population of working-class immigrants and aspiring actors squeezed ever tighter or squeezed out altogether. But despite the assault, the area's gritty industrial roots are stubborn and still plain to see.

I didn't know how far back the Manifesto's history went, but it was not a newcomer. It was long and narrow, clad in metal on the outside and in chipped green Formica inside. There was a long counter with worn green vinyl stools, a row of green vinyl booths along the front window, and another set of booths in a nook at one end of the counter. The ceiling fans were still, and the place smelled of grease, ammonia, and burnt coffee.

There were two Asian women in quiet conversation at the counter, and an old guy speaking Spanish into the pay phone, and the only other people in the place at three-twenty were the counterman and the cook. A black town car was circling the block. I'd counted four trips around when it stopped out front at three-thirty.

A skinny young man in khaki pants and a dark blue button-down shirt got out of the back and stepped into the diner. He was balding and he wore his remaining hair very short—shorter even than his narrow goatee. There was an annoyed, impatient look on his face as he scanned the room. His eyes stopped at me. He walked over.

"You March?" he asked softly. I recognized the voice—Brent. I nodded. "How about moving to the back?" he said. I slid out of the booth and picked up my coffee cup. I looked at the counterman and gestured toward the back. He shrugged.

"Just a sec," Brent said. He went out to the car. A big bald white guy in a black suit got out of the front passenger seat. Brent opened the rear door and Linda Sovitch stepped out. She took a last drag on a cigarette and tossed it in the gutter, and the three of them crossed the pavement and came inside. The big guy looked around and then stared at me. He had a face like a ham and skin the color of a turnip and he was wearing black wraparound shades. I ignored him. He and Brent sat at the counter. Sovitch came to my booth and took off her sunglasses.

She was smaller than I expected, about five-foot-two, and her features were somehow more intense out in the real world, but otherwise Linda Sovitch looked much as she did on television. She was wearing the same cream-colored jacket and the same sea-green blouse she'd worn on TV that morning; the same strand of pearls rested on her delicate clavicles. Her pale hair still fell in an artful curve, down to the base of her neck. Her lips looked, if anything, fuller, and her eyes even bluer. Besides the jacket and blouse, she wore torn faded jeans and black clogs, and a musky, flowery perfume—Shalimar, maybe. Her hands were small, with sharp pink nails, and she wore a big yellow diamond on one finger, above a platinum wedding band. I knew she was in her middle thirties, but she looked younger.

She slipped into the seat opposite me and checked her watch. "You wanted to talk about Greg?" she asked. Her voice was high but without accent, and there was nothing girlish about it. She looked me squarely in the eye.

"When's the last time you spoke with Mr. Danes?" Might as well cut to the chase. She tilted her head a little and thought about things.

"Five weeks ago, maybe. We had lunch. Why?"

"His wife—his ex-wife—is having a little trouble getting in touch with him."

Sovitch tilted her head again. "Has she tried his office?"

"He's on vacation and hasn't come back yet."

"Don't they know how to reach him at Pace?"

"Apparently not. I was given to understand that you two were friends. I thought maybe you had heard from him or that you might have some idea of where he's gone."

Sovitch looked puzzled and shook her head slowly. "I haven't seen much of Greg lately. That lunch was the first time in a long time."

"He didn't mention vacation plans?"

She shook her head. "Not to me. You sure he's not just avoiding her?"

"Why would he do that?"

Sovitch shrugged. "I don't know, to piss her off maybe. They don't exactly get along, you know."

I nodded. "What did you two talk about at lunch?"

Sovitch's mouth closed and her eyes narrowed. "Why does that matter?"

"I'm not sure it does, but I won't know for certain until you tell me about it."

She scowled and shook her head. "That sounds like bullshit to me, March."

"I'm curious about what was on his mind. If he talked a lot about music, for example, then maybe he went off to hear some music."

Sovitch looked impatient. "He didn't talk about music," she said. She checked her watch again and glanced at the counter. I was losing her.

"I heard he hasn't been in such a good mood lately. Did he mention that at all?"

Sovitch fixed her eyes on me again. "If you're getting at something, March, get at it. Otherwise, stop dicking around." It was a legitimate request. The problem was, I didn't quite know what I was getting at. I was fishing.

"I'm not trying to dick around, and I don't want to turn this into a guessing game either. I just want to know how Danes seemed the last time you saw him: what his mood was, what you talked about, that kind of thing. It may seem irrelevant to you—it may seem like gratuitous prying—but I've been at this long enough to know that useful things don't usually come with a label attached. They may not even be useful at first; they may only become significant later on, when you put them alongside five other things. Sometimes you just have to put stuff in a bag and shake."

Her mouth took on a skeptical twist. I continued.

"Look, I appreciate your time, Ms. Sovitch, and I don't want to bother you more than I have to, but what's the big deal about this lunch?"

Sovitch's eyes flashed and she gave me a hard look. After a while, she nodded to herself and took a deep breath. "There's no big deal. It just wasn't . . . particularly pleasant, that's all." She picked up her sunglasses and fiddled with the nosepieces. "I told you I hadn't seen Greg in a while. That's because he's been a little unhappy with me lately—with most things, really. When he called about lunch, I took it to mean we'd gotten past all that. But I guess not."

"What was he unhappy about?"

Sovitch's laugh was ironic. "Haven't you caught the news the last few years? It's been a little bumpy on Wall Street, in case you haven't noticed. Greg's got investor complaints up the ass, and his reputation has taken a serious whipping."

"I know that part. I meant, why was he unhappy with you?"

She looked at the tabletop. "He's angry—hurt, I guess—about some of the stories we ran on analysts. He thinks they were one-sided. I've told him a lot of people thought our coverage was pretty one-sided in the other direction, back when the Dow was at eleven thousand, but he doesn't want to hear that. And I've told him he should just forget it and move on—between nine-eleven and war, it's old news anyway—but that just makes him crazier."

"Is that what you talked about at lunch?"

"Yeah. And if I'd known that was going to be the topic, I'd have skipped the whole thing. But like I said, I thought we were done with that. It turned out Greg just had a different approach; he had an idea to pitch to me. A special segment of *Market Minds*—'An Analyst's Perspective,' he wanted to call it—with himself as the only guest."

She shook her head in disbelief, and an indignant tone came into her voice.

"You like that—an hour of Greg Danes telling his side of the story? Maybe we could get some harp music in the background and big blowups of his baby pictures. Can you believe I actually had to explain to him why that would never fly? Jesus, he could be so tone deaf about some things.

"And then he had the nerve to get all pissed off at me. He started in with how he felt *used,* how we treated him like a trained seal or a circus geek—something to sell tickets with—really fucking abusive. I finally got fed up listening to him and left." Sovitch straightened and tossed her hair back. It occurred to me that Danes might've had a point about selling tickets, but I kept it to myself.

"That was the last you heard from him?"

"The last I heard, and the last I hope to hear. Greg's a smart guy, but he's a fucking nut, too, and times have changed. He's just not worth the trouble anymore." She looked at her watch.

I nodded. "One last thing, Ms. Sovitch. Has anyone else called to ask you about Danes?"

She shook her head. "Lucky me, you're the only one." She glanced at Brent and cocked an eyebrow. He and the big guy got up and stood by the door. Sovitch turned back to me. "You got twenty minutes out of me, March."

"And I'm grateful for it. I'll try not to ask for more."

Sovitch smiled coolly. "Ask as much as you like," she said. "You won't get another damn minute." She slipped her sunglasses on and left, her minders close behind.

I walked home from there. There was a chill in the air, and faint traces of yellow and orange in the sky over New Jersey. I thought about what a great pal Linda Sovitch was, and about the little she had told me. Her story was consistent with the others I'd heard: that Danes was angry and bitter, fixated on his lawsuits and bad press and on the raw deal he thought he'd gotten.

But more interesting than what she'd said was what she *hadn't* said—or asked. For someone who called herself a journalist, Sovitch had been remarkably incurious about Danes being missing. Other reporters I knew would've been crawling through my socks and picking my pockets the instant they'd heard, and they certainly wouldn't have answered my questions without asking some of their own in return. But not Sovitch. All the way back to 16th Street, I wondered about her lack of curiosity and about why she'd agreed to see me in the first place.

It was after five when I got home, and there were messages. The first was from Simone Gautier, out in Queens. Danes's car wasn't at the airports and his body wasn't in the local morgues. Written reports and bills to follow.

The second message was from Danes's vacationing doorman. His voice was gravelly and full of Brooklyn. There were other voices in the background and what sounded like a ballgame on TV.

"This is Gargosian; you left a message with my wife. I'll try you later, or when I get home—be about ten days." Shit. I called his home on City Island and left another message with Mrs. Gargosian. I made a note of it on my pad and saw my earlier entry there, to call Anthony Frye, late of the Pace-Loyette equity research department. I flicked on my laptop and picked up the phone again.

It didn't take long to find a residential listing for Frye, and he answered on the first ring. He spoke with an upper-class English accent, and his voice was young and ironical. I explained who I was and what I wanted, and nothing that I said seemed to surprise him very much.

"I heard about Greg storming out," he said. "But I understood he'd decided to take some sort of impromptu sabbatical."

"Maybe, but his ex-wife and his son would like to get in touch with him. Were you there when he left?"

"No. I'd resigned the week before, and Pace likes deserters off the premises straightaway."

"Was that the last time you saw Danes—the day you resigned?"

"Yes," Frye said. "Though I barely saw him then, they had me out the door so fast." A doorbell chimed on his end and he called out. "Come ahead—it's open." There was a swell of voices and laughter on the line, and it became difficult to hear.

"It sounds like this is a bad time to talk."

Frye laughed. "Yes, an excellent time to drink, but a bad time to talk. How about tomorrow?" We agreed on a time and place and he rang off, to the sounds of reggae and clinking glasses.

I looked at my watch and took a deep breath. It was time to call Nina.

"We've got things to talk about," I said. "Can I come over this evening?"

"You found something?"

"Not Danes, if that's what you mean."

"Then what?"

"Something we need to discuss in person. Is this evening okay?"

"Very mysterious. But sure, come on over. Shit, you're becoming a regular here, March. Better watch it, people might start to wonder." She laughed and hung up.

I drank some water from a pitcher in the fridge and looked at Jane's tulips. The stalks hung bare and limp in their vase; the petals were turning brown on the counter. I hung up my suit and pulled on a pair of jeans and sat down at my laptop. I opened the file I had saved this morning and reread the details of *Sachs v. Danes.*

9

It was past seven when I got to Sachs's place. The temperature had continued to drop and the wind had teeth as it whipped between the old factory buildings. Across the East River, the downtown office towers were lit and limned with the last colors of sunset. There were lights in the windows of the I-2 gallery, too. I looked in and saw Ines's skinny hipsters rearranging the partitions around a new set of crates, but I saw no sign of Ines.

She was upstairs. She answered my knock, and tension washed through the doorway with the cigarette smoke and paint smell and too-loud music and raised voices. Ines was still and quiet in the tide.

"I don't care what the fucking guidance counselor says, I'm not staying in that shithole another fucking year!" Billy's voice came from the far end of the apartment. It was raw and hoarse. Ines didn't react.

"She's expecting me," I said. Ines nodded.

"Now may not be the best time, detective," she said softly. I heard Nina's voice. I couldn't make out the words, but the anger and frustration in them were clear. Billy answered at full volume.

"I don't care how good you say it is, you don't have to go there. You don't have to deal with those fucking assholes every day!" A door slammed.

"Fine!" Nina yelled. "Go to public school then! See how you like it when the fucking assholes have guns!"

"You think they don't have 'em at my school?" Billy yelled back. "You don't know shit."

There were fast footsteps and Nina Sachs crossed the apartment, an angry cloud of smoke swirling behind her. She glanced at me, snorted, and went into her studio without a pause. Ines and I looked at each other.

"Is he here to see me?" Nina called. "Might as well send him in. Things can't get much more fucked-up tonight." She laughed bitterly. Ines nodded slightly and I stepped inside. The piles of clothes were a little smaller than they had been last time and the half-eaten meals were gone. Ines was in the midst of cleaning. She disappeared into the kitchen and I made my way to Nina's studio.

Nina was at the drafting table, wearing jeans and a man's blue shirt with the sleeves cut off. Her auburn hair was tied back. A new cigarette was dangling from her mouth and there was a glass tumbler full of red wine on the cart beside her. She was sketching furiously. I went to the little stereo and turned The Ramones down a few notches. Nina gave me a dirty look.

"Don't fuck with my music." She sounded like Billy when she said it. I ignored her.

"Have you given any more thought to the cops?" I asked. She shook her head.

"No time. Maybe you noticed: I have my hands full here." She looked at me with narrowed eyes. "You have something to tell me?"

I nodded. "I spoke to Linda Sovitch this afternoon," I said, and told her about my meeting at the Manifesto. When I was through, Nina Sachs pursed her lips and stared at her sketching.

"You think she's going to put this on the news—about Greg?"

"I don't think so—though I couldn't tell you why not."

She smiled a little. "It seems like Greg was having a bad fucking day, doesn't it?" she said. It was the happiest she'd sounded since I came in.

"A bad day that got worse when he met with Turpin, later that afternoon. And Sovitch is just one more person—one more friend—who has no idea of where he's gone. Are you worried yet?" Nina didn't answer. We heard muffled voices, and Ines appeared in the doorway.

"I am going down to the gallery, and Guillermo is coming with me," she told Nina.

Nina frowned and shook her head. "No, Nes, he has homework to finish, and I don't want him bugging you."

Ines held up a slender hand. "He is no trouble, and he will finish his schoolworks downstairs." Ines looked at me and then at Nina. "And then perhaps you can get some work done here." They stared at each other for a while without speaking. Finally, Nina shrugged. Ines turned and left, and in a little while we heard the door close. I looked at Nina.

"Are you worried yet?" I asked again.

She frowned at me and shook her head. "What is it with you? You think I'm some kind of . . . bitch? Well, fuck you, March. You don't know me and you don't know my dear ex-husband, either. You have no idea what a vengeful little prick he can be. And dragging the cops into his life is just the kind of thing that would set him off."

"You're sure that's all that's stopping you?"

Sachs sat up straight on her stool. She took a long drag on her cigarette and looked at me through the smoke. "There something on your mind?"

I took a deep breath, to dissipate the anger that had clotted in my throat. "Just a little something you neglected to mention, Nina—that your divorce action was reopened four months ago, after ten years. That Greg is fighting you for custody of Billy."

Sachs screwed her face into an impatient grimace and waved her hand. "Yeah . . . and? What's the big deal?" she said. "And what the fuck is it to you anyway? I hired you to look for Greg, not investigate me." I took another deep breath and bit back my first response, which began with the words, *Listen, you stupid shit.* When I spoke, my voice was level and quiet.

"I *am* looking for him, Nina. One of the things you do in a missing persons case is look at any legal actions the missing person is involved in, the theory being that they might provide clues as to why the person disappeared—or why someone made him disappear."

Nina laughed unpleasantly. "Is that what's got you hot and bothered? You think I made Greg disappear?" She laughed some more. "And then what, I hired you to throw the cops off? Jesus, March, that's some conspiracy theory you've got there."

"What I'm saying—right now—is that you've withheld material information. Do I wonder why, and what else you might be holding back? Sure I do. And am I annoyed? More than a little. This stuff is hard enough without your games. But as far as conspiracy theories go, I haven't gotten started yet. And rest assured, mine are nothing compared to what the cops will throw at you if you screw around with them this way. You can drop me a postcard and tell me all about it."

Nina reached for the tumbler of wine and took a long swallow. "What the fuck is that supposed to mean?"

"That means I'm out of here, Nina—right now—unless you stop bull-shitting me."

We stared at each other, and neither one of us blinked. Finally, she shook her head.

"What do you want from me? I've got no big secret. I told you all I know about where Greg is. The other stuff . . . I didn't think it was worth mentioning. Greg's been pissing and moaning about custody on and off for years. The only thing that changed recently was his filing suit. But it's not like that's going anywhere. That's just Greg, grandstanding. We were talking about it. We were going to agree to something . . . just like all the other times."

"What other times?"

"The other times Greg's had a hair up his ass about custody. The other times he's gotten it in his head that he doesn't like how the kid's growing up or that he wants to play full-time dad. He gets himself twisted up, we yell at each other for a while, and we agree to something." Nina pulled hard on her B&H. The ash glowed orange, and the cigarette shrank before my eyes.

"What didn't he like about the way Billy was growing up?" I asked, after a while.

Nina made a wry face. "Figure it out, March. His only son and heir growing up with two dykes? And he's always had it in for Nes. He's con-vinced himself she was the reason our marriage ended, which is crap. Things had gone to hell for us long before I met Nes, and she and I were nothing more than friends when I split with Greg. But he never listens." Nina took another drink, and I thought some more.

"And when it's come up in the past, you've agreed—what?" Nina got up and walked to the little stereo in the corner. She squatted down and rifled through a stack of CDs on the floor and swapped The Ramones for something else. She turned up the volume: Bryan Ferry. She stood and turned back to me.

"We agreed that Greg could see more of him—at least while his inter-est lasted."

"It didn't, usually?"

"It didn't ever. But what the hell. We agreed."

"And what did you get out of it?" I asked. Nina Sachs frowned at me.

"What's that supposed to mean?"

"You just gave him more time with Billy out of the goodness of your heart?"

Sachs's face got white and hard, and her mouth became a tight line. "You have no idea what it's like raising a kid in this city, trying to make a living as a painter. Money gets tight, and if Greg bumps up the child support payments it helps. Am I supposed to be ashamed of that? Does that mean I'm holding him up? Or that I'm selling my kid, for chrissakes?" She took a hit off her cigarette and breathed out a boiling column of smoke. "You have a lot of fucking nerve, for the hired help."

I nodded absently. "If this time was no different, what made Danes reopen the custody suit?"

"He was in a bad mood about everything, he was mad at the whole fucking world, and he was complaining about money."

"So he'd rather spend it on a lawsuit?"

Sachs shrugged. "Go figure," she said. She ran her fingers along the base of her neck. "Maybe he thinks he can't do anything about his career being in the tank, but he can do something about Billy. Maybe he thinks this is a battle he can win." She sighed heavily and shook her head. "How do I know what goes on in his mind?"

She sat at the drafting table, stubbed out her cigarette, and rubbed her eyes with the tips of her fingers. Then she picked up a pencil and started sketching. From the little stereo, Bryan Ferry crooned. *I could feel at the time / There was no way of knowing* . . .

I watched her and listened to the music and we sat that way for what seemed a long time.

"Did you hire me to find Danes, or to find dirt on him for this custody thing?" I asked finally.

Nina let out an exasperated breath. "I told you, I don't give a shit about the custody case. There isn't going to *be* a goddamn custody case." She took a long drag on her cigarette and shook her head. "Look, the sad fact is Greg's still my main source of income. If something has . . . if that's going to change, I need to know. I hired you to find him; that's it. Now, are you coming or going on this?"

"Will you call the cops?"

"Jesus, you don't let up." Nina sighed. "Is that a requirement for you to keep working?"

"The requirement is that you don't lie to me, Nina, and that you don't hold out. Calling the cops is just good advice."

She looked down at her sketch and nodded. "I'm not lying to you, and I'll think about the cops," she said softly. She picked up a stick of charcoal and moved her arm in broad strokes.

I looked at the top of her auburn head. "Okay," I said. I left her apartment and made for the street.

I went past the gallery, rounded the corner, and collided with Billy Danes. He was leaning against the building, smoking a cigarette. He staggered backward and embers went flying.

"Goddammit," he whined, and turned his mother's irritated look on his broken cigarette and then on me. I brushed ash off my sleeve and Billy recognized me. "Oh, shit," he said.

"Hey, no need to apologize, Bill," I said.

He snorted. "Apologize? You're the one that crashed into me, in case you didn't notice."

I laughed. "And saved you from an early death by doing it."

Billy rolled his eyes. "Yeah, right," he said. He was wearing baggy fatigue pants and a baseball jersey with a mournful-looking manga character on it. He fished in his pants pockets for another smoke, found one, and looked up at me defiantly. "Got the lecture ready?" He looked maybe ten.

I shrugged. "Not me." He snorted again, and lit the cigarette with a yellow plastic lighter. I gestured at his T-shirt. "Cowboy Bebop?" I asked.

He nodded, grudgingly. "So, what—you're some kind of comic freak? Kind of old, aren't you? What do you do, hang in the stores and check out the little boys?"

"Not exactly. How about you, do you collect?" Billy shrugged. "Anything in particular?" I asked.

He puffed on the cigarette, suppressed a cough, and shrugged again. "Horror, mostly—old school stuff. *House of Mystery, House of Secrets, Dark Mansion*—that kind of thing."

I nodded. "How about *The Unexpected* or *Vault of Evil*?" I asked. Billy's face lit for a second and then regained its indifferent façade.

"Yeah, like that," he said, and coughed again.

He was staring out across the water and I stared with him.

"She take a chunk out of your ass too?" he asked after a while. His voice was softer and there was weary knowledge in with the levity.

"Just a small one—not so I can't walk or anything," I said.

Billy laughed. "Probably 'cause she'd already eaten," he said.

I chuckled, and we both were quiet again.

"She's not always this way," he said.

"Uh-huh."

"She's got shit on her mind. A show coming up and . . . shit with my dad."

"Uh-huh."

"You looking for him?"

"I am."

"You find him yet?"

"Not yet." There were footsteps on the pavement. Ines Icasa came around the corner and stopped. She looked at Billy and he sent the cigarette arcing into the darkness with a practiced flick. He backed up a little.

"What are you doing, Guillermo?" she said. Her voice was tight with anger.

"Nothing—just talking to him." The whine was back in his voice.

Ines shook her head. "Never mind. I know what you are doing, and we will talk about it later. Now get back inside and finish your schoolworks, please." Billy started to speak, but Ines cut him off. Her voice was sharp. "*Now*, Guillermo." Billy snorted and muttered and shuffled around the corner.

Ines looked at me. Her lithe body was tense, and her smooth face looked harder than stone. "What are you doing?" she asked. Her dark eyes were hot.

I felt like backing up too, but I didn't. "We were talking," I said, "mostly about comic books. I considered lecturing him on the evils of smoking, but I thought better of it."

Ines looked at me for a while, and the tension seemed to drain from her face and her body. She sighed and leaned against the building. "I apologize, detective," she said. She reached into a hip pocket and brought out a crumpled pack of Gitanes and a slim gold lighter. She inhaled deeply and breathed smoke into the sky. "I am a hypocrite, no?" The wind kicked up and she wrapped her arms across her chest. "It has been a trying evening."

"So I gather. What was the fight about?"

Ines sighed, and ran the toe of her shoe across the uneven pavement. A gypsy cab passed. It dropped a loud group in front of the club on the next block. Ines watched it pull away.

"About his school," she said. "He goes to a private school in the Heights, a very good one, but he is not happy there. It is difficult for him— not the schoolworks but socially. There are many gifted students there, but

Guillermo is one of the youngest. He is young in many ways and . . . a little angry. He does not make friends easily." She took another pull on the cigarette and exhaled with a quavering sigh.

"He thinks he would prefer a different school, perhaps a boarding school. Nina does not agree. She would like him to remain close to home. It is an old argument."

"And what do you think?"

"I also would like him close to home. But I am not certain we can give him all that he needs. We try, but I think that Guillermo is looking for a life more . . . predictable than what he has. More conventional, perhaps." Another puff, another sigh. "He is at an age where that has become important to him."

"What does his father think?"

Ines stiffened beside me. "I would have no idea of that, detective," she said. She stubbed her cigarette on the side of the building and walked around the corner.

Jane bought me dinner that night at Viva!, a high-end Mexican place in Chelsea with mango-colored walls and a pretty, peripatetic clientele. At nine-thirty it was filled with music and clatter and a thousand chirping conversations. We sat beneath a mural of grinning skulls and feathered snakes and ominous sunflowers and ate—salmon roasted with fennel for me and chicken mole for Jane. Ours was the quietest table in the place.

Jane was pale and there were shadows beneath her large black eyes. The little she said about her day and her deal was punctuated by pauses and yawns.

"Am I keeping you up?" I asked.

"Sorry," she said, shaking her head. "I'm getting tired of those guys. I'll be glad when this job is done." She drank some water and picked at her chicken. "Bad time in Brooklyn?"

"More weird than bad," I said, and I told her about my talk with Nina Sachs, and with Billy and Ines afterward. There was a little frown on her bow-shaped mouth the whole time I spoke and her eyes never left me.

"The kid sounds like a character," she said when I'd finished.

"He's that."

"You feel bad for him." It wasn't a question.

"It's a bad age, caught between childhood and whatever comes next.

You want to fit in but you don't know with what. You want to jump right out of your skin a lot of the time, and maybe there's some part of you that knows it's going to get worse before it gets better.

"And Billy's got problems on top of that. He's smarter than the other kids, and smaller, and his parents have been trading him like a poker chip for who knows how long. As far as I can tell, Ines is the closest thing he has to a grown-up in his life—the closest thing he's got to a parent."

Jane nodded. Her frown deepened a little and a small line appeared between her eyes. "Do you like him?" she asked.

I had to think about it. Certainly he was an irritable, awkward mix, of fear and anger and complaint and suspicion. And his attempts at teenage cool were still far off the mark, resulting mostly in a sullen truculence. But that's not all he was. I remembered the manic pleasure in his voice when I'd heard him over the telephone, calling Ines to dance. I recalled the spark of interest in his face when we'd talked about comic books, and his deadpan delivery when he'd shared his opinion of Batman. And I could still hear his earnest tone when he'd explained his mother's anger to me—and maybe to himself—and his gravity when he'd asked if I was searching for his father. I nodded slowly at Jane.

"I guess I have to," I said. "He reminds me of myself at that age."

"Unloved and unlovable?" Her tone was light, but she wasn't smiling.

"And wary," I said, "and untethered." Jane looked at me but said nothing.

The waiter cleared our plates and left us with dessert menus. We read them in silence.

"You want something?" I asked.

"To go home," she said.

10

Jane woke late the next morning and scrambled, cursing, out of bed, into her clothes and upstairs to her apartment. There was bumping and thudding from above, followed by high heels, followed by silence. I pulled the sheet around me and closed my eyes and tried to find a warm spot on Jane's pillow, but it was no good. Her heat had dissipated and I was awake.

I showered and shaved, pulled on a pair of khakis, and took my time over a bowl of oatmeal and the newspaper. Then I carried my coffee mug to the table, along with the telephone and a notepad.

The lawyer running Gregory Danes's renewed custody fight with Nina Sachs was Reggie Selden, and he was a big deal in New York divorce circles. The woman who answered his telephone reminded me of this and assured me that my call would go no farther until I told her who I was and what I wanted. When I did she laughed unpleasantly.

"Our understanding is that Ms. Sachs is represented by Margaret Lind," she said. "Until we hear otherwise, any communications you have for Mr. Selden should come through her office."

"I just want to know if anyone in your office has spoken to Gregory Danes lately. I—"

She cut me off. "That's our policy, and discussing it with me won't change things. I'm sorry I can't help you." I somehow doubted her sincerity. I finished my coffee and checked my watch and hoped that Anthony Frye would be a little more forthcoming.

I was in front of 60 Wall Street at eleven o'clock sharp. At eleven twenty-five, Frye came through the revolving door. He had a cell phone to his ear and he was talking quickly and looking at the pavement. I recognized the English accent and the sardonic tone.

"Maureen? . . . Yes, it's Tony. . . . Yes, I know I'm late, and I'll be later still, as I'm just now getting into a taxi. So tell them for me, will you? About thirty minutes, traffic willing. Thanks, Mo." He put his phone away and shook his head and began to cast about for a cab.

Frye was a slight handsome man of thirty or so. His dark hair was long and unruly, and his small regular features were unblemished except for the shadowed pouches beneath his eyes. He was rumpled but expensively so, in a gray suit, a red-striped shirt, and a blue tie worn loose.

"Frye?" I asked. He was only slightly surprised.

"Oh, Christ—you're March, aren't you?" he said, smiling. I nodded. "And I'm vastly late, I know. Sorry."

"No problem," I said, "if we can still talk."

Frye nodded absently. "As long as you don't mind doing it in the back of a cab."

We walked to the corner of Wall and Water, where Frye scared the hell out of me by wading into traffic and waving spastically at every cab in sight. It was an odd technique, and risky, but it was effective. Five minutes later we were rattling northward on the FDR Drive. I was asking questions and, in between listening to messages on his cell phone, Frye was answering them. He was less fond of Danes than Irene Pratt was, and more blunt about it.

"How long did you work for Danes?"

"Too long," Frye said ruefully. "Five years."

"I've heard he can be a difficult guy."

Frye smiled. "Whoever told you that was a master of understatement."

"From which I gather you didn't get along with him."

"That depends on your yardstick," he said. "By the standards of normal human interaction, I'd have to say we got on abysmally. By the Greg standard, though, I suppose I did quite well with him—better than most, in fact." He pushed a key on his phone and held it to his ear again.

"Which meant what, in practical terms?"

Frye held up a finger and listened intently for a moment, then shook his head. "That we spoke only when necessary and otherwise had as little to do with each other as possible."

"Not exactly chummy after five years. What was the problem?"

Frye sighed and pocketed his phone. He looked at the East River, bouncing by the cab window. "Greg doesn't deal well with dissent, Mr. March, and he requires a rather large quotient of deference from his colleagues. As it happens, I'm chronically long the former and short the latter."

"Is that why you quit?"

"That, and the fact that staying there was doing nothing for my career. Who wants to be the last rat off the ship, after all?"

"I didn't realize Pace-Loyette was sinking."

"The firm will survive, I expect, but the research department won't— not in its current form, at any rate. It's much diminished already, and it hasn't hit bottom yet. I am by no means the first person to realize that, and I won't be the last."

"Has Danes figured it out?"

"Of course he has, but being Greg, he puts himself at the center of the phenomenon. He sees it as another example of management's desire to tar his reputation and fix him with blame for all the excesses of the past."

"Is there any truth to that?"

Frye looked at me and nodded slowly. "Some, perhaps, but mainly the seniors at Pace just want to get on with things; they want to settle their claims and move along. Greg can't see that; he sees settlement as an admission of guilt—his guilt."

"So you don't think he'll up and leave any time soon?"

"No, not Greg. And until those claims are settled, I don't know that there'd be many bidders for him. No one wants the baggage."

"So I gather you two didn't discuss his vacation plans that last day you were in the office?"

Frye snorted. "Lord, no. Not on that day or any other. As I said, we didn't have that kind of relationship."

"Who does he have that kind of relationship with?"

"Friendship? Pleasant acquaintanceship? No one I can think of, though maybe Irene Pratt comes closest. Do you know Pratt?" I made a vaguely affirmative sound. "She's a diligent soul, and much better at deference than I." Frye's phone trilled. He made more excuses to Maureen and entreated her to do the same to whoever was waiting for him uptown, which gave me time to think.

"Forget friends, then," I said, when he got off the phone. "How about anyone that Danes has pissed off?"

Frye laughed. "That's quite a list. Greg is a plague on everyone, from the summer interns to half the occupants of the executive suite."

"He leave any of them particularly mad? Anyone holding a grudge?"

"I couldn't say, really. People learn to keep their distance when at all possible, and most of those fortunate enough to work directly for Greg develop rather tough hides."

"What about the ones who don't?"

Frye gave me a speculative squint. "Greg has a certain radar for them, Mr. March. They seem to attract more than their share of torment, and they don't stay around long."

"Which is a polite way of calling Danes a bully."

"I suppose it is." Frye smiled innocently.

"Bullies collect enemies, as a rule. Did Danes manage not to, somehow? Did none of these people stay angry with him?"

He shrugged. "None of them stays angry with the weather either, I imagine. And once you know Greg, you realize that's what he's like. He's like a force of nature: a natural bastard. But there's nothing personal in it— or, rather, it's personal but indiscriminate. Sooner or later, the rain falls on everyone." Frye raised an eyebrow. "Why the interest? Do you think Greg's run afoul of someone? Is that why he hasn't returned?"

I shrugged. "I don't know enough to think much of anything yet," I said. "All I have now are questions. Most of them will come to nothing, but I have to ask."

"Hell of a job," he said. I nodded. We were coming up on the UN, and traffic had come nearly to a halt. Frye swore softly and called Maureen again. I thought about some things Irene Pratt had told me. Frye rang off and I had another question for him.

"Winning personality aside, how is Danes as an analyst?"

"Greg is undeniably a very bright guy: keen insights into companies and industries, a very quick study, and a phenomenal memory. I'm the first to admit I learned a lot from him."

"Though not from his work on Piedmont, I'd guess."

"That again." Frye sighed. "People never tire of it. But in truth, it's unreasonable to expect that Greg—or any other analyst—would have known what Denton Ainsley was up to. Greg may have smiled in a few too many photo ops with Ainsley, and gone on a few too many Piedmont junkets, but that doesn't make him an accomplice. Foolish, perhaps, or vain, but not complicit."

"Piedmont was just one bad call; what about the rest? If Danes is so smart, how did he end up so wrong?"

"There are lots of smart people in this business, March, but smart isn't the whole story. Smart isn't always enough. You need insight into how the market moves and a feel for the people who move it."

"Danes doesn't have that?"

"Everyone has blind spots," Frye said. "Greg's, I suppose, are a reluctance to revisit his calls—even in the face of a changing market—and perhaps a certain susceptibility to manipulation by fund managers."

"I understand the first part more or less, but what does that last bit mean?"

Frye smiled. "One of the things an analyst does is talk to people who hold big positions in the shares of companies they cover. In part they do it to solicit investor views on where the companies are going, and in part it's to pitch their own ideas. But those conversations can be very tricky things.

"Say, for example, you cover Company X, and Mr. Smith, a hedge fund manager, holds a big stake in X. If you were getting ready to rate X as a *strong buy*, it would be nice to know that Mr. Smith was going to hold on to his shares of X—or perhaps even increase his position. So before issuing your report, you might go have a chat with Mr. Smith. With me so far?"

I nodded.

"Good. Now, Mr. Smith is no fool. He knows that if Company X gets a *buy* rating from so eminent an analyst as yourself, its shares are likely to rise. And he knows that if he sells off his position into that run-up, he can make a pretty penny for his fund. So given all that, and being a devilish and manipulative bastard like all his ilk, Mr. Smith might seek to mislead poor gullible you. He might try to convince you that he thinks your ideas about X are brilliant and subtle and altogether sublime and he agrees with them entirely. And if you were so deceived, you might trot back to your office and issue your *strong buy* report—and find yourself in for a nasty surprise when Smith unloads his position into your nascent rally, momentum swings south, and shares of X tank in a big way."

"Is that the sort of thing that happened to Danes?"

Frye nodded. "My example's simplistic, but it captures the flavor. In Greg's defense, it's a subtle game, with lots of permutations. And it's played against some very clever people whose cards are almost always better than yours. Even the best find themselves wrong-footed now and again."

"But with Danes it was more often than now and again?"

"He has a hungry ego. It makes him vulnerable to stroking from smart, powerful people."

I thought about that for a while. "Insightful, for a stock analyst," I said, and meant it.

Frye laughed. "I'm a strictly amateur psychologist, I assure you. But Greg's quite a specimen; it's impossible not to speculate. And that's *ex*–stock analyst, by the way."

Our cabbie had fought his way off the FDR and onto the midtown streets, but we were not moving fast enough for Frye. He cursed vigorously at each red light, and at 47th Street and Third Avenue, he tossed a bunch of bills through the Plexiglas divider and got out. He headed up Third at close to a trot.

"What are you doing now that you've left Pace?" I asked, following.

"What every analyst dreams of, of course." Frye grinned. "I'm starting a hedge fund." And he disappeared into Smith & Wollensky.

11

Fort Lee is perched high above the Hudson River, atop the wooded cliffs of the Palisades, and an easy drive from Manhattan: straight up the West Side Highway and across the George Washington Bridge. It's an old town, with a past that stretches back to the first English settlers and to the Dutch before them. The welcome sign at the town line boasted of it: *Rich in history,* it read, in flowery white script. Maybe so, but they kept it well hidden. Mostly the town seemed rich in on-ramps and off-ramps and parking lots, in shopping centers and drive-through banks, in video stores and copy shops and nail salons and pizzerias. What poverty it suffered seemed mainly in the areas of architecture and zoning.

It was midafternoon and raining when I crossed the GW, and traffic was heavy near the tolls. So I had plenty of time to gaze upon the tangle of highways where the toll plaza morphed into the New Jersey Turnpike and several other routes, and to study the thicket of indecipherable road signs posted there. Despite this contemplation, I had only the vaguest notion of where I was supposed to go. New Jersey does that to me.

I steered my rented Toyota to an off-ramp. The local streets were pitted and gray, and the local drivers had little patience with uncertainty, but I paid them no heed and eventually found my way to Lincoln Avenue.

It hadn't been difficult to come up with an address for Richard Gilpin's firm, Morgan & Lynch, though the one I'd found was not the one listed on the company's Web site—that address belonged to a commercial mail drop in one of Fort Lee's many strip malls. I'd plugged the Morgan & Lynch telephone number into a reverse directory, and out had popped a listing for something called Ekaterinberg Holdings, with an address on Lincoln.

It was a small office building, with a façade of white brick that was going brown and narrow metal-framed windows. The windows were dirty and most of them were dark. The building had only four stories, but it loomed above its neighbors on the block, which included a Korean restaurant, decked out in mirrored glass and white stucco, a travel agency with a torn red awning, a two-level municipal parking lot, and a surgical supply company with barred windows and a sign proclaiming the area's largest selection of latex gloves. Office space must've been tight down in the Caymans.

I drove past the building and pulled the Toyota into a space a block and a half down, in front of a bar called Roxy's. Rain was falling harder now, and slanting in the wind. A wet shoe box flip-flopped across the street, following a plastic grocery bag that drifted like a ghost. I turned up the collar of my field jacket and opened my umbrella.

The lobby was a little larger than a broom closet, and done in algae-green tiles and fluorescent lights. There was a dusty plastic plant to the right as I came in, and a building directory on the wall to my left, behind a cracked pane of glass. I consulted it but learned little, as the only plastic letters left there had been arranged to spell the word SHAT. The elevator was to the rear, and taped on the wall next to it, in red ink on cardboard, was a handwritten note to the mailman. From this I learned that anything for Ekaterinberg Holdings or EK Industries or Gromyko Construction was to go to the fourth floor. I figured that included me, and I wedged myself into the tiny car.

The elevator smelled like a taxi, only not as fresh, and the short hallway it opened onto smelled even worse: cigarettes, beer, old pizza, mildew, and piss, not necessarily in that order. The strawberry air freshener that someone had sprayed recently was hopelessly overmatched. The walls were paneled in fake wood, like a basement playroom, and murky light came from a glass fixture overhead. The carpet was brown and squishy, like moss, and I was glad it was a short walk to the only door there was. It was blank but for a mail slot, and it had no bell. I went in without knocking.

I was in a room not much bigger than the elevator. It was windowless and pictureless, paneled and carpeted like the hallway. The only other door was on the opposite wall, and it was closed. The only furnishings were a dented metal desk to the left, a plastic swivel chair behind it, and a black canvas director's chair in front. The desk was small, and the telephone and TV on top occupied nearly its entire surface. The director's chair was empty. The swivel chair was not.

She was sprawled in it, her legs stretched out before her and crossed at the ankles. She looked fourteen, going on forty. Her hair was white-blond on top and black at the roots. It was short in back and long on the sides, and an uneven fringe ran across her forehead. Her features were fine and childlike: a tiny red mouth, a small rounded nose, thin brows, narrow slightly tilted gray eyes, ears barely large enough for their half-dozen piercings and the hardware that hung from them. Her face was round and downy, the bones still hiding beneath a layer of baby fat, and her skin was a flawless white, but for the tattoos.

There was one at the corner of her right eye that looked like a little red teardrop, and another along the side of her neck that spelled the word *pain* in elaborate black print. The same fancy lettering appeared on her knuckles, spelling the word *white* on her left hand, and *bitch* on her right. A green snake wound around the length of her skinny right arm and flicked its red ink tongue at her wrist.

She wore jeans and a tight gray T-shirt, and the hard-looking store-bought breasts underneath seemed to belong to a much larger woman. They jutted from her body like a stone mantel, and made a convenient shelf for her ashtray. She took a cigarette from it, puffed, and raised her head to look at me. Her little eyes were vacant and flat. She stared at me for a moment and then went back to her TV show, something about women whose husbands loved sheep. When the advertisements came, she took the ashtray off her breasts and put it on the desk and sat up. Her gray eyes got smaller.

"You want something?" She had a heavy accent, and pronounced her *w* as a *v*. Eastern European. There was no hostility in her voice, or even suspicion, just a mild curiosity that someone had turned up at her door. I thought for a moment. I wasn't sure what name Gilpin went by here—assuming he was here at all.

"Richards around?" I asked. One of her brows went up, and something like a smirk crossed her young face.

"Dick?" She said it so it rhymed with *seek*. I nodded. Her gaze flicked back to the TV as the commercials ended. "In there," she said. She flicked a thumb at the door, perched the ashtray on her bosom again, and went back into her slouch. I opened the door and went in.

It was a rectangular room with windows along one side that looked out on Lincoln Avenue and the rain. And it was full of cigarette smoke and testosterone.

The men sat at tables arranged end-on-end, in three rows that ran the length of the room, and they peered into their monitors and spoke into telephone headsets. It was a mostly young bunch—twenty-somethings— and mostly unappealing, like a group of spring-break drunks spoiling for a fight. There were a lot of neck chains in the room, and wrist chains, and expensive watches too. There was a lot of hair gel, and a storm front of clashing colognes. The dress code ranged from jeans to leather to silk tracksuits and rumpled Armani. Besides ashtrays, coffee cups, and beer bottles, skin magazines were the most common desk accessories. A lot of heads turned as I walked in, but they soon turned back to their monitors and telephones. They had work to do.

They were dialing for dollars. Some of them read from scripts and some were winging it; some of them whispered into their headsets and some were shouting; some pleaded, others cajoled, and a few all but threatened—but ultimately it was the same pitch, over and over again: the opportunity of a lifetime, don't miss out, guaranteed returns, fully hedged, risk free, a sure thing. Send money now. The Morgan & Lynch sales force at work.

The guy closest to the door had a thick neck, shiny blond hair, and a red polo shirt that threatened to rip around his biceps. I stepped behind his chair.

"Where's Richards?" I asked. He clamped his hand over his headset mike and twisted in his seat to give me an ugly look. Then he turned back around and started whispering.

"I'm telling you, Mr. Strelski—can I call you Gerald?—it's all set to go. And when it does, it'll go like a rocket."

The guy next to him tapped my arm and pointed to the other end of the room, to a doorway partly blocked by one of the tables. I nodded and went over. The door was ajar and someone was talking on the other side of it. I recognized the deep, deeply sincere voice of Richard Gilpin.

He was on the phone and only glanced up when I came in. He was caught up in the rhythm of his pitch.

". . . We're pursuing some very exciting opportunities in the Latin American markets, Mrs. Trillo—some deeply undervalued companies. . . ."

I tuned him out and looked around. The office was no bigger than the reception area and it was furnished along the same lines, though Gilpin had a fancier phone and, instead of a TV and fake breasts, he had a computer and a big Styrofoam cup of coffee. There was a metal filing cabinet in the corner, next to a trash can and a swivel chair. I wheeled the chair over and sat and watched Gilpin.

He was a broad guy in his late thirties, with big arms and shoulders and a block-shaped head atop a heavy neck. He had wavy well-barbered brown hair that he wore in a modified Prince Valiant. It hung low over his forehead and nearly brushed his pale brows. His dark eyes were narrow and set deep in his beefy face, and they were gathered too closely around his wedge-shaped nose. His mouth was small and thin, and his cleft chin had begun to dissolve into a blurring jawline. His tan was very dark and looked machine-made.

Gilpin wore khaki pants and a blue button-down shirt with the sleeves rolled up over his hairless arms. He looked more like the football coach at a Sun Belt high school than a fund manager. In fact, he was neither. He stared off into infinity as he worked his mark, and his big hands carved the air as he spoke. He was wrapping up now.

"Absolutely think about it, Mrs. Trillo—but you need to know that the fund is almost closed at this point. The window is small and getting smaller." Gilpin listened and nodded. "Overnight is no problem, Mrs. Trillo, absolutely none at all. I'll call you first thing in the morning." Gilpin punched a button on his phone console, pulled the headset off, and sighed heavily. He rubbed the back of his neck and turned his head from side to side. Finally, he looked at me.

"What do you want?"

I was quiet for a moment, searching his face for some resemblance to Gregory Danes. I found none. "I want to talk about your brother."

Gilpin winced and hunched his shoulders. "Fuck . . . you're the guy on the phone. What the hell are you doing here?" His voice was still deep, but the smoothness was suddenly gone.

"You wouldn't take my calls, Richard, and I had an afternoon to kill." Gilpin wrinkled his brow and looked behind me, through the open door. He lowered his voice.

"You a cop?"

"Not lately."

"Private?" I nodded, and Gilpin relaxed minutely. "Working for who?"

I smiled at him and shook my head.

"I don't know what your business is," Gilpin said, "but I can tell you this isn't the place to do it. The office isn't open to the public, and management gets real nervous about visitors. From what I heard, the last guy who came sniffing around was lucky to get out with all his fingers attached. If I were you I'd hit the road, Jack."

"And where is your management today, down in the Caymans or down the block getting takeout? By the way, do I call you Gilford around the office, or Richard, or just plain Dick?"

Gilpin blanched behind his tan. He got up, shut the door, and retreated behind his desk again. He moved quickly for a big man.

"You're hysterical, buddy, a fucking riot. I figure you got about ten minutes before you're laughing out your asshole, so make the most of them."

I poked at the carpet with the tip of my umbrella. "I don't need long, Richard. Just tell me when you last heard from your brother."

"From Greg?" He snorted. "I never hear from that little prick, unless *I* call *him*—and I gave up on that a while ago." Gilpin picked up his coffee cup and took a sip. He made a sour face and put it down. "And he's my *half* brother."

"So the last time you spoke to him was when?"

Gilpin's mouth puckered with something worse than the taste of his coffee. "A year ago—no, fourteen months it was."

"And?"

"And nothing. That's the last time we talked. Full stop." Gilpin looked at the door.

"What did you talk about?"

He wrinkled his brow some more, and anger began to vie with nervousness in his small deep eyes. "What the fuck business is it of yours?"

"I said I didn't need long, Richard, but you're slowing things down."

Gilpin's thin mouth twisted. He pointed a stubby tan finger at me. "Screw you, buddy. You're nothing. I don't have to tell you shit."

I shrugged. "Of course you don't, Richard, it's your choice entirely. Just like it's my choice to call your pals down at the SEC—in the enforcement division, maybe—and tell them where they can forward your Christmas card this year. I'm sure they'd be fascinated to hear what you and your associates are up to."

Gilpin blanched again. "Hey, I don't know those guys from Adam," he said, pointing toward the door. "I don't know what the hell they do out there, and I don't ask; we just share the office." But even he wasn't convinced. He put his hands up and shook his head a little. "All right, all right: the last time I talked to Greg . . . I called him fourteen months ago, about some money, a loan I needed. My big brother ran true to form and told me to fuck off. I told him to screw himself, and that was the end. Conversation didn't last ten minutes."

"That the way it usually goes between you two?"

Gilpin made a mocking smile. "You're real perceptive, pal. You must be a pro."

"You know any of his friends? Anybody he's close to?"

He barked a nasty laugh. "You think I know shit about his life? You think he's had a goddamn thing to do with me since he went off to college? Christ, he barely had the time of day for me before then. Talk to his buddies on Wall Street if you want to know about him; talk to his dyke wife; talk to anybody but me." Gilpin took another swallow of his coffee and made another wretched face.

"So you don't know where he might go on vacation?"

The nasty laugh again. "I told you—I don't know about Greg's life, and I don't want to. I got my own problems." He gestured around the room and snorted. "I got my own fucking vacation to worry about, right here." Gilpin picked up his coffee cup and arced it into the trash can in the corner. Coffee splashed on the wall and ran down the paneling; Gilpin didn't seem to mind. He looked at me again.

"Greg's missing?" he asked. "Is that what this is about?" Before I could answer, he screwed his eyes shut and rubbed his thick hands over his face. "Fuck it, I don't want to know. Just do me a favor and get the hell out of here, will you?"

Gilpin slumped behind his desk, and I saw fatigue and chronic worry beneath his artificial tan. He was like a long-caged animal: exhausted and resigned, any fight left in him no more than reflex. He hadn't said much, but it was all he had. I got up.

Nothing had changed in the big room when I passed through; the boys were still smoking and working the phones, and this time no one raised a head. Something had changed in the reception area, though.

The girl was gone. In her place behind the desk was a compact man, wearing a green waterproof field jacket just like mine. He had short blond hair and precise handsome features on a narrow white face. His eyes were gray and slightly upturned and reminded me of the eyes of the girl who wasn't there. The TV was still on, but it was C-SPAN, not sheep, that he was watching. He looked at me briefly and impassively when I came through the door, and then his eyes went back to the screen. I paused for a moment, expecting him to say something, but he didn't. I crossed the room, and his hand dipped into his jacket pocket and came out with a phone. I left the office and found the elevator waiting in the empty hallway.

They were outside, just beyond the lobby doors, and there were three of them. Two were big, and the third was bigger. The two big men held wide golf umbrellas. One man was around thirty, with dirty-blond hair, tied in a ponytail. He had a lot of rings on his umbrella hand, and his high cheekbones, pointed nose, and V-shaped mouth made him look something like a shark. He wore a long canvas duster, fastened to the throat. The other man was older, with short dark hair, a neat beard, and suspicious eyes. He wore work boots and khakis and an expensive waterproof shell over a plaid shirt, and in other circumstances I might have taken him for an engineer or a geologist. They had a couple of inches on me, each, and an easy twenty pounds. The third guy was a different story altogether.

He was six-foot-six, at least, and nearly three hundred pounds, and his bald bullet-shaped head was mostly covered by an intricate tattoo: two dragons locked in mortal combat, their red fangs clashing at the top of his skull. A hint, perhaps, of what went on underneath.

His face was fleshy and hairless and fish-belly white. A pale blue scar ran from temple to cheek down the left side, and met up with another that ran across his chin. His brow was a shelf of bone above small black eyes and a nose that had been rebuilt several times. His mouth was a lipless wrinkle, and his arms looked like two sacks of rocks. He was dressed in black motorcycle leathers, black gloves, and heavy black boots, all soaked through with rain. Rain beat down on his bare head, and each drop seemed to enrage him. He seemed to like the feeling. His eyes were locked on me.

The geologist nodded. "Let's get out of the rain while we talk," he said. He motioned me under his big umbrella. He had an accent, but it was slight and I couldn't place it. My carry permit is no good in Jersey, my gun was safe at home, and my options were limited. I nodded back at him, rolled up my umbrella, and stepped under his. The shark stepped in beside us and Attila brought up the rear. They walked me into the parking structure next door.

Inside, the two big guys closed their umbrellas and led the way up a ramp to the second level. Attila walked behind me and made kissing noises. The only car on the second level was a massive black Hummer. It had smoked windows and a big chrome brush bar, and it glistened with beaded rainwater. The two big guys walked toward it but stopped when they were twenty yards away. I stopped too. They turned to face me. Attila paced behind me and made sniffing sounds. The big guys looked at me and I looked back, and we stood that way for a while.

"Shall we talk?" I said finally.

Attila came up close behind me and roared in my ear. "Shut up, bitch!" His voice was high—another steroid juicer, no doubt—and his accent was Eastern European. His breath had a burnt chemical odor, and the smell off his body was sour and powerful. He resumed his pacing and bumped me with his shoulder as he did. It was like getting sideswiped by a bus. I staggered forward a step but kept looking at the other two guys. A smile flickered across the shark's face. He shook his head slowly and put a finger to his lips and made a shushing sound. We stood silently for another couple of minutes and then we heard footsteps.

It was the compact blond man from the reception desk. His field jacket was zipped against the rain, and his corduroy collar was turned up. His head was down and his hands were in his jacket pockets, and he didn't look at us as he came slowly up the ramp. The two big guys shifted nervously as he approached and even Attila grew still.

He came to a halt between the two big men and opened his jacket and shook off the rain. Underneath he wore a black sweater over a gray shirt. He was about five-foot-seven, and he looked like he was made of rebar. He ran a small, strong-looking hand through his hair and flicked away the water. He looked at me.

"Are you Morgan or Lynch?" I asked. He ignored my question.

"What is your name and what is your business with Gilpin?" he asked. His voice was soft and flat and faintly accented.

"Didn't Gilpin tell you?" The two big guys shifted, and Attila came around to yell down at me.

"Bitch! You answer the questions!" The chemical smell was overpowering. A meth smoker maybe. Steroids and meth—the breakfast of champions. Great. The compact man cleared his throat and made a gesture to Attila with his small hand. Attila went around behind me again.

"Gilpin tells me everything, which I think you will come to see as a sensible course of action." He was quiet for a moment, and he tilted his head slightly as he looked at me. "What is your name, and what is your business with Gilpin?"

"I'm a PI, and I'm working a missing persons case. I thought Gilpin might have heard from the guy I'm looking for. Apparently he hasn't."

The small man pursed his narrow lips and gestured again to Attila, who came around in front of me. "Perhaps I have not made myself clear; perhaps that is why you have not answered my questions fully. Or perhaps you have not understood me." The rain was falling harder, and the small man's voice was nearly lost in the rushing sound of it. My heart was pounding. "I think Goran's questions would be more clear to you." Attila smiled hideously at me and made his kissing noise.

I looked at the small man and took a deep breath. "I'm happy to speak with you and maybe answer some questions too—and if you want to answer a few in return, I'll even spring for the coffee. But lock your freak back in the attic, and let's do this like civilized people." Attila's nostrils flared and his little black eyes got smaller and blacker. He took a step toward me and drew back his fist. He opened his mouth, to roar at me, but I interrupted.

I snapped my umbrella up into his crotch and drove the metal point into his balls. I'm not sure how much damage it did, but it got his attention—long enough for me to hit him twice in the throat with the stiffened fingertips of my right hand. The blows came up from under, from the legs and hips, and with plenty of twist and momentum. He made a retching sound and clawed at his throat, and while he did I pivoted and kicked him hard in the side of the knee. He went down, and his bald head made a wet cracking sound on the pavement.

I stepped back, breathing hard, and was surprised to find I still had my umbrella. The geologist was pointing a big automatic at me, and so was the shark. The small man was shaking his head slowly, and there was a look of weary disappointment on his neat face. He rested a hand on the geologist's arm and spoke softly in a language I didn't recognize. The two men lowered their guns and the shark knelt by Attila, who was still on the ground and whose eyes were unfocused. Blood was leaking from his nose. The small man looked at Attila and sighed and shook his head a little more.

"The drugs make Goran excitable and too easily provoked. He is less and less useful." He looked up at me. "Perhaps you are too easily provoked, as well. Perhaps if I were any less . . . *civilized* . . . you would be dead right now." I struggled to get my breathing under control and managed a shrug. Between them, the shark and the geologist hoisted Attila to his feet and half walked, half dragged him to the Hummer. They heaved him into the back seat and shut the door and waited by the car. I took another deep breath.

"If you were careful enough to want to talk to me in the first place, I figured you'd be careful enough not to escalate things needlessly. Not before you knew who I was, anyway—and who else might know where I went today."

He nodded. "That is a great deal of speculation . . . and risk."

I shrugged again. "Not that much," I said, and I smiled a little. "Not with a guy who watches C-SPAN and has such good taste in clothes."

A whisper of a smile passed across his face. "More than you think, I assure you," he said.

"You want to have that chat? My offer of coffee stands."

The small man shook his head. "We will talk here. You said that Gilpin was of no help to you—that he had not heard from your missing person, yes?" I nodded. "And you believed him?" I nodded again. "Gilpin said you threatened him . . . with certain regulatory agencies." Another nod. The small man looked at me, silent, waiting for more.

"He wasn't cooperative at first; I needed some leverage."

"So, your threats were empty?" It was one of those *Do you still beat your wife?* questions.

"My feeling about the Feds is that they should earn their pay," I said. "They don't need my help and they don't want it."

"So you have no reason to speak with Gilpin again or to disturb my business any further?"

"None that I can see."

"You have no reason," he said. His soft voice was cold and there was no question in it. I looked at him for a moment and nodded. The faint smile flitted across his face again, and he turned up the collar of his jacket. "So I will not see you again, Mr. . . . ." He held out his hand.

I looked at him and shook it. It was like a fistful of cyclone fencing. "March," I said.

He nodded. "Gromyko." He zipped his jacket and climbed into the passenger seat of the Hummer. The geologist got behind the wheel and the shark got in back, and they drove down the ramp and out into the rain.

I stood at the top of the ramp for several minutes and let the tension drain away, but my limbs still quivered with loose adrenaline as I walked to my Toyota, and I was edgy and alert. If I hadn't been, I might have missed the cars that followed me back over the bridge and into Manhattan.

12

A bad tail job has all the subtlety of a cold sore; a good one—an expensive one, with lots of cars, and drivers who don't get overeager—is delicate as lace. The guys who'd followed me from Jersey weren't bad—they'd used at least two cars, and they never crowded—they were just unlucky. Traffic over the bridge brought them in too close and I was already jumpy. They'd known the deal was done when I started a slow meander through the streets of Morningside Heights, and after a game half hour they'd broken off. But they weren't bad.

Which was why I took the long way to my brother's house on Saturday, and stopped frequently to check my back. My last checkpoint was a Starbucks on First Avenue. I sat near the window and scanned the afternoon traffic for faces or cars I'd seen too often. I caught no glimpse of the rusted brown Cavalier from last night, or of the black late-model Grand Prix, but that was little comfort. And I still had no idea of who they were or what they wanted—which was even less.

I'd called Neary this morning and told him what happened. He'd thought it was Gromyko. I had disagreed.

"It would surprise me somehow," I'd said.

Neary laughed skeptically. "From what you told me about your chat in the garage, I'm surprised he didn't dump you in the Hudson for cold-cocking his ape."

"I think he's a little more subtle than that—at least on a first date. He wanted to find out what I was up to and send a message about staying out of his yard. He did that, and we . . . reached an understanding. And there are practical considerations, besides. You think he's got the manpower for a professional car tail just waiting around?"

"I don't know who he is or what kind of manpower he's got, and neither do you. But I'll make some calls and maybe we'll find out." I thanked Neary and told him I owed him one. He muttered something about a long list, and asked if I had any kind of line on Danes yet. I told him no and told him about Pratt and Sovitch and Anthony Frye and what I'd found out about Danes's custody fight with Nina Sachs. When I was through, Neary whistled softly.

"Not exactly Mr. Congeniality," he said.

"Not exactly."

"Still, you'd think a semifamous guy like him would have a few more friends."

"If he does, they stay well hidden."

I finished my coffee, left Starbucks, and headed south and west. I watched the cars and the sidewalks as I went, and thought some more about the smallness of Gregory Danes's life, how sparsely peopled it was, how an absence of five—almost six—weeks could occasion so little notice and even less concern. I walked and thought about Danes's isolation, and by the time I reached Ned's I was somehow thinking about my own.

Ned lives on Park Avenue in the low seventies, in the big old apartment we all grew up in. It was just after two when the doorman trotted out, held the big bronze door, and greeted me by name—a sure sign I'd been visiting too often. A tall slender couple waited in the marble lobby: Lauren and Keith.

"Look at you, all prompt and everything," Lauren said, and she kissed me on the cheek. She wore a green cotton sweater and baggy pants. Her black hair was loose and parted in the middle. She brushed it from her angular face, and it hung straight and glossy down her back. There was a faint tan across her cheeks and her strong pointed nose. Her green eyes narrowed slightly.

"Where's Jane?" she asked.

"At the office," I said, "arguing with lawyers." I reached around her to shake hands with her husband. Keith Berger looked down from his six-foot-four elevation. He was wearing jeans and a plaid shirt, and he still had his Rockefeller University ID clipped to his pocket. He ran a hand through his tangled brown hair and grinned.

"You're getting good at this," he said. "You hardly grind your teeth at all now."

Lauren elbowed him and looked behind me. Liz came through the door. She wore a gray linen shift and a wry smile on her handsome face. She kissed Lauren and Keith and dug a finger in my ribs.

"You still need some meat on you," she said, and kissed me too. "Where's Jane?" I told her, and she looked at me skeptically for a moment and nodded.

Lauren checked her watch. "Let's go up," she said.

My nephew Derek had just turned seven, and it was his birthday party. Not the lavish one for schoolmates; that was next week, at the Museum of Natural History. This was the more relaxed version, for family. And as family functions went, it wasn't too bad.

There was a tangle of children in the den—Derek, his younger brother, Alec, and a passel of Klein cousins, once and twice removed. They were in the degenerated stages of a game of Twister, and most of the action seemed to be about pulling one another's socks off.

The grown-ups were scattered through the living room and dining room and on the brick-paved terrace that runs around most of the apartment. There were twenty or so of them: my Uncle Daniel and Aunt Marion, my Uncle Ben, a few of their kids—my cousins—and their spouses, a couple of Janine's siblings, my brother David and his unlovely wife. Elevator jazz was playing, and it got nicely lost in the sounds of ice on glass and silver on china. Someone handed me a glass of iced tea and a plate of food and started talking. I fastened a smile on my face and started nodding.

I drifted through the big apartment, through the crowd of family, through the afternoon, like a new suitor: benign, agreeable, and mostly silent. But I had no complaints. No cross words were spoken, no snide remarks were made about keyholes, motel rooms, or hidden cameras, and no one offered anything close to career advice. Maybe we were getting somewhere, my family and I; maybe we were finding neutral ground. Or maybe it was just that I managed to avoid my brother David all afternoon.

It was nearly four-thirty when Lauren and Keith came to get me. I was playing a video game with Derek and Alec and a bunch of other kids and failing badly at it, much to their great amusement. I kissed my nephews and we left.

As family functions went, not too bad.

I got home before five, with no one following me or staked out at the curb—at least that I could tell. I changed my clothes and went for a run before the streets got thick with Saturday-night crowds. There was a message from Jane when I got back. I took a pitcher from the fridge and poured a glass of water, and I listened to her tired voice on the telephone speaker with an odd mix of disappointment and relief.

"I'm just finishing up, but I have another session with these clowns tomorrow, so I'm going straight to bed. I'll be out early, so I'm not sure when I'll see you. Sometime, I guess."

I drained my glass and felt the cold spread through my chest and into my stomach.

"Sometime," I said softly.

13

I'd worried that Christopher might have second thoughts about letting me into Danes's apartment, but my worries were misplaced. He'd had a rough weekend, and the only thing on his mind on Monday afternoon was more money. We stood in the small alcove off the lobby and haggled a little over price and time. We finally agreed on three hundred for three hours, and he palmed me the key. I gave him half the cash.

"It's on twenty—Twenty-B," he said. "Just be real quiet, bro, and be real fucking careful." His body was stiff and his movements were jerky.

"Any neighbors around?" I asked. Christopher's eyes bounced around the lobby.

"How the hell should I know?" he hissed. He wiped his hands on his uniform pants and softened his voice. "I don't think so."

"Take a deep breath, Christopher. This will work out fine." I rode to the twentieth floor alone.

The doors opened onto a quiet corridor that made a square around the elevator shaft. The carpeting was thick and peach-colored, and the walls were ivory, with brass sconces. There were four doors in dark wood with shiny brass hardware. Apartment B was to my left, at eleven o'clock. There was a button on the doorframe and I pushed it. I heard a chime inside, but nothing else. I took a deep breath, put the key in the lock, and went in.

I closed the door softly and stood listening. I heard ticking sounds in the ductwork, the faraway *whoosh* of traffic, and nothing else. I was in a rectangular foyer, carpeted in pale gray. The walls were white, and there were tiny halogen lights mounted flush in the ceiling. To my left was a powder room in white marble, and to my right was a closet with double doors. The air was stale and still, but scented with nothing more malignant than carpet and dust. My pulse was fast and my shoulders were tight, and I was filled with the tense uneasy thrill I always got when I creeped a house. I slowed my breathing and snapped on a pair of vinyl gloves.

I started with a walkabout. Danes's was a corner apartment, laid out in a broad V, with the living room at the apex. Off the living room, down one leg of the V, were the dining room and kitchen. Down the other were the master bedroom, a guest room, and an office.

It wasn't a huge place, but it was well appointed. The doors were solid and the walls were thick; the switches and fixtures were European, and the kitchen appliances were top-of-the-line. Except for the brushed-steel kitchen and the marble baths, all the rooms were painted white and carpeted in the same gray pile as the foyer.

The rooms were furnished sparely with modern Italian pieces. Everything was sleek and aerodynamic-looking, and the colors were muted—grays and tans and olives—except for a cherry-red sofa in the living room, an acid-green armchair in the master bedroom, and a bank of neon-orange bookshelves in the office. The walls were mostly bare, and what was hanging was abstract and bland. The apartment looked not so much decorated as delivered whole from a showroom in Milan. I finished my walk in the kitchen and leaned against a counter and sighed.

"Fucking Christopher," I said aloud.

The place had already been tossed, and not carefully. It wasn't heavy-handed—the sofas hadn't been upended and the beds hadn't been gutted—but it was plain nonetheless. The apartment, though clean and neat throughout, was off-kilter, like a deck of cards that has been shuffled but not squared. The countertops were spotless and the wastebaskets were clean—even the soap dishes were pristine—but the closet doors were ajar and so were the drawers, and their contents, though hung and folded, were askew and misaligned. I lowered my expectations and started searching.

The refrigerator was sparse but not bare. There were condiments, a carton of eggs, a bottle of seltzer, ground coffee, and a magnum of champagne inside, but no leftovers and nothing with a short shelf life. That could mean Danes had emptied it out before he left, or that his cleaner had, or it could mean he didn't eat at home much. In New York City it was hard to tell. The freezer was empty but for the ice trays.

There was nothing of interest in the drawers or cabinets. The china and silver were good but not extravagant, and the pots and pans and cutlery looked unused. The pantry was stocked with Swiss breakfast cereal, tea bags, canned soup, and expensive cookies, but with no hints of Danes's whereabouts.

There was nothing in the dining room besides an aluminum and glass dining table, eight spindly aluminum chairs, and a sideboard in bleached wood. The sideboard was empty. I moved on to the living room.

The walls were glass at the crook of the V, with doors that opened onto a V-shaped terrace. The view was south and east, and the room was full of light. The thin clouds were close enough to touch. Besides the red sofa, the room was dominated by a gleaming black baby grand piano and a wall of built-in cabinets. I opened one of the cabinet doors. Inside was music.

There were shelves of it, from floor to ceiling—CDs and vinyl, lots of vinyl. I slid some records out. They were all classical, and each was sleeved in clear plastic. Behind other doors was the stereo, though that was hardly an adequate term for it. It was a wall of black metal technology: a pre-amp and amplifier—with actual vacuum tubes—an impossibly complicated equalizer, a disc player, a separate disc changer, and a black-and-silver turntable that looked like something you could mill plutonium with.

There were file-sized drawers at the base of the cabinets. I opened them and thumbed through the papers inside. It was sheet music, all for piano and organized by composer: Bach, Beethoven, Haydn, Mozart. The pages were well handled and annotated in pencil at the margins.

I headed down the hallway to the master bedroom and froze. There were voices in the corridor outside. They were muffled by the thick walls, but they were men's voices and they were coming closer. I heard keys jangle, and the voices got louder and someone laughed. Then the elevator doors opened with a clank, and the voices dimmed. They closed, and it was quiet. I started breathing again and felt sweat trickle down my back. My shoulders were stiff and I rolled them around and went into the bedroom.

It was a large room, with not much in it: a glowing green chair like something from a *Star Trek* episode, a king-sized bed with built-in nightstands, and more built-in cabinetry. A door to my right led to a deep walk-in closet, and another led to the master bath. The bed was made up. The bedding was pale green and felt expensive. There were no clothes lying around. I started with the cabinets.

Inside were a big flat-screen TV, a DVD player, and a cable box. Danes's DVD collection was modest, nothing like his music wall and distinctly lower-brow: action flicks, science fiction, some frat-boy farces. They were sorted by genre and title.

There were pictures on one of the nightstands, in silver frames: one of a younger Billy near the polar bear pool at the Central Park Zoo; another of Billy and Danes by the seal tank. It was blurry and looked like Danes had been holding the camera at arm's length when he'd taken it.

There was an alarm clock and a telephone on the other nightstand. I picked up the phone and hit the redial button. It rang four times and a heavily accented voice answered: "Garage." I stayed on long enough to establish that it was the place Danes parked his car and then hung up. The nightstand drawers held little of interest: pens, notepads, a bag of cough drops, a package of tissues. The shelves underneath were empty but for a slim red restaurant guide and a TV remote. There was nothing under the bed or under the mattress. I went into the bathroom.

It was a beige marble temple to the gods of hygiene and evacuation. There was a long counter with two fancy German sinks, a Japanese-style soaking tub, and a glass-walled shower with seating for six and more knobs, spouts, and hoses than a submarine. The toilet and bidet were sequestered in a little marble chapel of their own. They were low-slung and futuristic and seemed unsuited to human anatomy. The medicine cabinet was above the sinks, behind a mirrored panel. I pressed on it and it opened with a hiss.

Inside was a collection of toiletries and drugs. The toiletries were all high-end, and the drugs were over-the-counter and unremarkable: aspirin, antacids, eye drops, and vitamins.

There was a linen closet next to the soaking tub, stocked with sheets, thick towels, toilet paper, a first-aid kit, and a box of condoms. There was nothing exceptional about the condoms—they were a simple domestic brand, without bells or whistles—but they suggested that Danes had a sex life. I went back to the bedroom, to the big closet.

It was actually a wood-paneled room, done up like a little slice of Paul Stuart. Clothes hung in double racks on either side, and like his collections of music and movies, Danes's wardrobe was ruthlessly organized. Business attire on the left, casual clothing on the right, accompanied by appropriate belts and ties; everything sorted by season and color. His shoes were mustered in neat rows on shelves below the hanging clothes. There were empty hangers on the casual side, and gaps in the platoon of casual shoes—at least two pairs were gone.

There was a wide bureau at the back of the closet, with built-in shelves above it; a set of brown leather luggage was on the highest one. The bags were empty, but there seemed to be one missing from the set—something larger than an airplane carry-on but smaller than a trunk. I put the bags back and went through the bureau.

The top drawer held hardware: watches, cuff links, collar stays, belt buckles. The others held clothing: underwear in one drawer, socks in another, pajamas in the next. Then I opened the bottom drawer.

They were in matching sets—pale blue, pale gray, green, maroon, and black—all the same expensive Italian brand: bras and panties, neatly folded. I didn't think they were Danes's size. Along with the lingerie, there was a woman's green polo shirt in the drawer, a pair of faded jeans, and the faintest trace of a musky scent. Beneath the jeans, there was a green leather clutch bag with a silver clasp. The leather was soft and had a matte finish. The clasp was tarnished. Inside the bag was a leaky blue pen, a folded credit card receipt, a dusty roll of mints, and three quarters. I unfolded the receipt. It was from a little French restaurant on Lexington, a few blocks from Danes's apartment, and it was over a year old. The print was faded but still legible in the light, and so was the signature scrawled across the bottom: *Linda Sovitch.*

I let out a deep breath and looked at the receipt for a while. Then I folded it and put it back in the purse and put the purse back in the drawer.

I checked my watch. I had another hour before Christopher started going into cardiac arrest. The guest room went quickly. It had a double bed, a nightstand, a bureau, an armchair, and a TV—and nothing of any interest to me. I moved on to the office.

It was a small room, with narrow windows at one end. There was a sleek metal desk and a matching credenza on the left-hand wall, the orange bookshelves on the right, and barely room left over for the leather swivel chair. My predecessor's tracks were plain there—in the gaping file drawers and open cabinet doors and in the books that lay like toppled dominoes on the shelves. I started with the desk.

The desktop had nothing on it but equipment: a telephone and an answering machine at one end and, at the other, a flat-screen monitor and a mouse, both hooked to a docking station for a laptop. But there was no laptop in sight. I followed cables from the docking station to a cabinet in the credenza and found a printer-copier-fax combo and a modem, but still no laptop. It was impossible to know if it had left with Danes or afterward.

A blinking light on the answering machine caught my eye. I picked up the telephone. It had caller ID, and I scrolled through the recorded numbers. There were fifty of them, all the phone could hold. I thought for a moment about taking the phone and the answering machine with me but decided against it. There was a chance—maybe a good one—that this case could become a police investigation. If it did, the cops would take a very dim view of my walking off with evidence, so dim they might walk off with my license in return. I got out my pad and pen and sat down in the swivel chair.

It took me fifteen minutes to copy down the caller ID information from Danes's phone and another ten to listen to the dozen messages on his answering machine. I wrote down the names of the callers and when they called. All the messages were from people I knew: Nina Sachs, Irene Pratt, Dennis Turpin, Giselle Thomas, and Nancy Mayhew. The wording was different, but the content was all the same: "Where are you? Call me." One of the last calls was from Billy. It began with a long breathing silence after the beep, disappointment perhaps, at getting the machine. When he finally spoke, his voice was a choked mix of hurt and anger and low expectations bitterly fulfilled.

"You were supposed to pick me up," he said. And then, after a long pause: "Are you ever going to fucking call?"

Billy's message was fairly recent, just over a week old, and none of the messages went back much more than three weeks. I put my pad away. I pressed the redial button on the phone and after two rings got a Chinese restaurant that I knew was around the corner, on Third Avenue. Someone asked for my order and I hung up.

The desk had a center drawer, and I pulled it out and put it on my lap. Inside were paper clips, rubber bands, a roll of postage stamps, and—in the back—Danes's passport. It was dog-eared and swollen, full of stamps from countries in Europe and Asia and the Caribbean, and its presence here meant that Danes wasn't in any of those places. At the back of the drawer was a business card. The paper was heavy stock and the print was black and sober-looking. FOSTER-ROYCE RESEARCH. JUDITH PEARSON, ACCOUNT MANAGER. I put the card in my pocket and the drawer back in the desk and turned to the credenza.

The top drawer was full of file folders and so was the bottom. There were labels on the folders—phone, condo, utilities, bank, brokerage, insurance, legal—and nothing at all inside them. I pushed them aside and found only paper clips and bent staples on the bottoms of the drawers. I closed the drawers and heard a tearing sound. I opened them again and knelt down and reached my hand into the space behind the drawers.

Whoever had been here before me had searched a lot, but not well. I came out with papers: a bank statement. It was six months old and crumpled, but it was better than bent staples. I pulled the bottom drawer out and reached into the empty space and found another wrinkled sheaf: credit card bills and a brokerage statement. I smoothed the documents out and folded them and put them in my pocket. I went to the orange bookshelves.

Most of the books were on business and mathematics, though there was one shelf devoted to music: history of, theory of, and composer biographies. I pulled some volumes at random from the shelves, leafed through them, and found nothing there but pages.

There were silver-framed photos lying flat on the topmost shelf, and I took them down one by one to look at. There was a picture of Billy standing on the deck of the *Intrepid* and looking sullen, and another of him on the climbing wall at Chelsea Piers, looking embarrassed and angry. There was a photo of Danes in black tie flanked by several gray-haired executive types. He was holding a framed certificate that declared him to be 1999's analyst of the year, at least in the judgment of one prominent trade rag. Next to that photo was the framed certificate itself. It seemed to have aged well. There was a picture of Danes and an older man, standing on either side of a young Asian woman who was holding a violin. I recognized the woman from television and from the time I'd heard her play at Carnegie Hall. I didn't recognize the old man. He had sparse white hair on a tanned and freckled head, and his face was narrow and hollow-cheeked. His smile was tired but warm. The last photo was an old one—over ten years old. It was of Danes and Nina Sachs, and it had the same tropical backdrop as the one Sachs had shown me in her apartment. In this one, she and Danes stood side by side on a stone terrace above an empty bay. He wore a blazer and white trousers, and his hair looked blond in the sunlight. Nina wore the same gauzy caftan. Their fingers were laced and they smirked identically into the camera, as if at a private joke. They looked happy.

I checked my watch. Christopher was no doubt having seizures downstairs; it was time to go. I looked quickly through the front hall closet and the powder room and found nothing in either place. I listened at the front door. It was quiet in the corridor, and I slipped out and locked the door behind me. I took my gloves off, put them in my pocket, and took a deep breath.

The elevator came right away and I was about to step on when a tall broad-shouldered man came churning out. His head was down and he sideswiped me as he went past. I rocked backward but he seemed not to notice. He had a long coat on, too warm for spring, and jeans and work boots. There was an unkempt fringe of dark hair around his ears and collar, and a thin tangle across the top of his large head. His face was full, and shaded by a few days' dark growth. His mouth was small and puffy and it was moving as he stepped off the car, but only he could hear the words. His wire glasses were askew on his broad nose, and I caught only a glimpse of his eyes, which were dark and agitated and far away.

I stepped into the elevator and watched him go to the door next to Danes's—apartment 20-C—bend over the handle, and work a key in the lock. The doors slid closed and I descended. The elevator car had a rank smell.

14

It was four o'clock when the taxi dropped me at 23rd Street, and I took my time walking home from there. When I got to 16th I was reasonably sure I was alone. My block was quiet: a couple of dog walkers, two moms pushing strollers, a FedEx guy unloading, a light blue van pulling away from the curb, a dirty red hatchback pulling in. I went upstairs.

It was too warm in my apartment and the air was stale, and I opened all the windows while my voice mail played over the phone speaker. There was a message from Mrs. K, telling me, in somewhat cautious tones, that two more interviews had been scheduled at Klein for later that week and to consult my e-mail for details. And Nina Sachs had phoned, to ask—brusquely—that I call her with a progress report. I shook my head and wondered what she'd make of the lingerie.

I wasn't entirely sure what to make of it myself. The clothing and the receipt suggested that Danes and Sovitch had been having a thing—and an ongoing thing, at that. If that was so, it would cast a different light on what Sovitch had said to me—and maybe explain her distinct lack of journalistic curiosity. I wouldn't know until I had another chat with her, and maybe not even then. Maybe I'd find that the underwear belonged to someone else altogether. Maybe it belonged to Danes. I called Nina Sachs's number and let it ring twelve times before I gave up.

Jane had called too. "I've got time off for good behavior tonight. Want to do something? I'll ring when I'm ready to leave."

I flicked on my stereo. WFUV was playing Freedy Johnston, but I wasn't in the mood. I put a Ry Cooder disc in, something Cuban with guitars, poured a big glass of water, and carried it to the table. I took off my coat and emptied its pockets of souvenirs: my handwritten list of phone calls and messages, the business card, and the wrinkled collection of months-old documents—the bank statement, the brokerage statement, and the credit card bills.

I'd tried pressing Christopher for more current mail when I'd come downstairs, but he was no help, telling me only that Danes's box was empty and his mail was being held at the post office. He hadn't been completely useless, however, even if he was unwilling at first.

It had taken the threat of withholding the rest of his cash, and the suggestion that I might stick around and talk to the building super, to get Christopher to admit that this wasn't the first time he'd sold access to Danes's apartment. That had happened almost ten days earlier, he told me—the week before our first conversation—and the buyers were the same two nondescript guys he'd told me about before. But despite my arm-twisting, Christopher had continued to insist that he knew neither their names nor how to contact them. At least he was consistent. I drank some water, pushed up my sleeves, and picked up the bank statement.

It was six months old but illuminating nonetheless. For one thing, it explained why the lights were still working in Danes's apartment. Most of his regular bills—for phone, cable, electricity, condo common charges, parking, even his maid service—were paid automatically, by direct debit from his checking account. His paychecks came in the same way, two times a month, fat and automatic. If his current balance was anything like the one he'd had six months ago, his cable service was assured for years to come.

For another, the statement rendered Nina Sachs's concern for her ex-husband in concrete terms: six thousand a month in alimony and another six in child support. Nina would have to sell a lot of paintings to generate that kind of cash flow, and she would definitely notice when the check was late.

Danes's brokerage statement covered roughly the same period as the bank statement. His portfolio was a conservative mix of stocks, corporate bonds, and government bonds, with a market value at the time in the high seven figures. The companies he owned were big household names, and there were none on the list that I recognized as technology firms. Buy-and-sell activity in the account was quite low.

None of that was particularly surprising; as head of research at Pace-Loyette, Danes's personal investing would be constrained by layers of rules and regulations laid down by the Securities and Exchange Commission, the National Association of Securities Dealers, the New York Stock Exchange, and his own firm. His holdings would be subject to scrutiny by each of those parties, and every buy or sell order that he placed would require the prior approval of Pace's compliance department. Active trading—short-term speculating as opposed to longer-term investing—would be difficult, if not altogether prohibited, and for all intents and purposes, he'd be barred from owning shares in the technology companies that his department issued reports on and maybe even in companies in the same industries.

I looked at the month-to-date and year-to-date returns calculated on the statement. Its lack of flash had not inoculated Danes's portfolio against the vagaries of the market, and its performance, at least as of six months ago, was decidedly anemic.

A gust of wind sent pages flipping across my tabletop and I rose to shut some windows. Day was fading and the sky was pink and vaguely tropical looking. Sixteenth Street was in shadow. The sidewalks had filled and traffic was backed up behind a van parallel parking in a space across the street. It was a tight spot, but the van's driver was deft and traffic was soon moving again. I worked the kinks from my neck and looked at the van. Its taillights went out but no doors opened. I rolled my shoulders and wondered what color it was. Gray? Silver? Light blue? It was impossible to tell in this light.

I sat down at the table again and slid Danes's credit card bills over. They weren't quite as old as the two statements but they weren't current either, so there were no convenient, week-old charges from the Hideout Hilton or the like to be found in them. Scanning the pages, I saw that for the most part Danes took his meals on the Upper East Side, bought his clothes on Madison Avenue and his music on the Internet. But it wasn't all eating and shopping. There was a three-month-old charge, over a weekend, from a pricey bed-and-breakfast in East Hampton. There was another charge, four months back, from an inn in Lenox, Massachusetts. And earlier that same month, there had been what looked like a weekend trip to Bermuda.

I stacked the credit card statements together and put them next to the bank and brokerage statements. Like them, these had been illuminating but not immediately useful. My eyes felt gritty and dry. I was tired of looking at numbers. I picked up the business card.

I'd never heard of Foster-Royce Research, but I assumed from the name that it was a stock research outfit or maybe a corporate headhunting firm. I found it on the Web and found that I was wrong.

Research was apparently a polite English way of saying *private investigations.* Foster-Royce was a London-based detective agency and, apparently, an up-market one. Besides its headquarters on Threadneedle Street, the firm had offices in Paris, Zurich, Madrid, Rome, Hong Kong, Toronto, and New York—all the better, I guessed, to support its self-proclaimed specialty in international assignments. According to its Web site, Foster-Royce investigators had broad experience with such outfits as Interpol, the Metropolitan Police, the Gendarmerie Nationale, the RCMP, the FBI, and others, and maintained *deep local contacts* in all the countries where Foster-Royce kept offices. They promised thoroughness, professionalism, integrity, and, of course, discretion. I hoped that last bit was just talk. The corporate directory told me Judith Pearson was assigned to the New York office and gave me the number.

Judith Pearson took my call without delay. She had a pleasant southern voice and a friendly manner, and she was discreet to the point of mute. She wouldn't tell me if she'd ever met Gregory Danes or even heard his name before, much less admit that he was a client of Foster-Royce. But she did invite me to call her again if there was anything else she could help me with. Her good-bye was cheerful and self-satisfied. I sighed.

I got up and stretched and stood by the windows. The sky was dark now, and tinged with purple. The evening rush had merged seamlessly with the leading edge of the dinner crowd, and traffic was, if anything, worse. The streetlights were lit, and I saw the van still parked across the way.

I filled my water glass, turned on the television, and switched to BNN. *Market Minds* was on, and Linda Sovitch's blond image filled the screen. She was saying something about housing starts and mortgage refinancings, and I turned the sound off and watched her full lips move and her blue eyes shift back and forth. She gestured with her left hand, and the big yellow diamond on her ring finger flashed under the studio lights. I thought of something I had read somewhere.

I opened my laptop and went online, back to *LindaObsession.com*. I found what I was looking for on the bio page: a mention of Sovitch's marriage, ten years earlier, to real estate developer Aaron Lefcourt. It got just a single line—as if the Web site's authors couldn't bear to contemplate it any longer. It was the only reference to Lefcourt anywhere on the site, and I had to look elsewhere to learn more.

I didn't have to look hard. Aaron Lefcourt, while not a household name, was by no means anonymous. For the last dozen years, he'd been CEO of Royal Court Development, a real estate company started by his father back in the sixties. When Aaron took over, Royal Court specialized in cheesy "vertical malls" in New York City's poorer neighborhoods. Twelve years later, Royal Court had interests all over North America, including hotels, convention centers, golf courses, and ski resorts. According to a recent interview in *BusinessWeek,* Aaron had plans to expand into Asia and to take the company public "any day now." According to a companion piece that ran alongside the interview, Lefcourt's success in real estate was his second act. Before that, he had achieved a sort of fame in another sphere altogether—television.

Fourteen years earlier, Aaron Lefcourt had been an executive at AXE— one of the first of the upstart television networks—and a wunderkind in a business of wunderkinds. He'd developed such landmark series as *Showmom,* a sitcom about a kooky single mother, her smart-aleck teenage daughters, her lovable ex-con grandma, and her life as a Vegas showgirl, and *Taggers,* a drama about an attractive and racially diverse troupe of LA graffiti artists who were also undercover cops. Lefcourt had had the network's top spot all but locked up when his genius overreached.

According to the article, industry insiders now judged the show to have been far ahead of its time—a forerunner of reality television. Back then they had called it "shocking" and "beyond bad taste." The show had been Lefcourt's pet project, his brainchild, and it was called *Me! Me! Me!* Its premise was simple: three adorable orphaned children would compete in games of chance and skill and vie for the affections of a wealthy childless couple. At the end of the segment, the couple would choose one child for adoption and send the others back to their orphanages. It aired only once. A firestorm of angry print and chatter ensued, and culminated in Lefcourt's dismissal two days later.

The articles mentioned Linda Sovitch only briefly, and then only to speculate about her husband's influence on the steep upward trajectory of her TV career—a subject her husband declined to discuss.

I looked at the photo of Lefcourt. He was forty-three now. His face was full and shiny, with rounded features and deep dimples—cherubic but for the hint of anger around his small mouth, and the watchfulness in his dark eyes. His brown hair was wavy and gleaming.

I rubbed my eyes and drank my water. *Market Minds* had ended and two paunchy bald guys in expensive suits were yammering silently and pointing at each other. I turned the television off and walked back and forth in front of my windows and looked down at 16th Street, at the van still parked there.

So what if it is light blue? I asked myself. *There are plenty of blue vans in New York, and nothing sinister about them, right?* I slipped on my coat and went downstairs.

It was cool outside, and the sidewalks were full of couples and loud groups. The van was up the block, about forty yards away. At street level I could see that it was light blue and that its windows were smoked. I walked away from it, to the corner, and crossed the street and came up on the other side. I was half a block away when the van's tailpipe smoked and its lights flared and it pulled out of its tight spot and drove off. I tried to read its rear plate but it was caked in mud.

Plenty of light-blue vans in New York. Right. The jumpy off-center feeling that had hung behind my eyes like a nascent migraine since I'd spotted the tails last Friday blossomed now into full-blown paranoia.

I looked at the cars parked on the block, and at the crowd that filtered past, and I thought about how I might do it. I wouldn't leave it to just one car, and I wouldn't leave it to cars alone. I looked up and down the street, but I knew it was no use; if anyone else had been watching, they'd seen me make the van and seen the van take off. They would've dropped far back by now. Assuming the van had been watching me in the first place. Shit. Someone took hold of my arm and I reached out and spun around.

"Jesus Christ!" Jane said. She yanked her wrist from my grasp. "What's the matter with you? You scared the hell out of me."

"Sorry," I said. "You surprised me."

Her brow was furrowed, and a patina of anger lay over her tired, pretty face. She rotated her wrist and massaged it with her other hand.

"Sorry," I said again.

"You look like you just stuck your finger in a light socket. What are you doing out here?"

"Nothing . . . I was going to the store. I thought you were going to call before you left work."

"I was in a hurry to get out of there."

I took Jane's arm and walked her across the street and up the stairs to our building. Her eyes were narrow.

"You're sure you're okay?"

"I'm fine. What do you want to do for dinner?"

Jane shook her head and went inside. "I don't know," she said. "Let me shower and change first." I nodded. She pressed the elevator button and looked at me some more.

"Let me see the hand," I said. She held up her hand and I took it in mine and inspected it elaborately. I turned it over and kissed her palm. "Better?" I asked.

"It's a start."

15

Tuesday morning was wet and windswept—more like March than nearly May—and I was soaked by the end of my run and chilled to my fillings. My apartment was quiet and full of rainy light, and though her perfume hung faintly in the air, I knew that Jane had gone. I tapped some wall switches and the overheads came on, and the place was brighter but just as empty. I stripped off my clothes and toweled myself dry and stretched.

A shower and a decent meal had restored Jane last night, and the prospect of the days ahead, full of lawyers and wall-to-wall meetings, had filled her with a taste for freedom, and so we'd stayed out late. A jazz trio was playing at Fez, and we'd gone there after dinner for the ten o'clock set. We lingered for the midnight show as well, and then we'd strolled up Broadway and had dessert at an all-night place off Union Square. Then we'd come back here and taken off our clothes and made love until we were insensate.

And we did not once discuss my case or mention the scene on the sidewalk. Don't ask, don't tell. I finished stretching and got into the shower.

I was drinking coffee when Neary called. He was on his cell and he spoke loudly over traffic noise.

"I talked to some people about your pal out in Jersey," he said. He told me what some people had to say.

"His name is Valentin Gromyko, and he's from the Ukraine by way of Paris and Madrid. And apparently he's a real comer. He started here a few years ago with a crew of Slavs, doing hijack work around the Port of Elizabeth. From there he got bigger and branched out into protection, gambling, and loan-sharking. He's moved north too, into Passaic and Paterson and, lately, Fort Lee. And he's been giving the old guys a real pain in the ass—crowding them, undercutting them, stopping just short of out-and-out war. He took over a boiler-room operation from one of them a couple of years ago. Could be that's what you saw."

"Any idea how he's connected to Gilpin?"

Neary snorted. "Yeah," he said. "Gromyko owns the guy."

"*Owns* as in . . . ?"

"As in lock, stock, and barrel. It seems Gilpin is a big bettor, and a really stupid one, too. About a year ago, he got in over his head with his bookie— six figures over—and the bookie sold his paper to Gromyko. Gilpin's been working off the debt ever since, doing what he does best. But you know how that goes. With a nut that size and the vig on top, he'll never see the light of day. And it's not like he can call the cops."

Neary's voice dissolved into static, and the connection dropped. I hung up the phone and waited for a call back and thought about Gilpin while I did. I thought about what he'd told me of his last conversation with his brother—about the loan he didn't get—and I thought about Gilpin's exhausted caged-animal look. I felt sorry for the guy. The phone rang; it was Neary.

"These people you're talking to know a lot about Gromyko," I said.

"Not enough for an indictment," Neary said. "They tell me Gromyko's a cautious guy. He's not flashy and he keeps a close eye on things, and he doesn't make waves unless he has to. But when he does, he's thorough about it. Nothing floats back up." I was quiet and Neary swore at an unseen driver.

"You have any more company?" he asked.

"Not today," I said, and I told him about the van. It was his turn to be quiet.

"And you don't think this comes from Gromyko?" he said finally.

"I don't know," I said. "Maybe I should go over and ask."

"Ask nice."

"Nice is my best thing," I said. Neary snorted. "Ever hear of an outfit called Foster-Royce?" I asked him.

"It's a Brit agency, and they work a lot in Europe. I've never dealt with them but I hear they're pretty good. Why?" I explained how I'd come across the name, and Neary thought some more. "You think he hired them?" he asked.

"Could be, or could be one of their people came to talk to him about something. Nobody at Foster-Royce will tell me one way or the other." Neary made a sympathetic noise and rang off.

I finished my coffee and called Nina Sachs and once again got no answer. I thought about driving over to see Gromyko, but I didn't have nearly enough caffeine in me for Jersey just yet, and it was still too early. I went to the table and looked at the lists of phone numbers waiting for me there.

I filled my mug and switched on the laptop. I checked my e-mail, but there was no sign of the phone records I'd bought last week. I cursed to myself; phone records would make this a lot easier. I opened a spreadsheet and began to transcribe dates, times, names, and numbers from my notes and to match answering machine messages to the telephone numbers from the caller ID list. It was a tedious process, but coffee helped. I ticked and tied, and whenever I came across a number with no name attached, I consulted an online reverse directory to fill in the blanks. I hadn't paid much attention to the numbers as I'd copied them down at Danes's place—I'd just wanted to get them all, and quickly—but now, typing them into the spreadsheet, I saw a pattern.

Danes had gone on vacation just over six weeks ago, and the first of the fifty calls in his telephone's memory was dated two days after he'd left. But the messages on his answering machine went back only three weeks or so. Almost thirty calls had come in during those first two and a half weeks. Had none of those callers opted to leave a message? Somehow I didn't think so.

I recognized many of the numbers on the caller ID list, including Danes's own cell phone number. It appeared over and over again, at regular intervals of three days, and always around the same time of day: 6 p.m. And then, just over three weeks ago, just before the first message had been recorded on his answering machine, it stopped appearing. I was pretty sure Danes had been calling in to retrieve and erase the messages on his answering machine. But I had no idea of where he'd been calling from and no more than a bad feeling about why he'd stopped.

I listed the names that owned the numbers appearing on Danes's caller ID. It was a short list, and, other than Danes's divorce lawyer, I'd already spoken to all the people on it. But the names on the list didn't account for every call that Danes had received. Scattered across the six weeks of his absence, there were over a dozen calls that had registered on Danes's phone only as PRIVATE, with no number or name associated. Telemarketers maybe. Or maybe not. I looked at the short list of callers and wondered again at how small his world seemed to be.

I drove a Buick across the bridge. Other than that, things were pretty much the same in Fort Lee: asphalt and bad traffic, all covered in rain. The little office building was still there, with its white bricks stained the color of tea. The smell was still bad in the tiny elevator, and worse in the fourth-floor hallway. And the girl was still there, with her white skin and tattoos and scary breasts, smoking behind her desk and watching TV. She looked at me with tiny, empty eyes. After a while recognition came.

"What you want?" she asked, and blew smoke at me.

"I need to talk to Gromyko."

She looked at me some more and took a long pull on her cigarette. "Who's Gromyko?" she said.

I sighed and shook my head. "I'll be at the bar down the street." The girl blinked at me and said nothing, and I left.

Roxy's was empty, and dim enough that the décor was mostly hypothetical. Amber lamps shone behind the battered black bar onto the bottles and the glassware and the chromed cash register, and the only other light came from the EXIT signs and through the small front window. There was a gray-haired guy built like a fireplug behind the bar, and a shadow at the far end that might have been a waitress. I bought a club soda and took it to a table by the window. I drank slowly and watched the rain come down. It took Gromyko an hour to get there.

The black Hummer pulled up in front of the bar, and the big blond guy who looked like a shark got out of the passenger seat, opened the rear door, and held an umbrella. Gromyko stepped out and said something to the shark, who nodded. He got back in the front seat and Gromyko crossed the pavement and came in.

He ignored me and went to the bar and spoke quietly to the bartender, who passed him a steaming paper cup and a napkin. Then he walked up front and sat down across from me. Raindrops beaded on his short blond hair, and his pale narrow face was still. He dunked his tea bag in and out of the hot water and looked at me.

"I did not expect to see you again," he said quietly.

"Same here, but something's come up."

Gromyko took his tea bag out of his cup and put it on the napkin. He blew on the tea and swallowed some and looked at me, waiting.

"When I drove back to the city on Friday, I had some company. Two cars: a black Grand Prix and a brown Cavalier. Ring any bells?"

Gromyko sipped more of his tea. A tiny crease appeared between his canted gray eyes. "No."

"How about a Ford Econoline van, light blue, with smoked glass and mud on the plates?"

He raised his head slightly, then turned and motioned through the window. The shark climbed out of the Hummer and trotted into the bar. Gromyko spoke softly and rapidly and I understood none of it. The shark nodded and replied and Gromyko dismissed him.

"Did he know something about this?" I asked, but Gromyko ignored the question.

"Why do you bring this to me?"

"I thought there might be a connection," I said. "I picked up the tails after talking to you."

Gromyko shook his head. "Did it not occur to you that that was simply the first time you noticed them?" he asked, and he sipped again at his tea. "There are more profitable ways for me to allocate my resources than to following you, and more pressing business for me to attend to." He emptied his cup and crumpled it so quickly and completely that it seemed to vanish before my eyes.

"What about your colleague, Goran? Is he up to any freelancing?"

Gromyko's small mouth moved minutely. "Goran is no longer with me," he said. "It is not Goran."

"Are you sure about that?"

"Utterly," he said. I was quiet, thinking. Gromyko was poised to stand, but he didn't.

"Is it possible someone latched on to me while they were looking at you?"

A colder light came into his eyes, and the little crease on his forehead deepened. His voice grew quieter. "I think not," he said.

I nodded and gestured toward the Hummer. "Did he know anything about this?" I asked.

Gromyko nodded imperceptibly. "He was escorting Gilpin from the office on Saturday and thought a blue van might have followed him for a time. It broke off before he could act on it. The license was covered with dirt." I waited for more, but nothing more came.

"That's it?" I asked. "No theories on what it was about?"

Gromyko's face was as calm as an icon's. "It is possible that I could be of assistance to you, Mr. March, but I do not operate a charitable organization. My advisory services are valuable, and for them I expect payment in kind."

I laughed and put on my best Marlon Brando voice. *"Someday, and that day may never come, I will call upon you to do a service for me."*

Gromyko raised an eyebrow and gave me an icy microscopic smile. "It is not a currency I expect you wish to part with," he said, and he stood. "Your calculation in the garage, with Goran, bought you something, Mr. March, but do not be misled by that. Do not intrude on my business again. Do not come here." He picked up the crumpled cup, the tea bag, and the napkin and placed them on the bar and left. The shark was out of the car again, umbrella in hand, before Gromyko was through the door.

I took a deep breath. A television came on at the far end of the bar. A soccer game was in progress, before a large crowd in a sunny clime. The play-by-play was in a language I didn't recognize, but it was lively and plentiful and the barman seemed to find it amusing. Outside, the street was wet and ugly, and the prospect of walking to my car and driving back to the city seemed, all of a sudden, a hideously complicated thing.

I ran a hand over my face. I was tired, and only some of it was lack of sleep. Too many hours at the laptop had left me with bleary eyes and a bad feeling about Danes, but little else, and this trip to Fort Lee had been only slightly more productive. I believed Gromyko when he said he wasn't having me followed—even if there was more to the story that he hadn't told me. That let me take his name off my list, but it got me no closer to whoever was following me, and certainly no closer to Danes himself.

I drank off the melted ice at the bottom of my glass and rubbed my eyes. It was warm in the bar and soothing in the dim light. The images of running men were bright and cheery, and the foreign words were animated and friendly sounding. The shadow at the end of the bar began to move around the room, lighting the little candles on the tables. It was a waitress. She was black-haired and lithe, and I wondered what her name was and what her voice might sound like. The barman put two shot glasses on the bar and pulled a bottle from beneath the counter. Vodka. He filled a glass and looked over at me and held up the bottle.

"You want?" he asked. "On house."

I was scared by how long it took me to tell him no.

Nina Sachs had called while I was in Jersey, and when I called her back she actually answered the phone.

"Where the hell have you been?" she said. "I left a message over a day ago." Her voice was scratchy and fast and made me grind my teeth.

"And I've called you back—but no one picks up."

"I'm working," she snapped. I heard her lighter spark.

"So am I, Nina."

"Yeah—for me."

"For the moment."

Nina Sachs sighed and cleared her throat. "All right, all right, let's stop pissing at each other. Just tell me what's going on."

I started with Gilpin. Sachs smoked and listened while I told her about my trip to Fort Lee, and her only response was mild surprise that Danes had had any contact at all with his half brother. I tried the name Gromyko out on her, but she'd never heard of him.

I moved on to Danes's apartment and the evidence I'd found of a relationship between him and Linda Sovitch. The news brought laughter rather than surprise.

"Christ, is that how she lines up her guests?" she said, with a nasty chuckle. Then she thought about it some more. "You think Sovitch was bullshitting you when she said she didn't know anything about where Greg is?"

"I don't know, and I don't know for sure that there was anything going on between them. That's why I want to talk to her again."

"Trust me"—Sachs snickered—"she leaves her underwear, there's something going on. What else did you come up with?"

"A business card," I said, and told her about Foster-Royce. "It's a detective agency, based in London. They have offices in New York and a bunch of other places, and apparently they do a lot of international work. And they're at least good enough at it not to tell me whether Danes is a client of theirs. You have any idea why he'd hire an outfit like that?"

There was silence, and then Nina sighed. "How the hell should I know?"

"Has he hired PIs before?"

"I told you, I have no idea. What else did you find?"

I took a deep breath and told her that Danes's apartment had already been searched, and that someone had been following me, at least since my first trip to Fort Lee. Sachs went quiet, and all I heard for a long while were the soft sounds of her smoking.

"What the fuck is going on?" she asked eventually. Her puzzlement was genuine.

"Someone else is looking for him. I haven't figured out who yet, or why."

Frustration boiled in Sachs's voice and spilled out as anger. "I thought I paid you to figure things out, for chrissakes. But all I get from you is speculation and more fucking questions!"

I didn't hang up on her, but I thought hard about it. I took another deep breath and let it out slowly.

"That's the way this works sometimes, Nina. In fact, that's the way it works most of the time—and getting mad about it doesn't change things."

She started to speak, stopped herself, and swallowed everything but a derisive snort. "Fucking racket," she said under her breath. "Do you have any actual progress to report?"

"I have more fucking speculation," I said. "You can decide if it's progress." I told her about the phone messages on Danes's machine, and the calls on his caller ID, and the pattern I'd seen. Saying it out loud made it more troubling.

"He was calling in on a regular basis, Nina, every three days, for over two weeks. And then he just stopped."

She was quiet for a moment. "When was this again?" she asked finally.

I read her the date of the last call from Danes's cell phone. "The messages on the answering machine start piling up right after."

"Maybe he was waiting for a call," she said softly. "Maybe he finally got it, so he stopped checking in."

"I suppose that's one possibility."

"And the other is what, that something happened to him?" The irritation and petulance were back in her voice. "And I suppose you're going to lecture me again about calling the cops? Well, I don't have time for it." I heard her suck a lungful of smoke.

"You have to make time soon, Nina, because I've only got a few more people to talk to, and if they don't lead anywhere I'm going to be out of things to do for you—not without spending a lot more of your money."

Nina Sachs swore to herself. "Look, I'm working right now. Give me a day or two and we'll talk about this, okay? Come by on Thursday." I sighed and agreed and she hung up.

I put my phone on the counter and looked out the window. The rain had stopped and a breeze stirred the water that pooled at the curbs and on the rooftops. Umbrellas had vanished and people moved more easily on the sidewalks. Traffic was light and nicely unfamiliar.

16

"You've got to take it outside, sir," the security guard said. "And there's no loitering anywhere on this block." He was six-foot-five and about 275 pounds, and his maroon blazer was strained to tearing across his shoulders. Of the dozen or so armed guards in the stone lobby of BNN's fortresslike West Side studios, he was the most petite. He held his big arms wide and made a little pushing motion in the air, in the direction of the revolving doors. I was not inclined to argue. Besides, I was used to it; people had been telling me to get lost for much of the day. I walked over to Broadway and found a coffee place.

I'd spent the morning trying to reach Linda Sovitch and failing miserably at it. Her supersecret cell phone number was no longer in service, and if she'd gotten a new one it was either not in her name or not yet for sale on the gray market. The number I'd found for Lefcourt's place in Greenwich, Connecticut, was answered by an officious-sounding woman who'd informed me that unsolicited phone calls were unwelcome and refused to take any messages.

My calls to BNN were received less warmly still. I didn't get as far as Sovitch's assistant, Brent; I didn't even get as far as Brent's assistant. Going down to the studio itself had been a desperation play, and not one I'd put much faith in. I'd been right not to. The big guys in the lobby would not, of course, let me see Sovitch or anyone who worked for her, nor would they accept messages. And there was no chance of catching a glimpse of her, as all BNN talent came and went from the studio through a distant and well-guarded garage entrance.

I'd had better luck with Danes's maid service: Maid for You. I'd pulled the name from Danes's credit card bill and called the number early this morning. With only a little coaxing, an obliging fellow named Les had confirmed that Danes was a client, and told me that he'd suspended his weekly cleanings about six weeks before. Danes had told him that he was going out of town for a while and would call to resume service when he got back. He hadn't called yet.

I paid for my latte and slouched in a big chair and watched a couple of twenty-somethings type furiously on their laptops. I thought about Linda Sovitch, and eventually I had an idea. It wasn't novel, and I wasn't sure it was good, but I knew it would read better on my invoice than napping at Starbucks would. I hauled myself out of the chair and took my coffee home.

I powered up my laptop and went online to the BNN Web site. It was badly designed and festooned with blinking advertisements, and I had to hunt for the icon that would open an e-mail window I could use to send a note to Linda Sovitch. While I was hunting, I got lucky. Under a banner that read *Today on BNN.com,* and next to a little picture of Linda, I read: *Chat live with Market Minds host Linda Sovitch. Today at 2:30.* It was 2:20.

I found my way to the chat page and registered, and then I waited. At 2:40, a message flashed on my screen and the moderator introduced virtual Linda. I typed my question into the chat window and let it sit for the next fifteen minutes, while people with monikers like *muniluv* and *buynsell* and *stockgal* asked Sovitch questions about equities and bonds and interest rates—none of which, it seemed to me, was she qualified to answer. Which didn't stop her. When the moderator informed all concerned that time was running out, I hit *enter.*

I didn't expect my message to show up on the chat board and I wasn't disappointed. Linda took a final question and the moderator thanked all the participants, plugged Linda's show, and ended the exchange. Ten minutes later my phone rang.

"What the fuck are you doing?" It was Linda Sovitch. "You call my house, you call the studio, you show up here, and now this shit. This is coming damn close to harassment—and maybe stalking too." Her voice was brittle and tight, like nothing I'd heard on her TV show.

"You didn't like my question?" I asked.

"You think you're fucking funny?" she said, and she read my question aloud, with plenty of bile. "'*What do you say to critics who charge that members of the business press are hopelessly compromised by conflicts of interest—that they are cheerleaders for business and too close to the people they're supposed to be covering—that they are, in essence, in bed with their subjects?*' You think that's cute?"

"I thought it was a pretty good question—and relevant, too."

"Relevant to what?" she asked. I didn't answer and after a while Sovitch's breathing was audible. "Come on, asshole, spit it out. Relevant to what?"

I sighed. "Relevant to you and Danes."

Sovitch started to say something but stopped. "What the hell do you want from me?" she asked eventually.

"I want to talk to you about Danes. I want to know where he is."

Sovitch snorted. "I'm tired of this," she said. "Keep bugging me and you'll be talking to my lawyer." She hung up. I shook my head and closed down my laptop. I thought it was a good question.

Perhaps, upon reflection, Linda Sovitch thought so too. An hour after she'd hung up on me, and not long before *Market Minds* was due to go on the air, she called back. She was brisk and efficient.

"Tomorrow morning at ten," she said.

"Where?"

"Give me your address; I'll send a car." I gave it to her and she was gone.

I put the phone down and wondered what had changed Sovitch's mind. Worry about how much I knew, or about what I wanted? Worry about who else I might be talking to? All of the above, most likely.

I yawned and went into the kitchen. My footsteps were loud on the wood floors. I heated some coffee in the microwave, but it was bitter and muddy and made my stomach feel the same. I looked down the length of my apartment. Late-day light fell in big yellow rectangles across the room but didn't seem to warm it. It was quiet, and quiet upstairs too. I hadn't seen Jane since yesterday morning, and she'd told me that I wouldn't see much of her for the rest of the week, but I was listening for her footsteps nonetheless.

I'd spent a lot of time alone in this apartment—a lot of time alone, period, in the past few years—and I'd wanted it that way. Alone was quiet and predictable. Alone was disciplined and organized and safe. It was sticking to my job and to my running and to an even keel. It was the opposite of static in my head and glass in my chest and aimless, calamitous motion and incinerating anger. It was the opposite of chaos. And if the cost of that stillness had been a certain austerity, even bleakness, then it was no more than I'd been willing to pay. It was getting off cheap. Alone was what I knew. It worked for me. But lately—since Jane—it didn't work as well.

I turned on the stereo. Jane had left a disc in: Flora Purim singing "Midnight Sun." I flicked through the others in the changer—Nikka Costa, Lucinda Williams—and switched to the radio. The Iguanas were playing something funky on WFUV, but even they couldn't dispel the mood that had overtaken me. I browsed my bookshelves and ran my hands across the spines, but the titles slid by unread. I opened my laptop and made a half-hearted attempt to update my case notes. One hour and two sentences later, I closed it again and went for a run.

A town car pulled up in front of my building at ten on the dot, its black skin gleaming in the morning sun. There was a small man with gray hair behind the wheel. I got in back and we drove off. We headed uptown, but we did not make for the Manifesto Diner or the BNN studios. Instead, we slid onto the FDR Drive.

"Where're we going?" I asked him. He started a little, as if I'd roused him from a nap, and checked some papers on the seat next to him.

"I got here that I'm taking you up to Greenwich. North Street, it says." The Lefcourt residence.

I sat back and watched the Triboro Bridge and the Bruckner Expressway slide by. He got on 95, and there was construction and chaos and lots of dodging and swerving and sudden braking. I was glad I wasn't driving. Fifty minutes later, he got off in Greenwich, near the train station.

Downtown Greenwich was crowded in the warm late morning, and we picked our way slowly past the low office buildings near the turnpike and through the shopping district to the north. The shop buildings were brick and stone and meticulously maintained, and the shops themselves were gently rusticated versions of their cousins on Madison Avenue. The streets and curbsides were crowded with saurian SUVs and shiny sedans, mostly German. The sidewalks were filled with prosperous matrons and slender young mothers, mostly blond.

We wound our way onto East Putnam, and homes began to appear.

They were large and old and Victorian, and comfortable-looking on their well-barbered lots. The lots got larger as we went up Maple Avenue, and larger still on North Street, and the houses receded farther from view. We passed over the Merritt Parkway and drove under a canopy of branches and new leaves, and the lots and houses vanished altogether behind thick hedges and high stone walls.

The Lefcourt spread was a few minutes north of the Merritt, and bordered by a tall, undulating brick wall. We stopped at the wrought-iron gates and a security camera looked us over. The driver spoke to an intercom and the gate swung open and we pulled in. The winding gravel drive was bordered by a blazing cloud of forsythia. It ended in a rising loop around a large circle of lawn and a gnarled oak. On the far side of the circle, at the top of the rise, was the house.

It was a great wedge of fawn-colored shingle, with sage-green trim on the windows and doors, and a foundation of rough gray stone. The façade was asymmetric and busy, studded with window bays and eyebrow dormers and with a deep veranda on the right. Four broad steps led to the front door. The car crunched to a halt by the steps, and I got out.

"I'll be over there," the driver said, and he pointed to a low shingled car barn, farther around the gravel circle. I nodded and he drove off. The sun was warm on my shoulders, and the light breeze carried the scents of grass and earth and cedar. It was quiet but for some birds chirping and the soft growl of a distant mower. The front door opened and a woman stepped out and stood at the top of the steps. It was not Linda Sovitch.

She was about five-foot-two, and her gray suit was crisp and angular, like her short dark hair and pale face. She folded her arms across her chest and regarded me with something that might one day—in the distant future—thaw to suspicion. I was wearing a black polo shirt, gray trousers, and black loafers, and I'd left my gun at home. I was presentable, even by Greenwich standards, but she peered at me and sniffed as if I'd been sleeping in the stables.

"Mr. March? I am Mr. Lefcourt's assistant. We spoke on the telephone." I recognized the cold officious voice. "Mr. Lefcourt is in his office." She turned and went back inside. I followed.

"I'm actually here to see Ms. Sovitch," I said.

She didn't turn around. "Yes, well . . . this way."

The entrance foyer was bright and wide, with paneled walls painted white and dentil molding. The plank floors were a dark shiny brown, and the Persian rugs were mostly red. The coffered ceilings were far away.

I followed the woman into a broad hallway. A stairway with slender balustrades swept along the wall to my left. Straight ahead, its entrance framed by a pair of columns, was a sitting room with tall windows and a marble fireplace, and silk-covered sofas that looked ornamental. I saw a broad swath of lawn through the windows and, in the distance, a flagstone-bordered swimming pool. Two men were working on the pool, peeling back its green covers.

The woman led me down the hall to the right, past more tastefully decorated rooms that bore no signs of use. The hallway ended in a pair of paneled doors. She paused with her hands on the doorknobs and looked as if she were waiting for a drum roll. Finally she pushed the doors open and we went in.

The room was long and low, with a brick fireplace at the far end and a row of French doors to the right that opened onto the porch I'd seen from outside. Near the French doors was a seating area, with a green silk sofa, armchairs, and low tables, all gathered around a large Persian rug. To the left was a wall of built-in shelves in glossy white wood and, toward the far end of the room, a big mahogany partners desk.

Aaron Lefcourt was behind the desk, in a soft-looking leather chair. He had a phone receiver in one hand and a TV remote in the other, and he was talking to someone as he surfed through channels on the big screen mounted behind his desk. He looked much as he had in the *BusinessWeek* photo—the same dark, wavy hair, the same angry, cherubic features—only fatter and with a tan. He had on linen pants and a raspberry-colored polo shirt that was tight over his round belly. His arms were brown and hairless and thinner than his stomach might suggest. He wore a gold chain on one wrist and a thin gold watch on the other. He glanced at us as we came through the doors and then went back to the TV. His assistant led me into the middle of the room. I looked at the shelves behind Lefcourt.

They were a shrine to Lefcourt and Sovitch, and festooned with testimonials from charities they'd supported, awards bestowed on them, and photos of them with politicians, celebrities, and captains of industry. There were a lot of photos of Sovitch with guests from her show. I didn't see any with Danes. Lefcourt swiveled in his chair and scowled at my guide and me. The woman herded me toward the sofa. I sat in a chair; she stood.

"You're worried about nothing, Mikey," Lefcourt said into the phone as he flicked past Court TV. His voice was medium-deep, with a distinct New York accent. "He'll go for it 'cause he wants to be a part of the deal. It makes him feel good—like his dick is longer than two inches." While he listened he shot past BNN and CNN and CNBC, and came to rest on an infomercial for a tooth bleaching device. Lefcourt laughed into the phone. "Trust me, Mikey, will you? Jesus, you're like a fucking old woman. I'll be in the office later—call me." He laughed again and hung up and looked at me. He tapped a button on his phone console.

"Yeah, he's here now. Send Jimmy in." Lefcourt hung up the phone and came out from behind his desk. He was about five-foot-ten, and his movements were clumsy but energetic. He went to the end of the room, to a sideboard near the fireplace. There was a chrome carafe on it and china cups and saucers. Lefcourt started pouring.

"You want coffee, March?"

"Black is fine," I said.

He turned to his assistant. "You just going to hang around like the maître d'?" The woman's pale face was opaque. She turned and left without a word. A moment later, the double doors opened again.

A big guy came in. He was bald and ham-faced, and his coloring was bad. He was the guy I'd seen with Sovitch at the Manifesto Diner, still dressed in black. Lefcourt paused in the middle of the room and watched as the big guy produced a digital camera. It was nearly lost in his huge hands. He peered at me through the viewfinder and flashed away. I sat still and said nothing. He took five or six shots and looked at Lefcourt, who nodded and looked at me as he spoke.

"That's good, Jimmy. Make sure everybody gets copies."

"Maybe you'd like some profiles," I said.

Jimmy looked a little confused. Lefcourt looked annoyed and motioned with his head toward the door. Jimmy left. Lefcourt put my coffee on a small table and took his to the sofa. He drank his coffee and looked at me.

"I guess you don't mind having your picture taken," he said. I smiled. "And I guess you won't mind if we hand it out, to the local police, maybe, or the security guys at the studio."

I smiled some more. "Not to be rude, but I'm actually here to see your wife."

Lefcourt drained his cup and slid it onto a side table. He crossed his legs and draped his hairless arm along the back of the sofa and tried to look relaxed, but whatever engine ran inside him didn't like to idle, and his foot bounced around on the end of his leg.

"What do you want to bother my wife for, March?" he asked, smiling.

I drank some coffee. "I don't want to bother her. I just want to talk to her about her friend Gregory Danes."

"What about him?" Lefcourt asked. He was still smiling, but his dark eyes were locked on my face.

"That's something I'd rather discuss with your wife."

Lefcourt gave a nasty laugh. He shifted his bulk on the sofa and ran his fingers over the upholstery. "Well, she doesn't want to discuss that, or anything else, with you. So your choice is me or get the fuck out."

I finished my coffee and thought about that. "I'm not sure she'd feel that way if she knew what I wanted to talk about." Lefcourt made a skeptical face and shook his head; I continued. "And I'm not sure you really want to hear this."

"I'm a grown-up, March," he said. "I can handle it." I nodded. It's what everyone says—before they see the pictures. Maybe Lefcourt meant it.

"I want to know about her relationship with Danes. I want to talk to her about where he might be."

"She went through that crap with you already." He wasn't making this easy; he wasn't trying to.

"Sure. I just want to go over some of it again."

"You think her answers will be different?"

I sighed. "I have reason to believe she may not have been . . . entirely frank with me the first time."

"What reason?" Lefcourt snapped. "Where'd you get this *reason* from?"

"That's not the issue—"

He cut me off and pointed at me. "Bullshit! Don't call my wife a liar and make allegations, and then tell me you don't have to substantiate them. If that's how you do business, it's a good thing you got yourself a trust fund." Lefcourt watched me for a reaction, but I had none. I wasn't surprised that he'd had me researched; I'd have been surprised if he hadn't. I watched him, too, and saw that there was no real anger beneath the shouting, just posture and tactics.

"I'm not trying to do business with you," I told him. "I'm trying to talk to your wife."

Lefcourt carried his cup to the sideboard and filled it with coffee. I didn't think he needed any more, but I kept my opinion to myself. He stood at his desk, drinking it, while he ran through channels with his remote. He stopped at a music video and watched two girls grind their pelvises together.

"You spoke to her once," Lefcourt said. "What are you going to hear different the second time around?"

I was getting tired of the back-and-forth. "I don't know. The truth, maybe."

"Listen, March—"

I cut him off. "Was she or was she not having an affair with Danes?"

Lefcourt took a deep breath and let it out slowly. His voice was softer when he spoke, and his words were very distinct. His dark eyes glittered above his round cheeks. "It's not just gossip when you say that about somebody like my wife. That kind of talk calls her professional ethics into question—and her judgment. That kind of talk has an impact—on reputation, on ratings, on contract negotiations. It's not schoolyard bullshit anymore, March, it's serious business." He tapped his small mouth with his finger.

I sighed again. "I don't give a shit about her ethics or her sex life. I just want to know where Danes is."

Lefcourt tossed the remote on the desk and came back to the sofa and stood behind it. "She can't tell you anything."

"You're sure about that?"

"A husband knows things," he said, and there was a grim little smile on his little mouth.

"Things like where Danes might be, maybe?"

"That's not something I keep track of."

"Not now," I asked, "or not ever?"

Lefcourt smirked. "What's got you so convinced that something was going on between them anyway? What've you seen?"

He was relentless in his fishing, and I decided to tug a little on the line. "She left stuff at his place," I said.

Lefcourt's face got tight. His tanned forehead was shiny. "What stuff? And what proof do you have that it's hers?"

I shook my head. "I'm not interested in proving it."

Lefcourt paced behind the sofa and pointed at me, trotting out the anger again. "You'd better be prepared to, if you're going to go around talking like that. You're a deep enough pocket, March. You screw up Linda's earning capacity, and I promise I'll fucking empty you out." I stood up and Lefcourt seemed startled. "Where are you going?"

"It seems a safe bet that your wife isn't showing up anytime soon, and we're going round and round here and getting nowhere, so I figured it was time to leave."

Lefcourt stared at me for a few seconds. "Have you heard a word that I've said?" he asked.

"You know, I was about to ask you the same thing."

I was at the door when Lefcourt called to me. "I meant it, March, about leaving her alone. Any more crap like your chat-room stunt, and there'll be a flock of lawyers picking on your bones." I looked back at him but said nothing. "I meant it about Danes, too. Neither one of us knows where he is, and neither one of us gives a shit."

17

"Sure, I remember the guy," Phyllis said. "A few more customers like him, I'll burn the place down and go back to being a parole officer." It was late afternoon, and I was calling the hotels that had appeared on Danes's credit card statement. The Copper Beech Inn, in Lenox, Massachusetts, was first on my list. Phyllis was the owner, and her voice was rough and friendly through the telephone.

"He was a real piece of work," she continued, laughing. "Had something to say about everything, from the pillows, to the coffee, to the water pressure, and none of it was good. We love guests like that—they make it all worthwhile."

"Was he there with anyone?"

"Nope, it was just him and his sunny disposition."

"Had he ever been there before?"

"Not before or since, thank God."

"Any idea what he was doing up there? That time of year isn't ideal for leaf-peeping."

Phyllis laughed again. "Back in January, it would've been more like snow-peeping. But folks do come up then, for cross-country skiing or just to get away. I have no idea what Chuckles was doing, though. Can't say he seemed real relaxed."

I thanked Phyllis and made my next call, to the Maidstone Tavern in East Hampton. A guy named Tim answered. He was arch and breathy and kept putting me on hold, and it took him a long while to tell me very little. Eventually, he confirmed that Danes had been a guest there about three months earlier and that he'd not been back since, but he had only vague memories of Danes himself and couldn't say if he had been alone during his stay. I got off the line before a headache took hold.

I sat back from my long oak table and looked at the TV screen. Linda Sovitch's muted image appeared. Her mouth moved, her white teeth flashed, and then she was gone, replaced by an ad for a German car. I thought—again—about my morning visit with her husband.

Aaron Lefcourt hadn't registered much shock at the notion of his wife carrying on with Gregory Danes; the closest he'd come was an imitation of indignity. He was much more interested in how I knew about the affair and in how much noise I planned to make. Which, when I considered it, made a kind of pragmatic sense: the fact that she'd been sleeping with one of her regular guests—especially one as tainted as Danes—wouldn't do Sovitch's career any good. An imaginative plaintiff's lawyer could even use it to turn her—and her network—into collateral damage in one of the investor suits still floating around. Reason enough, I supposed, for a practical man like Lefcourt to want things kept quiet. But was it also the reason Danes hadn't come home?

That theory might go down easier if Lefcourt had been just plain jealous—though I knew just plain greed was at least as popular a motive for murder. Hell, maybe he was greedy *and* jealous, both.

It was absolute conjecture, but it was irresistible, too. I knew Danes wanted to restore his reputation, and I knew he wanted Sovitch to help him do it. I also knew—because Sovitch had told me—that he was pissed off at her for not giving him airtime on her show. What if their lunch conversation had been a little different from what Sovitch had described? What if Danes had threatened to go public with their affair? From what I knew of him, Danes wasn't above that kind of threat; it might even be his style. And if he had done that, would Sovitch have run to Lefcourt, as she had when I'd come sniffing around? And what might Lefcourt have done?

"Speculative bullshit," I said aloud, and of course it was. But Danes had checked his messages every three days for nearly three weeks, and then he had stopped. There was nothing theoretical about that.

I picked up the phone again. The woman in Bermuda had a lovely voice and an odd, mid-ocean accent, and she was so pleasant in her refusal to answer any of my questions about Danes's stay at her hotel that I was nonetheless glad I called. When I hung up, it was time to go to Brooklyn.

I don't often sit down to dinner with families—not my own or anyone else's—and I wasn't sure what to expect at Nina Sachs's place. Certainly not *Ozzie and Harriet,* but not, I hoped, something out of Eugene O'Neill either. As it happened, it was an entirely pleasant evening. Right up until the end.

I bought a bunch of irises at a market near the Clark Street subway station, and I walked over to Willow Street and down toward the water. The western sky was drenched in impossible color and the breeze was warm and full of blossoms and the smells of supper on the stove. Laughter and scraps of conversation drifted out of open windows into the darkening air, and the evening streets seemed intimate and somehow full of promise. I took my time walking down.

The I-2 Gallery was closed, and white shades covered its big windows. I looked up and saw that Nina's windows were opened wide. I pressed the intercom button and the lock buzzed right away. Music tumbled down to meet me as I climbed the stairs: Motown. Nina's door was ajar.

Billy was sitting cross-legged by the windows, between two stacks of comic books and in front of a pile of plastic bags and cardboard backing sheets. He wore camo pants cut off into shorts and a green T-shirt. His feet were bare and his legs were bony and white. He was bagging comics and bopping to the music, and he waved when I came in. Nina and Ines were in the kitchen, and they put me to work right away.

Ines was at the fancy stove, chopping peppers and onions and fixing them on skewers with cubes of beef. She smiled at me. Her black hair was up in a loose shiny pile, and she wore a long apron over a fuchsia linen shift. Her feet were bare, and her fingers and toes were nicely manicured and painted to match her dress. There was a small silver band on the second toe of her right foot.

"Detective," she said, and she surprised me by kissing my cheek. "The flowers are lovely." Her face was warm and she smelled of lavender.

Nina was at one of the steel-topped counters. Her hair was loose and she was wearing gray shorts and a sleeveless black T-shirt. Her legs were pale but firm and nicely shaped. She stood before a cutting board and the mangled remains of a tomato. She had a paring knife in one hand and a stem glass in the other. There was something red and slushy in the glass, and she took a drink of it.

"Can you chop?" she asked me.

"More or less."

"That's better than me," she said. "I'll trade you." She handed me the knife, hilt first, and took the flowers. "Do I have something to put these in, Nes?" she asked.

Ines chuckled. "In the cabinet, above the glasses, there is a tall vase."

I held up the paring knife. "Got something a little bigger?" I asked Ines. She smiled and pulled an eight-inch knife from a wooden block on the counter.

"This should do, detective."

Nina made a mock scowl. "Everybody's a fucking critic," she said. "I'll stick to driving the blender. It's better for all concerned. You want a strawberry daiquiri?" I shook my head. "Come on, it's our Memorial Day warm-up—you've got to have one."

I shook my head again. "I don't drink."

Nina tilted an eyebrow at me. "I'll fix you a virgin, then."

"That's all she lets me have," Billy called from the living room. "They're not bad."

"With that kind of testimonial, how can I refuse?" I said. Nina dumped strawberries, sugar, and ice into the blender, capped the steel pitcher, and hit the button. I leaned toward Ines and spoke over the din.

"What am I chopping for?"

"Tomato and onion salad, so not too fine." I nodded and started slicing. Nina shut down the blender and handed me a drink.

"We're out of umbrellas," she said. "I figured we could talk after dinner, and since you two have everything covered, I'm going to sneak into the studio for a while." Ines nodded and Nina carried her drink away. I watched as she crossed the room and ruffled Billy's hair as she passed. He looked up at her and smiled.

Ines and I worked side by side. She swayed gently to the music as she chopped and skewered, and she sang along softly and sipped at her daiquiri. Her knife work was fast and precise, and there was something almost hypnotic in the movements of her long, strong fingers. Even with the windows open and the fan running it was warm in the kitchen, and there was a faint sheen on Ines's forehead. The broad, flat scar on her arm looked slick. Her perfume and the delicate aroma of her sweat mingled pleasantly with the smells of cooking food.

I was slow but managed not to make too much of a mess. I finished with the tomatoes and moved on to the onions, and when I'd hacked those up sufficiently, Ines swept them into a big glass bowl and tossed them with oil and vinegar and some basil leaves.

"What else can I do?"

"Just relax, detective."

I took my drink to the living room and sat on the edge of the sofa. Billy was just finishing his bagging.

"New stuff?" I asked.

He nodded. "Yeah. I've got the complete run of *House of Anxiety* now—all mint—and I'm only missing five issues for the full set of *Perturbed*. I got something that's up your alley, too." Billy sorted through the pile and handed me a stack of seven comics. I looked them over. "*Detective Comics,* issues 437 through 443, from 1974, when *DC* brought back the Manhunter and brought your buddy Batman into it. All very fine or near-mint condition. Be careful with them; I got them to trade with a guy, for the first three issues of *Dreadful Landscape.*"

Billy watched me closely as I studied the comics, and I must have shown the right degree of reverence, as he was soon talking me through his whole stack. He expounded on the artists and writers of nearly every issue in the pile and went on at length about the fine points of quality grades— what separated a near-mint-minus, for example, from a very-fine-plus. He had a vast array of facts at his disposal, and he was pleased with his esoteric knowledge. He was as finicky and proud as any collector of stamps or fine wines, but his sense of humor—sarcastic and self-deprecating—saved him from pedantry. I thought about Gregory Danes's record collection and wondered if monomania ran in families. Whatever its source, Billy reveled in it. His thin face lost its usual dour cast, and his blue eyes were lively and sharp. Words tumbled out of him, and his hands danced around. The Motown disc ended and Billy interrupted a pronouncement on pricing to change CDs.

"Can we at least hear something *close* to this century?" he said. Billy went to one of the tall shelf units, to a messy heap of discs next to the CD player. He picked through it, passing cruel but amusing judgments on his mother's taste in music, and eventually found something he liked. He loaded the disc and fell into a deep slouch at the other end of the sofa. The music was funky and jazzy, with plenty of horns, a twanging electric guitar, and beefy keyboards. It sounded familiar.

"I know this," I said. "Who is it?" Billy looked pleased.

"Band's called Galactic, the album is—"

"*Crazyhorse Mongoose*," I interrupted. "I haven't heard this for a while." Billy was taken aback, and maybe a little impressed. And that got us onto a whole other topic.

Billy's taste in music was not the typical twelve-year-old's, and it was catholic, to say the least. It ranged from sixties and seventies soul to jazz fusion to ska to old-school punk and hip-hop, and he talked about musicians and bands with a fervor that surpassed even his comic book discourses. Many of his favorites were obscure, but I knew a few of them, which surprised Billy some more.

"Do you play anything?" I asked.

Billy shrugged. "A little bass, but I don't spend enough time with it." He looked at me and hesitated. "My dad's always trying to get me going on the piano."

"That's what he plays, right?"

Billy nodded. "Shit, yes. He's been playing since he was five or something, and he's amazing. He's into classical stuff. I told him he should listen to some jazz, but he thinks it's bullshit. I told him to check out Monk, but he doesn't want to know."

He looked down and thought about something and laughed to himself.

"Check this," he said, and he sprang off the sofa and trotted down the hall toward his room. From the kitchen, Ines watched him go. Then she looked at me and brushed a strand of damp hair away from her face. Billy was back in under two minutes, holding a glossy photograph.

"This is what my dad knows about jazz," he said, and handed me the photo. It was a picture of three men in black tie, standing side by side. On the right was Gregory Danes, and in the center was a world-renowned bassist, an aging jazz icon and darling of the NPR set. On the left was a white-haired man with hollow cheeks whose name I didn't know, but whose face I recognized from a similar photo I'd seen in Danes's apartment. The famous bassist had autographed the picture in black marker: *To my buddy, Bill—keep swingin', man.* Billy laughed.

"Personally, I think the guy plays elevator music," Billy said. But I could tell he was pleased to have the photo, and proud that his father had met the great man—and too full of adolescent cool to admit to either.

"Who's the other guy?" I asked him, but Ines called to him and interrupted any answer he might have given.

"Guillermo, set the table, will you?" Billy rolled his eyes dramatically but hoisted himself off the sofa and into the kitchen. I followed him.

"Need some help?" I asked.

"I got it," he said. He made a stack of plates and flatware and carried it to the living room, to the green glass table near the sofa. Ines and I watched him.

"He's in a better mood," I said quietly.

Ines laughed softly. "For the moment. We went to visit a school in Manhattan this afternoon. It is very small and it caters solely to gifted children, and they have a very impressive maths program. The atmosphere there is very . . . welcoming."

"He liked it?"

She smiled. "His exact words were, *It doesn't suck.*" Her imitation of Billy's disaffected, cracking tenor was spot-on, and I laughed and so did she.

"Will he go there?" I asked.

Ines's face grew still. "I do not know," she said. She turned back to the stove and the skewers of beef. "The grill is hot and these will not take long to cook. Could you call Nina please, detective?"

Nina and Ines sat on the sofa, and Billy and I sat on cushions on the floor. The food was delicious. Besides the salad and the kebabs, Ines had made a couscous, and Nina whipped up a few more batches of daiquiris—virgins for Billy and me.

Dinner conversation started with Nina's upcoming show at a small but influential art museum in Connecticut, meandered around to the sorry state of the New York City art scene, and somehow found its way to the love lives of the half-dozen or so galleristas who were sometimes in Ines's employ. Billy speculated freely on who was doing what to whom, but he grew silent and squirmy when a girl named Reese was mentioned. Nina teased him.

"Reese is this little blond thing from Santa Barbara," Nina said to me. "She goes to Cooper Union, and she works for Nes on the weekends. She's nineteen and she's got this snaky little bod and Billy's totally hot for her." Billy colored deeply. "I'm telling you, Bill, she's single again and I think she's into younger stuff." Billy slurped the last of his daiquiri and flipped her the bird.

Throughout, Billy was the DJ, spinning Curtis Mayfield, The Radiators, The Tom Tom Club, and more Galactic, and he and Ines slid, spun, and bumped to all the danceable tracks. Billy was wild and comic and Ines was liquid. They dragged Nina up a few times and made an earnest go at me too, but I was resolute.

Ines brought out coffee and a big bowl of cut fruit, and when these were gone I did the clearing. Billy surprised Ines and Nina by volunteering to help. We were in the kitchen when he asked, in a low voice, about his father.

"You know where he is yet?"

I shook my head. "Not yet," I said. "You have any thoughts about it?"

He was scraping food into the trash and he didn't look up. "Not a fucking one," he said softly.

Billy finished loading the dishwasher and I went into the living room. Ines and Nina were on the sofa, leaning into each other and laughing at something. Nina trailed a finger up the curve of Ines's bare calf, and Ines closed her eyes.

"We should talk," I said. Nina and Ines disengaged. Ines stood and gathered up some stray glasses.

"I need smokes," Nina said. "Walk with me."

The sun was gone and the tropical-chemical colors had bled from the sky, and only the pinkish city glow remained. But it was still mild outside and the streets were still benign. There was a cluster of people down the block, standing outside a chic-looking bar. They were drunk and cheerful, and they assumed everyone else was too. They were wrestling with the question of what to do next and confusing each other deeply in the process. One of the girls called out to us.

"Hey, what do you think? Williamsburg? Or do we go to the new place on Smith Street?" We didn't answer, but Nina shot them a sloppy salute and they all laughed. We went around the corner, and our heels made a knocking sound on the cobblestones. Nina was wobbly on the uneven paving and she steadied herself on my arm. She bought Benson & Hedges at a twenty-four-hour grocery and slit the pack open as soon as we got outside.

"Want to sit by the ferry landing?" she asked. She didn't wait for an answer but headed toward the river. I followed.

There were a lot of people in the little park by the water—packs of teenage boys and girls looking for each other and something to do, couples strolling hand in hand, dog walkers, tourists, and more than a few photographers, trying hard to capture the dizzying view. The Manhattan skyline rose, glittering and wet, from the black river, and the office towers seemed to lean toward us. My eyes were drawn to the empty patch of sky downtown, and I felt my throat close up and my teeth clench.

We found a bench. The seating slats were badly splintered, and we perched on the back rests. Nina smoked in silence, and after a while I gave her my report. I told her about my meeting with Lefcourt and about my futile attempts to track Danes to the Hamptons, the Berkshires, and Bermuda. I didn't have much to say and it didn't take long to say it, and when I was done Nina kept quiet.

"Have you thought any more about the cops?" I asked eventually.

She sighed heavily and took a last drag on her cigarette and flicked it into the darkness. It landed far off, in a burst of orange cinder. "Yeah, I've thought about it." Her voice was tight.

"And?"

She sighed again. "And I don't want to do it." I drew a breath to speak, but Nina kept on going. "I don't want to do any of this anymore." She looked at me and I looked back. "You know what I'm saying? I want to stop. I want you to stop." She turned away and popped another B&H out of the pack and lit it. The smoke vanished in the night air.

"You want me to stop looking for Greg?"

She stared at the black water and the cityscape and nodded. "I appreciate what you've done, but—"

"What's this about?" I said. Nina looked at me again. Her mouth was tight and her eyes were narrow. She ran a hand through her hair and looked down at her clogs.

"I didn't realize I had to explain myself to you," she said, and the nasty familiar edge came up in her voice.

"I've been working hard on this thing for nearly two weeks now, Nina—and getting poked at and threatened and tailed in the process—and all of a sudden you tell me to drop it. I think you owe me some explanation of where the hell this is coming from."

"Don't throw that crap about threats and being followed my way," she snorted. "It seems to me all that shit comes with your job description. And as far as what I *owe* you, I owe you what's on your fucking invoice, pal, and nothing more."

She blew out a big cloud of smoke and glared at me. Then she held up her hands and shook her head.

"Christ, we really push each other's buttons, don't we? I haven't gone at it like this with anyone since Greg." She puffed some more and rubbed the back of her neck. "Look, this isn't out of nowhere, March. I told you up front I didn't want to sink a lot of money into this, and you said yourself you've done almost everything you can without it costing me a lot more. I decided I don't want to spend a lot more." She took another pull on her cigarette and it sizzled and shrank noticeably.

"So it's just the money?"

Nina shook her head. "It's the money . . . and the fact that I'm tired of this back-and-forth about the cops. I know what you think and you know what I think and I doubt either one of us is going to change. Am I way off base about that?" She wasn't.

"There's something wrong, Nina," I said quietly. "There's something wrong about Greg. The fact that he stopped calling, the fact that other people are out there looking—"

"Jesus, again with this!" She massaged her forehead with her fingertips. "I don't want to hear it, okay?" Her voice was loud, and a couple of dog walkers looked at us. She traded stares with them but took the volume down a notch. "I don't give a damn about whatever else he's involved in. I'm not going to the cops, and I don't want you to either. Can I be any clearer than that?" I didn't answer. "You promised me confidentiality," she said. "And that's what I expect."

"That's what you'll get," I said.

Nina sighed and climbed down from the back of the bench and stood before me. "You'll send a bill?" I looked at her and nodded. She flicked her cigarette away and put her hands in her pockets. "For chrissakes, don't take it so personal."

I took a deep breath and started to speak. And stopped. Why bother? "Tell Ines thanks for dinner," I said. "And tell Billy good-bye." Nina nodded and walked away, already fishing for another smoke. I heard her lighter spark behind me.

18

Warren Bradley was saying something about the CIA, but my mind was wandering. In fairness, it wasn't Warren's fault. He was an excerpt from a job interview textbook: well groomed, well spoken, confident, and poised. His dark hair was going gracefully gray at the temples and was expensively cut, and if he were any more distinguished-looking, he'd have to run for office. His white shirt was spotless and his blue suit was pristine. Even the racehorses that galloped on his necktie did so with calm assurance. And as far as I could tell, he was entirely sober. I was the one having problems.

". . . of course, that was before counterterrorism became a growth industry," Warren said. He looked at me expectantly, an uncertain smile on his handsome face.

I wrenched my thoughts away from Nina Sachs and the ferry landing, and back to the conference room at Klein & Sons and the interview with Warren. I was pretty sure he'd been making a joke, and I smiled back at him. I guessed right, and he looked reassured and kept on talking.

I read through Warren's résumé again. Like him, it was perfect: Ivy League college, law school, a stint in the air force, another with the Bureau, and ten years at a big Wall Street firm, where he'd risen steadily through the ranks to the number-two spot in their internal security department.

"Tell me about your assignment in London," I said. That kept him going for another ten minutes.

Warren was my second interview of the day. Alice Hoyt had been my first, and she too had been sober and confident and eminently presentable, though that's where the similarities ended. Alice was medium height and broad-shouldered, and there were a lot of laugh lines around her full mouth and dark eyes and a lot of gray in her short Afro. She had graduated public high school in the Bushwick section of Brooklyn, and although she had served in the military too, it had been in the army as a lance corporal. From there she'd joined the NYPD and attended Queens College at night for a BS and, later, an MS in criminal justice. She'd spent over twenty years on the job, fifteen as a detective and five as the boss of a detective squad in Midtown North. From there she'd gone private, to a DC firm that did a lot of corporate consulting and, as Alice told it, employed at least as many publicists as it did operatives. After five years, she was tired of the travel and of the time away from her husband and three kids.

"I've been away from Brooklyn too long," she'd said, with a wry smile.

Warren's deep voice wound down. It was my turn to talk again.

I went back and forth with him for another twenty minutes, and I mostly paid attention. We exchanged firm handshakes and Mrs. K showed him out, swooning only slightly as she did. I went into Ned's office.

Ned wasn't there, but my sister Liz was. She was sitting on Ned's sofa, her shoes off and her long legs propped on the teak coffee table. She looked up from a sheaf of papers and pushed narrow reading glasses onto her forehead.

"Where's your boss?" I said.

"Lunch meeting. You do more interviews?" I nodded, and Liz grinned. "Any bodily fluids spilled in there?"

"Not today."

"Off your game, huh?" Liz dropped her glasses back on her nose and returned to her papers. I took off my suit jacket, loosened my tie, and sat. I put back my head and closed my eyes. I heard Liz turn some pages, and after a while she spoke.

"What's wrong with you?"

I answered without moving. "I didn't sleep much last night."

"I take it there was no upside to that."

"Not that I could tell."

"What was the problem?"

I opened an eye. She was still scanning her papers. "I got fired yesterday."

She looked up. "Surely not for the first time."

"It doesn't happen so often that I'm used to it," I said. "And this time I'm not even sure of the reason."

Liz stared at me for several moments without expression. "Well . . . you can always reconsider Ned's offer. We'll find you a nice little office down the hall, maybe a cute assistant . . ." I flipped her the bird and she went back to her papers. I closed my eyes, and thoughts of Nina Sachs and her case spun in my head.

An hour of sitting at the ferry landing and another few spent turning in my bed hadn't improved my understanding of why Nina had given me my walking papers, or brought me any closer to figuring out where Danes had gone to or why he hadn't come back. I'd gone over and over what I knew about him and what I could only guess at, and no matter how many times I did, it never amounted to much.

I had come to know that Danes was an unpleasant and difficult man, with a knack for putting people between a rock and a hard place. I knew also that his basic orneriness had been salted in recent years with anger and resentment over his damaged career and his thwarted attempts at salvage. I knew that on his last day at Pace-Loyette, that anger had been on the boil. He'd argued with Linda Sovitch at lunch and argued some more with Dennis Turpin, and then he'd stormed out. And gone home. And packed a bag. And stopped his mail and maid service. And the next morning he'd gotten in his car and driven away.

After that it was all question marks and conjecture. Where had he gone? Why had he stopped calling for his messages? Why hadn't he returned? Who else was looking for him, and why? The big questions swirled with a host of smaller ones. I was fairly certain that Danes had had an affair with Linda Sovitch, but I didn't know for how long or how it had ended, if indeed it had. The only version I had of their lunchtime argument was the story Sovitch had told me—and it was not one I had a lot of faith in, any more than I had in the little show that her husband had staged for me.

The door opened and Ned came in, my brother David trailing behind.

"They want twenty percent," David said, "but I think they'll go for—"

Ned cut him off. "We're overpaying as it is. If they're trying to hold us up, then I say wish them luck and show them the door." Ned's voice was tired and impatient. He went behind his desk and scrolled through his e-mail. David stopped in the center of the room and looked irritable. Then he saw me, and his irritability became scorn.

"Sorry I'm late, Johnny," Ned said. He looked over Liz. "Am I late for you too?"

"I'm early," she said.

He nodded and went to his wall of shelves and produced a glass of ice water from somewhere. "Want some?" he asked us. I raised my hand and Ned brought me a glass. Then he sat next to Liz and looked at me. "How did it go?"

"Yes, do tell," David said, perching on the edge of Ned's desk. "I hear such interesting things about your interviews." His eyes sparkled meanly. Ned frowned.

I drank some water. "Bradley looks better on paper, and you'd probably feel more comfortable with him at first, but Hoyt will do a better job for you." Ned's brow was creased and he pursed his lips. I reached over and handed him the two résumés, and we were quiet while he scanned them. David interrupted.

"How can that be?" he said. "I looked at those CVs. Bradley has just the kind of experience we want."

"Bradley's an empty suit," I said, too quickly.

Ned looked up, his face blank. "Is that why you assume I'd be more comfortable with him?" he said. David grinned nastily. Shit.

I shook my head. "No, that's why I think he appeals to David. But the reality is that Bradley's cut from more or less the same cloth as a lot of the people around here."

"And that's a bad thing?" David said.

"I'm not going to debate that with you. But one thing it doesn't mean is that he's the best person for this job."

Ned looked at the résumés some more. "And you don't think he is?"

"In my view, he's strictly a hands-off guy. Most of his Wall Street experience seems to be in self-promotion and empire building; it sounded to me like he delegated everything else. I didn't think that's what you were after." I looked at David. "Of course, I could be wrong."

"And Hoyt?"

"She's less buttoned down—a little rougher around the edges—but she's a whole lot more hands-on. She's run a detective squad, she's run high-profile cases, and she's run task forces too. And after twenty-plus years in the NYPD, I think you'll find her political skills are up to snuff."

"But she's never done this kind of job before," David said.

"Neither have I, but you were ready to give me a shot." Liz snorted behind her papers, and I thought I saw Ned smile.

David colored and looked at me. "*He* was ready; I didn't get a vote."

My eyes were hot and I was suddenly very tired. I got up and pulled on my jacket and headed for the door. "You have my opinion," I said to the room. "Do what you want with it. Hire Bradley; I'm sure he'll work out fine. Better yet, hire that Tyne guy. With him you get a floor show."

"Johnny . . . ," Ned said, but I didn't stop. I closed the door behind me and didn't glance at Mrs. K on my way out.

"It sounds to me like she gave you her reasons for calling it off," Jane Lu said. "You just didn't like them." She walked across my bed and sat cross-legged next to me and didn't spill a drop of what she carried on the tray. There were two mugs of coffee, a bowl of quartered oranges, croissants, and a crock of jam. Jane was wearing one of my sweatshirts and nothing else. It was Saturday morning and it was pouring rain outside. I rolled over and rested my cheek against her thigh. It was warm and smooth and I would've been happy to spend the day there, but it was not to be. Jane was going into the office.

"It's not a question of like," I said to her thigh, "it's that her reasons don't make sense."

"Not wanting to spend more money isn't an unreasonable thing," Jane said, biting into an orange slice.

"If that's what she's worried about she could go to the cops; they do this work for free."

"You didn't like her explanation for wanting to steer clear of them?"

"That it would piss Danes off? I don't know. I've learned never to underestimate just how twisted things can get between exes, but even so . . ."

I ran my palm across the sole of Jane's foot. She laughed and tore a croissant in half and spread some jam on it.

"Even so, what? What's the problem?" The smell of coffee merged with Jane's perfume and made me hungry. I nibbled gently at her thigh and she giggled.

"The problem is, she could've decided this a while ago and saved herself a lot of money. So why pull the plug now, right after I find out about Sovitch and about Danes's phone calls? Why stop when I've finally found things that could be substantial?" I moved my mouth up to Jane's hip, and she shifted on the bed. I slid my hand along the inside of her thigh. She laughed and brushed it away.

"I guess this opens up your schedule a little," she said.

I propped myself on my elbow and looked at her. "What do you mean?"

"I mean you don't have a case right now, and you have time on your hands—time to go somewhere, maybe." Her eyes held mine, and after a while her smile began to fade.

"I guess so," I said, and sat up. "I hadn't thought about it."

"No?"

"Besides, Sachs is volatile. There's a chance she'll cool off over the weekend and rethink things."

Jane swung her legs over the side of the bed and sat on the edge. Her back was stiff and perfectly straight. Her voice was soft and full of sarcasm. "Hope springs eternal," she said, and she went into the bathroom and shut the door.

It was past noon when I awoke again, and I was alone. The breakfast tray was on the floor and breakfast was still on it. It was dark outside, and rain fell against the tall windows in a hectic clatter. It slid down the glass in sheets and cast twisting shadows on the walls. I rolled on my back and watched them and tried not to think about Jane.

A gust of wind rattled the glass. I pulled on my shorts and stood at the window. Low clouds scrambled across the sky and caught on the jagged edges of the cityscape. I looked down and saw the tops of many umbrellas, bumping at each other like clumsy fat men. I rubbed my hands over my face and got into the shower.

I owed Nina Sachs a final report, to go with my invoice, and I poured a cup of coffee and opened my laptop to write it. After forty-five minutes I pushed back from the table and read over my work. The INVESTIGATION section was a straightforward chronology of what I'd done, where I'd gone, and whom I'd spoken with, and the FINDINGS section was a recitation of everything relevant that I'd learned. It was depressingly short. I drank off the last of my coffee and went to the kitchen to brew a fresh pot.

Despite my best efforts, I'd been unable to wrestle my worry about Danes into anything like a theory, and the CONCLUSIONS section of my report was still unwritten. Maybe I should keep it simple: *Something bad has happened.* I put the paper cone in the coffee machine and spooned coffee in and thought again about Billy. I could still hear his nearly whispered question: *You know where he is yet?* I flicked the switch on the machine and the phone rang.

"You fucking bastard!" she said. She was nearly breathless with anger, and it took me a moment to place the voice. "You fucking son of a bitch! I trusted you—I talked to you—I spilled my goddamn guts—and you do this?"

"Calm down, Irene, and tell me what it is you think I've done."

Irene Pratt huffed at the other end of the line. "Don't give me that crap. You're the one who was looking for him. You're the one who was sniffing around his office. You know what you did, you lying shit."

I thought for a moment and listened to the coffee trickle into the carafe. "I have no idea what you're talking about, Irene, so why don't you take a deep breath and tell me what's going on?"

Pratt started to speak and stopped herself a couple of times and settled into a furious silence. When she finally spoke the edge was off her voice, and something tentative had replaced it. "You're serious?"

"I'm serious that I have no clue what you're talking about."

"You're serious you didn't do it?"

"Didn't do what?"

She seemed not to hear the question. "But if it wasn't you, then . . . who did it?"

I clenched my teeth. "Who did *what*, Irene?"

It took her a long while to answer. "Who broke into my office . . . and into Greg's?"

19

I met Irene Pratt in the lobby bar of the Warwick Hotel. There were lots of plump armchairs in there, and big windows that looked out on Sixth Avenue, and soft incandescent lighting that gave the place a snug feel against the rain. Irene Pratt wore jeans and sneakers and a school-bus-yellow rain slicker, and she looked young and scared. She was perched at the edge of a bar stool, nursing a Coke and fidgeting with a bowl of peanuts, when I came in. She looked up and looked ready to bolt.

"Tell me again how you had nothing to do with this," she said. Her voice was low and taut. She pushed a strand of wet hair away from her face.

I shook the water from my shoulders and hung my jacket on the back of a bar stool. "I told you, Irene, I haven't been near your office since you saw me there with Turpin. This isn't me." The bartender came by and laid a small napkin in front of me. I ordered a cranberry juice and club soda and turned back to Pratt. "What happened?"

She took a swig of her soda. "I came in just before noon and my office door was unlocked and I knew something was wrong."

"Because of the door?" I asked. Pratt nodded. "You're sure it was locked when you left last night?"

"Last night and every night," she said. "And then I looked at my desk, and I knew that things were . . . different. Not obviously different, but . . .

neater than I leave things. A little more squared off." Her shoulders were rigid beneath the yellow slicker, and she kept shifting in her seat.

"The cleaners couldn't have straightened things up a little and maybe forgotten to lock the door?"

Pratt shook her head. "They don't have keys to our offices, and they don't clean them unless we're there. I was still working when they came last night. They just emptied the trash, vacuumed, and left." She took a peanut from the bowl and chewed it nervously.

"What else besides the door and the desktop?"

"My credenza—behind my desk—it's got a set of file drawers in it and they were opened."

"Unlocked or actually pulled open?"

"The lock was still locked, but it wasn't latched on to anything, and you could just pull all the drawers open."

"And you're sure—"

"I always lock it. Always."

"Anything missing?"

"I don't think so."

"Your PCs were okay?"

"As far as I could tell." A big group of tourists came into the bar. They were loud and took up a lot of space, and they seemed to make Irene Pratt even jumpier. I leaned toward her.

"And what about Danes's office?"

"It was locked, but the knob was loose in my hand, and the little metal thing—in the doorjamb—was dented. And when I put the key in the lock, it didn't turn at first."

"It's always locked?"

"Always, when Greg's not there."

"You know who's got keys?"

"I've got one; our assistant, Giselle, has another; and security's got one. I think that's it."

"What did you find inside?"

"It was neat as a pin in there, just like always: desk clean, everything very orderly. . . ." She took off her glasses and wiped them with a bar napkin and put them on again. Her dark eyes moved back and forth across the crowd behind me. "But he has the same credenza as I do, and it was opened just like mine."

"When's the last time you were in there?"

"Wednesday or Thursday, to get a file. And don't even ask if the drawers were locked then, because they were—and there was nothing wrong with his door either."

"Who has keys to his credenza?"

"As far as I know, just me," Pratt said, and she chewed another peanut into dust.

I drank my drink and thought for a while. "You're pretty careful about keeping things locked up."

"Everyone is, in this business. An advance copy of a research report, or even of a draft, could be worth a lot to some people. It's like betting on the Sunday football games when you've already read the Monday papers. So—yeah—we're pretty careful."

"Has Pace had that kind of trouble before?"

"Leaked reports? God, no—that's all we need."

"What made you go into Danes's office today?" Her eyes fixed on mine for a moment and then flicked away.

"I . . . I don't know," she said. "When I thought someone had been in my office, I guess I just got worried." She looked at me, and there was color in her pale face. "The first thing I thought of was that it must've been you."

"I'm flattered." I laughed. "But why me?"

She looked down at her knees. "You'd called me, and come around the office and had that scene with Tampon, and then you showed up at my place. Who else was I supposed to think of?"

"Am I the only one who's been asking about Danes?"

Pratt was quiet for a while. "You're the only one who's come to the office or come to see me," she said.

"But am I the only one who's been asking?"

"A lot of people call us," she said. "Some of them ask about Greg."

"People like who?"

"People we do business with," she said, looking around the room. "Industry contacts, fund managers, people from the companies we cover—the same people who called before he went away."

"Anyone who's been calling more often lately?"

She looked intently into her glass and swirled the crushed ice around. "No one I can think of," she said finally. "I told you, a lot of people call us; I don't keep track of them all. But I know you're the only one who's come around."

"Until now," I said. The bartender came by and offered Pratt a refill on her soda. She nodded. "When you thought this was me, what did you think I was looking for?" I asked.

Pratt shook her head. "I don't know . . . nothing specific. Something to help you find Greg, I guess."

"Any ideas on what that might be?"

She peered at me from behind her smudged lenses, and there was irritation in her voice. "I don't know. I don't know any more about where he is than I did the last time we talked. Isn't finding him supposed to be your area of expertise?"

I let that go and drank some of my drink and thought some more. Behind me, laughter erupted from the group of tourists.

"You report this to anyone at Pace?" I asked.

Pratt's dark eyes were wide. "No. No one."

"Who are you supposed to tell?"

"Security, I guess—and Tampon. He wants to know anything about people looking for Greg."

"So why haven't you called him?"

"I don't know. I was . . . worried, I guess."

"About what?"

She looked at me for a long while. "I talked to you too much that night, and I shouldn't have. And I've been worried ever since about Tampon finding out. I was afraid if I told him about this, one thing would lead to another . . ." She sniffed and rubbed her nose with the back of her hand. "It could be my job," she said softly.

I nodded at her. Pratt sank her hands into the pockets of her slicker and sat hunched and silent. It was warm in the bar, but she looked as if she were tensed against a cold wind. A tourist barked out a loud guffaw and Pratt started.

"Are you okay?" I asked.

Pratt stared at me. Her nose was red and her lips were chalky. She nodded. "This whole break-in thing is . . . creepy," she said. Her voice was nearly a whisper. "When I thought you'd done it I was mostly mad, but now"—she swallowed hard and shook her head—"now it's got me thinking and . . . I'm scared."

"Of what?"

She looked beyond me, into the noisy crowd. "Four or five days in the last week, I've seen this car parked near my place, and a guy in it that I think is watching me."

I put my glass on the bar and spoke very quietly. "What kind of car, Irene?"

Pratt's eyes narrowed and came back to mine. "It's black, a Pontiac I think, and new-looking."

I thought of the cars that had trailed me over the bridge, the night I'd come back from Fort Lee. One of them had been a black, late-model Grand Prix. "And the guy in it?"

She shook her head. "I don't know . . . a white guy with dark hair and a mustache . . . in his thirties, maybe. Just a guy." Her face was taut, and she dug her hands deeper into her pockets.

"Was he there today?" I asked. She nodded. "Has he said anything to you, or done anything?"

"Nothing. He's always reading a paper or a book; he's never even looked at me. It's just a feeling I get." Her shoulders twitched as if a chill had rippled through her. "What's going on, March?"

"I don't know," I said. "But someone besides me has been looking for Danes, and someone—maybe the same someone—has been tailing me and staking out *my* place. It could be the same person who creeped your office, or the same person who's been watching you."

"Jesus Christ," Pratt said, and she rose quickly and clumsily. Her voice was an angry rasp. "What the fuck is going on? What did you get me into?"

The bartender looked at us and frowned. "Sit down, Irene," I said, and I took her arm. She shrugged my hand away, but sat. "I told you, I don't know what's going on, but whatever it is, it probably has more to do with Danes than with me."

"That's great to hear," Pratt said. "It'll be a real comfort the next time I see that car, or when somebody breaks into my office again." She ran her fingers through her hair, over and over. "So what the hell am I supposed to do?"

It was a fair question, and I thought about it for a while. "You do three things," I said finally. "First, you try to calm down. I know it's not easy; I know this break-in thing is scary as hell, and being tailed is even worse, but I think whoever's doing this is interested in Danes, not in you."

"You *think*—"

"Second, you go back to work and report the break-in at Danes's office to everybody you're supposed to, but you leave your office out of it." Pratt took a breath and started to speak; I ignored her. "You've already signed in at your building today. If Turpin and his pals find out about the break-in, and that you were at work but didn't report it, they'll start to wonder about you. If they also find out you've talked to me, you'll be in deep shit." Pratt sputtered but I held up my hand. "Don't worry. They won't hear it from me, but that doesn't mean they won't hear it. I assume you called me on your office phone today." She went white.

"Shit. Oh, shit."

"That's why you don't want them wondering about you. You tell them about Danes's office and nobody gets suspicious; nobody has a reason to check the calls from your phone."

Pratt put her hand on her forehead. "Oh, shit."

"Third, after you report this, you go home. If that car is parked outside your place, or if you see that guy again, you call me."

She cursed softly for a while and then went silent. After about a minute she took a deep breath and sat up. Her voice was steadier when she spoke. "And if I see him and call you, then what?"

"Then I'll come over and have a chat with him."

"*Have a chat with him.* What the hell does that mean? Is that like *cement overshoes* or something?"

I laughed. "It means I'll talk to him and see if I can find out what he's doing and why."

"Christ, I can't believe this," she said, and shook her head. "You'll get there quick if I call you? You won't leave me hanging?"

"I won't leave you hanging, Irene, but I don't think this guy is any threat to you. I think he's staking you out in the hope that Danes will turn up. But if you get scared or feel threatened, call the cops."

She cringed and shook her head some more. "The cops? Oh, Christ."

I put my hand on her arm, and this time she let it stay there. "Call Turpin, tell him your story, and keep it simple. You haven't done anything wrong, Irene; this will all be fine. Just calm down."

Pratt took another deep breath and squared her shoulders. She stood and drained her soda and looked at me. Her dark eyes were rimmed with red. "All right . . . all right," she said, and she managed something like a smile. "I can do this. But when you figure out what the hell is happening, you tell me, okay? Don't leave me hanging, March."

"Okay," I said, and she nodded at me and walked out of the bar. I watched her yellow slicker sift into the crowd.

Something was going on—I had known that—but now I knew that whatever it was had some organization and size. Whoever followed me had also tailed Richard Gilpin out in Fort Lee and staked out Irene Pratt's place too. More likely than not, they were also the same guys who'd been sniffing around Danes's apartment. And now they'd broken into the Pace offices. They were not perhaps the most skillful operators in the world, but they didn't seem to want for manpower.

I signaled for the check and thought about Pratt and her conflicting fears. The break-ins and the tails had scared her, but she was also wary of me and anxious about her own indiscretions. It was only because her alarm had outweighed her other worries that she'd called me at all, and I got the sense there were things she hadn't said. Which made her no different from most people I meet.

I'd meant what I said about whoever was watching her—that their interest was probably in Danes and not her—but the break-ins worried me. They implied an unhealthy appetite for risk, or maybe a certain desperation. I shook my head.

A familiar buzz was running through me, a palpable mix of anticipation and anxiety. It was the leading edge of recognition, the sense that something was emerging from murky waters, but whether wreck or sunken treasure, I still had no idea. And it was inchoate worry, too—about Irene and Nina and Ines and Billy. About Danes. I paid the tab, found a quiet corner in the Warwick's lobby, and pulled out my cell phone.

Nina Sachs was in a foul mood when she answered, and it only got worse when she realized who was calling. She flatly refused to see me at first, and for a while it was all I could do to keep her on the line. But I was insistent and, despite herself, she grew curious and a little anxious. She was downtown, at Ines's SoHo gallery, and she agreed to meet me at a bar on Broome Street. I took a cab there.

Siren was a hip, high-ceilinged place done in blues and sea greens, and outfitted like a Philip Johnson aquarium. The lighting was cool and dim and shifting, and the background music was Brian Eno. The tiny aluminum tables were topped in frosted green glass, and at just past five on a rainy Saturday they were mostly empty. Nina was seated at the back of the room, with a bottle of merlot, two glasses, and Ines. They were vigorously ignoring the city's smoking ban, but no one at Siren seemed to care.

"What is it with you?" Nina asked as I approached. "You can't take rejection?" Even in the submarine light I could see the veins in her eyes and the grainy texture and sallow cast of her skin. Her hair was loose and limp, and her hand shook as she raised a cigarette to her lips. Hangover. Her jeans and shirtsleeves were stained with paint and charcoal.

Ines sat close by, and though she was better groomed than Nina, and more recently washed, she too looked unwell. Her coloring was gray, and her face was gaunt and dyspeptic. She motioned to one of the little metal chairs.

"Please sit, detective." Her voice was furry. Nina drank off her merlot and refilled her glass and looked at me belligerently.

"This better be fucking good, March."

I took a deep breath. "I told you that someone besides me has been looking for Danes—sniffing around at his apartment, out in Jersey, maybe other places too—and I told you that someone has been tailing me. Well, it seems I'm not the only one." Nina Sachs looked at me over her wineglass and Ines was perfectly still, and neither one said a word as I told them about Irene Pratt. When I finished, Nina blew smoke at me.

"That's the big deal: Irene the librarian thinks someone's been peeping at her window and stealing her office supplies, and she calls on you to protect her?" Nina took a gulp of wine and I looked at Ines. Her face was empty and her eyes were far away. I sighed.

"This is an organized thing, and—"

"That's old news," Nina said.

"—and if they've been watching me and Pratt, there's a good chance they're watching other people too—people like you, for instance."

Ines drew an audible breath. Nina waved her hand dismissively.

"This is bullshit."

"You may think so, but it doesn't change the fact that they're out there. And judging by what's happened at Pace-Loyette, they may do more than just watch."

A deep crease appeared on Ines's forehead, and she touched her long fingers to the side of her neck. Nina pointed across the table with her cigarette. Her mouth was an angry wrinkle.

"This is crap, March; this is about you being pissed off because you got fired. This is about you looking for work."

A knot of tension formed at the back of my neck. "Believe what you want, Nina. I'm just asking if you've noticed anything."

Nina snorted derisively but Ines leaned forward, worry in her eyes. "Anything like what, detective?"

"Don't encourage him, Nes," Nina said.

"Any strange cars parked nearby, any strange people hanging around your block or around your building—that sort of thing."

Nina's laugh was nasty and forced. "Strange people? We live in New

York City, March—we got nothing but strange people. We *are* strange people, for chrissakes." She looked at Ines, who worried her lower lip and looked at the floor.

"What about break-ins?" Ines asked.

Nina slapped the tabletop. Smoke exploded from her mouth. "Jesus Christ, Nes, how many times do I have to tell you? That was not a break-in. That was nothing." Ines ignored her and so did I.

"What break-in?" I said.

"It was two weeks ago—no, longer: the week before you came," Ines began. Nina rolled her eyes and muttered something; Ines paid no attention. "It was midday. Guillermo was at school and Nina was in Manhattan. I was working in the gallery and I had gone upstairs for my agenda. I had some calls to make and I had left it in the kitchen. I had taken the elevator, and as the doors opened on our floor, someone ran past very quickly—down the hall and into the stairwell.

"I was more startled than scared when it happened, and I did not know what to think of it. I went to our door and put my key in the lock, but it would not go in all the way, and it would not turn. It was as if something was jammed into the lock."

Nina shook her head. "You are so fucking dramatic sometimes, I swear. The lock was busted—"

"The locksmith said there was something broken off in it. He said it looked as if someone had tampered with it."

"Which means shit," Nina said. "It's not like that's the safest neighborhood in the city. It's not like nobody ever gets robbed there."

"Has it happened before?" I asked. "To you or to anyone in your building?"

Nina gave me a sour look and sucked in more smoke. Ines answered my question.

"No, detective, it has not happened to anyone in our building, before or since."

"Did you get a look at the guy?"

"He was just a blur," Ines said.

"Did you report this to the police?"

Ines shook her head and looked down. Nina snorted. "You and the fucking cops again," she said.

I sighed. "Why didn't you tell me about this before?"

"Why the hell should I?" Nina said. "It was nothing then and it's nothing now—despite your scare tactics, and Nes's hysteria. It didn't have anything to do with what I hired you for."

"I think you may be wrong about that."

Nina shook her head and drained her wineglass. Ines took a cigarette from Nina's pack, pinched the filter off, and lit it. Her movements were very slow and her eyes never left the tabletop.

"Has there been anything else?" I asked.

"Not that I have noticed," Ines said. She looked up at me. "What shall we do now, detective?"

"I know some people who could watch your block for a while, to see if anyone is staking out your place."

"What are you, nuts?" Nina's laugh was contemptuous.

Ines's face was still. "*Mierda,*" she whispered.

"I told you," Nina said, "this is about him looking for more work—and now he's bringing his friends into it."

Ines turned to me. "Is there danger . . . to Guillermo?"

"I don't think so. Whoever is doing this is interested in Danes. If they're watching you, it's because they think he'll turn up."

"Which means they're fucking stupid." Nina snorted. "Nes, you can't seriously believe this crap?"

Ines was silent.

"It won't take long to find out if I'm wrong," I said.

"It won't take any time at all," Nina said quickly, "because it's not going to happen."

Ines looked up, and she and Nina stared at each other. "Nina—"

Nina put her hands on Ines's knees. Her voice fell to a whisper. "Forget it, Nes. I've had enough of this guy—enough of this whole thing. I don't want people snooping on us and scaring Billy. It's just not going to happen." She turned to me, and her tone sharpened.

"Are you clear on that, March? It's not going to happen. Now take your conspiracies and your friends and clear the fuck out of here. I'm sorry I ever hired you, and if you don't leave us alone my lawyer will make *you* sorry too." Nina stubbed out her cigarette. Red patches of anger flared on her cheeks. "Clear out, I said. What's the matter—you have nothing else to do? You have nothing else to fill your time?"

Ines sat still and very straight and stared hard at nothing. I stood and rolled my shoulders to work out the stiffness, but it didn't help. I walked away.

My building was quiet when I got home, and I was wet and angry. I toweled off my hair and changed my clothes, and then I was just angry. I brewed a fresh pot of coffee and sat in the dark and watched the night come on, and the rain turn into thunderstorms, and the storms engulf the city. After a while I switched on a light and picked up my phone and called Tom Neary.

20

By Sunday morning, the storms were east of Cape Cod, the sky was empty and blue, and I was downtown, following Tom Neary through the darkened halls of Brill Associates. He led me through the high-rent client district, past mahogany-clad conference rooms, and down corridors lined with gilt-framed paintings, to a pair of metal doors. We went through and came out on the other side of the tracks: fluorescent lighting, dingy walls, threadbare carpeting, shabby cubicles, and—as a general rule—no clients allowed. Neary's office was in a corner.

It was a good-sized room but spartan in its fittings, which consisted mainly of metal furniture and unsteady piles of paper. His office artwork was a whiteboard, covered by the faded arrows and boxes of an unintelligible diagram. I sat in a straight-backed chair in a big square of sunlight. Neary sat at his metal desk and put his sneakered feet up. He took the lid from a cup of coffee and blew the steam away.

"Getting fired twice in three days and by the same client—that's impressive, even for you." He sipped his coffee. "You may have hosed my weekend, but at least you're entertaining."

"Happy to oblige," I said. "But I'm not sure the second time really constitutes a firing. It was more like a validation of her original decision."

"I won't split hairs," he said. "Did Irene Pratt ever call you back?"

"Last night, to say she'd spent a couple of hours telling her story to the Pace security people and again to Turpin—who jumped to the same conclusions about the break-in that she had."

"She see anything at her apartment?"

"Nope. No sign of the Grand Prix or the guy with the mustache."

"Which doesn't mean there wasn't someone there." Neary looked into his cup and then at me. "You hear from Turpin?"

"No."

"You will."

"You don't think they'll just call the cops?"

"Not over this," Neary said. "They call the cops and they have to tell the whole Danes story. No way his management wants that attention—from the cops or the press." He upended his coffee cup to get the last few drops, and looked at me. "You sure you want to do this?" he asked.

"I'm sure."

Neary shook his head and smiled. "People who work for a living don't do this shit, no matter how curious they are." I nodded. "This is how people get the idea you're a dilettante, you know? Not me, mind you. I don't make a habit of turning away business, and I'd never bad-mouth a client—at least not to his face."

"That's where you and I differ," I said. "That, and the fact that my professional discount is better." I looked at my watch. "Think they'll be here soon?" As I spoke, two men appeared at the office door. I recognized them both.

Juan Pritchard was about my height and half again as wide, with coffee-colored skin and black hair cut short. He had a broad friendly face, a square chin, and a mouth always set in a half smile. The impression of affability was tempered by his large calloused knuckles and by the scar that ran from his left temple to below his collar line and was dissipated completely by the look in his stony black eyes. He wore khaki gabardines, a black linen shirt, and sleek rimless glasses, and he nodded at me as he came through the door.

Eddie Sikes came in behind him, wearing wilted pants and a long-sleeved brown shirt. He was five-nine and wiry, and his black hair was long and unkempt. There was a gold hoop in his right ear and a day's gray growth on his lean face. His pale eyes gave away nothing.

"Hey," he said to Neary. His voice was a scratchy whisper. Sikes carried a white paper bag, and from it he produced two cups of coffee. He handed one to Pritchard and the two of them sat on Neary's sofa.

"Got a couple more of those?" It was a woman's voice and it was full of the Bronx. Lorna DiLillo was tall and dark and limber-looking. Her full lips were glossy, and there was a skeptical light in her brown eyes. She swept a wave of shiny black hair from her shoulder and took off her denim jacket. There was a black automatic holstered butt forward at her hip.

Victor Colonna was with her. He was small, fine-featured, and grave, and his smooth hair was precisely cut and combed. His white shirt was immaculate and bright against his skin. His eyes moved quickly around the room.

"Always got your back," Sikes rasped, and he drew two more coffees from his paper bag. DiLillo and Colonna crossed the room to collect them. Pritchard held out a massive fist and DiLillo bumped it lightly with her own as she passed. Colonna sat next to Sikes and DiLillo leaned on Neary's cluttered windowsill. She sipped her coffee and looked at me and then at Neary.

"Thanks for coming in," Neary said, and he folded his hands on his desk. "You all remember March?" They nodded. "Well, he's *Mister* March now, because now he's a client, and actually paying for the privilege of fucking up your Sunday." DiLillo snorted.

"For now, the job is surveillance, at four different sites. I've got fact sheets for you here." Neary tapped a thin stack of paper on his desk. "But the short story is, John wants to know if anybody's got these sites—these people—staked out. And if so, he wants to know who. So we want photos, names, plates, and affiliations if you can get them."

"That's for now," Sikes whispered. "What comes after?"

"Can't say at this point," Neary answered. "We just have to wait and see. Read and react."

DiLillo pushed herself off the sill and took the sheets from Neary's desk. She handed copies to Colonna, Sikes, and Pritchard and started reading her own.

DiLillo looked at me. "You've got vehicle descriptions here, and something sketchy on one guy. Does this mean you've seen them?"

"I've seen some cars and a van, and one of their subjects—Irene Pratt—has seen the mustache guy."

DiLillo scowled. "Which answers my question about how good they are."

"Some of them clearly suck; maybe all of them do. And maybe there are some I haven't seen that don't."

DiLillo nodded.

"This could take more feet on the street than just ours," Pritchard said.

"I'll give you more if you need them," Neary said, "but get out there first and tell me."

Sikes folded the sheet and tucked it in his breast pocket. "I'll take Brooklyn."

"I'll take Mr. March's place," Colonna said.

DiLillo looked at Pritchard. "I'll take the chick on the West Side. You take—what's-his-name—Danes's place, Juan. You got those Upper East Side rags for camo."

Pritchard smiled at her and looked at Neary. "We on the clock now?" he asked. Neary nodded.

"You called the motor pool?" Colonna said.

Neary nodded again. "They're expecting you. Call my cell when you're on station."

Sikes and Pritchard followed Colonna and DiLillo out.

Neary turned to me. "You know how this shit goes; it could take a few hours or a few days. I'll call when I have something."

It was still early when I left the Brill offices. The air was bright and clean, and a morning calm still lay on the city streets. Across Broadway, a shopkeeper hoisted a metal gate that made a noise like raucous birds. Up the block, at Duane Street, a single drunk moved carefully across an intersection and around a steaming manhole. A flight of taxis cruised by, headed south. They were off duty, and they moved slowly and with an odd dignity. Some Wallace Stevens lines ran through my head: *Complacencies of the peignoir, and late / Coffee and oranges in a sunny chair.* Then the drunk stopped, opened his pants, and pissed on an office building. The poetry changed from Stevens to Bukowski and vanished altogether. I kept walking north and thought about what Tom Neary had said.

People who work for a living don't do this shit, no matter how curious they are. He was right, of course, this was an indulgence—though not just of my curiosity. Certainly, I wanted to know who else was interested in Danes and what the hell was going on; you don't get into this business without an itch to solve puzzles. I also realized that whoever had me under surveillance had no way of knowing that I'd been canned—and hence no cause to call off the dogs. I hated the feeling of being watched, and I wouldn't rest easy until I'd had a little chat with whoever was holding the leash. But there was, I knew, more to it than that.

I crossed Broome Street and looked west and saw the still-shuttered front of Siren. I thought about seeing Nina Sachs there yesterday, and about her parting shot. *What's the matter—you have nothing else to do? You have nothing else to fill your time?* The words had been steeped in scorn, but I couldn't say they were wrong. The prospect of empty time—of rest-less, dangerous hours filled with nothing but myself—was making me more nervous than usual lately. I wasn't ready for it just then; in fact, I was afraid of it.

The city was wide awake by the time I reached 16th Street, and the side-walks were full. I didn't look for Victor Colonna in the crowd, and I caught no glimpse of him. I went upstairs and let some air into my apartment while it was still fresh. Then I changed into shorts and a T-shirt and went out for a run.

I was gone for over an hour, and there were messages when I returned. The first was from Lauren.

Hey, Johnny, it's me. Liz told me about your little dustup with David. She said Ned was pissed as hell at him because of it. I know he really appreciates your help on this interview thing. Give me a buzz, will you? I shook my head and skipped to the next message. It was from Jane, and there was no hint of yesterday's cool sarcasm in it.

I knocked on your door this morning but you'd already left. Can you believe I'm stuck here on a day like this? I'll be back and forth between the office and the lawyers, but I'll try you later. Maybe we can do something. There were muffled voices in the background and then Jane again. *Okay, got to go.* Then Irene Pratt's voice came on the line.

March? Are you there? Pick up if you're there. There was a long pause, full of nothing but Pratt's breathing. *All right, I guess you're not in. Well, call me back—I want to know what's going on. So . . . call me, okay?* I showered and pulled on jeans and a T-shirt and punched her number.

"Finally!" she said.

"Everything all right? Have you seen that car again, or that guy?"

"I haven't seen a thing. Of course, I haven't been outside today." She sounded tired.

"You don't have to hide, Irene."

"Easy for you to say—nobody broke into *your* office. Did Tampon call you yet?"

"No."

"He's going to."

"So I figured."

"You'll be . . . discreet when you talk to him, right?" Her voice was tinged with embarrassment.

"I won't even say your name."

"Thanks," she said. "You find out any more about who's been watching me—about who's doing all this?"

"Not yet, but I'm working on it, and now I'm not the only one. I've asked some people I know to give me a hand." Irene Pratt made an affirmative noise and went quiet. She'd run out of things to say, but she was reluctant to get off the line. Nerves.

"It's a nice day, Irene, you should go out and enjoy it."

"Yeah, okay," she said, without conviction. "But you'll call me if you find something out, or if your friends do?"

"I'll call even if I don't, just to check in."

Pratt's voice brightened fractionally. "Talk to you later, then," she said, and hung up.

I rummaged in my fridge and came out with a bottle of water and a container of yogurt. I took them to the table and switched on my laptop, and while I ate and drank I went over my final report to Nina Sachs. I read through it several times, and each time I did, the CONCLUSIONS section was stubbornly blank.

21

"You really thought you could get away with it?" It was six-fifteen on Monday morning, and Dennis Turpin's New England accent was grating even through the telephone. "You didn't think we'd know it was you?"

I woke up enough to play along. "Who is this?"

"Turpin, from Pace-Loyette, and you haven't answered my questions, March. What did you think you were doing?"

I sat up and rubbed my eyes. Jane was nowhere in sight. I went for confused and indignant. "I thought I was sleeping," I said.

Turpin let out a disgusted sigh. "Go ahead, play games if you want. I'm just calling to find out why I shouldn't report you to the police and start proceedings to have your license yanked. You're making the decision easy. If you want a chance to explain yourself, this is it. I'd take it if I were you."

I stifled a yawn and ran a hand through my hair. "You're the one playing games, and it's way too early in the morning. I have no idea what this is about, and I'm not going to guess."

Turpin's laugh was harsh. "You expect me to buy that when I practically witnessed your first break-in attempt?"

"Break-in attempt?" It was my turn to laugh. "That's bullshit and you know it—and it's old news besides. Why the hell are you calling about that now, at the crack of dawn, for chrissakes?"

"You call it bullshit; I say all that stopped you before was our security. But we weren't so lucky this time."

I gave him a dramatic pause. "What *this time* are you talking about?"

"You're right, March, it is too early for games. So instead of playing around with you, I'm going to hang up and pour myself another cup of coffee and call the police." He went quiet, but he didn't hang up.

I sighed into the phone. "Let me go out on a limb here, Turpin, and guess that there was some kind of break-in at Pace and you think I had something to do with it."

Turpin snorted. "And I suppose you're going to tell me that you didn't, and that you can account for your time."

He was as subtle as a hand grenade, but I managed not to laugh. I worked something irate into my voice. "You're damn right I had nothing to do with it. And what time am I supposed to account for, exactly?"

Turpin huffed, but his confidence was fading. "Screw around, then, but when you hear a knock on the door, remember that you had your chance. And tell your client the police might want to talk to her too. There are conspiracy issues, if she put you up to this."

I sighed again, and this time I meant it. "For chrissakes, Turpin, give it a rest. I'm not the guy you want, and I think you know it. I'm still looking for Danes and I guess you are too, but we're not the only ones. If you'd stop threatening me for five minutes, we might be able to figure out who else is working this." Turpin thought about it for a while, but ultimately it was no sale.

"You had your chance, March," he said, and hung up.

I put the phone down and pulled the covers up and tried to sleep and didn't. After ten minutes I got into the shower.

I took myself to breakfast at the Florida Room, an airy spot around the corner from my place, and called Irene Pratt while I drank my orange juice. She was whispering and nervous, but relaxed a little when I told her that my conversation with Turpin had been brief and predictable.

"And he didn't ask about me?"

"He didn't ask and I didn't tell."

She sighed audibly. "Will he really call the police?"

"I doubt it. I'm pretty sure that was mostly for my benefit. Any sign of the mustache man or his car this morning?"

"Not that I saw. Have you heard anything from those friends of yours, the ones giving you a hand?"

"Nothing yet," I said. I promised, again, to keep in touch and rang off.

I took a slow walk home, and the whole way I fought the urge to check my back. I was a couple of paces off the corner when I saw him. He was at my building, at the top of the short flight of iron steps that leads to the front door. He was smoking a cigarette and looking at his feet and swinging his backpack absently against the iron railing. His jeans were black and baggy, and his gray T-shirt bore a picture of a robot monkey wearing a gi and swinging a pair of nunchakus. Billy.

"School holiday?" I asked. He looked up and took a long drag on his cigarette.

"No," he said. He made it sound like a challenge. His narrow face was stiff and his cheeks were red. He took another drag and flicked the butt down the stairs. It landed at my feet and dribbled smoke.

"Something the matter?" I asked. I flattened the cigarette with the toe of my shoe.

He snorted. "Yeah, something's the matter—with you. It turns out you've got a terminal case of asshole."

"Sounds painful."

Billy made a mocking smile. "I hope so."

"Billy, what the hell is this about?" Billy dug in his back pocket and came up with a crumpled pack of Marlboros and a yellow plastic lighter. He pulled out a bent cigarette and lit it.

"I told you, it's about you being an asshole. It's about you saying you were going to find my fucking father and then up and quitting on us." He blew a stream of smoke down at me and looked much like his mother as he did it. "That's what it's fucking *about*, asshole."

I took a deep breath. "Who told you I quit?"

Billy scowled and nodded and blew more smoke in my direction. "My mom, asshole. My mom told me."

Shit. I shook my head. "You had breakfast yet?" I asked.

Billy flicked a hand at me, as if he were brushing off a fly. "Don't give me the fucking big brother act, okay? No more comic book talk, no more music, no more buds and pals, all right? Just keep that crap to yourself."

I looked at Billy and he looked back, angry and a little scared. "I didn't quit this, Billy."

"Don't bullshit—"

"That's enough," I said. My voice was low and tight, and it brought Billy up short. A quiver rippled through his lower lip and his eyes looked wet, but he didn't look away. "I didn't quit," I said, more softly. "Last Thursday night, your mom told me she'd decided she didn't want to go on with this.

You'll have to ask her what her reasons were and decide for yourself if they were good ones. But they were *her* reasons, Billy, not mine. I didn't quit."

Billy let out a long breath and ran the back of his hand over his eyes and forehead. "You're so full of it," he said softly.

"I'm not, Billy."

He looked down and his voice got softer still. "Don't bullshit me about this," he said.

"I'm not."

He shook his head. "Fuckin' A," he said. His voice quavered and his nose began to run. "Fuckin' A." He dragged on his cigarette and coughed and spluttered.

"Throw that thing out," I said. "I'll buy you breakfast."

We went back to the Florida Room and sat in a booth. Billy ordered pancakes and French fries and a cream soda. I had coffee. He pulled a pile of paper napkins from the dispenser and blew his nose and wiped his eyes. There were big fans revolving on the ceiling. Billy tilted his head back on the banquette and watched the slow blades turn.

"She fucking lied to me," he said, and managed a rueful laugh. "She fucking lied to me again." The waitress brought my coffee and a can of cream soda and a glass full of ice.

"Does that happen often?" I asked.

Billy shrugged. "Sometimes . . . when it's easier for her."

"Easier than what?"

"Easier than explaining something or having an argument. Easier than the truth." He poured a little soda into his glass and watched it insinuate itself between the ice cubes.

"What was easier about this?"

"It was easier than telling me why she doesn't give a shit about finding him, I guess." He filled his soda glass and drank some off and filled it again. He did this over and over, until the can was empty.

"Did you talk to Ines about it?" I asked. Billy shook his head. "Maybe you should. Is she usually straight with you?"

Billy spoke carefully. "Nes is no bullshitter."

I nodded and his face relaxed. "You've known her a long time," I said.

"My whole life, basically."

"She does a lot for you guys."

Billy made a wry smile. "My mom can find her smokes by herself, and her studio. For anything else she needs Nes."

"Does Ines take care of things for you too?"

His smile warmed. "All the school stuff, and soccer, and when I go to the comics conventions—she does all that. Nes does pretty much everything that takes a grown-up." Billy crunched on an ice cube and watched a very tall woman in a very small dress walk by our table. When she was out of sight he turned back to me.

"My mom gave you a hard time?" he asked.

"Pretty much," I said, smiling.

"It's like her best thing."

"Is she that way a lot?"

Billy shrugged. "I guess."

"With everyone?"

"Everybody's eligible."

"Including you?"

He shrugged again and gazed someplace over my shoulder. "Nes says it's because she's afraid of stuff, and that she needs to control things or something—I don't know if I get it all. But Nes says when you fight back it just makes her more scared and she gets more pissed off and it all just gets worse. She says when my mom gets going like that you have to be sort of a chameleon; you have to blend in and fade away and not give her anything to hit at. Nes says it's like mental kung fu." He looked into his soda glass and blinked hard. "I'm not much good at it, though. I don't see it coming a lot of the time, and mostly I fight back."

I started to speak, but my throat closed up and I couldn't. I drank some coffee and took a shaky breath.

"Does she give Ines a hard time too?"

"It's different with Nes. She knows a lot of stuff—about painting and art and business things—and my mom respects that. And she knows Nes does a ton of stuff for her—for both of us. And, you know, they're . . . together." Spots of color came up in Billy's cheeks and he looked over my shoulder again. "Besides, Nes is patient. And she's really good at the kung fu stuff."

He looked around the room and then stared down at his silverware for a while. The waitress brought another can of soda and refilled my coffee and went away. Billy's eyes came back to mine, and there was a trace of embarrassment in them.

"She's really not so bad, you know—my mom, I mean. She's really smart, and she's a great painter. Everybody says so—magazines and newspapers and all those collectors and stuff. And she can be really funny too. She just . . . has a lot of shit on her mind sometimes." He nodded as he spoke, and guilt and pleading were all mixed up in his voice. I swallowed hard and nodded back and he smiled at me, relieved. I drank some more coffee.

"When's the last time you heard from your dad?" I asked.

"Last time I talked to him was weeks ago, right before he left. I was supposed to see him, and he called right before and canceled."

"What did he say exactly?"

Billy shook his head. "Mom's the one who really spoke to him. By the time I got on the phone he was mostly full of his *sorry, sorry, sorry* bullshit. He said something had come up and he was going away for a while, and he said he was bad company right then anyway. He said he'd pick me up when he got back, and that we'd be spending a lot more time together." The waitress came by again and slid a plate of pancakes the size of steaks in front of Billy. She put a plate heaped with fries alongside.

"Did he say what it was that had come up?" Billy shook his head and ate a fry. "Any idea why he said he was bad company?"

"Who knows? He's in a bad mood like ninety percent of the time." He laid thick ribbons of syrup over his pancakes and started eating.

"That business about spending a lot more time together—what do you think he meant by that?"

Billy washed his pancakes down with cream soda and took a breath. "I thought he was talking about the whole custody thing," he said.

I hadn't realized Billy knew about the custody battle. "Did he talk a lot about that?"

Billy's cheeks colored again. "He used to. He used to say all kinds of shit about my mom—and Nes—until he figured out it was just pissing me off."

"What kinds of things did he say?"

He flushed more deeply and looked away. "Just some stupid shit about . . . I don't know."

I could guess about what, and I let it go. "Do you get a vote in the custody thing?"

"You mean about who to live with?" he said. I nodded. Billy shook a few cups of salt on his fries and glued them down with a quart of ketchup. He plucked some fries off the heap and ate them. "I guess so," he answered.

"So, what is it?"

"My vote? I don't know. I guess it might be okay to stay with my dad for a while, or at least it would be different, but . . . my mom and Nes would be all bent out of shape. They'd miss me and shit."

He ate more fries and looked up.

"My dad was talking about boarding school, and I thought that might be cool . . . to go someplace else . . . to get away." Billy shrugged. "I don't know. Mostly I just wish they'd stop the fucking fights. Or leave me out of it, anyway."

I nodded, and we sat in silence for a few minutes.

"That phone call—that was the last time you heard from him?"

Billy nodded. "Yeah. Besides the messages, that was it."

I managed not to spit my coffee out. "What messages?"

Billy answered with a mouthful of pancake. "The messages he left on the machine—phone messages."

"How many messages were there?"

"Just two."

"Do you know when he left them?"

"The first one was like a week after he left town, and the second was a couple of days after that."

"What did he say?"

"Not much. Just *calling to say hi*, or something like that."

"But you didn't actually speak to him?" Billy looked at me like I was stupid and shook his head. "Do you remember what time of day he called?"

"While I was at school, I guess. I played them when I came home."

Billy carved his way through the pancakes and I was quiet, thinking about the messages.

"Did you tell your mom he called?"

Billy hesitated. "I . . . I guess not. He didn't say anything really, and . . . sometimes it's better if I don't talk to her about him."

The waitress came by and held up a coffeepot and raised an eyebrow. I shook my head and she walked away. I watched her go and looked at the back of her T-shirt, at the picture of a pit bull demolishing a wedding cake that was emblazoned there. A little plastic groom in a little plastic tux teetered precariously atop the cake, and it made me think of something. I looked at Billy.

"You remember that picture you showed me at dinner last week, of your dad and the bass player and that older guy, all of them in tuxedos?" Billy nodded. "You know who the old guy is?"

He nodded some more. "I don't remember his name—Joe something, maybe. He's a friend of my dad's. He lives in the same building."

"He a music fan like your dad?"

"I guess. I know they go hear stuff together." That was all Billy could recall about the man, and I had no more questions. No more that Billy could answer, anyway. He finished his pancakes and the last of the fries and wiped his mouth on a napkin. He didn't look like he was about to explode, which was baffling to me.

"I've got to get you home," I said.

Billy winced. "I can go myself. I—"

"Don't waste your breath," I said. "I'm taking you." He didn't argue.

There was no answer at the Sachs apartment, but Billy gave me the gallery number and Ines Icasa was there. Her voice was taut with worry and she let out a long breath when I told her that I was bringing Billy home.

"*Dios mío*," she said softly. "Thank you, detective, I will be here." She hung up and I pocketed my phone. I looked across at Billy.

"You want anything else?" I asked. He shook his head. "You ready to go?"

He rubbed the back of his neck and stared at me. His blue eyes were large in his narrow face. "Will you look for him anyway?" he asked.

"I'll look for him," I said. I didn't know what else to say.

It wasn't quite noon when Billy and I walked into the I-2 Gallery. The shades were up on the windows and the place was flooded with light and empty except for Ines. There was a half-filled glass of red wine on the long counter and a scattering of papers. A cigarette smoldered in a metal ashtray. Ines's pink shirt was clean and starched, and her hair was combed and shiny, but her coloring was still off and there were shadows under her eyes. Billy started to say something but she cut him off.

"Upstairs, Guillermo," she said. Billy opened his mouth again, but Ines pointed at him before he could speak. "Now." He glanced at me and shrugged and went. Ines sat on a stool behind the counter and sighed deeply. She reached for her cigarette and took a long drag. It smelled like a brush fire. Her elegant fingers slid aimlessly along the countertop.

"The school telephoned this morning," she said, "to ask if he was ill. He has done this before—several times. But it is always very . . . worrying. He came to see you?" I nodded. "Why?"

"To ask me why I'd stopped looking for his father." Ines stepped back, as if balance had deserted her. "I told him he'd have to talk to Nina about that. Or to you." She puffed on her cigarette and shook her head.

"I am sorry," she said softly. "Nina should not have . . . It was a mistake to say that to Guillermo."

"Maybe you should tell her."

Ines stabbed her cigarette into the ashtray and picked up her glass and drank half of what was in it. Her laugh was short and unpleasant. "Perhaps you have noticed that Nina is a difficult person to tell things."

"If not you, then who?"

She shook her head. "It is complicated."

"Apparently."

Ines looked at me sharply. "I can do some things for Guillermo, but I am not his parent. I could teach him to use the toilet and to throw a ball. I could show him how to ride a bicycle. I can be sure I am here when he arrives from school, so he does not come to an empty apartment. I can know when he is late . . . or when he is truant. Those things I can do, detective, but I am not his mother, and I cannot tell his mother what is best for him. On some topics, my opinions are irrelevant." Her lovely oval face sagged and she drank from her wineglass again. "Do you have children?"

"No."

"Then you cannot know the complications," she said, and smiled bitterly. "Perhaps neither one of us can."

The wineglass was empty and Ines's eyes were clouded. She leaned heavily on the counter and rested her head on her arms. I saw the razor-straight part in her black hair and I saw her shoulders quiver. There was no traffic in the street beyond the big windows, and it was very quiet in the gallery. There was a new exhibit hanging—massive canvases with large, vaguely floral shapes in deep purples and reds and pinks—and I stood and looked at them while I waited for Ines to raise her head. After a couple of minutes she did.

"I must check on him now," she said. She took her heavy key ring from the counter, and I followed her to the street. She locked the glass doors and looked at me. "You should not be here when Nina gets home."

22

I spent the rest of the afternoon at home, waiting for word from Neary and thinking about Billy. I thought about the tension in his narrow frame as he looked down from the steps of my building, and of the hurt and confusion etched around his eyes. I remembered what he'd said about his mother, and how, when he knew he'd said too much, he'd made excuses for her and looked to me for agreement. I recalled Ines's advice to him—to simply fade away—and I clenched my fists. I thought about parents and children, and about how kids survive and at what price. I thought and I waited, but no answers came to me and Neary never called.

Jane appeared late Monday night, bleary-eyed and subdued, and bearing Indian food. She hung her suit jacket on a chair and kicked off her shoes, and we ate mostly in silence. When she did speak it was in angry fragments about her deal, which had hit an eleventh-hour snag over her participation in the company after its sale. The buyers wanted her to run things for two more years, but Jane wasn't interested. They were insistent and threatening to make it a deal-breaker; Jane was getting mad.

"I don't come with the copier and the paper clips," she muttered over her tandoori. "I'm not a piece of fucking office furniture." She got tired of talking about it halfway through dinner and flicked on the television. She surfed through the channels and leafed angrily through the pages of another fat travel magazine and finished her meal in silence. I carried the trash to the chute down the hall, and when I got back Jane was sitting on the sofa. The travel magazine was in her lap and the TV was off. She was staring at me.

"So, have you figured out what you want to do about this vacation thing yet?" she asked. Her words were quick and taut, as if she'd had too much coffee, and her eyes—though tired in her tired face—were looking for something. Like a fight.

"What do you mean?"

"You said there was a chance your client might reconsider over the weekend—that your job might come back. Are you still waiting for that to happen, or has something else come along?"

I sighed. "Is this really the best time? Don't you want to get some sleep?"

"Sleep's overrated," Jane snorted. "I just want to know where I stand with this trip. How much time can that take?"

I went into the kitchen and poured a glass of water. I drank some of it and cleared my throat and looked at her over the counter. "We've talked about this. We—"

"No, we haven't. We've talked *around* it—for weeks now. Now I actually want to talk *about* it." Her dark eyes narrowed and color rose in her face. "Did your job come back?"

"Not exactly."

"That's nice and direct," she said. Her laugh was short. "Is there an explanation to go with that?"

"Sachs hasn't changed her mind, but there was a break-in at Pace-Loyette over the weekend, in Danes's office. I'm looking into that."

"They hired you?"

"Not exactly."

Jane's brows came together. "Has *anyone* hired you?"

"I told Irene Pratt I'd look into it. And I told Nina's kid, Billy, that I'd keep looking for his father."

"So they're your clients now?"

"It's more of a pro bono thing."

Jane shook her head. A tiny smile, equal parts incredulous and bitter, played on her perfect lips. "*Pro bono* is right. The question is: good for who, them or you?"

"They need—"

"What do *you* need, John? What is it that *you* want?"

I put my glass down. "I've told you, I don't think a trip is a bad idea, I just—"

"I'm not talking about the trip anymore," Jane said. The silence afterward was ringing.

"I was starting to suspect that," I said, after a while.

Jane's face darkened. "Don't be funny," she said quietly. "Not now."

"What do you want me to say, Jane?"

Jane looked down at her stockinged feet for a while. Then she raised her head and locked her eyes on mine. "You can say what it is we're doing here, for starters. You can tell me what this is supposed to be. Whether it's just something convenient, that fits into the time you can't fill up with work, or . . . something else." Jane's fingers were white at the edges of the magazine, and a pulse was beating quickly on her neck.

"I've never thought of this as just handy," I said softly.

She took a deep breath and dragged a hand through her cropped hair. "And was there some way I was supposed to know that? Was there a sign I missed? Maybe it's the lack of sleep—or maybe I'm just no good at parsing the oblique stuff—because the only signal I get from you says *convenience*."

I drank some more water, but it didn't relieve the churning in my gut. My ears were full of a rushing sound. "Convenience is a two-way street," I said.

Jane's mouth tightened. "What's that supposed to mean?"

"It means that your work is important to you, and you like your life organized a certain way, and all of this is pretty convenient for you too. It fits nicely into what little free time you give yourself. It's close to home and to the office, and—"

"You really think that's why I'm here, because of . . . *geography*?" she asked. Her magazine had fallen to the floor but she didn't seem to notice. Her face was very still.

I shrugged. "I think we're alike, Jane. Both of us like things neat, and we like them on our own terms."

Jane looked at me, and after a while she sighed. "I think that's facile bullshit," she said. "And what's more, I think you know it." She went to the table and picked up her jacket and slipped her feet into her shoes. "I think you know there's a difference between being dedicated to your work and hiding inside it. And an even bigger difference between being self-sufficient and . . . whatever it is that you are."

She slung her bag over her shoulder and turned when she reached the door.

"But you were right about one thing," she said. "This wasn't a good time to talk." She closed the door softly behind her.

I ran long on Tuesday morning, and worked my way through the weight stations at the gym a few times, and stood under the shower afterward until the wobbly feeling in my limbs passed. I called Irene Pratt from a diner on Eighth Avenue, over my first cup of coffee. She answered right away, but when I told her who it was she said she couldn't talk and to try her later. I finished my oatmeal and read the paper, and over my last cup of coffee, I called again. She kept me on hold for five minutes.

"Just checking in," I said, when she came back on the line.

"Uh-huh. Well . . . thanks, I guess."

"Everything all right with you?"

"Me? I'm fine—great, in fact."

"Any more signs of that guy?"

"I haven't seen anything or anybody. In fact, I'm thinking now that I was just being paranoid."

"The break-in wasn't paranoia."

"Yeah, but the business of people watching me—"

"A black Grand Prix followed me too. I don't think you imagined that."

"How do you know? There are probably hundreds of cars like that in New York—maybe thousands."

I was quiet for a moment. "What's wrong, Irene?" I asked finally.

"Nothing—nothing's wrong," she said. "I just need to get some work done, that's all. I think I was being paranoid, and now I need to cut it out and get back to work."

"I won't keep you, then. I'll call if I hear anything."

"Don't bother," she said quickly. "I mean, not on my account. Like I said, I'm fine and I just want to get back to work. I don't want to think about this stuff anymore."

"I can understand that, but these guys may have other ideas."

An edge came into Pratt's voice. "*These guys?* You talk like there's some big conspiracy, but I'm telling you I'm not sure I even saw anything, okay? Now let me get back to work." The line went dead.

I pocketed the phone and the waitress dropped a check on the table. I sat there and looked at it and thought about Pratt. On Monday morning she'd been scared and worried and had taken comfort in hearing from me. Twenty-four hours later, she wanted me to go away. I had no idea why.

Plenty of people have taken sudden dislikes to me before, but I didn't think that was Pratt's problem. Fear was a possibility. Fear of getting any more involved in whatever was going on, perhaps, or of having anything more to do with me. Fear of Turpin finding out. Fear of losing her job. Pratt had had a bad case of nerves when I'd seen her on Saturday, and I was willing to bet it had only gotten worse and more corrosive with each passing day. Maybe she figured to put it all behind her with a hearty dose of denial. Or maybe she just had a lot of work to do.

I paid the bill and walked home. And kept right on walking, past my building. I didn't feel like sitting in an empty apartment just then, or hearing the echoes of Jane's voice, or the silence upstairs, so I headed east—to Union Square—and spent much of the day roaming in a very large bookstore. I wandered the science fiction and the history aisles, and read some essays on contemporary politics and world affairs, and when I was sufficiently disheartened I drank a lot of coffee.

I checked my voice mail when I got home. There was nothing from Neary, but there was a message from Paul Gargosian.

"Don't know if you still want to talk, but I'm home now. You have my number." I did and I used it, and left him yet another message. Then I checked my e-mail. At long last, Gregory Danes's phone records had arrived. I clicked on the attachments and scanned through the reports and felt my heart sink.

"Shit," I whispered.

Neary called on Wednesday morning, and I was downtown in twenty minutes. DiLillo and Sikes were sitting on his office sofa. I leaned on the windowsill and Neary nodded at DiLillo.

"There's surveillance at all the locations," she began. "Four out of four. They're using a lot of people, and they must be burning through a lot of cash. They're running three eight-hour shifts at each site, and a round-robin deal with the cars, switching them from site to site, so the same one doesn't show up at the same place two days in a row. As far as we could tell, the surveillance is static; we don't think they're tailing anybody. But we'd have to work it with more guys to be sure." She held up a fat manila folder. "I've got the stills for you."

I opened the folder and leafed through it. It was full of photographs, of men and cars. There were crisp daylight shots and grainy nighttime ones, from long distances and from close up and at odd angles, but all of them were clear enough to ID faces and read plate numbers. The men in the pictures were of various types: white and black and Hispanic, young and old, fat and lean. They didn't look like brain surgeons, but then again they didn't look like junkies or flashers or racetrack touts, either. Except for a certain wariness around their eyes, they were a mostly unremarkable bunch. There were a lot of different men in the pictures, and I stopped counting after a dozen. I didn't recognize any of them, though I saw a black Grand Prix, a brown Cavalier, a dirty red hatchback, and a light-blue van that all looked familiar.

I was quiet for a while, and the three of them looked at me. My jaw felt tight and I heard a pulse thrumming in my ears. It wasn't a surprise; I'd known they were out there. Still, it galled.

"At my place too?" I said. My voice sounded far away.

DiLillo nodded. "Uh-huh," she said. "But they're being real careful about it, if it's any consolation. At least two cars, and they never park on your block."

"Who are they?" I asked.

"We're still working on IDs for some of them, but what we have so far is that they're all independents—small-time, one-man shops, like you. No offense."

"We think they're subcontracting," Neary said.

"For who?"

Neary looked at Sikes, who gazed out the window as he spoke. "I know a few of these guys, and one of them owes me. I braced him last night. He doesn't know the client—he swears up and down he doesn't—but he knows the prime contractor, the guy that signs his check. It's Marty Czerka."

My brow furrowed. "Who's that?"

Sikes shook his head regretfully, and he and DiLillo exchanged sour smiles.

"Marty?" DiLillo said. "Marty's the guy who put the *sleaze* in sleaze-ball."

Sikes's laugh was almost a whisper. "Yeah. The guy who put the *douche* in douche bag."

DiLillo giggled. "The guy who put the *fat* in fat fuck."

Neary shook his head. "Thanks," he said to them. "That was helpful." He turned to me. "Marty's a PI. He's got a small agency, him and a brother-in-law and an idiot nephew, all in an office on Canal Street. About a thousand years ago he was on the job uptown, working vice. His fifteen minutes of fame came when he busted some aging rock star in a suite at the Carlyle, with a carry-on full of coke, two semiautomatics, and an underage hooker with a busted arm. Got Marty on television and everything. It took him all of a week to fuck it up.

"First, he gets caught peddling pictures of the bust to some supermarket tabloid. Then another of those rags claims he promised *them* an exclusive on the photos, and they sue the shit out of him. And finally it comes out that Marty and the hooker have a longterm thing going, and the two of them maybe set up the whole show. He's lucky they didn't fry his large ass, but as it was that was his ticket to the private sector.

"Since then he's made a specialty of any slimy thing that comes along: ugly divorce cases, ugly custody fights, ugly sexual harassment claims—a real dog parade. And whatever side of the shitpile Marty is on, it's never the right one. He's a fixture in some circles, the way Fresh Kills Landfill is, only Marty smells worse. I'm surprised you've never run across him."

"I don't breathe the same rarefied air as you big corporate types," I said. "Who's he working for now?"

Neary shook his head. "That's the question, isn't it?"

I turned to Sikes. "Your pal didn't know, but what about these other guys? Think one of them might have a name?"

Sikes lifted a skeptical brow. "I'd guess Marty would keep that card pretty close to the vest; he wouldn't want any of these geniuses going direct to the client and cutting him out of the deal. But shit does happen, especially in a group this big; the hens get together and get to gossiping. I wouldn't bet on anybody talking, though—not without some serious leverage."

"They're all such good soldiers?" I asked.

DiLillo shook her head. "Marty buys a lot of freelance help, so he's a regular meal ticket for a lot of these guys. They won't want to fuck that up. And half of what they're selling is their ability to keep their mouths shut. Nobody wants a rep for being a talker; it sucks for business."

She had a point. "Anybody have leverage with one of these guys?" I asked.

"I shot my wad yesterday," Sikes said. DiLillo shook her head.

"Think some cash would motivate them?"

Sikes smiled. "They'll all take your money—no doubt about it—the problem is knowing who to give it to and what the hell you're getting in return. Finding that out could be expensive."

"How about Czerka himself?"

"You never know with Marty," Neary said. "He's a creep, and as a general rule you've got to figure he's always for sale. On the other hand, he can't afford to burn too many bridges. I think with Marty it'll depend on how much he's making off the client, what he thinks the blowback would be from burning him, and how much you're willing to grease the rails."

I thought about that for a while. "Surveillance still going?" I asked.

"Until you say otherwise," Neary said.

"A couple of days more, then." I looked at Sikes. "You think that friend of yours will give Czerka a heads-up?"

A chilly grin spread across Sikes's face. "He's not that stupid." He and DiLillo got up and left. Neary sat back in his chair.

"Somebody's spending a lot of money on this," he said.

"You mean besides me?"

"Besides you. And that means somebody with deep pockets and motivation. It also means that Marty will suck at this tit for as long as he can."

"If buying him doesn't work, there's always charm or deceit—or both."

"Charm's no good on Marty; he's got no receptors for it. And I wouldn't put too much faith in trickery either. He's no rocket scientist, but Marty has a sewer-rat kind of shrewdness."

"How about a nice beating, then?"

"You're not paying nearly enough for that. No, I think we take a walk up to Marty's office and have a talk. He'll either negotiate or he'll tell us to fuck off. And if he does, we can still make a run at the hired help."

We were quiet for a while and Neary gave me a speculative look.

"I figured you'd be a little more excited about this," he said.

"I'm smiling on the inside. I got Danes's phone records last night—his home and his cell."

"Were they worth the wait?"

I nodded. "They cover a thirty-day period starting about five weeks ago, just a few days before he last called in for his messages."

Neary nodded. "And?"

"The home number was no surprise; no calls made from there during that time. The activity was on his cell. There were a couple of calls to Reggie Selden, the lawyer representing him on the custody thing, and calls to his own home, to get messages. There was a call to Nina Sachs's number—"

Neary cut me off. "I thought she hadn't heard from Danes."

"So did I, but according to Billy his father left a couple of messages for him on the answering machine. He didn't mention them to his mother."

Neary nodded, and I continued. "Then there's that final call to his home number—which corresponds to the date and time on his caller ID—and that's it. There are no other calls."

Neary's brows came together. "That was the last one?"

I nodded. "Not only did he stop calling in for his messages, he stopped making calls altogether."

Neary sat back in his chair. He tapped a finger lightly on the edge of his desk. "He could have another phone," he said.

"I guess so, but I haven't turned up another number in his name."

"It could be one of those prepaid throwaway things."

"It could be."

"You talk to Sachs about this?"

"She's made it pretty clear she's not interested."

Neary shook his head and drew a big hand slowly down his jaw.

We walked north on Broadway. A skim coat of pearly cloud had spread itself across the sky, and glare and heat and intimations of summer had begun to build beneath its shell. Bus fumes and car exhaust and the smell of ripening trash stayed close to the pavement, and I was sweating a little when we turned east on Canal. Both of us were thinking about Danes's phone bill and what it might mean, but neither of us put it into words.

Czerka's office was in a soot-gray building near Centre Street, and convenient to the House of Detention. The lobby walls were green and the linoleum floor was sticky underfoot. The lone desk guard barely glanced at our IDs when we signed in. We took a dim elevator up.

The ninth-floor corridor was fluorescent-lit and painted a nasty blue. It was empty and quiet and smelled powerfully of disinfectant. The doors to the office suites were metal-clad and bristled with locks. Czerka's office was to the left, tucked between a bail bondsman and a bathroom. The plastic sign on the door read CZERKA SECURITY BUREAU. There was an intercom box mounted on the wall, and Neary leaned on the buzzer.

Nothing happened for a while and then a storm of static erupted from the speaker and abruptly stopped. Neary hit the buzzer again and was rewarded by another burst of noise and then nothing.

"If you're talking, I can't hear a word you're saying," he shouted into the box. A feeble buzzing came from the vicinity of the doorknob. Neary pushed and we went in.

It was a cramped, windowless room with fluorescent lights and a smell of cigarettes, old food, and flatulence. The walls were lined with battered metal file cabinets and most of the floor space was taken by two metal desks, facing each other across a narrow aisle in the center of the room. There was a computer on the left-hand desk, with a huge monitor, a modem, and a rat's nest of cabling that snaked away behind the cabinets. The right-hand desk was covered in food wrappers and magazines—Burger King, KFC, and Krispy Kreme, *Soldier of Fortune* and *Maxim*. A sound mind in a sound body. There was no one in the room, but there was a doorway straight ahead, and a voice shouting out from it.

"Who the fuck is it?" It was a man's voice, deep, wheezy, and wet and with a strong Long Island accent. I followed Neary in.

The inner office was larger than the outer one, and was graced by a dirt-fogged window, but it was no less crowded and smelled even worse. It too was lined with file cabinets, and all of them were topped by dusty heaps of newspapers and magazines. To the right was another big workstation, perched on a frail-looking card table, and in the corner was a half-sized refrigerator with a coffeemaker on top. In the center of the room was a scarred oak desk. Its surface was obscured by layers of file folders and newspapers and glossy catalogs, and by an immense glass ashtray that overflowed with cigarette butts and spent matches. In front of the desk were two plastic guest chairs, and wedged behind it was the man I took to be Marty Czerka.

He was spread out in his green leather chair like a toad on a lily pad. His big head was liver-spotted and mostly bald, and the fringe of hair at the sides was coarse and gray. His skin was mottled pink and white; it fell in deep folds around his eyes and meaty nose and flowed over his shirt collar. More gray hair bristled over his hooded blue eyes and above his thick upper lip.

His shirt had once been white, and from its size it might also once have been a spinnaker. Now it had French cuffs and gold cuff links shaped like little nightsticks. A stained yellow tie hung limply down its front, the knot obscured by Czerka's double chin. His pale hands were veined and speckled, and his fingers looked like bad sausage. He stubbed out a cigarette, and ash dribbled over the sides of the ashtray. He looked at Neary and his thick brows came together.

"Neary, right—ex-Feeb, with Brill?" he said. Neary nodded.

Czerka shifted his big head and looked at me. There was a spark of recognition and surprise in his hooded eyes, but he doused it quickly and put on a game face of indifference and lethargy. It was deftly done. He looked back to Neary.

"Who's he?" he asked.

Neary smiled and sat in one of the guest chairs. I sat in the other. Czerka didn't seem to mind not getting an answer to his question. He found a cigarette in the wreckage of his desk and lit it with a wooden match. He sighed in some smoke and coughed wetly. He rolled the cough around in his throat and savored it, as if it were the best part of smoking.

"You're not on my calendar today," Czerka said.

"I thought I'd drop in," Neary said, "just on the off chance."

Czerka nodded. "Sure," he said slowly. He looked at me again. "And you?" I smiled and said nothing.

"I thought maybe you could help me out, Marty," Neary said.

Czerka took another drag and coughed a little more. "Help," he said absently. He shifted in his seat, and a greasy popping sound issued from somewhere below his desk. A moment later, a noxious sulfurous smell filled the room. Charming. I looked at Neary, who kept on talking.

"I have a friend who's feeling a little bit crowded lately."

"*Crowded*, huh? What, he needs a bigger apartment? Or a laxative maybe?" Czerka's blue eyes glittered. He cleared his throat loudly and for a long time. "You the friend?" he asked me, when he finished. I was quiet. Neary ignored the question too.

"We're in the market for a name, Marty," he said. "We can buy it or swap for it or whatever, and nobody has to know where we got it from."

Czerka played one of his fat fingers along the edge of his mustache and then slid it into his nose. "What name?" he said finally.

Neary was full of elaborate disappointment. "Come on, Marty. The name of whoever's paying for the small army you've got on the street these days."

Czerka treated himself to another drag and another ripe cough and was about to speak when the outer door opened and banged shut. There were heavy footsteps and a man stood at the office door.

He was young, no more than twenty-five, and medium height, but with the neck and shoulders of a serious gym rat. He wore shiny gray warm-up pants and a black T-shirt from someplace called the Platinum Playpen, and a heavy odor of sweat and leathery cologne preceded him. His dirty-blond hair was buzz-cut on his small head, and his eyes were pale and vague and set close below a bony brow. The left eye was blackened. There was a bandage across his pulpy nose, stitches at the corner of his undersized mouth, and bruising along his jaw. There were foam-and-metal splints on three fingers of his left hand. He held a couple of paper bags in his right, and he put them on Czerka's desk.

"I got the smokes, Uncle Marty, and the sandwich and the lottery tickets," he said. His voice was cracking and adolescent. He looked at us and wondered who we were, and it seemed like a lot of work for him. He fixed his gaze on me, and after a while a dim light came into his eyes. He didn't try to hide it, or even realize that he should. There was irritation on Czerka's face and in his voice.

"Yeah, great work, Stevie. Now go watch the front room—and close the door behind you."

Stevie stared at us harder, in what I realized was supposed to be a tough look. "You got a problem here, Uncle Marty? Something I could help with?"

"Go!" Czerka barked. Stevie colored but did as he was told. Czerka stubbed out his smoke and looked at Neary and chuckled. It was moist and mocking.

"Since when are we such old pals that you waltz in here calling me *Marty*? And since when do I give a shit about you or your friends or their problems or whatever the hell you're in the market for? You may not be a Feeb anymore, but you still got that Feeb attitude, that's for damn sure."

He took a loud breath and laughed some more.

"You got a lot of fucking nerve coming in here, thinking I got something to sell you. What, you think you're the only stand-up guys in the world? You think the rest of us lowlifes are just looking for a chance to roll on a client?" Czerka got winded and his laughter dissolved into a racking cough.

Neary nodded at him. "I didn't realize your sensibilities were so refined, Marty," he said. "You have my deepest apologies. And now we can talk cash money, or I've got some business I could push your way, or we could do some of each. Or maybe you're interested in something else. But if you are, you've got to tell me, because I can't read minds." Neary paused and smiled. "So, do you want to do yourself some good here or not?"

Czerka flicked at us dismissively and dug through the bags on his desk. He pulled a brick-sized package in white butcher's paper from one, tore back the wrapping, and hoisted a sloppy pastrami on rye to his mouth. Grease bled down his hands and left his chin and mustache wet, and the smell of meat and fat rose to mingle with the other delicate aromas in the room. He put the sandwich down and pulled a cigarette from somewhere and lit it even as he chewed, open-mouthed, on the pastrami. Jesus.

"Forget it, Neary," he said, and bits of food fell from his mouth to the desk. "Your pockets aren't deep enough to make it worth the trouble." He glanced at me and shook his head. "Even his aren't deep enough. Now get the fuck out of here and let me eat my lunch." He picked up his sandwich again.

Neary looked at me and shrugged. I took a deep breath and tried not to choke. I spoke quietly. "Mesmerizing as it is to sit here while you smoke and fart and smear yourself with lard, I'd be more than happy to go get myself steam-cleaned and leave you in peace, believe me. But I've got a client who'd really like to know what's going on, and frankly so would I. I know you don't give a shit about who wants what, but my client has some resources, and I do too, so maybe you shouldn't be so quick to dismiss. Maybe you should get your brains out of your fat ass and reconsider."

Czerka stared at me, his sandwich poised above his desk. He was quiet and his blue eyes were hard beneath their folded lids. Red patches spread over his cheeks, and his shoulders and fat arms began to shake, and then a gurgling sound came from his open mouth. Czerka put his sandwich down and shook and laughed for almost a minute, until his face grew dark and there was a hissing in his breath. He wiped his mouth with the back of his hand.

"Son of a bitch!" Czerka laughed, "Fucking steam-cleaned, huh?" He looked at Neary. "See—your pal thinks I'm dog shit, just like you do, but he comes out and says it. He can barely stand to breathe the same air as me, but he puts it right out there. I got to say, I kind of like that. But sweet talk won't get you into my pants, March." He looked at me as he said my name, but I managed to keep my composure. Czerka laughed a little more and took hold of his sandwich again. After a while he glanced up.

"Door's right there, boys," he said.

We walked out of Czerka's office, past Stevie and his bandages. He tried to give us another hard stare as we went by, but it came off looking like constipation.

On the elevator, Neary sighed loudly. "Not just another pretty face, is he?" he said.

"But a great personality. My guess is he won't have a lot of second thoughts."

"He won't have any. We'll pull together a list of the people my crew has

ID'd and see if anybody in my shop knows any of them. If they do, that might give us a place to start."

It was warmer outside, but compared to Czerka's office the air seemed fresh and clean. We walked back to Broadway in silence and stopped outside the subway station.

"What do you think happened to Stevie?" I asked.

"Tripped over a barbell maybe?"

"Maybe it outsmarted him."

I was still trying to clear my lungs when I pushed open the glass and wrought-iron door of my building and stepped into the entry vestibule. And then I stopped. There was a large manila envelope taped to my mailbox. It was blank except for my name, which was printed in capitals, in black marker. I peeled it off the mailbox door. It was light. I opened the flap. There were just a few sheets of paper inside. I slid them out and felt a rush of heat in my face and a surge of blood through my temples.

They were photographs, in color, printed on plain paper. Their quality was mediocre at best, but the subjects and their surroundings were clear enough and so were the little date-and-time stamps in the corners.

"Jesus." My legs felt shaky and my heart was pounding, as if I'd just run a long way. I leaned against the wall for a moment. "Jesus." I pulled out my cell phone.

My fingers felt clumsy as I punched her number. Jane's phone seemed to ring forever, and I looked down at the photos while I listened. Her assistant finally answered.

"Jane Lu's office."

"Is she there?" My throat was tight and it was hard to get the words out.

"Hi, John. I'm afraid she's not available right now."

I ground my teeth. "Is she *in*, though—actually in the office now?"

"Oh, yes. She's in the conference room, in a meeting."

"You're sure of that? You've seen her?"

"I just saw her go in." She sounded puzzled. "Is something wrong, John?"

Something loosened in my chest. "No, nothing. Just have her call me when she gets out. First thing, okay? Tell her it's important." I hung up and punched another number. Janine answered.

"Johnny—you must've read my mind. I was just about to give you a call."

"Are the boys at home, Janine?"

"They just this minute walked through the door," she said.

I let out a deep breath.

"They're still washing up, so they haven't opened them yet."

My throat tightened up. "Opened what?" I said.

Janine laughed. "The presents you sent. They came about an hour ago. But what's in them, Johnny? And what's the occasion?"

23

"Tell me what the hell this is if not a warning shot," I said to Tom Neary. I tossed the envelope in his lap and got into the back of the Volvo sedan. It was double-parked in front of Jane's office on West 22nd Street, and Sikes and Pritchard were sitting up front. "And tell me who it's from, if not that bloated bastard."

Neary took out the photos. There were three of Jane—leaving our apartment building, entering her office building, getting into a cab some-place in midtown—and three of my nephews, Derek and Alec—outside of their apartment building, in the park, and leaving their school. Neary studied them carefully and I looked along with him, until another wave of anger came over me and I turned away and stared out the window. But it did no good. The scene uptown kept playing in my head.

Janine had met me in the lobby of her building. Her face was pale and she was rigid with worry and embarrassment. Her voice was a stiff whisper.

"What is going on, John?"

"Where are the boys?" I asked. The doorman and the concierge were casting sidelong looks at us, and Janine took my arm and led me to the sidewalk.

"They're around the corner, at the Miltons'. What is this about?"

"You left the packages upstairs?"

Janine's blue eyes narrowed and flashed. "Yes. Now for God's sake tell me what's happening."

"I don't know who sent them, but those packages are a message—a warning—to me. They go along with some photos I received today."

"Photos of what?"

I took a deep breath. "Some were of Jane . . . and some were of the boys." Whatever color was left in Janine's face drained away. Her eyes went wide and her hands went to her mouth.

"Jesus Christ," she said, and stepped away from me. A long black car pulled up to the curb and Ned got out of the back. His face was rigid. He looked at Janine and then at me.

"What the hell is going on here?" he said. I told him about the photos and the packages and what I thought they meant, and as I did he shook his head and ran his hand through his gingery hair. When I finished he stared at the pavement for a long time and said nothing. Then he turned to Janine.

"Why don't you sit in the car, Jan?" he said softly. Janine murmured something and moved to the curb. Ned's driver jumped out and held the door. Janine glared at me coldly as she climbed inside.

"If you give me the keys, I'll get the packages and get out of here," I said to Ned. He nodded and fished in his pocket.

The packages were in the foyer, in a plain brown shopping bag, and both of them were wrapped in gold paper. They were rectangular, about the dimensions of a medium-sized phonebook but much lighter. Janine was still in the car and Ned was still standing by the curb when I returned. His face was lined and sagging. I handed him his keys.

"I'm sorry about this," I said.

"You know, you've terrified Janine and the kids. And you've certainly scared the hell out of me. My God, Johnny, what kind of a life are you leading that this sort of thing happens? What kind of thing have you brought to our door?" He stopped and took a deep breath and softened his voice a little. "Janine's upset right now and so am I, and she—we both—think maybe it's best if you don't come around for a while."

I looked at Ned for a moment and nodded. "Sure," I said, and walked away.

. . .

"What was in the packages?" Neary asked, bringing me back to the car.

"Jigsaw puzzles, one of a talking train and another of that furry dinosaur. Somebody's idea of funny." I looked over at Neary. "Tell me it's not a warning shot," I said again.

"To back off of Danes?"

"It's the only thing I'm working on."

Neary shook his head slowly. "I'm not so sure it's Marty."

"Who else can it be? Are you saying that somebody else is running a tail on me, and your guys somehow missed it?"

Neary sighed, and Sikes and Pritchard shifted uncomfortably in the front seat.

"Marty's boys were the only ones we saw out there, and I'm pretty sure they're the ones who took these photos. But I'm not sure Marty organized all this. And if you'd calm down a little and think about it, you might agree."

I took a deep breath and ran my hand across the back of my neck. It was warm and sticky. "Okay, all calm now. What am I supposed to think about?"

"The timing, for one thing," Neary said. "Not even an hour went by between the time we left Marty's office and when you found those pictures. Do you think he had that stuff ready and waiting and that he sent Stevie racing uptown to deliver it as soon as we left?"

I shook my head. "I think he'd set it up already. Our showing up when we did was a coincidence."

Neary raised his eyebrows at me. "You think Marty could be that cool, knowing what was happening while we were sitting in his office? He's not a total idiot, but he's also not that smooth. And what about genius-boy Stevie? He clearly recognized you, even though it took him a while and he didn't know enough to keep it to himself. You think that's the response you would've got out of him if he knew this shit was going down today?"

I rubbed my eyes. "Maybe he didn't know about it," I said. "Maybe Czerka doesn't trust him to know about this stuff."

Neary wasn't buying. "I don't know that Marty trusts anyone, but I do know Stevie does all his fetching and carrying. If Marty arranged this bullshit, Stevie would've known about it, and he would've pissed his pants when he saw you today."

I looked out the window at the doors of Jane's building, and thought about what Neary had said, and grudgingly agreed. The timing didn't make sense and neither did Czerka's behavior, or Stevie's. But my anger wanted a focus, and if not Czerka . . .

"Then who?" I said aloud.

"If we assume Marty's boys took the pictures—and I don't know who else would have—there are only two choices as to who set this up: one of Marty's guys or Marty's client."

"His guys would have no reason to do it," I said.

"None that I can figure."

"Which leaves his client."

"Which leaves his client."

A surge of frustration closed my throat, and I slapped my palm against the window glass. "Which leaves us exactly where we were before—with no fucking idea of who that might be."

"Maybe not exactly where we were," Neary said evenly. "If Marty doesn't know about the pictures, I can use them to shake him up a little and maybe shake something loose." My cell phone trilled and I answered it. It was Jane, ready to leave.

"I'll meet you out front," I told her. I hung up and looked at Neary. "I notice you said *I can use them,* not *we can use them.*"

Neary sighed and was quiet for a while. "I think you're wound a little tight right now, John," he said finally. "I wouldn't want you doing any-thing . . . counterproductive."

I stared at him. "How hard will you go at him?"

Neary's eyes narrowed and Sikes and Pritchard shifted again in their seats. "As hard as I need to," he said. We were quiet for a moment, watching the street.

"When are you going to talk to him? It should be soon—"

"Today," Neary said, cutting me off. "I'll do it today."

"How about the nephew, Stevie? He might go easier than Czerka. He—"

"I'll do what needs doing, John." Neary's voice was tight.

"And that means what?"

"That means part of what you're paying for here is my judgment. That means I'm not going in there high on my own adrenaline and with my head up my ass. That means if what you're looking for is somebody to kneecap these guys, you're on your own." Neary stared at me, and his eyes were flat and unmoving.

I took a deep breath and let it out and nodded. "I don't know if I could take that office again anyway," I said.

Neary smiled a little. He looked beyond me, out the car window. "Here she comes," he said. He slipped the photos into the envelope and passed it to me.

I climbed out of the Volvo. "Call me when you've talked to Czerka. And thanks for sitting out here."

"It'll be on your bill," he said. "You sure you don't want a shadow home?" I shook my head and closed the door and the car pulled away. Jane was watching. She hitched her big black bag higher on her shoulder. There were tight lines around her mouth.

"Was that your friend Neary?" she asked. I nodded. "What was he doing?"

"Waiting for me to get here."

Jane pursed her lips. "What's going on?" she said. We started toward 16th Street and I told her. We walked slowly and Jane listened, and when I was done she didn't speak for several minutes. When she did, her voice was soft and flat.

"The boys were okay?" she asked.

"Probably a little confused, but okay."

"That's good," Jane said.

She was quiet for another half a block.

"And you think this thing is a warning to you—about Danes?" I nodded. "From whoever hired—what's-his-name—Czerka?" I nodded again. "I guess they don't know that you were fired."

"I guess not."

She went silent again, and as we reached the corner of Fifth Avenue and 17th Street, she stopped. "What's the warning?" she asked. "I mean specifically, what message is he sending with those pictures?"

I looked at her and she met my gaze and waited. "I suppose it's a message that he knows what's important to me and that he can . . . get at those things if he wants to. I suppose it's a message about what's at stake if I keep pushing."

"And is he right about what's important to you? I know your nephews are, so he's right about that much." Her face was blank, and her dark eyes were empty.

"I didn't want this, Jane. I don't want anything to happen to you."

"Something already happened to me."

I took a deep breath. "I know."

Jane started walking again. "Why didn't you tell me someone was following you—maybe following both of us?" she said.

"I didn't think they were a threat—until recently I wasn't even sure they were there. And I never thought they were interested in you. You had a lot on your mind, and I didn't want to upset you."

Jane stopped again. She almost spoke, but she bit back the words. She looked at the manila envelope in my hand. "Let me see them."

I shook my head. "You don't—"

"Just give them to me, goddamn it." Her voice was icy. We moved into the doorway of a small office building and I handed her the envelope.

Jane slipped the pictures out and looked at each one. Her face was still and ashen; only her dark eyes moved. She leafed through the stack three times and leaned against the building and was quiet for a while. When she did speak, it was almost to herself.

"They were so close . . . I had no idea."

"Neither did I."

She handed me the envelope. "But now you know," she said. "You have no case and you have no client, but now you know about this. So what will you do?" Her voice was even and without emotion.

"I need to find out who sent this, Jane."

She nodded, unsurprised. "Why?"

I studied her unreadable face and thought about all the answers I could give—that the best way to keep her and my nephews safe was to find whoever made this threat and send a message of my own, that I didn't like being pushed around, that I needed to know what the hell was going on, that I needed to keep working. All of them were true and none of them seemed adequate and finally I said nothing.

After a while we walked again. Jane slowed as we came to 16th Street and looked down the block. I followed her eyes as they scanned the people and parked cars, and I saw a grimace cross her face and a shudder go through her shoulders.

"Let's get something to eat," she said, without looking at me.

We kept going south, to a coffee shop off Union Square, and had a silent meal amid a chattering crowd. We went back to 16th Street afterwards, and Jane's steps were quick and resolute down the block and into the lobby of our building. I rang for the elevator and she dug in her bag and pulled out her house keys. We got in and I pressed four. Jane pressed five. She watched the numbers light as we rose. The doors opened on four and I got out.

"I don't want these things in my life," Jane said. I started to speak, but the doors began to close, and as they did something shifted in Jane's face.

Her mouth got smaller and the fine creases around it curved downward. And something happened in her eyes like a shutter opening. They grew darker and larger and brimmed for an instant with anger and disappointment. And then the doors shut and the car rose again.

I heard Jane moving around upstairs and I heard music come on: Chrissie Hynde, turned up loud. I checked my messages. There were three from Lauren and I didn't bother to listen.

I poured myself a large glass of water and drank it while I paced the room and let my anger steep. I thought about Marty Czerka's mystery client and what he might want with Gregory Danes. I thought about the small handful of people I'd found in Danes's life and wondered which of them might care enough to hire a guy like Czerka.

I thought about Neary, too, and wondered how his conversation was going. I wasn't optimistic. It wasn't that I doubted Neary's skill at the back-and-forth; I didn't. I've seen him play the good guy, the tough guy, the burned-out-doesn't-give-a-shit guy, and the fucking-crazy guy, and he's better at it than most. But Czerka had no doubt played those parts himself, and while Neary might surprise him, I didn't think he'd get him talking.

No, Stevie was definitely the weak link in that shop; he was the guy I'd go at first. But Stevie might need a little encouragement, and that's where Neary would draw the line.

I stopped my pacing and thought about Stevie's broken nose, and about his bruises and stitches and splinted fingers, and I remembered what Richard Gilpin had told me, back in Fort Lee. *The office isn't open to the public, and management gets real nervous about visitors. From what I heard, the last guy who came sniffing around here was lucky to get out with all his fingers attached.*

The phone rang and I jumped. It was Neary. He was calling from a car and he sounded exhausted.

"I took a run at Marty," he said, "and got nowhere." Neary waited for me to say something, but I didn't. He went on. "He was surprised, no question about it, but you saw—he dances pretty good for a fat man and he wouldn't admit to anything. In fact, he seems to know less now than when we saw him this afternoon."

"What about Stevie?"

"There was no sign of him in the office. I had Juan check out the neighborhood watering holes, but he had no luck. I sent Eddie out to his place in Queens. We'll keep an eye out there and at the office until he turns up." Neary yawned deeply. "I'm sorry about this, John."

"You should get some sleep."

"We'll find him, if not tonight, then tomorrow or the day after."

"Sure," I said.

Sure, unless Uncle Marty finds him first and tells him to shut the hell up and runs him out of town for a while. I thought some more about Stevie and his broken fingers and about what Gromyko had said, the last time I had seen him.

It is possible that I could be of assistance to you, Mr. March, but I do not operate a charitable organization. My advisory services are valuable, and for them I expect payment in kind.

I sat at the table and thought about how long it might take to locate Stevie and how much coaching he might get by then. I rubbed my eyes and thought about Goran and Gromyko and deals with the devil and payment in kind. I thought about the manila envelope and about the pictures inside. I punched the number for Morgan & Lynch in Fort Lee, and a woman answered. She sounded like the tattooed girl.

"This is March," I said. "I want to talk to Gromyko." I gave her my number and she hung up. I sat and waited for a call back and listened to the music coming through the ceiling. It was louder now, and punctuated by the angry staccato of Jane working combinations on the heavy bag.

24

I slept badly that night and met Gromyko the next morning in the Conservatory Garden in Central Park. I took a long and elaborate route to ensure that I got there unescorted, and I arrived early, at just after eight. I entered at 105th Street, and the sound of morning traffic on Fifth Avenue faded behind me as I passed through the Vanderbilt Gate and into the Italian-style section of the garden. It was a warm morning, with a breeze and some fat clouds in a Wedgwood sky, but it was just past opening time and the garden was nearly empty. There was a well-dressed elderly couple making their slow way south, toward the English garden, and a willowy woman with long blond hair and a flowing flimsy skirt standing near the wrought-iron pergola. I headed north, past a row of blossoming crab apple trees and into the French-style garden. The tulips were still in bloom, and their bright heavy heads bobbed a little in the little wind.

Gromyko was early too, and he was standing by the fountain. He wore loafers and loose white trousers and a band-collared shirt with the sleeves rolled up. He was looking at the bronzes—three dancing maidens—and at the water that rose and fell between their elegant arms, and his blond hair shone in the sunlight. The Ukrainian Jay Gatsby. He walked toward me and his movements were precise but also graceful and relaxed. His canted gray eyes were as cold as ever.

"You are more than prompt, Mr. March," he said.

"It's a nice morning."

Gromyko nodded. "And the gardens are particularly nice in this season." We walked slowly down the path, flanked by vast beds of tulips, and a little of yesterday's heat seemed to come up at us from the soil. "I walk here every morning, but spring mornings are the best." Gromyko saw my surprise and a smile disturbed his pale features. "It is not a long walk, Mr. March, I live just over there." He pointed south and east.

"Not in Jersey?"

Gromyko snorted a little. "No, not in New Jersey," he said. He came to a stop by a stone bench and put a foot on its edge and folded his arms across his chest. "And now business. You said last night that you wished to consult me." I nodded. "And you recall that I operate on a quid pro quo basis, yes?"

"I recall."

"And when the time comes that I require payment?" Gromyko fixed his gray eyes on me, and despite the sunlight a chill spread through my limbs.

"I pull my weight," I said. "Within reason."

Gromyko smiled a little. "Always within reason, Mr. March."

"Let's not get ahead of ourselves here. I haven't asked you anything and you haven't answered. So it remains to be seen how much help you can be."

Gromyko smiled again, patiently this time, as if at a quarrelsome child. "I am at your disposal," he said quietly.

"That day in the garage, you weren't surprised when I told you I was working a missing persons case. And you didn't press me about it. You didn't ask who was missing, or much of anything else."

The little smile stayed on Gromyko's face. "No, I did not."

"I think that was because you already knew who I was looking for."

A nod. "I did."

"Because I wasn't the first person to come looking for this guy and wanting to talk to Gilpin. Someone else had been there before me."

Gromyko's smile widened slightly. "Someone much less . . . *civilized*, Mr. March."

"Stevie," I said.

Gromyko shrugged. "I do not recall his name. He was a bodybuilder, impolite and stupid—an unfortunate combination."

"But he worked for Marty Czerka?" A look of disdain came and went across Gromyko's face, and he nodded. "How did you meet?" I asked.

"He accosted Gilpin outside the office, but failed to notice that two of my men were with him at the time. They sent Gilpin upstairs and called me."

"And you questioned him—somewhat vigorously." Gromyko said nothing. "And he told you . . . what?"

"Everything he knew. Which was very little."

"But he told you he was working a missing persons case."

Gromyko nodded again. "Yes. He was looking for Gilpin's half brother, Gregory Danes," he said.

"And he also told you who his client was?" I held my breath waiting for the answer.

"Yes, he told me that too," Gromyko said.

"And?"

"And now we agree that I have been helpful to you, yes, Mr. March?" His eyes narrowed again and caught mine. The breeze picked up and blew around a heavy scent of topsoil.

"We agree."

"Just so we are not ahead of ourselves," Gromyko said, and he smiled icily. "Jeremy Pflug. His client is named Jeremy Pflug." Gromyko spelled it for me.

"Who is he?"

He shook his head. "Google him, Mr. March; you will find out all you need to know."

"You don't know anything more about him than that?"

Gromyko sighed. "I satisfied myself that Stevie was telling me what he believed was true. And Gilpin assured me that he has nothing to do with his brother, and that he knows nothing of this Pflug. And Gilpin knows better than to lie to me. So I satisfied myself that this matter did not concern me.

"My business is growing rapidly, Mr. March, and it is demanding of my time. Where no clear need or benefit exists, I do not meddle in the affairs of others—a practice you would be wise to consider." Gromyko straightened and checked his watch. "If there is nothing else . . . ?"

"When did you have this talk with Stevie?"

"Some time ago—ten days, perhaps, before your visit."

"Any more signs of a tail since your man saw that blue van?"

"No," he said, and looked at his watch again. "And now I must go." His pale face was expressionless.

"Thank you," I said.

He nodded slowly. "Indeed," he said, and he turned and went south, into the Italian garden. I watched him walk past the line of crab apple trees and pause near the Vanderbilt Gate. The willowy blond woman unfolded herself from a bench and drifted across the garden to join him. She was just his height, and she leaned into him and took his hand and whispered something in his ear. Gromyko nodded at whatever she said, and the blond woman clutched his arm and kissed him. A swatch of laughter, high and girlish, fluttered across the garden like a leaf. And then they were through the gate and out of sight.

I sat on the stone bench and listened to the distant traffic sounds and thought for a while about the bargain I had struck with Gromyko. I wondered what he would ask in return for his favor and when he would ask it, and if our ideas about what was within reason would be even remotely similar. And what I would do if they weren't. And what he would do. I shook my head. It was pointless to speculate now, pointless to worry; the deal was done and I had a name. When the time came, I'd pull my weight— one way or another—but right now I had a name. The sun was warm on my shoulders and the bench was warm beneath me, and in a minute or two the frost seeped from my arms and legs.

I walked across the park to 96th Street, and caught a subway downtown. The Brill offices were still quiet. Neary was clean-shaven, clear-eyed, and blue-suited, and only mildly surprised to see me. I shut the office door.

"There's nothing yet on Stevie," he said.

"Don't worry about it. I've got a name."

"From who?" he asked.

"From somebody reliable."

"Somebody who's currently in one piece?"

"He was the last time I saw him."

Neary smiled a little. "I'm relieved. What's the name?"

"Jeremy Pflug." I spelled it for him, as Gromyko had for me. "No one I've heard of, but Google will reportedly tell us all we need to know."

Neary rolled over to his keyboard. "All we need to know for free, anyway, but it's a place to start. Drag a chair over."

We were at it for two hours, at first on Google, then on a variety of subscription services, and finally in a proprietary Brill database. It may not have been everything there was to know about Jeremy Pflug, but it was enough—and it was strange.

If you believed the overheated prose on the Web site of Scepter Intelligence, the company he had founded and of which he was president and chief executive, Jeremy Pflug was a larger-than-life character, a unique hybrid of Sir Richard Burton, Wild Bill Donovan, and the hero of a very thick paperback thriller.

According to his corporate bio, Pflug was in his late forties, Ivy educated, and a polyglot, with graduate degrees in economics and international affairs. He was a veteran of the U.S. Navy, where he had been a lieutenant commander and served with Special Forces teams. After the navy, he did stints as a war correspondent, a CIA analyst, and a bond trader, all as prelude to founding Scepter. His hobbies included sailing, caving, and martial arts. There was no mention of his favorite color.

There were many photos of Pflug on the Scepter Web site, in many valiant poses. There was Pflug as T. E. Lawrence, standing by a sand-pitted jeep, squinting out over a dusty steppe; swashbuckling Pflug, at the helm of a storm-tossed sailboat, squinting out over the merciless waves; Pflug as master of the universe, leaning insouciantly on a Bloomberg terminal, squinting out over a chaotic trading floor. There was Pflug the corporate pitchman, touting Scepter's services to a clutch of rapt executives; Pflug the inspirational leader, exhorting a roomful of fresh-faced young suits; and Pflug the expert, lecturing some plump Rotarians about homeland security. In all of them, he looked tall and lean and, if not exactly handsome, then at least rugged, tough, and daring. The vanity was unabashed and amusing.

The small portions of the Scepter site not devoted to Pflug himself were given over to a lot of drivel about the equivalence of commerce and war, the competitive advantage of knowledge, and the value of timely intelligence. It was unoriginal and sometimes incoherent stuff, heavily laced with—though not redeemed by—Pflug's musings on warfare, strategy, and tactics, all of which were mangled paraphrasings of Sun Tzu, Carl von Clausewitz, and Vince Lombardi. I read that Scepter was *an intelligence firm for the new millennium* but otherwise had no clue of what it did. Neary scanned the screen and shook his head. He laughed outright when we got to the other stuff.

The other stuff came mostly from a lengthy article, published a couple of years back in an irreverent monthly magazine, on the qualifications of some of the experts engaged by the cable news channels to provide color commentary on the last war. One of those so-called experts was Jeremy Pflug, and there was apparently much less to him than met the eye.

Starting with his academic background. Under the reporter's close inspection, Pflug's Ivy education became a freshman year in New Haven and a bachelor of arts from a West Coast diploma mill, the same fine institution that later awarded him his graduate degrees. The language skills consisted mainly of high-school Spanish, and—according to an unnamed source—the ability to bargain with hookers in French and German.

Pflug's claims of military service were slightly more legitimate. He had in fact been in the navy and had achieved the rank of lieutenant commander. But his service with Special Forces teams might more accurately have been termed service *of* Special Forces teams—as his primary duties had been those of a supply officer.

His CV stretched the truth even thinner when it came to his career after the navy. His experience as a war correspondent amounted to six months as a mostly unpaid stringer for a now-defunct news service. His beat was Singapore—not exactly downtown Beirut, as the author of the magazine article pointed out. His claim to have been a CIA analyst was even more tenuous. In fact, Pflug was a temp at a DC consulting firm that was hired by the Agency to analyze administrative costs. Similarly, "bond trader" was Pflug's spin on his nine months as a trader's assistant at a second-rate broker-dealer in Baltimore. The article, apparently, marked the end of Pflug's career in broadcast.

The subscription services and the Brill database confirmed some of what was in the article but shed no light on Pflug's company, Scepter Intelligence. As it was a privately held firm, there was no information available on its other officers, its revenues, its employees, or its clients, and what little we did come across was a rehash of what was on their Web site:

*Offices in Washington, New York, and London. Practice areas
include financial services, technology, media, and energy. Strategic
and tactical engagements.*

Neary leaned back in his chair and stretched. "I've got to get this guy to work on my résumé," he said, laughing. "A little tweaking, and it can read like I was attorney general."

"Or even postmaster general. But who is this guy, and what does he actually do? And what's his interest in Danes?"

"Assuming it is *his* interest," Neary said.

"As opposed to . . . ?"

"As opposed to a client's interest."

"Another fucking cutout . . . great." I shook my head. "So who's his client, and what the hell does *he* want with Danes?"

Neary smiled. "First things first," he said. "Let's start with who this guy is and what he does. What was the name of the magazine reporter?"

I looked down at my pad. "George L. Gerber, out of LA," I read.

Neary's fingers were busy again and he was quiet for a moment, reading his screen. "There we go. Think it's too early to call out West?" But he was already working the phone.

It wasn't too early for George L. Gerber. He was awake and alert over the phone speaker, and there was a prickly hint of Brooklyn in his voice. But he was pleasant enough, until we told him what we wanted to talk about. Then there was silence on the line, followed by some very careful questions about who we were. We gave him answers, and he said he'd call us back. Neary started to give him his direct number, but Gerber stopped him.

"I'll find the number for Brill in New York," he said. "If I can't reach you there, I don't want to talk to you." Five minutes later he was on the line again.

"So what's your interest in him?" Gerber asked. There was still plenty of caution in his voice.

"We tripped across him in a case we're working," Neary said. "We're looking for some background on him and thought you might help us out. You're the closest we've come to a Pflug expert."

"You got that right," Gerber said, with a bitter laugh. "But if you read my article, you already know the important stuff—that he's a lying, self-aggrandizing creep. I don't know what I can add."

"What can you tell us about Scepter Intelligence?" I asked. "You didn't say much about the company in your piece."

"Besides Pflug, there isn't a lot to say about Scepter. I mean, Pflug *is* Scepter."

"Their Web site sure makes it sound that way," Neary said. "Of course, it makes it sound like a lot of the civilized world depends on Pflug, just to hold things together."

Gerber didn't laugh. "I wasn't joking, Neary. He really *is* the company. I mean, from everything I learned, Pflug is the only employee of Scepter Intelligence."

Neary looked at me and I looked back, and we were quiet for a while. Gerber helped us out.

"The Web site's a Potemkin village, and all the offices—in DC and New

York and London—they're just serviced space. For a few hundred a month he gets a respectable address, a phone number, a receptionist, a place to get mail, and a decent conference room when he needs to have a meeting. As far as I could tell, the company mainly exists in Pflug's condo, out in the northern Virginia burbs."

"So he does all the work?" I asked.

"He's more like a contractor. He gets the gigs and hires on whatever help he needs—day labor, specialists, even other companies—for however long he needs them. He manages them and slaps a big markup on every job."

"What kinds of jobs, George?" Neary asked. "What's he selling, and who's he selling it to?"

Gerber snorted. "He calls it *private intelligence* and *opposition research* and a few other pretentious euphemisms, but what it is, is spying—dirty tricks, creeping and peeping, buying and selling secrets, smear campaigns—all that good stuff. Pflug's a corporate spook, and despite what a creep he is—or maybe because of it—he's a good one." Neary looked at me and raised his eyebrows.

"And his clients?" Neary asked.

"He keeps that a secret," Gerber said. "And the people and companies that buy his services tend not to talk about it much."

"You never ran across any of them doing your research?" Neary said.

"The closest I came were some guys who did freelance work for him over the years. They're how I first got on to what his business was really all about. Pflug never let them anywhere near clients, but they knew who their targets were. They wouldn't share any names with me, no matter how many drinks I bought them—I think they were afraid of being implicated in anything—but two of them said the list included *a lot of Wall Street assholes*. And that's a quote."

Neary and I looked at each other again. "Think we could have a chat with some of those guys?" I asked.

Gerber laughed. "Sorry, boys, that's how somebody like me loses all his reporter merit badges. Pardon my French, but no fucking way."

Neary shrugged, and we were quiet for a while, thinking.

"How do you know he's good at it?" I asked Gerber finally.

"What?"

"If you never spoke to any of his clients, how do you know that Pflug is good at his work?"

There was a long silence on the phone speaker.

"You still there, George?" Neary asked.

"I'm here," Gerber said. His voice was a little choked.

Neary looked at me and raised his eyebrows. "You doing okay?" he said to the phone.

"I'm all right," Gerber said.

"Did we hit a nerve, George?" Neary asked. "Was that a bad question?"

Gerber coughed a little. "No, no, it was the right thing to ask," he said. "It's what I would've asked." Another cough. "I know that Pflug is good at what he does because for a while, after that article came out, I was one of his targets."

"What happened?" I asked.

Gerber sighed. "It was little shit at first: hang-up phone calls in the office and on my cell and at home. And then I began to notice that they were timed—just when I'd get to my desk in the morning, just when I'd get in my car, just when I'd get home—as if someone was watching me. Then my mail started getting fucked up. Bills came late, and the envelopes looked like they'd been tampered with. Some bills never came at all. Then one day I got no mail at all, just a mailbox filled with dog shit.

"After that he moved on to the office. A woman down in sales started getting harassing e-mail—pornographic e-mail—that looked as if it was coming from my computer. From me. And just like the phone calls, they were timed; she'd only get them when I was at my desk. And then . . ." Gerber paused and coughed some more. "Then, my editor gets a fax—anonymous—that purports to be from an employee who's too frightened to come forward directly. The fax tells him he should check out my computer, that I've been downloading all sorts of . . . pictures . . . of kids, for chrissakes . . ." Gerber paused again and sighed heavily.

Neary spoke to him, and his voice was surprisingly gentle. "You must've had some idea where this was coming from, George. You must've thought of Pflug first thing."

"Of course I did," Gerber said. "As soon as the phone calls started. And I told my editor and our lawyers and the cops about them right away. That's probably what saved my ass. Because these e-mails and the shit they found on my computer—the pictures—they all looked like the real deal. And there were no signs of tampering, no traces of intrusion, no traces of anything—not on my computer, or my phones, or my mailbox. Nothing."

"When you told the police about the phone calls, did they put traps on your line?" Neary asked.

"Sure they did, at which point the calls stopped. And that was the pattern: I was always playing catch-up. As soon as I talked to the postal inspectors about my mail, the mail tampering stopped and the e-mail shit started. When that happened, our tech guys put some sort of monitor on my account, after which there were no more harassing messages. And then my boss got the fax."

"Did anybody ever confront Pflug?"

"Several times. He claimed to have no knowledge of anything, of course, and he could prove he was on the other side of the country when this shit was happening. There was no evidence that pointed to him—or to anyone else, for that matter."

"Are you sure it was Pflug?" I asked.

Gerber was quiet again and I worried that I'd angered him, but when he spoke his voice was soft.

"After the business with the fax and the pictures, things went quiet. A week, a month, two months go by and nothing happens, and I'm thinking it's finally over. And then . . ." Gerber coughed softly a few times and took a deep breath. "Then one night I come home and my dog—his name was Murrow—is gone. He was a fat old Lab, arthritic and deaf and half blind, who'd sleep all day in the back yard. He barely got himself up to take a leak anymore, and on his best day he couldn't have jumped my fence, any more than he could've opened the gate by himself. But he was gone.

"I called the cops, and ten minutes later a prowl car came to my house. They took me up the ridge to the edge of a ravine, and . . . down below was Murrow." He paused again and sniffed. "A jogger had phoned it in just an hour before, and she was all freaked out. And why not? I mean, how often do you see a headless dog?"

Gerber sighed heavily. Neary looked at me and shook his head.

"The cops told me it was probably local kids. They said they'd had problems with pet killings in some neighborhoods on the other side of the canyon, and this was probably the same thing. They said they'd be working it, but they didn't sound hopeful."

"What did you think?" I asked.

"Not much of anything, just then. I was . . . I was pretty much in shock. But afterward . . . I knew."

"What happened?"

"About a month later, I was having lunch with a friend of mine at a place in Santa Monica and the waiter comes over and tells me I have a call on their pay phone. I pick it up, and on the other end is Pflug. He tells me he's calling to say how sorry he was to hear about my dog, and isn't it terrible about kids today, and what's wrong with our cities anyway? And then he laughs like a maniac, and says I can change my underwear now because he's done with me. And then he hangs up."

"*Was* he done?" Neary asked.

"Nothing else happened—except I didn't get a decent night's sleep for about a year afterward."

"You go to the cops about it?" I said.

"And say what? I had no proof of anything, and by then I knew Pflug didn't leave a trail." Gerber was quiet for some time, and then he found his voice and his bitter laugh again. "So that's how I know Pflug is good at his work. That's my cautionary tale. Any other questions?"

Neary and I looked at each other. We were out of questions, and we told Gerber so and thanked him for his time.

"I can't say it was a pleasure, but if it serves to screw up Pflug a little, I'm glad to do it. Any chance you guys want to tell me a little more about what's going on?"

Neary smiled. "Sorry, George, but in the words of a fine journalist I know: *no fucking way.*"

Gerber laughed. "Then I wish you luck—and if you get the chance, give that bastard a kick in the nuts for me . . . and give him one for Murrow too."

Gerber hung up and Neary rubbed his eyes. "Hell of a guy, this Pflug," he said. "Maybe I *won't* let him work on my résumé." I nodded. "Those pictures—of Jane and your nephews—from what Gerber said, they seem to be right up his alley."

"It seems so."

Neary looked at me. "Chances are, he won't tell us shit about who his client is."

"Nevertheless, I'm looking forward to the discussion."

25

Neary said he would work on a meet with Pflug, and I didn't object. Chances were, Pflug would be more receptive to his approach than to mine, and I knew Neary didn't entirely trust me to manage it without bloodshed anyway. I took a subway uptown, and the ride to Union Square was filled with the memory of those photographs, the look on Jane's face as the elevator doors slid shut, and the choked sound of George L. Gerber's voice. By the time I got home, my head was aching and my teeth were clenched.

The only things new at my place were the phone messages. One was from Lauren.

"It's me again. Will you please just give me a call?" No. The next one was from Paul Gargosian. His gravelly voice was full of amusement.

"This is one hell of a game of phone tag we got going. Call me back or stop by the building if you want. I'm pulling double shifts the next two days."

And that was all; there was nothing from Jane or anyone else. I looked around my apartment, at the dust motes and the empty space, and thought about the prospect of waiting there for Neary's call. I decided to take Gargosian up on his invitation.

. . .

A couple of weeks in Florida had left Paul Gargosian deeply tanned, and his teeth were very bright when he smiled. He was fifty-something, and broad-shouldered, and his black hair was dense and curly and dusted with gray. His thick nose was starting to peel. It could've been the lingering effects of vacation that made him seem so relaxed and affable, but somehow—from the spray of laugh lines around his eyes and the timbre of his voice—I suspected he was always that way.

"I wasn't sure you were for real," he said, smiling. His hands were wide and calloused, and his handshake was strong. "I figured maybe you were just a recording."

"Some days I think the same thing," I said. "You have time to talk now?"

"Sure," he said. He held the door and ushered me into the lobby and over to the concierge station. "What's so important you had to call a dozen times?" he asked.

"I'm looking for Gregory Danes," I said. His eyebrows went up. I lied a little and told him I was working for Danes's ex, who hadn't heard from him since he'd left weeks before, and who was getting worried. "The guy filling in for you—Christopher—said you knew most of the tenants."

At the mention of Christopher's name, Gargosian rolled his eyes. "A recommendation from Chrissy—there's a career highlight."

"You know anything about where Danes is?"

Gargosian shook his head. "The last time I saw him was, I guess, the morning he left. It was early, and I brought his bags down and held them here while he went for his car. Then I loaded him up and he drove away. I haven't seen him since."

"No mention of where he was headed or when he'd be back?"

Gargosian grimaced a little. "He's not real talkative—not to the guys who work here, anyway. He said he was going away for a while—that's what he said, *a while*—and he was having his mail held. That was it."

"Has he ever gone away this long before?"

"He's been away two, three weeks at a time before—maybe a little longer—but not like this."

"He have a lot of luggage that morning?"

"A couple of bags, a briefcase—no problem fitting 'em in the trunk."

"And he was alone?"

Gargosian's eyes narrowed momentarily. "Yep."

"Was he usually?"

"What's that mean?" His voice was fractionally less friendly.

"It means, did he have a lot of visitors? A lot of houseguests? Girl-friends, boyfriends—that sort of thing?"

Gargosian's voice chilled by another few degrees. "What is this, anyway? Are you looking for a missing guy or is this some kind of divorce thing?"

"It's not a divorce thing," I said. "I don't care what Danes does or who he does it with, I'm just trying to find the guy."

Gargosian nodded slowly and relaxed a little. "It's just that I went through a fucking evil time with my own ex, so I'm a little touchy. I don't want to go telling tales."

"Sure," I said, and kept looking at him.

"He didn't have a lot of visitors. His kid was probably the most regular; he'd come by every few weeks or so."

"No girlfriends?"

"Not lately."

"How about before lately?" Gargosian hesitated, and I helped him out. "How about a pretty blonde who's shorter than she looks on TV?"

He looked relieved. "What do you need me for? You seem to know it all already."

"Confirmation helps," I said. "Anybody besides Sovitch?"

"No, just her. But for a while now, not even her."

"How long a while?"

He shrugged. "It's got to be six months at least."

"She was a pretty regular visitor before then?"

"It was kind of tapering off, I think. But for a while there it was two or three nights a week." Gargosian's eyes shifted to the doors and he loped across the lobby and held them for an attractive blond woman pushing a baby carriage. He walked them to the elevators and came back to the concierge station.

"Danes have many friends in the building—anybody he might've told where he was going?" I asked.

Gargosian shook his head. "He's not a real sociable guy."

"According to his son, he's got at least one friend in the building—someone he goes to hear music with."

Gargosian thought for a moment and began to nod. "He *had* one friend, more like: the old fellow, Mr. Cortese—Joseph—and a nicer guy you'll never meet. Hell of a sad thing when he passed. He was a real music buff, and friendly with Danes. They went to concerts together and stuff."

"White-haired guy—mostly bald on top—with a narrow face and hollow cheeks?" I asked. He nodded. "When did he pass away?"

"Last year, right around Thanksgiving. Bad heart."

"He live alone?"

"All alone. The missus was long gone."

A FedEx truck double-parked in front of the building. The driver waved at Gargosian and started stacking boxes on a hand truck. Gargosian waved back.

"I got to get the service door," he said, and went out to the street.

I leaned on the marble counter and thought about Danes and his late friend. Now I had a name to go with the face in the photos—Joseph Cortese—but I wasn't sure what that led to besides another dead end. My head was aching again and I was tired, and I wondered how Neary was faring in tracking down Pflug. I pressed my fingers to my temples but it didn't help. Gargosian returned and I hauled my thoughts back to Danes and Cortese.

"You said they went to concerts together." Gargosian nodded. "Here in the city?"

"Carnegie Hall, Lincoln Center, up at St. John's—the old guy talked about it all the time. And in the warm weather he'd go someplace up in Westchester. And he went to the mountains, too—the Berkshires. He had a house up there, and he'd go for big chunks of the summer. Danes went with him now and then."

"You know if Cortese had family? Anyone he was close to?"

Gargosian tilted his head a little. "We're getting kind of far from Danes, aren't we?"

"I'm looking for someone to talk to about this place in the Berkshires."

"The old guy had a nephew, but I don't know how close they were. He'd come around sometimes; he still does."

"Cortese's apartment hasn't been sold?"

"The nephew owns it now. Like I said, he comes by once in a while."

"Any idea where he lives?" Gargosian shook his head. "How about a name?"

"Don't know his first name, but his last name's Cortese."

I pulled a card from my pocket. "Can I leave this for him, for the next time he comes in?" Gargosian looked skeptical but took the card. "What about neighbors?" I asked. "Does Danes get along with his?"

Gargosian looked puzzled for a second. "I didn't explain it right, did I? Mr. Cortese was in apartment Twenty-C; he *was* Danes's neighbor, pretty much the only one. The other two units up there are owned by a corporation, and they're empty most of the time."

I thought about that for a while, and about the disheveled-looking man I'd seen coming off the elevator and going into 20-C, the day I'd creeped Danes's apartment. "What does the nephew look like?" I asked.

Gargosian thought for a moment. "A very big guy, not young . . . balding, with some dark hair around the sides . . . a big face . . . glasses. Kind of . . . messy." That was him. Gargosian looked at his watch. "If there's nothing else, I've got to get to the mail."

I nodded. "Thanks for your time."

"Hope I was worth the wait," he said, and held the door for me.

I hailed a cab on Lex and rolled the window down. We pulled away from the curb and a diesel wind rushed in at me. I thought about what Paul Gargosian had told me. Joseph Cortese seemed to be the closest thing to an actual friend of Danes that I'd come across so far. Except that I hadn't really come across him, as he'd been dead for going on six months.

That six-month period couldn't have been a pleasant one for Gregory Danes. Cortese died; Sovitch stopped coming around; a custody battle erupted with Nina Sachs; and Turpin had shown up at Pace-Loyette with a mandate to settle the claims that Danes wanted to fight. Not an easy time. Who could blame the guy for going away? Who could blame him for not coming back? I thought about how I might find Cortese's nephew, but I was tired and my mind kept wandering to Neary and Pflug.

The phone was ringing as I came through the door. It was Neary.

"I found him," he said.

"Where?"

"Here, in town."

"Is he willing to meet?"

"He said he'd be more than happy to. He even invited us to his rented conference room."

"When?"

"Six o'clock this evening," Neary said. I wrote down the address.

"Doesn't sound like it was too hard to get hold of him."

"I just called the numbers on his Web site."

"Was he surprised to hear from you?" I asked.

"Not even a little."

I met Neary in front of an undistinguished glass box on Park Avenue and 38th Street. We signed in and rode up together in silence. The company that provided Pflug with his New York address occupied the entire twelfth floor. The reception area was windowless and softly lit. The magazines were plentiful but out-of-date and the plump furniture was slightly shabby, and it looked like the business-class lounge of a failing airline. But for two receptionists preparing to leave, the room was empty.

They were making final adjustments to hair and makeup when we came in, and they eyed us warily. The short redhead with the diamond chip in her nose buzzed Pflug and led us to a conference room.

"It'll be just a minute," she said, and left us alone.

I sat in a scuffed leather chair at the long scuffed conference table and took a few slow breaths to bring my heart rate down. I looked out the window at the dim view of 38th Street. Neary sat across from me.

"I should do the talking," he said.

"Sure." I kept looking at the view.

"You should mostly just sit there."

"Sure."

"And not say much."

"Uh-huh."

Neary looked at me and sighed. Five minutes later the conference room door opened and Pflug walked in.

He was a lanky six-two, and there was a lot of elbow and knee in his gait as he shut the door and moved to the head of the table. His khaki shirt had epaulets and many pockets, and his olive-drab pants were held in place by a wide leather belt, adorned near the buckle with the brass end of a shotgun shell. His long head was topped by a brush of salt-and-pepper hair, and his sunburned face was meaty, and acne-scarred on one side. He pulled out a chair and folded his long arms and legs and sat. He looked at us with pale eyes and showed a lot of horsy teeth when he smiled.

"Tom, John, what can I do for you gentlemen today?" His voice was deep and theatrically haughty, like a bad Bill Buckley impersonation. He tapped at the side of his pockmarked nose. Neary looked at me and I said nothing.

"Mr. March is my client, and he would like to know why you've hired people to have him watched."

Pflug turned to me and grinned and shook his head. "Where does this come from, John? What could I possibly know about this?" He spread his large hands in staged confusion. I said nothing.

"He'd also like to know what your interest is in Gregory Danes," Neary said.

Pflug's toothy smile got larger and more disingenuous. Again he turned to me. "As a matter of professional curiosity, John, do you discuss your cases with just anyone who comes in off the street? Not that I know anything about this Danes, mind you, or about people following people; I'm just curious. Is that all it takes for you to bend over, John—just someone asking?" His pale eyes locked on mine and sparkled like broken glass. I stayed quiet.

Neary cleared his throat. "Mr. March recently received some photographs of a threatening nature. We have reason to believe you sent them, and we'd like to know why."

Pflug's smile stayed wide, and he didn't take his eyes off me. "Well, I guess everyone's got a right to their beliefs, even here in godless New York City. But belief is one thing and fact is quite another. Now, what was in these photographs that could be so threatening to a strapping fellow like you, John? Or are you just the nervous kind, perhaps, the kind that scares easily? I suppose that's no surprise, considering what you've been through, upstate and all. I suppose that's enough to leave anyone a little . . . skittish."

Neary rapped on the table. "Hey, squire, over here," he said.

Pflug turned his head slowly and smiled at Neary, but when he spoke it was to me. "Is that why Tom has come along today—because you're easily frightened?"

"Those photos could constitute harassment, Pflug," Neary said. "Maybe worse, with a sympathetic prosecutor. And this little display doesn't help. But we know you're just a hired man. Let's talk about who put you up to this."

Pflug smirked. "That was probably more effective when you were with the Bureau, wasn't it? It's easier when you've got a badge." He turned back to me. "So what *was* in those frightening photos?" I took another deep breath and let it out very slowly. I pursed my lips but kept quiet.

Neary shook his head and changed tack. "What are you doing in New York, anyway? From what I heard, you work out of Virginia—in your garage or something."

Pflug didn't like that. His brow wrinkled momentarily and his thin lips curled in a scowl, but he recovered quickly.

"You know, I ask myself the same question: *What are you doing in this city, Jeremy?* Between the foreigners and all the domestic whiners and complainers, I feel as if I'm in another country when I come here. Lord, I feel as if I'm on another *planet.* I don't know how you stand it. But hang on—you're actually *from* here, aren't you, John? You actually *grew up* here. Well, maybe that explains it." He showed me more teeth, and his eyes found mine again.

"You don't like leaving the country?" Neary asked. "Then what's with all the foreign-correspondent CIA bullshit on your Web site? Or is this Long Island lockjaw routine the bullshit part?"

Pflug's eyes narrowed and his face clouded with brief irritation. "Your friend is taking us away from our conversation, John. Let's get back to those photographs. Maybe if you'd tell me what was in them, it would stir some memories."

I nodded slowly.

Neary rapped on the table again. "Look. We know you're interested in Danes, and you know we are, too. Maybe we can cooperate here."

Pflug laughed. It was loud and braying, and it went on too long. "Well, that's very generous," he said finally. "But I don't think I could hold up my end of the bargain. I've got nothing to say about this Danes, and—truth be told—I'm not really a very *cooperative* fellow. At any rate, I don't think John here has his mind on that business anymore. I think he's got his mind on those photographs." He turned to me again. "Now, how about telling me a little about what was in those pictures. There was nothing of a *personal* nature, was there? No pictures of you and that Chinese girl of yours? Because from where I sit, that would be rude."

I looked at Neary. "This is pointless." I sighed. "He isn't going to help himself." I shook my head and got up from my seat. Pflug laughed loudly and stood up too, and as he did I whipped my right forearm into the side of his head. He went backward over the top of his chair and came down loud and hard, and before I could do anything else Neary had his hand on my chest. I leaned against it for a moment and then stepped back. My heart was pounding and adrenaline was careening through my veins.

Pflug rolled to his feet. He came up quickly and gracefully, a step out of my range and with his hands in front of him. His eyes were unfocused for a moment, but he shook it off and bent his legs and balanced nicely. A red welt was growing along the left side of his face. He touched it with his fingertips.

"*Now* we're getting to the point," he whispered.

Neary turned to him and put out his other hand. "Right there is fine," he said softly. He turned back to me. "You done now?" His voice was calm. "You satisfy your inner idiot?" I looked beyond him, at Pflug, and nodded minutely. Neary followed my gaze. "And you?" he asked. Pflug grinned. I was pleased to see there was blood in his mouth.

"I'm just fine," he said. He was breathing hard and fighting to control it.

"Then I think we're done here," Neary said to me. I nodded. He moved to the door and Pflug opened it. He stepped aside and made a little bow and started tucking in his shirt. Neary went through and I followed, and as I passed him, Pflug twisted his hips and his left arm snapped out and up at my face. I was looking for it but not at that speed, and he tagged me hard under the eye with the back of his fist. My head jerked sideways and filled with flares of pain and light and I shuffled back. I heard rather than saw him closing and I brought my hands up and tucked my chin down. I turned my body and his boot smacked my right arm, just above the elbow. It was like a brick shot from a cannon, and I staggered back. Numbness spread up to my shoulder and into my hand. I shook my head and my vision cleared and I saw Neary holding Pflug, one-handed, against the conference room wall.

"I thought we were done, Jer," he said softly.

Pflug managed a little smile. "We are now," he said.

Neary shook his head and took his hand from Pflug's throat. "Let's go," he said to me.

I looked at Pflug and didn't move. My knees were twitchy and so were my arms, and I could barely hear Neary over the rushing sound that filled my ears.

"John," he said more sharply.

I walked out and Neary followed. The reception area was deserted when we passed through, and quiet except for the sound of a vacuum cleaner running somewhere out of sight. The elevator came quickly and we got on. The doors were sliding shut when we heard Pflug's braying laughter.

26

I banged some cubes from an ice tray and wrapped them in a dish towel and held the towel to my face. Neary popped a can of ginger ale and drank half of it and took the rest to my long table. He sat down and looked at me.

"What is it with you?" he said finally. "What are you, thirty-something going on fifteen? I should know by now—every time I work with you, I end up with some kind of agita." It was the first time he'd spoken since we'd left Pflug's office.

Cold water ran down my neck and soaked into my shirt. My sinuses were frosting up, and the pain in my cheek was spreading across my face. I didn't say anything.

Neary took another long pull and drained the can. He sighed. "Did you somehow miss that this guy was *trying* to get into your head? Did you not get that he *wants* your mind on your nephews and Jane—and on him? That he wants it on anything besides who his client is and where the hell Danes went? I know Pflug's a subtle guy, but did that somehow escape you?"

"I got it," I said, from behind my towel.

"And you thought letting him goad you into a fucking bar brawl was the best way to handle it?"

"That wasn't my plan going in."

"I think that's probably bullshit," Neary said, and he crushed his soda can. "But I won't argue the point."

I wrung my towel into the sink and fiddled with the cubes and held the pack to my face again. I looked at Neary. "Sorry," I said. There wasn't much more to say: He was right, and we both knew it. Neary snorted. He tossed his soda can to me. I caught it and dropped it in the trash.

"Pflug is not a cream puff," he said. "We're not going to scare a name out of him."

I nodded. "And there's no one like Stevie in his shop, whose shoes we can squeeze."

"Anybody you particularly like, of the people that you've talked to?"

"For hiring Pflug? I don't know. . . . Not Pratt—she was genuinely freaked by the surveillance and by the break-in at the Pace offices. Turpin—it's hard to say. I don't know why he'd do it, and if it was him why the break-in? Why wouldn't he just give Pflug's guys the keys? Sovitch and Lefcourt—I suppose they're a possibility. . . . Of course, it would help to have some idea about what Pflug was hired to do."

"You don't think he's trying to find Danes?"

"Maybe. Or maybe he's trying to make sure no one else does."

Neary nodded. "You didn't mention your Ukrainian buddy."

"Gromyko? It's not him."

"You sound pretty sure."

I shrugged. Neary walked over to the windows and looked out on the shadowed rooftops.

"You think Czerka is typical of the kind of guy Pflug hires?" he asked, after a while.

"What do you mean?"

"I mean, if Pflug hires a guy like Marty to do his shitwork in New York, you think there's a chance he hires a similar kind of guy down in DC?"

I thought about it. "I guess it's possible."

"I guess so too. So maybe we could do what Gerber did: dig up one of Pflug's ex-freelancers. The guys in my DC office know the local players—including the local versions of Marty."

"Even if they can find someone who worked for him—and someone who's willing to talk—Gerber said Pflug kept the day labor away from the clients."

"Maybe. But maybe one of these guys was a little more enterprising than Pflug expected . . . or a little more cautious. Maybe Pflug wasn't as careful as he thought." Neary shrugged. "Hell, maybe one of them has a good guess about who Pflug's clients are—in which case they'd be one up on us."

I took the ice off my face and prodded my cheek. It was numb. "It's a plan," I said.

"Close enough, anyway," Neary said, and he looked out the window some more.

I poured a glass of water and drank it down and sat at the table. "As long as we're speculating, Gerber's sources said there were a lot of Wall Street people on Pflug's target list. It's possible that Greg Danes was one of them. It's possible that Danes pissed someone off badly enough that they sicced Pflug onto him."

"The pissing-off part is plausible," Neary said.

"I can go back at Pratt again, and see if she knows of anyone that was particularly angry with Danes. I can try Tony Frye, too. It's thin, but it's better than waiting around."

Neary nodded and stretched. He collected his suit jacket from the kitchen counter. "How are your nephews doing?"

"Fine, last I heard."

"And Jane?"

"Somewhat less fine," I said. He looked at me but said nothing.

Neary went back to his office, to start making phone calls. I showered and ate tuna fish from a can, and in between bites I left messages for Tony Frye and Irene Pratt. Then I read for a while from a book by Paul Auster, and then I went to bed and didn't sleep. The night was filled with shouts and car horns and sirens from the street. From upstairs there was only silence.

Friday morning was gray, and heavy with rain that never quite fell. I tried Irene Pratt twice more and got her voice mail and no calls back. I drank coffee and read the paper and poked absently at the little purple knot under my eye and at its larger cousin on my arm. Anthony Frye phoned me at noon.

"Mr. March," he said, with mock formality. "I was so pleased to get your message. What can I do for you today?"

"More gossip about your old boss," I said.

"Greg still hasn't turned up?"

"Not yet."

"Well, I'm happy to oblige, though it's fortunate you're getting me now. I'm rapidly forgetting my days as a lowly analyst."

"I'll talk fast," I said.

I asked him again about anyone who might have had an ax to grind with Danes, anyone who might be nursing a grudge. Frye gave it some thought but came up with nothing more than he had the last time I'd asked.

"Sorry to disappoint," he said, "but have you spoken with Pratt? She might have an idea."

I made a noncommittal noise. "How about people interested in Danes? Has anyone called you lately, asking about him?"

Frye snorted. "Only you, March, but again, I'd think Pratt would know better."

I thought back to when I'd asked Irene Pratt that same question, in the bar at the Warwick. She'd taken a while to respond, and when she finally told me no, her eyes had skittered around the room, looking at anything but me. At the time I'd marked it down to nerves, but was it? I remembered what she'd said when I'd asked what kind of people had been calling about Danes.

"People we do business with: industry contacts, fund managers, people from the companies we cover—the same people who called before he went away."

"You told me last time that Danes wasn't always adept at dealing with big investors," I said. "That there were fund managers who got the better of him."

"Indeed," Frye said.

"Were there any who did it on a consistent basis—any who Danes might have had a gripe with?"

Frye was quiet for a while. "I suppose there were," he said. "I don't know how Greg felt about them, but certainly whenever it would happen—whenever he would find that one of these people had blown smoke up his ass—he'd be angry and as near to embarrassment as he ever got."

"Why did he keep dealing with them?"

"Well, it was a part of his job, after all," Frye said. "Beyond that, I couldn't say."

"No psychological theories?"

Frye chuckled. "Greg fancied himself a player—someone who could move markets and reshape industries and that sort of thing. Perhaps dealing with those fellows on a regular basis was a part of that fancy; perhaps it helped him to believe his own PR."

"The people you're thinking of are all fund managers?"

"The three I have in mind ran hedge funds. Three of the biggest, in their day."

"But not anymore?"

"Two of them are out of the markets. Julian Ressler cashed out nearly three years ago, and Vincent Pryor was called to that big investor conference in the sky about eighteen months back."

"And the third?"

"The third is Marcus Hauck. He's still around and making a bloody fortune again."

"I've never heard of him."

"Not many have outside the industry."

"You know him?"

"Only slightly, and only over the phone; Greg dealt with him mainly. Hauck runs the Kubera Group—as in the Hindu god—and he's got over five billion under management, all told. He's smart and aggressive and very private, both professionally and personally. His funds hit a few bumps in the road at the end of the bubble—late into tech and late out—but over the past year or so he seems to have gotten the old magic back."

"And Danes still talks to him?"

"He did while I was at Pace, though not very frequently—perhaps every few months. You think he might know something about Greg?"

"I have no idea," I said honestly. "Is he based in town?"

"In Connecticut. Kubera's offices are in Stamford, and Hauck himself has some massive place in Greenwich. Why, are you off to see the wizard?"

"Maybe he can fix me up with a brain," I said.

Frye laughed. "From what I know of Hauck, he's more likely to set the flying monkeys on you."

Frye rang off. I poured myself another cup of coffee and opened my laptop, and after about an hour I found that Frye's description of Marcus Hauck as very private was an understatement. There was next to nothing about him online: a one-paragraph biography, a brief four-year-old article from a trade rag, and a more recent piece from a business weekly that added little. I learned that Hauck was forty-six, Swiss by birth, and the only child of a banker from Basel. He was educated in the States—at MIT and the Kellogg School—and from there he went to the investment bank of Melton-Peck, where he spent the next five years as the star of its proprietary trading desk. And then he started Kubera.

His first investors were former Melton colleagues, who'd liked the way Hauck had traded the firm's money and thought he could do as well with theirs. As it turned out, he did even better. In his first year out he posted returns over 15 percent, and for the next several he matched or bettered that—until the bump in the road that Frye had mentioned. Up to that point, his assets under management had grown steadily, as had his fees and his reputation.

The Hauck legend revolved mostly around his remarkable intelligence, his voracious appetite for market information, and an obsession with privacy that some said bordered on the pathological. He granted no interviews and refused all speaking engagements, and all of his employees—current and past—were bound by strict nondisclosure agreements, as were his two ex-wives. And that was it. There wasn't even a picture.

I read the articles over again, but repetition didn't make them more informative. I paced around my apartment, in the close gray air, and thought about Marcus Hauck and Jeremy Pflug. And I wondered some more about Irene Pratt and why she'd stopped taking my calls.

I picked up the phone a few times, to call Neary, and each time I put it down again. Asking him how things were going wouldn't make them go any faster. I thought about calling Jane at the office, and didn't. What would I say after *I wanted to hear your voice*? I pulled on my running shorts and shoes and got the hell out.

I ran for forty-five minutes through a fine mist that did nothing to cool me down but instead basted me in a sauce of bus fumes and soot. My shirt was soaked through when I turned onto 16th Street, and I slowed to a trot as I came to my building. There was a car double-parked out front, its hazard lights blinking. It was a Volvo sedan. Neary ran the window down.

"Good run?" he asked.

"Better than banging my head against the wall upstairs. You have something?"

Neary shook his head. "Barely. I talked to my guys in DC about tracking down one of Pflug's freelancers and using their local shitbags to do it. They had some ideas—came up with four or five guys in the Marty Czerka mold—but consensus was that it was going to take some time, a few days at least." I groaned and Neary held up a hand and continued. "So I switched to Plan B."

"Which was . . . ?"

Neary smiled a little. "I called up George L. Gerber again and begged."

I laughed. "And that worked for you?"

"I was just pathetic enough. Gerber gave me one name, a guy called

Santos who used to work for Pflug. I got off the phone with him a little while ago."

"And?"

"And that's where my good news ends. Santos didn't know much, not much more than what Gerber told us: that his subjects—his *targets*—were Wall Street people and that Pflug was very private about his clients. Or *client*, I should say."

"*Client*, singular?"

"That's what Santos said. He didn't have a name, but he was under the impression there was only one of them. And he thought it was some sort of big-deal financial guy."

Neary took off his glasses and rubbed his eyes. I told him about my conversation with Frye and he listened and thought about it.

"So Danes might have had some sand in his shorts about this guy Hauck—okay—but how do you get from there to Hauck hiring Pflug?"

"Maybe I don't," I admitted. "But Hauck is the name I've got to work with, and he qualifies as a big-deal financial guy. I want to try him out on Irene Pratt—assuming I can get her to talk to me."

Neary's eyes narrowed. "Why Pratt? Last night you didn't think she had anything to do with Pflug; you said the break-in had freaked her out."

"That was last night—now I'm not so sure. She wasn't particularly happy to hear from me when I called her on Tuesday morning. Mostly she told me she had work to do and she'd been overly paranoid about people following her, and she just wanted to forget the whole thing. She hasn't taken my calls since, and I'd like to know why."

Neary smirked. "You have that effect on people sometimes," he said.

"This is different. I got what might have been a weird vibe off her when I asked about people interested in Danes's whereabouts. At the time I wrote it off to nerves, but now I wonder if she had someone in mind."

"Maybe Hauck?"

"I'm hoping she'll tell me."

Neary nodded. "If you can get her to cop to that, there's something else you can ask." I looked at him. "I checked in with my guys on the way over here. Nothing's changed at Nina Sachs's place or at Danes's or yours; Marty's geniuses are still doing their thing. But not at Pratt's place. At her place, they've packed up and left. Maybe you can ask her why."

27

"This is it for me, Irene," I said into my cell phone. "This is all that's on my agenda today—just sitting here, waiting for you." It was Saturday morning, and I was outside the bar at the end of Irene Pratt's street, watching the door of her building. I had come there on a fishing trip, but there'd be nothing patient or quiet about it; I was wading in with big boots and a club.

Pratt's voice was tiny and mad and scared. "I knew it. I knew I should never have talked to you. I knew it was a stupid thing to do. What is wrong with you, anyway? Why are you harassing me?"

"We haven't gotten to the harassing part yet, Irene. Right now I just want to talk."

"Is that supposed to convince me? Because all it makes me think of is calling the police."

I laughed. "Sure, Irene, give them a call. And while you're doing that, I'll ring Turpin. We can all meet at your place and have a little party."

She drew a sharp breath. "You bastard," she said.

"Whatever. Can we talk now?"

She huffed for a while and then went quiet. "Come up, dammit," she said finally.

Pratt was waiting at the door when I got off the elevator. She wore jeans and a T-shirt and an anxious, angry look. Her hair was caught in an unwilling ponytail, and her face was paler than usual. She said nothing as I walked in.

There was a kitchen straight ahead of me, with white cabinets and stone counters, and a long hallway to the left. To the right was the dining room and, beyond that, the living room. The walls were white and the floors were gleaming wood. The apartment was sparsely furnished, with bland rustic pieces that seemed to have come from the same catalog. Except for the dining table, which held a massive PC and stacks of paper, it was tidy.

I followed Pratt into the living room. It was long and narrow, with windows at the far end and a treetop view. There was a brick fireplace on one wall, with a striped sofa nearby. Pratt crossed the room and perched on a bench beneath the windows. She looked at me warily, and her eyes flicked from the bruise on my face to the envelope under my arm.

"So . . . talk," she said.

I leaned against the sofa and looked down at her. "I didn't sleep well last night, Irene. In fact, I haven't slept well for a few nights now."

"This is what you came here to say?"

I smiled. "On the one hand, lack of sleep has made me a little slow on the uptake; on the other, it's given me time to think about things. Things like why you were so hesitant, back at the Warwick, when I asked you who had been calling about Danes. And what happened between Monday, when you were happy to hear my voice, and Tuesday, when you weren't. Things like who it is that you've been talking to, Irene—who it is that got to you."

Pratt's brows came together behind her wire glasses and she turned her head a little, as if she had a crick in her neck. "I don't know what you're talking about," she said evenly.

I smiled at her some more. "I think the break-in really shook you up. I think you were genuinely scared. But not so scared that you stopped thinking, right? Not so scared that those gears stopped turning."

Pratt sighed and rubbed her hands on her knees. "Am I supposed to understand some part of this?"

I kept smiling. "I think something occurred to you, when I asked who had taken an interest in Danes's absence. I think a lightbulb went on, Irene. You had someone in mind."

Pratt shook her head but said nothing.

"I don't know exactly what happened on Monday, though. Did you just wait for him to call the office again, or did you take the initiative and phone him—and offer up a little something?"

Pratt shook her head some more.

"I'm thinking it was the latter, and that you maybe started off talking about the break-in. That strikes me as an attention-getter."

"This is . . . I don't know what the hell to call this."

"And once you got his attention, then I imagine you got into the meat of things—your conversation with me maybe, the fact that I knew someone had been tailing me, and that I intended to find out who it was. The fact that I'd called in some people to help me do it."

"This is nuts—"

"I expect you probably got through to him right away, and you liked that. And why not? He's an important guy, right? And a good friend to have in the industry, too: someone who could really help a career. A person wants a friend like that at any time, but especially when things are a little . . . uncertain . . . at work. When her boss has up and left—maybe for good—and left her without a career path. I can understand wanting to ingratiate yourself with someone with his kind of clout."

Pratt chewed her lower lip. Color was rising on her white cheeks. "Are you almost done with . . . whatever this is?" Her voice was quieter and less steady.

"It's understandable, I guess, but if you're going to sign on for this sort of thing, you should make sure you know who you're working for."

"I work for Pace-Loyette. No one else."

I shrugged. "Have a look at those," I said. I tossed the envelope into her lap. She flinched as if it were a dead fish.

"What's in it?" she said after a while.

"Open it up."

"I don't—"

"Open it." My voice was sharp.

Pratt's shoulders twitched and she looked up at me. The corners of her mouth were tight and there was fear in her eyes. She unfastened the little metal clasp and slid the photos out.

"It's nothing gory, Irene, nothing messy. Just two little boys and a young woman, going to school, going to work, going about their business. Nothing scary." Her fingers were clumsy as she leafed through the pages, and her hands were trembling.

"Who are they?" she asked.

I ignored her. "Nothing scary, right? But look at how close some of those shots are. Whoever took them must have been very near, don't you think?"

"Who are they?" Her voice was quiet now.

"That shot there—they had to be right alongside her for that. But she had no idea that anyone was watching her. And there—they couldn't have been more than a few paces away from the boys for that one."

"Who are they, for God's sake?" She was staring down and her face was hidden from me, but her voice was a harsh whisper. I kept my tone conversational.

"The little boys are my nephews. The older one is Derek; he just turned seven. His brother is Alec; he's four. The young woman is a friend of mine. Her name is Jane. Someone delivered these to me on Wednesday afternoon. Around the same time, they delivered a couple of packages to my nephews—ostensibly from me. What's that, maybe two days after you had your conversation?"

Pratt drew a sharp breath. "I didn't . . . Are they . . . all right?"

"Sure, Irene." I laughed harshly. "They're just fine."

She looked up at me. Her eyes were red and watery behind her glasses and she wiped them with her fingertips. She put the pictures back in the envelope. "You don't know that this has anything to do with me," she said. I laughed again and it was nasty, even to my own ears. I reached over and took the envelope from her. She drew back.

"The people who took these are just foot soldiers, Irene, just hired hands. They work for a guy named Jeremy Pflug, who works for your . . . employer, so I suppose that makes him your colleague. Have you met him yet? He's a swell guy, and I'm sure you'll like him. His hobbies are invasion of privacy, intimidation, and decapitating dogs." Pratt gasped and I smiled at her. "I guess you haven't come across him yet, huh? Maybe at the Christmas party."

Pratt stood suddenly and crossed the room like she was leaving for good, but she stopped at the fireplace. She turned to me. "You make it sound like I'm a . . . spy. All I did was talk to him. He's not my boss." Pratt sniffled and I let out a deep, long-held breath. "And *he* called *me*—just like he has I don't know how many times before. He asked about Greg, and what was going on, and I told him about the break-in. So what?"

"And you told him about me."

She swallowed hard. "Is that supposed to be a crime? I've known him longer than I've known you."

I laughed. "You make it sound so innocent, Irene, almost as if you had no inkling that he might have been the guy who orchestrated the break-in and had both of us followed."

Pratt blushed deeply and looked away. "You don't know what I was thinking," she said after a while, but it was choked and without conviction.

"Why don't you tell me, then?"

Pratt snorted. "You don't know what it's like. If Greg doesn't come back, I've got no future there. Even if he does, it's a good bet he'll be out on his ass before long, and then it's just a matter of time for me. And it's not like analyst jobs are plentiful out there. I have to look out for myself; I have to network. It's not like anyone's going to do it for me. It's not like anyone at Pace gives a shit."

My eyebrows went up. "Is that what you call this—*networking*? Is that how you rationalize selling me out—at the same time that I was trying to keep Turpin off your back?"

A wave of color rose up Pratt's neck. "I didn't sell you out," she said softly.

"Of course not, you just reported our conversations to the man you thought might be behind the break-in and the tail jobs and neglected to mention any of it to me. Tell me, what did you get out of the deal? The promise of a job? Funding for a new business? Thirty pieces of silver? I hope it was something good."

Pratt's lip was trembling again and there were tears welling in her eyes, and I didn't give a shit. "I didn't know for certain that he had anything to do with . . . anything. I still don't. It was just a conversation."

"Sure, Irene. And part of that conversation was about how you shouldn't talk to me anymore, wasn't it?"

She glanced at me and then down at the floor. "I didn't know he would . . . do anything. I—"

"For chrissakes, they threatened my nephews, Irene. They came after my *family*! Please don't talk to me about what you didn't know—or didn't want to know."

That did it. A sob bubbled up from Irene Pratt's chest and her shoulders shook and she hung her head and cried. I let her go for a while, and then I went into her kitchen and found a glass and filled it with tap water. I went back to the living room and guided Pratt to the sofa and gave her the glass. She held it with two hands and rested it on her knees, and after a minute or two the tears began to subside. She sipped at the water and wiped her face with her hand. She looked up at me and looked away again.

"You all right?" I asked.

She nodded. "I . . . I'm sorry . . . I don't know what to say. Things are just so fucked-up . . ." Her voice was tentative and hoarse.

"I know, Irene. I know they are."

"He asked about me . . . about how I was doing. He wanted to know what all this . . . with Greg . . . would do to my job." She took a shaky breath and another swallow of water. "He said I shouldn't worry, that I could do much better. He's . . . practically a legend, and he never talked like that to me before." She looked up at me and her eyes were wet again. "That's how it started."

I nodded. This was the tricky part. I took a deep breath and tried to keep my voice even. "Did you ever talk to Pflug, or was it just Hauck that you spoke with?"

Pratt looked at me and grew very still. Her brows were furrowed and her small mouth was pursed. "Just Hauck," she said softly, and my heart started beating again.

"What's he got going with Danes?"

She shook her head. "Nothing . . . I . . . I don't know."

"But there is *something* going on?"

More head shaking. "I don't know—really, I don't. But . . . it's like you said. Ever since Greg went away, Mr. Hauck has called a lot more often and I'm not sure why."

"You have a phone number for him?"

"Yes," she sniffled.

Forty-five minutes later I left Irene Pratt, red-eyed, in her living room and walked the few blocks to the subway station at 72nd Street. I had a gut full of soured anger and self-disgust, and a meeting the next morning with Marcus Hauck.

28

The Kubera Group was headquartered in a low unmarked building of fieldstone and glass that sat atop a rise about ten minutes from downtown Stamford. It was hidden from the street by a screen of fir trees and thick plantings and surrounded on three sides by parking lot. The lot was empty at 8 a.m. on Sunday, and I parked my rented Ford about fifty yards off the building entrance and ran the windows down. It was a mild breezy morning, and the air around Kubera was scented with pine and new-cut grass. It was quiet in the parking lot, for the two minutes it took security to show.

"Can I help you?" the guard said. He was in the driver's seat of the unmarked white sedan that rolled up alongside me. He was young and crew-cut.

"I'm meeting with Hauck at eight-thirty. I'm early."

"Yes, sir. If I could have your name, please." I gave it to him and he thanked me and wrote something on a clipboard and drove off. I fiddled with the radio and found a college station playing Josh Rouse. I stretched my legs out and propped my feet on the dash. I closed my eyes and listened to the music and tried not to think about last night. I failed miserably at it.

After browbeating Irene Pratt into phoning Marcus Hauck, and forcing a meeting with him through thinly veiled threats to call the press and the police, I'd spent the rest of the day in a futile online search for more information about Hauck and the Kubera Group. By five o'clock I'd been frustrated and restless, and I took myself for a long walk, down to the Battery and up along Water Street. I'd lingered for a while at the Seaport, amid the tourists and the strings of white lights, and looked at the Brooklyn waterfront. I picked out a corner of a building that I thought was Nina Sachs's and wondered how they were doing over there—if Nina was still angry and Ines still scared, if Billy was still worrying about his father. I could still hear the pleading in his reedy voice: *Will you look for him anyway?*

I'd continued north from there and stopped for dinner at a tavern in the East Village. It was a dark tin-ceilinged place, with a scarred black bar along one wall. I'd sat at the bar and drunk club soda and picked at what passed for a tuna sandwich while the place filled up with regulars. Their faces were animated and unfamiliar and their conversations swirled around me like smoke. I listened to their words without comprehension and found the murmur of voices somehow comforting. I walked home through a thin rain.

The lights had been on when I'd come back to my apartment. There was a black umbrella by the door and a gray raincoat on the coatrack. Lauren was standing at the kitchen counter, drinking tea and turning pages of the Sunday *Times Magazine.* Her black hair was pulled into a loose ponytail, and her sharp features were pale.

"Am I intruding?" I asked, but my sarcasm made barely a dent.

"You're wet," she said.

"Wet, tired, and not up for this."

Lauren smiled thinly. "I notice your fingers look okay, though, and your phone is still working—so it must be your brain that's out of whack. That must be why I don't fucking hear from you."

I tossed my keys on the counter and went into the bathroom and came out with a towel. I dried my face and hair. "What do you want, Laurie?"

She closed the magazine. "I don't want anything, except to know that you're all right. I heard about what happened . . . with those photos."

"Well, I'm fine—superb, in fact."

"So I see."

"Is there something else?"

She looked at me and sighed. "Things will cool off with Ned and Jan. Just give it a little time."

I threw the towel on the counter. "Sure, things will be fine. In no time they'll be as warm and fuzzy as ever."

"They'll be okay, Johnny. They—"

"No, they won't. When this passes, assuming it passes, there'll just be something else and something else after that; it's inevitable. Because they're right—Ned and Jan and David—they're right. I'm not like them, my life isn't like theirs, and I'm not good company. And none of that is going to change."

Lauren shook her head. "They just don't get what it is you're doing with yourself, Johnny. I'm not sure I do either, but so what? We're your family."

"That's a nice sentiment, but it's not real life. The world is full of brothers and sisters who have nothing to do with one another. Maybe we should take a page from their book." I went around the counter to the fridge, pulled out a bottle of cranberry juice, and took a glass from the cabinet. "I'm best left alone, Laurie. It was stupid for either of us to think otherwise."

"Meaning what?" she said softly. "You're saying *adiós* to all of us?"

"I'm just being realistic."

"Is Jane a part of your new realism?"

I filled the glass and took a drink. "You're out of bounds now," I said, but she didn't care.

"You know she's been staying with me the last couple of nights? She's not comfortable here while those people are still . . . watching. She said it creeps her out."

"That makes two of us."

"It's not just the being followed, it's that you didn't tell her anything about it. And that you keep working on whatever this is, even though you have no client—and even with this threat."

"This is really not your business, Laurie."

"You can understand why she'd be a little scared."

"I understand perfectly," I said slowly.

Lauren looked down at her white hands for a while, and then she looked at me. "You won't meet a lot of people like her, Johnny. She—"

"*Jesus Christ!*" I said. "Don't you have someplace else to be? Don't you have a husband somewhere, and a job? Go spend your time on them. Go have a kid or something. Go lead your own fucking life." My voice was tight and harsh, and Lauren went quiet. She turned away from me and stood near the windows. The rain had grown heavier and made a sound like ice on the glass.

"That's pretty funny, from someone who barely has a life himself, who runs away from any chance of having one, who'd rather poke around in someone else's life than lead his own. It's pretty funny—in a sad, pathetic kind of way."

I sighed. "Do you have even a clue of what you're talking about?"

"Of course not. How could I have a clue? How could anybody? That would mean you let someone intrude on you and your anger. That would mean you actually told someone what the hell happens inside your head."

I laughed nastily. "I'll leave the psychobabble to you; you have a knack for it. I think chemistry is my ticket to better living."

"Right, right, it's a big joke, getting help. Who the hell could possibly need that? Certainly not you. You've got your own personal twelve-step program going, a perpetual one-man meeting. Tell me, do you serve yourself doughnuts and coffee and give out little tokens for each day of joylessness? Probably not doughnuts, I guess; those might be too much fun. And they might somehow interfere with getting those precious miles in. Now, in which step do you pledge yourself to complete and utter isolation? Is that before or after the hair shirt and the self-flagellation?"

"You're pretty funny yourself," I said quietly, but it didn't slow her down.

"I guess you've made it work for you, though," she said. "I mean, I can't remember the last time I heard you mention Anne."

"*Jesus*—"

"Do you talk about her to anyone, Johnny? Can you even bring yourself to say her name?"

I stared at Lauren's back. Her shoulders were stiff and her head was bent. "You should get the fuck out of here," I said.

Lauren laughed bitterly and turned to face me. "That might carry more weight if I didn't actually own this place," she said. Her green eyes were wet, and she ran a hand over them and looked at me. "But you're right, I should go. There've got to be better ways for me to spend my time." She'd walked to the door and pulled on her raincoat and picked up her umbrella. "You don't get that many chances, Johnny," she'd said from the doorway. "You should try not to fuck this up."

I heard the hiss of tires on asphalt. A gray Mercedes pulled up to the building's entrance, and even before it stopped a security guard came out at a run to open the glass doors. Two men climbed out of the car. I recognized one as Jeremy Pflug. The other, I assumed, was Hauck. They spoke briefly with the guard and Pflug glanced my way, and then they went inside. I took my feet off the dash and locked the car and walked across the lot. Nobody ran to hold the doors for me.

The lobby was stone—smooth and pale on the floor, rough blocks of gray and tan on the walls—and it was spare, with no art or corporate logo or sign of any kind hanging, and no waiting area for visitors. The only adornment—if you could call it that—was the guard station, like a stone fortification at the far end of the space. A guard was waiting there, and so was Pflug.

"The early bird," Pflug said. He looked at my cheek and put a finger to his own and smiled. It was wide and toothy and entirely unappealing on a Sunday morning—or at any other time. The Long Island lockjaw was less pronounced today, and he'd traded his duck hunting look for something more corporate: gray trousers, blue blazer, white shirt. He wore the jacket open, and I could see a shoulder rig under his left arm, and the butt of something heavy hanging there.

"Assume the position for me, John," he said, and gestured toward the guard station.

I was wearing jeans and a black polo shirt, and unless you were blind or stupid it was pretty clear I wasn't carrying. Pflug was yanking my chain, and I stared at him.

He shook his head and smiled. "Rules are rules, my friend, and we've all got to live with them. So be a good scout or go away—I don't care which—but you're not going in without a pat-down."

I sighed and held my arms out. The guard came around the stone counter with a hand-held metal detector. He was maybe twenty, and tentative, and he ran the wand quickly along my sides and legs and around my waist. It warbled at the car keys in my pocket and at my belt buckle but was otherwise quiet. I put my arms down and he stepped back and looked at Pflug.

Pflug shook his head. "No, no, no," he chided the guard. "Where did you learn to do this, at Wal-Mart? You can't rely on that little gizmo; you've got to lay hands on him. You've got to grab him." A blush and a pained expression spread across the guard's face, and he looked from Pflug to me and back again. I helped him out.

"Take me to Hauck or go explain to him why not," I said to Pflug. "That's *your* choice. I'm done with this sideshow." The guard went back behind the counter and studied his clipboard intently.

Pflug smiled and shook his head. "Don't get yourself in a twist, John, we're going, we're going." He went around the guard station and into a corridor on the left. I followed.

The corridor was paneled in shiny blond wood. The lighting was soft and the carpeting was thick. We progressed in silence, past darkened offices and around corners, to a smoked-glass door. Pflug pushed it open.

There was an elaborate secretary's desk to the left, in blond wood that matched the wall paneling, and a waiting area with tan leather sofas to the right. Straight ahead was a set of double doors with sleek brass handles. The doors were shut.

"We wait," Pflug said, and sat on one of the sofas. He crossed his long legs and patted the seat next to him. "Come on, take a load off, John. Don't be shy."

I looked at him but said nothing.

He laughed. "Peevish today? What's the matter, not seen enough of your little friend lately? She is a *busy* beaver." I stared at him. He cracked his knuckles and showed me more of his big teeth. He held his hands in front of his face like an imaginary camera and moved his finger up and down. "Click-click," he said. I shook my head and the double doors opened.

Marcus Hauck was my height but heavier, and his close-set features were half a size too small for his round pink face. His hair was blond gone gray, cut close and slicked down, and his brown eyes were moist and guileless behind wire-framed glasses. He wore an oxford shirt that was tight across the belly and khaki pants that were an inch too short, and his careful mouth was set in a tiny smile. Hauck was deep in his forties, but despite the graying hair and spreading gut, he had an unripe, somehow fussy look, like an over-large choirboy.

"Come in," he said. His voice was soft and had no accent.

It was a long room with a desk at one end, in front of a wall of windows that looked out on a stone terrace. The desk was a broad slab of maple with sharp edges and tapered legs, and there was a tan leather chair behind it and two Windsor chairs in front. The desktop was bare except for a leather blotter, a black telephone, a coffee mug, and a crystal sphere the size of a baseball.

A maple console sat along the wall to the left, its surface mostly covered with flat-panel monitors arranged in a strict row. There was a green rug on the floor, with a geometric pattern. It ran the length of the room, and at the far end, facing the desk, was a large weathered statue of a plump four-armed man.

He sat cross-legged on a stone plinth, and his stone features, and the elaborate carvings of jeweled strands on his arms and across his belly, were blurred and indistinct. His four hands held a club, a cup, a bowl, and a pouch, and there was something at once comic and sinister about him.

I took a seat in a Windsor chair. Pflug shut the doors and leaned against them. Hauck sat behind the desk and clasped his hands in front of him. They were pink and pudgy and perfectly still.

"I think I gave Ms. Pratt the wrong idea, perhaps—or maybe she was confused on her own." Hauck gave a hesitant smile. "In any event, between her and our Mr. Pflug here, I think you have gotten a mistaken impression as well." He shrugged his shoulders and the smile turned wry. Just a regular Joe, with five billion under management. I looked at Pflug. His eyes were fixed on me. I looked back at Marcus Hauck.

"What impression was that?" I asked.

Hauck laughed softly. "Something . . . sinister, perhaps? Something conspiratorial?" He smiled at me some more, but I didn't reciprocate and didn't speak.

Hauck was a quick study. He looked down at his clasped hands, and when he looked up again and spoke every trace of levity had vanished from his face and from his voice. "I understand your feeling that way," he said. "Those photos must have been quite upsetting." He looked over at Pflug and scowled. "I don't condone those tactics, and regardless of the outcome of our business today, I want you to know that you have my deepest apologies." It was an impressive change of tack—sudden, but with enough sincerity that it didn't seem jarring. I picked up the crystal baseball and turned it over in my hand. It was heavy and cool to the touch. Hauck's eyes followed it.

"That's comforting," I said. "But I'd like to know why it happened."

Hauck nodded gravely. "Mr. Pflug was working for me, doing what I gather you have been hired to do: searching for Greg. He actually started his work ahead of yours, Mr. March, but when he learned that you were on the job—and when he learned of your reputation—he thought he might leverage your efforts. Ride your slipstream, as it were."

"In other words, he thought he'd follow me around and see if I led him to Greg."

Hauck nodded encouragingly. "Yes—though unfortunately your results don't seem to have been much better than his." Hauck paused and looked at me, but I kept still. He went on. "And then you became aware of his people."

"They became hard to miss."

Hauck looked pained. "I've already spoken to Mr. Pflug about the quality of some of his resources."

I looked over at Pflug. If any of this was bothering him he hid it well. I rolled the ball from hand to hand above my lap. Hauck's eyes followed it, back and forth.

"And then?" I asked.

"And then some unfortunate decisions were made."

"Starting with the break-in at Pace-Loyette?"

Hauck cleared his throat. "I have no comment on that, Mr. March."

"Then which unfortunate decisions were you talking about?"

"When he learned of your determination to identify who was following you, Mr. Pflug elected to send those photos. And when you were undeterred and traced them back to Mr. Pflug and made contact with him, he became . . . hostile. Again, you have my apologies, Mr. March."

I nodded and rolled the crystal ball in my palm. I looked at Hauck. "As entertaining as that was, I'd figured most of it out already. What I was asking was why you were looking for Danes in the first place."

Another change came over Hauck, more subtle this time but just as quick. He sat back in his chair and his shoulders stiffened. His eyes cooled distinctly. The sincerity remained in his voice, in full measure, but the empathetic undertones dropped out and were replaced by something that hinted at indignity. He crossed his arms on his chest.

"Gregory Danes is a friend of mine, Mr. March, and I was worried about him; I still am. As you may have gathered, he has few friends and no family to speak of. If I didn't do something, who would?"

It was a credit to his performance, not to mention my self-control, that I managed not to shout *bullshit*. "Who indeed," I said, and nodded some more. "But why the secrecy? Why send Pflug sneaking around? Why not call the cops?"

Hauck smiled a little. "In retrospect, perhaps I should have, Mr. March. Perhaps things wouldn't have gotten so . . . out of hand. It would certainly have saved a good deal of misunderstanding. But at the time, I'm afraid, that just didn't seem possible.

"For one thing, I had—I *have*—no reason to think that anything untoward has happened to Greg. I'm still hoping that he's just decided to go on another of his unannounced retreats, and that the phone will ring and it will be him on the other end. If that's all this is, and I call in the police and create a furor in the press . . ." Hauck shook his head and smiled. "Well, I don't think Greg would appreciate it.

"And I have my own interests to consider, and those of my investors. Media attention is at best a double-edged sword for someone in my business, and I've made a habit of avoiding it. A story of this sort—hedge fund manager calls police in search for missing analyst—would be irresistible to the press. I have no wish to be linked to such a story, Mr. March, and neither do my investors. We simply couldn't afford it."

I couldn't suppress a laugh. "And this business—with photographs and threats—this was supposed to be the discreet approach?"

Hauck shook his head. "It seems absurd from this vantage point, I know."

Absurd and unbelievable, I thought, but I didn't say it. "And now what?" I asked.

Hauck smiled benignly and leaned forward. "And now, I hope, we've cleared things up between us, Mr. March. Now, I hope, you realize that this nonsense with the photos was simply Mr. Pflug's ill-advised attempt to cover his tracks—a desire for discretion taken to ridiculous and upsetting lengths."

"Like Watergate," I said. Hauck frowned for an instant, and then his smile returned, brighter than before.

"And knowing this," he continued, "I hope you'll forget about talking to the press—or whoever—and move on with me from here." His eyes were wide behind his glasses.

"Move on?"

Hauck nodded. "I'd like to hire you, Mr. March, to find Gregory for me."

I looked at him and he kept nodding. I looked over at Pflug, who was utterly indifferent. I looked back at Hauck. "You want to hire *me*?"

"To find Gregory, yes."

I sat back and sighed. Hauck looked at me eagerly. "What about *him*?" I asked, and flicked a thumb at Pflug.

"Mr. Pflug and I have discussed methods and tactics, and we've come to an understanding. Mr. Pflug will continue his work, but there will be no further incidents like the ones that brought you here."

"What do you want with Danes?"

Hauck's smile turned quizzical but never faltered. "I thought I explained, Mr. March—Greg is my friend. I just want you to locate him."

"And if I do, then what?"

"Then you call me, and let me know that he's well and where I can find him."

"What if he doesn't want to be found?"

"You have a dark turn of mind, I can tell. I simply want to talk to Greg. I simply want to know that he's well." I was quiet for a while, looking at Hauck. When his smile began to fray, he cleared his throat. "I realize the money may not be important to you, Mr. March, but this could be a quite lucrative engagement—and no different from what you're already working on."

I nodded and tossed the crystal in the air a few inches and caught it again. Hauck fought to keep his eyes on mine. "When's the last time you heard from him?" I asked.

He seemed relieved by the question. "We spoke on the phone several weeks ago—almost six weeks by now. I can get you an exact date."

"But it was after he left work?" Hauck nodded. "What did you talk about?"

He smiled. "It was just a chat between friends."

"Did you have an argument?"

"It was a chat, Mr. March, nothing more."

"He called you?" Another nod. "On his cell?" Nod. "Any idea where from?"

"None at all," Hauck said.

"You asked him?"

"He didn't care to say."

Pflug made a snorting sound and I turned to look at him. His face was still without expression and his eyes were still on me.

"Why not?"

"Greg could be . . . stubborn. I can't claim to know his thoughts."

"He say anything to you about his plans before he left?" Hauck shook his head. "What was his mood like?" Again the quizzical smile. "Was it stable? Did he sound depressed, elated, detached?"

Hauck hesitated, choosing his words. "It was stable—yes, and not depressed. Angry, perhaps, but not depressed."

"Angry at what?" Hauck smiled and shook his head and said nothing.

"What are you into with Danes?" I asked. "What's going on with you two?"

Hauck sat back and sighed, the picture of patience wearing thin. He folded his fat hands in his lap. "Really, Mr. March, I don't know how else to say it: I am Greg's friend. There just isn't anything I can add to that."

"No, of course not," I said, and rose from my seat. Hauck leaned forward and Pflug pushed off the door and moved his feet apart and balanced himself.

"You're leaving us?" Hauck asked. I nodded. "We haven't worked out the details of my offer yet." His eyes got smaller and his voice lost some of its softness.

"I don't think I can accept your offer," I said, and Hauck changed again. There was nothing subtle about it this time. His eyes narrowed to slits and his features took on a nasty, porcine look. His voice was flat and cold.

"I assumed from your questions that you already had accepted," he said. I still held the crystal baseball. I tossed it from my left hand to my right and said nothing. Despite himself, Hauck watched it travel.

"I feel that I've been misled, Mr. March," he said, and his face reddened to the collar line. "I really don't think you appreciate the *gravity* of this. Perhaps it would be best—for all concerned—if you would reconsider." He glanced behind me at Pflug.

"Which *all* is that?" I asked. "Are we talking about my family again?" I tossed the sphere from my right hand to my left. It was Hauck's turn to keep silent, and he did. His gaze was icy. I moved toward the door and Pflug shifted, blocking my way. He smiled at me and unbuttoned his jacket and shook his head. I looked at Hauck.

"I've answered your questions, Mr. March, and it's only fair that you answer some of mine."

I took a deep breath and let it out slowly. I pursed my lips and nodded. And then I pivoted and lobbed the crystal sphere at Pflug, who was game but never had a chance.

I tossed it up above his head, and against his will his eyes flicked upward and his hands moved to follow and I kicked him in the balls. The breath came out of him in a sickening bellow and he folded up around his pain, but even as he did, Pflug lunged at me. He groped in his jacket for his gun and pointed his shoulder into my gut and I turned and took the hit on my left arm. There wasn't much behind it and Pflug clawed at me with his left hand and snapped his head up, trying to connect. But his grip was loose and his timing was way off and I stepped away and hammered twice, hard, on the side of his neck with the side of my fist. Pflug went heavily to his knees. His eyes were rolling in his head, but still he flailed at me and dug for his gun. I threw my elbow into the center of his face, and his nose exploded and he went over backwards. He lay still, with his long legs bent beneath him.

I knelt over him and pulled a semiautomatic from under his arm. It was a shiny cannon, a Desert Eagle, and it weighed about fifty pounds. I turned to Hauck. He was standing behind his desk. His cheeks were flushed and his eyes darted from me to his black telephone and back.

I went to the desk and unplugged the phone and put it on the floor. I slid the clip out of the Eagle and put it in my pocket. My hands were shaking and I took some deep breaths and concentrated on keeping them steady. I checked the chamber. The shithead had a round up there, and I jacked it out and put it in my pocket with the clip. I sat again in the Windsor chair and put the gun on the desk.

"Sit down," I said. Hauck sat. Pflug groaned and rolled on his side. Hauck and I looked at him. Hauck shook his head and swallowed hard.

"Wasteful," he said. "You've damaged a valuable asset, and for nothing." His voice was soft again, but not yet steady.

"Not for nothing, Marcus, but to make a point."

Hauck's eyes narrowed. "And that is . . . ?"

"That you should keep your dog on a leash, Marcus. Because if he gets loose again, I'm holding you responsible."

"Is that a—"

"Your little story about how he got out of hand is a pile of crap, and we both know it. He does what you tell him to do. For all I know, you even tell him how to do it."

Hauck took another breath and started to speak but I cut him off again.

"But be clear on one thing: If I see him again—or anybody who works for him—around me or anyone I know, I'm talking to you, Marcus. Whether you sent him or not, I'm talking to you. You understand that?" Hauck was still and silent for a moment and then he nodded once. "And you'll make sure that he understands?" Another nod. I stood.

"What about my offer?" Hauck said. I looked at him and didn't know whether to laugh or spit. I settled on a bitter chuckle and headed for the door.

As I went past him, Pflug pushed himself to kneeling and launched himself at me. His movements were surprisingly fluid for someone whose nose was spread all over his face, but they were also slow and I had about a week to react. I twisted his wrist and kneed him in the jaw and sent him back down to Hauck's geometric rug. He landed with a grunt and rolled slowly on his back.

I looked down at him and remembered George L. Gerber and his murdered dog out in LA, and thought about booting Pflug in the nuts once more. But his face was bloody, his wrist was bent and likely broken, and he was altogether too wretched. I picked up the crystal sphere, which had come to rest, unscathed, against the console, and I looked at Hauck.

He was still seated at his desk, with his fat hands clasped before him. His brow was furrowed and his mouth was a blister of concentration. His eyes were fixed across the room on the weathered stone face of Kubera. I set the glass ball on the table and closed the door behind me and left him there, waiting for a sign.

29

The Surrogate's Court is at the end of Chambers Street, near Centre Street and in the wide shadow of the Municipal Building. It's a frilly Beaux-Arts palace with a huge mansard roof, arched entranceways, Corinthian columns, and plenty of statues of dead city elders. The lobby is multicolored marble and lavish in its adornment, and the sweeping double staircase looks like something out of the Paris Opéra. I went through security, up one side of the staircase, and down a long hallway. I followed signs and asked directions, and the farther I went the less things looked like Paris and the more they resembled Motor Vehicles.

I found my way to a green high-ceilinged room and a table stacked with requisition forms. I filled out a form and went to the end of a very slow line. At the other end of the line was a file clerk named Larry. He was tall, thin, and dusty, and he might have been forty or seventy. He stood behind a high counter, at the head of a phalanx of filing cabinets arranged in long shadowed rows. He took my form without comment and pointed to a bench. I took a seat with the paralegals and junior associates who'd preceded me in line, and while I waited I took out my subway map.

That's what it reminded me of, anyway. Intersecting colored lines, tick marks, lots of names and numbers—it could have been a diagram of the Fulton Street station. In fact, it was the time line I had drawn that morning—my graphic rendering of the little I knew about Gregory Danes's disappearance and of the many questions I couldn't answer. The theory was that in putting it down on paper, I'd see something I hadn't seen before. It had worked for me in the past, but not this time. This time, it was the subway to nowhere. I unfolded the paper and took another look.

It started eight weeks ago—in mid-March—with marks for Danes's lunch with Linda Sovitch, his argument with Dennis Turpin, and his abrupt exit from the offices of Pace-Loyette, and it ended on the present day in a big question mark. In between were Danes's call to Nina Sachs, canceling Billy's weekend visit; his call to Irene Pratt, telling her he was going on vacation; his departure from New York the next morning; his periodic calls to retrieve messages from his answering machine; his calls to Billy; and his final call for his phone messages. I'd recorded Danes's activities in blue ink. I'd used green for Pflug's men—their trip to see Gilpin, out in Fort Lee; their presumed visit to Nina Sachs's place; the break-in at Pace-Loyette; the tails on what seemed like half the city; the photographs. The questions were in red.

My meeting with Hauck yesterday had given me a few more tick marks for my picture, but it had added at least as many question marks. I knew now that Hauck, too, was searching for Danes, and that he had no better idea of where to look than I did. And I was all but certain that Hauck and Danes were into something together. But I had no idea of what that something was, or why Hauck wanted Danes, or what he might do if he found him.

I scanned the time line again, but repeated viewings didn't help. It remained history without narrative, a massing of dates and events that told no story. It captured nothing of Danes's barren personal life, and it caught none of the pressures that had been driving him in the months before his departure—the golden career turned to lead, the thwarted attempts at professional redemption, the failed relationship with Sovitch, the custody battle with his ex-wife, and the death of the man who might have been his only friend. Danes had ridden a long stretch of bad road before he'd ever gotten in his car that morning, and I couldn't believe that where he'd gone had nothing to do with where he'd been.

I'd drawn a red circle around the mark for Danes's last call home. Whatever else went on before—whatever his reasons for leaving, whatever he had going on with Hauck—that was when he'd stopped calling; that was when something had happened. And I couldn't shake the feeling that it was something bad.

Neary had called this morning to say that Hauck had made good on his promise to pull the surveillance from my place, and I'd tried some of my questions out on him. He'd been no help with them, but he had a couple of his own for me.

"Where do you go from here?" he'd asked.

"The doorman, Gargosian, gave me something about Danes's neighbor, a guy named Cortese. He was a music buff, and maybe the single honest-to-God friend Danes had—until the old guy died. It's the only lead left, and I guess I'll see what I can make of it."

"Why?"

"I told you, it's the only lead."

Neary sighed. "I know it's the only thing left to do. I meant, why are *you* doing it? Pflug and Hauck have backed off, and I doubt they're coming around again anytime soon, on top of which you have no client. And while I'd be pleased as punch to know where the hell Danes has gone, I just don't see that you have a dog in this fight anymore."

I'd been quiet for a while, looking around at my empty apartment, thinking about Jane and about Billy, and finally I'd said nothing. It was another answer I didn't have.

I'd spent the rest of the morning looking for Joseph Cortese, and though he'd been dead over six months, he wasn't a hard man to find.

Cortese was seventy-eight when he passed away, widowed, childless, and very rich. The money had come from the sale of his plastics company, over twenty years before. Since then, Cortese had been a generous patron of the arts and had served on the boards of half a dozen museums, music conservatories, and dance companies around the city. According to the *Times* obituary, he had maintained homes in Manhattan, on Sanibel Island, Florida, and in Lenox, Massachusetts. He was survived by his nephew, Paul Cortese.

Besides the obit, I'd found traces of Cortese on the Web sites of cultural institutions all over town—in meeting minutes, on lists of major donors, and in dozens of testimonials and expressions of sorrow. They all said essentially the same thing—that Joseph Cortese was a great guy, whose company and generosity would be greatly missed. If I wanted more, I'd have to go downtown. And so I had.

Larry beckoned with a dusty finger, and I folded my map, hoisted myself from the unforgiving bench, and hobbled to the counter. He had a single sheet of paper in his hand.

"You got no standing in the case, and no court order," he said. His voice was wheezy and soft. "So you can't see the whole package. This is what I can give you." He handed me the sheet. "Come back when you got some standing." He disappeared down one of the aisles and left me to my reading.

It was the top sheet of Joseph Cortese's estate package, the cover page of his probated last will and testament. What it revealed wasn't much, but it was what I had come for: the name and address of his estate's executor.

30

"We didn't do the will," Mickey Rich said. "Jerry Litvak—over at Litvak, Gant—did that. We do real estate here, exclusively real estate." He was a stout man with a deep weathered voice, a warm smile, and a cool gaze. There was a little brown left in his wavy white hair, and a little more in his thick beard, and he looked to be somewhere in his middle sixties. He was the senior partner at the law firm of Rich & Fiore and the executor of Joseph Cortese's will.

His office was furnished in oak and green leather, and it was comfortably frayed at the edges, broken in but not broken down. Family photographs covered every available surface, and an old lithograph of the Brooklyn Bridge hung behind his desk. He had a nice view of the Flatiron Building and a corner of Madison Square, and he had time on his hands. He'd agreed to see me when I told him that I wanted to discuss Joseph Cortese, and hadn't pressed much about why.

"I know Joe forty years—from when I got out of law school and he first gave me work. We were friends ever since, so when he asked me to be his executor, what was I going to say? Besides, there wasn't much for me to do. Joe kept his affairs neat as a pin and Jerry made a real clean will. The whole thing went through probate in under four months, which for an estate that size is some kind of record in this town."

"I gather he didn't have much family."

Rich shook his head. "No. His brother and sister-in-law passed away a long time ago. And when Margie, his wife, passed, that was it."

"The obituary said he had a nephew."

A pained look flitted across Rich's face. He nodded. "Paul."

"I guess the bulk of the estate went to him?"

He nodded carefully. "The Philharmonic, City Ballet, Juilliard, the Boston Symphony, some bequests to friends, and Paulie. Paulie was well taken care of."

"You know how I can reach him?"

Rich's cool gaze turned downright chilly, and he sat back in his chair. "Paulie's a little hard to locate sometimes. Why?"

I ignored the question. "He's a big guy, balding, with dark hair and glasses?"

"You know him?"

I shook my head. "Somebody pointed him out to me, over at Mr. Cortese's apartment building."

"When was that?"

"Not too long ago. He seemed a little . . . agitated to me."

"Paulie's like that sometimes," Rich said.

"How come?"

He shook his head. "You told me you wanted to talk about Joe, and now you're asking about Paulie. What do you want, March?"

"Do you know Mr. Cortese's friends?"

Rich smiled, and some warmth came back into his eyes. "That's a big group. People liked Joe and he liked people. I know some of them, but not all."

"Do you know Gregory Danes?"

The warmth vanished again and his face stiffened. He ran a hand over the front of his white shirt and fingered his red tie. "Not well," he said. "Is that who you want to talk about?"

I nodded. "Did you ever socialize with Mr. Cortese and Danes?"

Rich shook his head. "Danes was one of Joe's music pals. Me, I go in more for the ponies, so I never saw Danes with Joe."

"But they were close?"

"Close enough, I guess. Joe loved music and he knew a lot about it— I mean theory and history and everything—and I guess Danes does too. I guess they liked the same kinds of things. And Joe felt . . . bad for him."

"Why bad?"

"He thought Danes was a sad guy—that he was lonely and his life was . . . crappy." Rich shook his head and smiled a little, remembering something. "Joe knew about people."

"Was he right about Danes's life?"

"Probably. From the little I've seen, I can believe he's lonely. The guy's such a prick, nobody with sense would want anything to do with him. But what the hell do I know?"

"I guess Mr. Cortese didn't mind him."

Rich laughed some more. "Joe was a special case. He always did good works—more so after Margie passed away—and Danes was one of them. And probably the guy wasn't such a prick around Joe. Joe had that effect."

"So was Danes Cortese's friend or his project?"

"They were friends. Joe felt bad for the guy, but he genuinely liked him too. They had a good time at concerts and such. It was something Joe and Margie used to do, and I think he liked having somebody else to talk to about it." Rich thought of something and smiled ruefully. "Besides, you don't leave that kind of property to a casual acquaintance."

I had another question, but it vanished from my head like breath on a cold day. "What property?" I asked softly.

"The house, up in Lenox."

"Cortese left Danes property? In his will?"

Rich beetled his brows and looked at me like I was slow, which maybe I was. "Up in Lenox," he repeated.

"And Danes has taken possession of it?"

"About two months ago."

Two months ago—eight weeks, more or less. My heart was pounding, and I felt a vein throbbing in my neck.

"What the hell is this about, March?" Rich asked.

"I've been trying to locate Danes," I said slowly, "for his ex-wife. I didn't know about any property in Lenox, though. It didn't show up in any of the online searches."

Rich shrugged. "Transferred too recently, maybe? Or maybe they're slow in updating their computer records up there, who knows? I never trust those Internet things anyway. Give me a walking, talking county clerk any day."

"When's the last time you saw Danes?"

"When we did the filing and made the transfer—about two months ago, up in Lenox."

"Have you talked to him since?"

"He called me a few days later, asking if I knew who Joe had used for landscaping. I told him I'd check my files and call him back."

"You have a phone number for him up there?"

"He didn't have a phone hooked up. He told me to call his home number and leave a message, which I did. Why, you thinking he's up there still?" I nodded. Rich nodded back. "Could be. He had luggage with him when I saw him. He could've been planning to stay for a while. You try calling him, leaving a message?"

"Yes." Two months ago . . . eight weeks. "Tell me about the property," I said, and Rich did.

It was a 110-year-old Victorian farmhouse and an even older barn, on twenty acres that bordered October Mountain State Forest. Cortese had given it a name—Calliope Farms—and for the past ten years he'd spent much of every summer up there. And he had left all of it—furniture and record collection included—to Gregory Danes. Rich gave me the address.

I wrote it down and thought some more. "That's a pretty hefty bequest to make to a friend," I said eventually.

Rich shrugged. "It was a small piece of a hefty estate. And other people besides Danes got some nice stuff. Me, I got a Chagall. Anyway, after Margie, what else did Joe have in his life? He had his friends, his charities . . . and Paulie. Joe left something for everybody."

I was quiet again. Rich steepled his fingers and watched my face. "You said the estate went through probate quickly. Does that mean no one contested anything?" Rich nodded. "Not even Paul?"

Rich looked at me for a while. "Paulie was taken care of in the will," he told me finally. "He won't ever have to worry about keeping body and soul together."

"Does that mean he didn't contest anything?"

He sighed. "Not in any . . . organized way. He had every opportunity—I made sure of that—but Paulie . . . He complained a little, and he had some . . . *theories,* but ultimately he didn't contest it. And like I said, the will was clean, and he was well taken care of."

"What kind of theories did he have?"

"Paul gets ideas about things sometimes. For a while he thought that Danes had done him out of the place in Lenox. But it was crazy, and there was nothing to it."

"Where's Paul now?"

"I don't know. The apartment went to him, and so did the house on Sanibel, and I know he's shown up both places from time to time, but he doesn't stay at either one. Right now, if I had to guess, I'd say he's living in his car."

"What's the matter with him, Mr. Rich?"

Rich shook his head and looked out the window. "He was diagnosed paranoid schizophrenic, a long time ago," he said finally.

"Is he on meds?"

"Sometimes. And they work for him—when he takes them. He's had some real good stretches, where he's held a job and paid the rent and everything. And then he goes off and has some bad stretches."

"How bad?"

"He gets fired; he gets evicted; he drops out of sight for months at a time and winds up in a shelter or on the street." Talking about Paul seemed to make Rich tired. He twisted his hands together on the desk.

"Does he need to be institutionalized?"

Rich made a resigned shrug. "I don't know. Joe and I talked about it. I think maybe it's headed that way." He sighed some more and shook his head. "What does any of this have to do with Danes?"

"Does he ever get violent, Mr. Rich?" Rich looked down at his desk for a moment and then looked up at me. His eyes were worn and old and worried under his white brows. He nodded his head very slowly.

31

I was packing when Jane showed up at my door. She was still dressed for work in a navy suit, and her face was thin and tired-looking. She had an opened bag of barbecue potato chips in her hand. She tipped the bag toward me.

"Want one?" she asked.

"No, thanks," I said. She followed me back to the bedroom and leaned against the wall. She put a potato chip in her mouth and looked at my overnight bag, open on the floor.

"I got your message," she said. "I appreciate your letting me know." I nodded and put a pair of boxers in the bag. "Do you think they're gone for good?" she asked.

"I think so."

"You're not sure?"

I looked up at her. "Pretty sure is the best I can do," I said. "I can't guarantee anything for anyone."

She looked at me for a while and gave a tiny nod. "I appreciate your letting me know," she said again. She ate a potato chip. "Did you call Ned too?"

"Yep."

"He must've been relieved."

"I guess. I left a message, and I haven't heard back." I laughed a little, but it came out sounding choked. "Lauren said to give him time. I figure a year or so might do it."

I packed a polo shirt and jeans and tucked my shaving kit next to them. I took a black nylon waist pack from my closet and opened its two pockets. I put a flashlight, a small pry bar, a couple of screwdrivers, a Swiss army knife, a putty knife, and a couple of pairs of vinyl gloves in one. I took the Glock 30 from my bureau and slipped it in the other. I zipped the waist pack and put it in a side compartment of my overnight bag. Jane watched, and her face was very still.

"Where are you going?" she asked.

"Lenox. It's in western Mass, in the Berkshires."

Jane crunched loudly on another chip and nodded. "I used to go there in the summers with my parents. It's a little early for the music, but I guess you're not going for that."

"It turns out Danes inherited a house up there, from his late friend and neighbor Joe Cortese. The final transfer took place two months ago, just before Danes split. There's no phone in Danes's name in that neck of the woods, and Cortese's old number is out of service. I'm going to knock on the door."

Jane looked at the bag again. "And if there's no answer?"

"I'll let myself in."

She glanced at the clock on my nightstand. It was six forty-five. "It'll be late by the time you get there."

"I'll wait until tomorrow to go calling."

She picked another chip from her bag. "Renting a car?" I nodded. "It's—what?—a three-hour drive from here?"

"Three and a half," I said.

"Where are you staying?"

"A place called the Ravenwood Inn, right in town. The woman there said she'd keep a light on for me."

"Cancel your rental. I'll give you a lift."

I zipped up my bag and looked at her. "Don't you have to work?"

A tiny smile crossed her face. She shook her head. "We're all but done. We've got final versions of the agreements, and all we need now is board approval. Our board said yes today; the buyer's board is meeting at the end of the week. Until then, I don't have much to do. Besides, I've had my car for three months now, and I've used it maybe five times. It's going to go stale or something if I don't let it run."

I took a deep breath. "I don't know what I'm walking into up there, Jane."

"It's not like I'm going with you on your house call. There's a nice spa up there. I'll go get myself wrapped in something, or maybe I'll look at some real estate. Or maybe I'll just lie in bed all day and eat bonbons."

I shook my head. "Really, it could be . . . complicated."

"I consider myself warned. You want me to sign a release or something?"

"I'm serious."

She folded down the top of the potato chip bag and tossed it on the bed. She brushed her palms together and dusted off the crumbs. "So am I. I know what you do for a living, John; I'm a big girl." She crossed her arms on her chest. "Those guys following us took me by surprise—they freaked me out. And those photos . . ." A shiver rippled through her, and she shook her head.

"I'm sorry that that happened, Jane. I wish—"

She held up a hand. "I know. I know you're sorry. It was a passing thing, and now it's past. But you can't keep that stuff from me, okay? You have to let me know what's going on."

We were quiet for a while and I looked into her dark, weary eyes. "Are we taking the chips?" I asked.

It took Jane twenty minutes to shower, change into jeans and a T-shirt, and pack a bag. Twenty minutes after that we were in her gray Audi TT in a fast-moving stream of traffic, northbound on the Henry Hudson Parkway. Jane was behind the wheel; I manned the CD player and doled out the potato chips.

The Hudson River was black below us and empty, but for a tug pushing south toward the harbor. Yellow light spilled from its bridge and vanished on the oily water. The Palisades rose like a stone wave across the river, beneath a mass of purple clouds.

Jane squinted into the oncoming headlights and drove fast and well. And though she was tired, she was full of a nervous energy that could only dissipate itself in talk. It was lurching, lopsided conversation that lingered on no one topic but skittered among several without segue.

"We deferred the issue of my ongoing participation," she said. "We took it out of the deal agreements and the buyers are making a separate offer."

"They really think they can convince you?"

"They really think so."

"And?"

"And they're really wrong," she laughed. An SUV swerved into our lane without a signal. Jane punched the horn and the Audi made a sonorous bark. She downshifted, slid left, swore softly, and passed the SUV.

"I don't know what went on with you two," she said, "but you should give Lauren a call." I didn't answer, and she glanced at me sideways. "Whatever it was, it left her pretty upset." She glanced at me again. "She really worries about you, and she looks out for you. She spoke to Ned the other day, and he told her he'd hired that woman you liked for the security job—the ex-policeman, Alice something."

"Ned hired Alice Hoyt?"

Jane nodded. "Lauren thought you'd like that."

"I do—she'll do good work for Klein—but I didn't expect Ned to see it that way. Especially after what happened."

"Lauren was funny when she told me; she does a great Ned imitation." Jane puffed out her cheeks and lowered her voice. *"I may not like what he's doing with his life, but there's no denying he knows his business."* Jane looked sideways again and smiled. "You should call her."

We took the Henry Hudson into the Bronx, to the Saw Mill River Parkway, and we took that into Westchester. Traffic was heavy all the way. I put on a Steely Dan disc, and when Fagen started singing "Janie Runaway," Jane talked about vacation plans.

"I was thinking about Europe—maybe Venice or the lake country—but then I thought that's too much work, and maybe what we could use is some serious vegetable time. To me, that means ocean." She glanced over. I nodded. "It's late to find something on the Vineyard or Nantucket, but we could get something on the Maine coast or maybe farther north, like Nova Scotia. Or we could go out West—northern California maybe." She glanced over and I nodded once more. "Bermuda's nice too," she added.

"Uh-huh," I said. I knew by the silence that followed that that wasn't enough. Or maybe it was too much.

Traffic thinned when we got on the Taconic Parkway, and it thinned some more as we drove in silence through Briarcliff and Ossining. As we crossed the Croton Reservoir, Jane spoke again, and the sound of her voice startled me.

"I'm getting tired. You better drive."

We pulled off the Taconic in Jefferson Valley and switched places in the parking lot of a shopping center. Jane tilted her seat back. She kicked off her loafers and tucked her feet beneath her. I adjusted the driver's seat and checked the mirrors. Jane looked at me and spoke very softly.

"Do you want to go on this vacation with me?" she asked. "Just tell me, yes or no."

"Yes, I do . . . sure I do. We just need to see about the timing, that's all. I've still got this case—"

"But you want to go?"

"We just need to work out the timing."

Something crossed Jane's dark eyes, too quickly for me to read. She looked out at the parking lot and then at me, expressionless, for several moments. And then she yawned hugely and closed her eyes.

Jane was asleep before we got back on the parkway. I fiddled with the CD changer until I found a Pharoah Sanders disc. "In a Sentimental Mood" came on, and Jane murmured. I turned the volume down. We crossed into Putnam County, and the Taconic grew darker and altogether empty. The Audi threw a cone of hard blue-white light on the road and on the heavy curtain of trees alongside. I thought about Joe Cortese and his nephew and Gregory Danes, and I tried not to think about what I might find at Calliope Farms.

Jane sighed and shifted on the passenger seat. The scent of her filled the car. I looked over. She had one hand wrapped around a slender ankle, and the other beneath her head, like a pillow. Her face was pale in the instrument lighting, and very beautiful, and I was filled with an aching want.

Light rippled across the western sky and a peal of thunder followed. Jane shifted on the seat again. Her brow furrowed for a moment and her lips moved silently, and then she drifted into a deeper layer of sleep. My throat was tight and I shook my head and drove on, through an ever-receding tunnel of light, through the pitch-black wood.

The Lenox town center is just a few blocks square, and it's a New England postcard of massive trees, handsome houses, and neat sober storefronts and churches. The houses are a mix of white clapboard and painted Victorian, and though many were long ago converted to inns, they are confident nonetheless on their well-groomed lots. The granite and red-brick storefronts were uniformly dark when we drove by at ten forty-five. The churches looked smugly on the empty streets.

The Ravenwood Inn was a turreted Queen Anne, just south of the obelisk in the center of town. It was large and pink and laden with ornamentation, and there was a light on above the wide front porch. I put my hand on Jane's knee and shook gently until she opened her eyes.

A bleary-eyed girl, barely out of her teens, checked us in and led us to our room. It was in the turret, on the top floor, and it had a high beamed ceiling and a smell of musty lavender. The furniture was dark and elaborately carved, and the windows looked out on black clouds and thunder.

The storm came at 2 a.m., in bursts of blue light that seared through my eyelids, and in rolling explosions of sound that shook my bones, and whose aftershocks rippled in the walls. The wind thrashed wildly through the trees and the sky was an ocean of madness. I stood at the window and watched the world come apart.

"Jesus," Jane said softly. She came up behind me, and her body was bare and smooth against mine. The air sizzled and the whole room was lit for an instant and then was black. The floor shook. Jane shuddered and gripped my arms. "I don't like lightning." I felt her lips and her breath and her nipples on my back. Her hands were very warm, and she slid them across my belly. "Come back to bed," she whispered.

32

I bought coffee and doughnuts on Tuesday morning, from a place that made them fresh and that had managed to eke out a few batches in the intervals between power failures. The old-timers behind the pink Formica counter had a Pittsfield station on the radio, and the announcer told us that the storm had downed trees and power lines all over Berkshire County. We were advised to expect sporadic blackouts throughout the day and—based on the latest forecasts—more storms by evening. In the meanwhile, he said, road crews were out in force, making what progress they could with chain saws and cherry pickers.

I'd passed some of those crews earlier that morning, when I'd driven north and east of town to case Calliope Farms. I'd found the place on an otherwise empty stretch of muddy washboard, off something called Roaring Brook Road. It was near the Housatonic River and at the base of a steep, densely wooded hillside that I knew from the map I'd bought in town was part of October Mountain State Forest.

The house and barn sat on a rise, well back from the road, behind a ragged stone wall and beside an unmown meadow. There was a white wooden post with a white wooden sign at the head of the gravel drive. The blue script letters were faded but legible: *Calliope Farms*. The drive was rutted and empty but for puddles, and the house looked closed up. I'd driven by slowly and kept on going for a mile or so. Then I'd turned the car around and waited ten minutes and driven by again. Nothing had changed when I passed the second time except my stomach, which felt tighter and more uneasy.

Jane was getting out of the shower when I returned with breakfast.

"The lights keep going on and off," she said, as she wrapped herself in one of the inn's terry robes.

"Reliable sources tell me they'll be doing that all day."

"That's what the spa people said when I called. And without power they can't heat the seaweed or something, so it's no wrap for me—and no real estate either. It looks like it'll be a bonbon day after all."

"Sounds appealing." I put the coffee and doughnuts on the bedside table and picked up my overnight bag. I unzipped the side compartment and took out the black waist pack. Jane blew on her coffee and watched me carefully. "I just need you to give me a lift," I said.

It was after two when we turned off Roaring Brook Road and onto the washboard track. I killed the music and a few minutes later we rolled slowly by Calliope Farms. The driveway was still empty. Jane pulled over about a quarter mile past the white sign. Her face was tense.

"Leave your cell phone on," I said. "I'll call when I'm done and I'll meet you back here."

Jane flipped her phone open. "My signal's spotty."

I opened mine. "I'm okay if I point in the right direction." I reached behind my seat and grabbed the waist pack.

"If you want me to, I could wait," Jane said. "In case you knock and he happens to be there."

I smiled and shook my head. "If he's there, I'm going to have a talk with him."

"What if he doesn't want to talk?"

"Then I'll be calling you pretty soon."

Jane pursed her lips. "What if somebody else is at home?"

I smiled a little harder. "I'll call you when I'm done," I said.

Jane nodded but looked no less worried. "Well, be quick about it, okay? I don't want to be sitting in that turret by myself if there are more of those storms coming." I opened my door and Jane caught me by the sleeve and pulled me toward her. "Just be quick," she whispered, and kissed me.

I climbed out of the car and waited while Jane turned around and drove off. Then I headed up the road to Calliope Farms.

The sky was a low restless mix of blue and white and stony gray, and the light shifted quickly from daytime to evening and back again. Wind seemed to blow from all points of the compass, by turns warm and cool, in light breezes and heavy gusts. Water fell from the leaves of the maples and lindens across the road and tumbled through the heavy undergrowth and ran in a stream along the roadside. Everything smelled of wet wood and grass and earth. The temperature was in the low sixties and I should have been warm enough in jeans and a sweatshirt, but somehow I wasn't. I shook my arms out and flexed my fingers.

I buckled the waist pack around me and thought about what Jane had said and wondered again if I should have brought my gun. But my carry permit was no better here than it was in Jersey, and the Massachusetts laws were even stricter. Besides, I wasn't planning on throwing down with anyone. If someone was at home, I'd talk—assuming they were in a talking mood. If they weren't, I'd leave without a fuss. If no one was around, I'd get in and out as fast as I could. By the time I made it to the signpost I'd convinced myself, again, that I didn't need the Glock.

The drive ended in a rough circle of packed earth and gravel, bordered by wet lawn and maple trees. The farmhouse was straight ahead. It was two neat stories in white clapboard, with green shutters, a green shingle roof, and two brick chimneys. There was a flight of wooden stairs from the path to a deep porch and the front door. The barn was to the left and set farther back from the turnaround. It had a low stone foundation, and its sides were wide white vertical boards. It had a hayloft and a big sliding door—both shut—and only a few windows, all high off the ground. The meadow I'd seen from the road stretched out beside and behind it.

I got closer to the house and saw that shades were drawn on all the windows. I climbed the porch steps and peered through the front door glass, but it was covered in a white curtain and I couldn't see a thing. I pressed the bell, heard it chime someplace distant, and waited. After a minute or two I pressed it again. And again. Then I knocked loudly several times, and called out hello. And then I opened my pack.

The hardware and the doorframe were for shit, and I was inside in less than two minutes with no damage done. I closed the door behind me and looked down a dim hallway that ran through the house all the way to the kitchen. The walls were pale yellow, and the wide plank floors were dark and smooth. A stairway climbed along the wall to the right. The wind picked up outside and I heard raindrops tapping at the windows, but nothing else. Light filtered through curtains and shades, but it was gray and somehow subterranean. I pulled on vinyl gloves and sniffed the air. It was musty and damp and smelled a little of ammonia, but of nothing worse. I took a deep breath and a quick walk around and satisfied myself that no one was home. Then I took it from the top.

The attic was small, unfinished, drafty, and damp, and it was lit only by a single bulb and by the gray light that came in through the dormers. I pulled out my flashlight and flicked it on. Besides some storm windows and broken screens, and a box of moldy paperbacks, it was empty. The rain was steady now and loud above my head. I went down the narrow stairs to the second floor and into a bedroom.

It was simply furnished with a pair of wrought-iron beds and a bureau in green painted wood. There were green chenille spreads on the beds, with bare mattresses underneath. The floor was partly covered with a green and gray hooked rug, and a large aerial photo of what looked like the Tanglewood grounds hung on the wall. The windows looked out on the back of the house, on lawn, a small grove of apple trees, and the dark wooded hillside beyond.

The next bedroom was outfitted as an office, with oak file cabinets, a rolltop desk, and an oak swivel chair. There were framed *New Yorker* covers on the walls and dust and empty space in the cabinets and desk. There was even less in the small bathroom next door.

Next door to that was the master bedroom. I stood at the threshold and looked it over and felt my pulse quicken. It was larger than the other rooms, and it had a little more furniture: a big cherrywood bed, a cherry bureau, a small black writing table and chair, a hooked rug on the floor, a black-framed mirror on the wall. But where the other rooms had been tidy and battened down, this one was scrambled.

The king-sized mattress was stripped bare and lay askew on the bed frame. All but one of the bureau drawers stood open and empty, and that one was missing. I found it under the bed, and it was empty too. The closet door was ajar. There was nothing inside but a few hangers scattered on the floor, next to a pillow. The mirror was crooked and cracked.

The master bath was more of the same. It was larger than the one in the hallway, and equipped with expensive new fixtures that looked very old.

But all the drawers and cabinet doors hung wide and gaping, like a lot of missing teeth. I went downstairs.

There was a study off the entrance foyer to the right. It was a narrow room with windows that looked onto the front porch, and it was furnished with a pair of green love seats, an oriental carpet, and Joseph Cortese's music collection. The collection of vinyl, CDs, and DVDs filled six built-in floor-to-ceiling cabinets, and made what I'd found at Danes's place look like a starter kit. The sound system occupied a seventh cabinet, and it was arcane and ominous-looking. The speakers were hung on the walls, along with a dozen photographs of a smiling Joseph Cortese, standing with musicians and conductors and friends. I'd seen two of the photographs before—one at Danes's apartment and the other at Nina Sachs's.

The living room was across the hall, and it connected through a wide entranceway to the dining room in the rear of the house. The furnishings were casual and comfortable-looking—slipcovered chintz sofas, fat leather chairs, a cherry coffee table, and brass lamps. There was a small linen chest beside one of the sofas, but it held nothing more than a deck of playing cards and a box of matches. Behind its brass screen, the fireplace was clean and empty.

I heard a rumbling sound, and the dim light coming through the shades grew dimmer. I went to a window and looked outside. The sky was a tumbling mosaic of gray on gray, and rain was falling even harder. Leaves were flying sideways from the trees.

I stood at the entrance to the dining room. A four-branch brass chandelier hung from the ceiling, above an old oak table and six oak chairs. There were three windows on the back wall and a connecting door to the kitchen on the right. There were moss-green curtains on wrought-iron rods over two of the windows. The third window, near the kitchen door, was covered only by a roller shade.

I pushed up a wall switch, and the chandelier came on. It shed a thin yellow light from bulbs shaped like flames. I crossed the room and looked at the bare window frame. There were empty ragged screw holes in the upper left-hand corner, and in the upper right were the bent remains of a bracket. The smell of ammonia was more pronounced. I knelt down and played my flashlight along the floorboards. There was a long irregular patch of wood that was scuffed and scratched and lighter than the rest of the floor. The ammonia smell was even stronger, and there was a smell of bleach too.

I took the putty knife out of my waist pack and worked it into the gap between the floorboards. I brought it out and there was something grainy, crumbly, and nearly black on the end. I shined the light along the irregular patch, in the seams between the floorboards. They were mortared with dried blood.

"Goddammit," I said aloud. My voice sounded shaky and strange in the empty house. I got to my feet and went into the kitchen.

The kitchen was large and well appointed, with limestone countertops, glass-fronted cabinets, a green tile floor, and a pine table. I flicked on the overhead light. There was nothing in the big sink, but there was a new-looking coffeemaker on the counter and opened packages of paper plates and cups and plastic cutlery in one of the cupboards. The other cupboards were bare, and so was the refrigerator.

A half-glass door at the far end of the kitchen led to a mud room, with a washer and dryer, a utility sink, and a door to some wooden steps and the back lawn. There was a plastic gallon bottle of bleach in the sink, and another of ammonia. Both were nearly empty. There was a metal bucket beneath the sink with a big scrub brush inside. Its worn bristles were stained a dark brown.

Across from the dryer was another door, to what I thought was a closet. But I was wrong. It was a small rectangular room—a pantry—with deep shelves that wrapped around three walls and a rank smell that rushed up into my face. I ran my hand along the wall and found a light switch, and I felt an icy lump land in my gut.

It was a nest.

The floor was covered by a dirty blue gym mat and a sleeping bag and piles of wadded gray clothing, all surrounded by a berm of wet newspaper, greasy paper bags, and soda bottles. There was a large electric lantern on the lowest shelf, and a red portable radio, and on the shelf above that was a heap of torn and taped and badly folded road maps. The other shelves were bare. The odor was stinging—a humid, feral mix of decayed food, body odor, urine, and feces. And there was no mistaking it for anything else; it was a concentrate of what I'd smelled that day in Danes's apartment building, when I'd gotten onto the elevator as Paul Cortese was getting off.

"Christ," I whispered.

I turned off the light and closed the door and went back into the kitchen, and as I did there was a flash at the windows and a deep rumbling in the sky. The lights flickered out and then came on again. I looked at my watch and looked outside. It was after four, but the sky looked more like midnight. The storm was early.

I pulled out my phone and flipped it open. No signal. I went to the window. No signal. I moved around the room. No signal.

"Shit."

I went to the entrance hall and doused the house lights behind me.

The porch was no shelter from the sideways rain, and I was soaked in less than a minute. I turned the flashlight on and the beam leapt forward six feet and vanished in the swirling air. I went down the steps and onto a path that was fast submerging, and I headed for the barn. Gravel and mud squelched and slid under my boots. The barn was thirty yards up the path, and no more than a sketchy silhouette until the lightning. Then, for an instant, it loomed above me, stark and flat and bone white—like an X-ray against the metal sky—and then it was dark again. I leaned into the wind. My hair was plastered to my head and rain ran down my back. I pointed the flashlight at the path and avoided the larger potholes and fell only twice.

I planted my boots in the mud and heaved on the sliding door, and it moved not an inch. I tried it again with no more success, and went around the corner of the barn, to the right. The building shielded me from the wind and a little of the rain, and I stayed close as I worked my way over stones and low vegetation toward the back end. I found another door about halfway along. I played the flashlight over it. It was a wide Dutch door with black iron latches and black iron hinges, and a shiny new hasp set into the doorframe. There was a shiny new lock hanging from it. I opened my waist pack and took out the pry bar.

This doorframe was not for shit and neither was the hardware, and I put a lot of back into it and wasn't subtle. There was a tearing sound and the hasp came away from the frame, along with some long galvanized screws. I pushed the door open and stepped in.

It was black inside, and quiet, and it smelled of damp timber, damp earth, wet hay, and compost. There was a garage smell, too, of metal and rubber and gasoline and exhaust. And faintly, below these odors, was the scent of something else. I found a switch along the wall.

Lights hung from the big central beam, but they were few and dim, and heavy shadows were everywhere. Still, the high points were plain: the black timber bones of the place and the packed earth floor; the ladder to the hayloft at the front of the barn, near the sliding door that was chained and locked; the row of open stalls on the long wall opposite me; the large open space in the middle, and the big black Beemer parked there. My heart was pounding.

I walked to the car and the smell was stronger. I walked around the car. It had New York plates, of course, and of course they were Danes's. The window glass was fogged inside, but not so clouded that I couldn't make out the body in the back seat.

33

He was long gone, and stewed in his own juices—bloated, loose, and coming apart. And he'd been rolled, like an obscene sausage, in heavy plastic sheeting that was sealed at the ends with duct tape. The wrapping was stiff and translucent, and it clouded any features that might have been left on the body, but through it I could see a black irregular patch where the chest used to be.

The car and the plastic had kept the animals out, but it couldn't keep the smell in. It was suffocating and thick, and it boiled out of the open rear door and filled the barn in an instant. I closed the door and staggered back a few paces and ground my teeth to fight the heaving in my stomach. I blotted my eyes with my sleeve and pulled the collar of my sweatshirt up over my nose and stood for a while, taking shallow breaths. I thought about Nina and I thought about Billy.

"Goddammit," I whispered.

I looked at the car. It was a crime scene—this whole place was—and I knew I should leave it in peace. But I'd left *should* behind a while ago—when I'd creeped the house and broken the lock off the barn door, or maybe much earlier than that. I shook my head. My vinyl gloves were wet and tearing, and I pulled them off and jammed them in my pocket. I reached into my waist pack and pulled out a fresh pair.

"In for a penny," I said to myself.

I opened the driver's door, and a fresh wave of dead smell rolled out. I ground my teeth against it and looked into the front seat. It was a mess. It was as if a cyclone had passed through the compartment and dropped the jumbled contents of a linen closet and a wardrobe and a medicine chest in there. Bedsheets and blankets and towels were tangled with trousers and underwear and shoes; shirts were knotted with pillowcases and socks, and the whole chaotic pile was shot through with toiletries: toothbrush, vitamin bottle, razor blades, dental floss, shaving cream. It was debris from the storm whose tracks I'd seen in the master bedroom of the farmhouse.

There was a suitcase jammed into the foot well on the passenger side. It was brown leather and expensive-looking, just like the luggage I'd seen in Danes's apartment. There was a brown plastic medicine bottle with a white cap near the brake pedal. I knelt down and shined the flashlight beam on it. It was for a prescription antibiotic, and it was made out to Gregory Danes. The trunk release was near the driver's seat and I pressed it and the trunk lid went up an inch.

I closed the car door and went around back. There was a flash of blue light through the high barn windows, and a sizzling sound, and an almost simultaneous crack of thunder. The building shook and I felt the pressure wave in my shoulders and I was sure that the windows had shattered. The weak lights failed and found themselves again. I looked up at the windows and saw they were intact. I lifted the trunk lid.

The first thing I saw was the missing curtain rod from the farmhouse dining room, and the missing green curtain. The rod was bent and the curtain was stiff with dried blood. Beneath it was another insane pile. Rather than linen closets and wardrobes, it looked as if someone had whirled a refrigerator together with a desktop. The food was on top—a carton of milk, eggs, butter, a foil bag of coffee, bread, a box of Swiss breakfast cereal, a bottle of red wine—all curdled and rotten and gone to mold. The smell wafted up at me, competing with—and momentarily defeating—the dead smell. It was a small reprieve. Below the food was hardware.

I saw the cell phone that was never answered, an electronic organizer the size of a deck of cards, and the laptop that was missing from the docking station in Danes's apartment. I saw a wineglass, cracked and dark with dregs and mold, and a snarled skein of black power cables wrapped around it all. The papers were underneath.

Some of them were newspapers—*New York Times, Journal, FT*—and some were magazines, and some of them were glossy pamphlets and catalogs. But the milk carton and wine bottle had drained on the pile, and left the electronics sticky and spotted with odd pink scabs and the papers mostly illegible. I picked carefully through the mess and stopped when I got to the briefcase. It was a black leather satchel, and it was empty except for an accordion file. The file was red, with a long flap and an elastic band, and it was mostly unscathed. I slid it out and opened it up.

There was a thick sheaf of papers inside. I thumbed through them and my heart started to pound. There was a bench behind me, near the Dutch door, and I sat on it and read.

Mostly, they were stock research reports, with titles like "Fly Me to the Moon: A Survey of Online Travel Agents," and "Going, Going, Gone: Valuation of Internet Auction Houses," and I recognized the names of the authors—Irene Pratt, Anthony Frye, others—as members of the Pace-Loyette equity research department. The reports were in chronological order on the pile—oldest to latest—and every page of every report was marked CONFIDENTIAL in dark capitals in the upper left-hand corner and DRAFT in the upper right.

The report at the top of the pile had been written by Irene Pratt, and it was fifteen months old. It was eight pages long and surveyed stocks of video-game software companies, and it ended with a recommendation to buy the shares of three different firms. Stapled to the bottom of its last page was a rectangular strip of paper. It was from a fax machine, and it confirmed the transmission, some fifteen months back, of an eight-page fax from a number with a 212 area code—a New York City number—to a number with a 203 area code—a number in Connecticut.

The last report on the stack was barely three months old. It had been written by Anthony Frye and another man from Pace, and it concluded with sell recommendations on the shares of four companies. It was six pages long, and it too had a fax confirmation stapled to its last page—six pages sent to a number in Connecticut. In fact, each of the twelve reports in the stack had a fax confirmation fastened to it. The sending phone numbers were different in each case, but the receiving numbers were all the same. They suggested that someone had been faxing drafts of Pace-Loyette's confidential research reports to someone else in Connecticut, and that whoever it was had been doing it for well over a year.

It was the pages I found tucked between the research reports that told me why. There were twelve of them, one following each of the research reports, and they were typed—not printed—on the simple yet elegant letterhead of the Kubera Group. They were investor statements.

The dates corresponded roughly to the dates on the research papers, lagging them in each case by a week or so, and they reported the performance of only one investment: a 15 percent share in a fund that had the innocent-sounding name of Kubera Venture Twelve. It was an investment, apparently, that had done quite well. On the first statement, dated fifteen months back, the investor's stake in Kubera Venture Twelve was worth just under five million dollars; on the last, its value had more than doubled. I guessed that the investor must have been quite pleased with that performance, but as he was currently wrapped in plastic and dissolving in the back seat of a car, I'd never know for sure. But maybe Marcus Hauck could tell me—it was, after all, his signature on each of the statements.

I let out a long, slow breath. The way I read it, they were in business together, Danes and Hauck. In violation of about a zillion securities laws and NASD rules, and who knew how many of Pace-Loyette's company policies, they were in business together. Danes's end of the deal, apparently, was to provide Hauck with advance copies of Pace-Loyette's research reports. Hauck's part, I assumed, was to use that information to place bets for his funds. Pace-Loyette's reports might not have the same oomph in the markets these days as they once had, but with the size of the positions that funds like Kubera took, even small moves up or down could mean serious money. And Danes, in return for his faxing services, had apparently cut himself in for a piece of that action—and never mind conflicts of interest or little things like insider trading. I remembered what Anthony Frye had told me about Hauck—about the bumps in the road that his funds had hit, and about the magic he'd somehow reacquired over the past year—and I was pretty sure I knew where he'd found his sorcerer's stone.

I looked through the sheaf of papers again. The file was damning to Hauck and Danes both, and while it might not be the whole of their paper trail, it was enough to set even the most sluggish investigator on the right track. It was a smoking gun, and I wondered why Danes had compiled it. And then I recalled what I'd heard about Danes—from Irene Pratt and Anthony Frye and even from Neary—about his reflexive mistrust of people, his tendency to see conspiracy everywhere, and his habit of keeping a firm grip on his management's balls. Whatever else Danes had intended the file to be, it was also an insurance policy. If he'd ever gone down for any of this, he wouldn't have gone alone.

I wondered if Marcus Hauck knew the file existed. He couldn't have been sleeping well if he did, and it could explain why he'd mobilized Pflug and his army of contractors when Danes dropped out of sight. Having something this explosive in the hands of a co-conspirator as difficult and volatile as Danes was bad enough. Having the co-conspirator go missing was infinitely worse.

There was a long rumble of thunder and a gust of wind, and the Dutch door blew open. I jumped. I looked at my watch; it was closing in on six o'clock. I took a last look at the papers and put them in the file folder, and another burst of light and shattering noise exploded overhead. The rafters rattled and glass chattered in the windows. The lights flickered—off and on and off again—and stayed off. I switched on my flashlight.

Shit. I wasn't going to get much more searching done in the dark, and in truth I thought I'd found what I'd come for. It was time to call the cops. It was time to go.

I went to the car and slid the file folder back into the briefcase and closed the trunk. I pulled out my cell phone and tried to find a signal, but the ether was empty no matter where in the barn I stood. I put the phone away and headed for the door.

The rain and wind were heavy when I stepped outside, and the rush of water and the cold ozone tang of the air were a shock and a massive relief. I took a deep breath and looked up at the sky and let the rain wash down my face and through my hair. I needed to burn my clothes and take a long hot shower, but this was a start.

I stood there for a minute or two, and then I pointed my flashlight down and began to work my way along the side of the barn toward the house and the road. I wondered what the power failure had done to cell phone service, and if I'd find a signal down by the road. I thought about the cops who would come in answer to my call—assuming I could make one—and what they'd think about being dragged out on a night like this, and about finding me here, and about what I'd found. And I thought of Jane, and how she was doing in the storm. I stumbled on a stone but kept my feet. I rounded the corner to the front of the barn and smacked my knee on the bumper of the car parked there.

I backed away and ran my flashlight over the car. It was a Chrysler—a K-car—twenty years old at least, and it was brown and heavy with rust. I looked around and reached into my waist pack for the pry bar, but I was too slow and too late and I didn't see it coming.

34

Something like a two-by-four came down between my shoulder blades, and my flashlight went spinning into the rain and dark. He grabbed me by the neck and by the belt and I went spinning too, face first onto the hood of the Chrysler, with a sound that dwarfed the thunder. I slid to the ground and he grabbed my left arm and something popped in my shoulder and I was flying again, into the side of the barn. I didn't register the impact or the pain until I was slumped in the mud, and by then they were abstractions.

I didn't black out, not completely, but I couldn't move much—or not dependably, anyway—and my thoughts were slow and haphazard. I felt him grab me by the belt and drag me. I felt the stones and shrubs I was dragged across, and there was a jagged pain in my shoulder with every jolt. I felt the wind gusting and the rain sweeping over me in sheets, and I felt it stop as I was dragged across a threshold. I smelled the thick, cloying scent of death again, and a rank familiar odor much closer by. Then he swung me, and I skidded and tumbled on the packed earth floor and came hard to rest against something made of wood. And then I blacked out.

There was light when I came to. It was from an electric lantern that was sitting on the roof of the Beemer, and it cast a milky circle around the car and a heavy shadow beyond it. I was crumpled in that shadow, in one of the open-ended stalls that lined one side of the barn. There was blood in my mouth, and maybe dirt, and the side of my face was swollen and numb. There was a faint ringing in my ears and my left shoulder was dislocated. My left arm hung useless beside me like an empty sleeve, and just inhaling caused it to throb and burn. I lay without moving and breathed slowly, and watched Paul Cortese pace back and forth beside the Beemer, into and out of the light.

He was bigger than I remembered—at least six-foot-five—and broader, and he was more disheveled and crazed. His work boots were soaked and splattered with mud, and so were his khaki pants and threadbare brown sweater. His thin tangled hair was plastered to his head, and there was a week's worth of dirty beard on his wide face. There was tape on his glasses and mud on the lenses and I could see nothing of his eyes. He made jerky splay-fingered gestures with his thick blunt hands, and I saw that they were covered with dirt and cuts. His small mouth was moving and I could just hear him over the storm.

"You see? You see what happened? He left another. I see it, and I know you see it too. You see it all. He leaves them, and now I have to put them away." His voice was quick and droning, and the rises and falls and pauses in it had to do with breathing and not with meaning. It was oddly liturgical somehow.

"You know he did it, you know it. He left another—like the last one, but outside, at our car. He left him at our car. He looked at our car." Cortese went still and stiff, and after a moment he twisted his face and shook his head, as if in painful denial of something. "I do—I do have to put them away now. I put them away before—I got it all out. So I have to clean now. He leaves it for me, so I take care of it." Cortese resumed his pacing and wild gesticulating.

I came cautiously to a sitting position and leaned against the back of the stall, and I bit back a gasp of pain when I put weight on my left arm. I reached for my waist pack, but it was gone. I felt around for it but found only dirt. Cortese slammed his fist on the Beemer's roof and the light jumped and so did I.

"We cleaned it all last time—all of it—the whole house. And now he left another. I have to take care of it now." He assumed a wide ragged orbit around the car, and after a few circuits he walked stiffly toward the far end of the barn. He returned with a long roll of plastic sheeting balanced on his shoulder and a six-pack of gray duct tape in his hand. Shit.

He leaned the plastic sheeting against the car and put the duct tape on the hood and disappeared into the shadows again. I got my feet under me and stood slowly in the darkness. My heart was pounding and my arm was throbbing. I heard Cortese rummaging somewhere off to my left, but with the bubbling sound of rain, and the wind in the rafters, it was hard to localize. The lightning flashes only served to blind me. Cortese exclaimed something and it sounded far away. He was big and crazy and he had two good arms. I wasn't sure I'd get a better chance.

I kept low and kept quiet and headed toward the car, skirting the circle of light. I crouched by the front bumper and listened for a moment and heard only wind. I went around the car and headed toward the Dutch door—or where I thought the door was. The barn was black just a few feet from the car and I moved slowly and with my hand outstretched. My knuckles brushed wood and my fingers found the doorframe. I ran my hand along it, feeling for the latch, and heard a shuffling behind me and an angry mutter and an iron clamp closed around my neck.

A spike of pain shot down my shoulder and into my arm and I kicked out and back and connected with something. There was a grunt of surprise but no loosening of his grip. I twisted and brought my right forearm around and banged it against his. It was like hitting a fence post, but his hand slipped off me. And then something came out of the dark and slammed into the side of my head. My knees sagged and he caught me by the belt and threw me into the side of the Beemer. The breath flew out of me in a stinging gasp, and I lost my footing and went down.

Paul Cortese stepped into the circle of light. He was bent over slightly and rubbing the side of his knee and whimpering softly. Tears rolled down his big face and left pale tracks on his skin. I came up fast from a crouch and drove my right fist into his midsection, just below the sternum. He yelped and coughed and staggered back half a step and I stepped forward and threw my elbow into his windpipe. Or that was the plan.

Cortese brought his thick hands up and caught my arm and grunted and pushed. I skidded into the car and hit it with my shoulder and yelled. Cortese looked down and rubbed his gut and made a mewling sound that chilled my blood. Tears spilled from his cheeks. He looked up, and his face was clenched and dark with rage. His eyes were black and full of madness. I turned and slid over the Beemer's hood, and as I did I stretched out my good arm and knocked the lantern off the roof of the car. The barn went black.

I rolled and scrambled in the dark and stopped when my back hit a wall. My heart was hammering and my breathing was ragged and the rushing in my ears blotted out the rain and the wind and whatever sounds

Cortese might be making. I inhaled deeply to slow things down, and I stared into the blackness and strained to hear.

Cortese was sniffling and crying and moving around, but he was near the car and he didn't seem to be looking for me. I heard a clinking sound, like tools bumping together, and a click, and a thin white beam of light moved across the Beemer and onto the ground nearby. Shit.

Cortese put a flashlight on the car hood and stood in its light. His shadow was huge and misshapen and he looked like a golem as he bent to his work. He lifted the roll of sheeting easily and unfurled a large swath on the floor. Then he reached into what looked like a tool bag at his feet and came out with a carpet knife and cut the plastic. He cut open the package of duct tape, pulled out a roll, and tore strip after strip of tape from it. It made a noise like static.

I stood and leaned against the wall. Hitting Cortese was like hitting wet clay, and my right hand and arm were sore. I shook them out and thought about doors. To my right somewhere was the sliding door that was chained and locked, and that would get me exactly nowhere. Nearby to that was the ladder to the hayloft, where my chances were little better—assuming I could get up the ladder in any reasonable time. Somewhere to my left and across the barn—somewhere on the other side of Cortese—was the wide Dutch door. If I got out, it would be through there. If I didn't, I'd be dead.

I tucked my left elbow up against my ribs and tucked my left hand into my belt. I took a deep breath and began to edge forward. Outside, the rain and wind suddenly subsided and it grew quieter in the barn. There'd been no lightning for a while now, and the thunder was rolling away. I heard Cortese's mutterings plainly, and the rattling noise of stiff plastic. If I could hear that, he could hear me—and the longer I waited the quieter it would become. I needed to move. I edged forward again and to the right—and I saw light.

It was a hard blue-white color, and for an instant I thought it was lightning. But it swept in an arc through the barn's high windows and across the walls and I knew that it was a car. And then I heard the engine.

Cortese heard it too, and he stood very still and listened. The engine grew closer and the sound of tires on gravel came with it. Cortese picked up his flashlight and moved away from me, to the door, and I heard the scraping of the latch. And then the car horn sounded—once, twice, three times—each time a sonorous bark. It was the Audi. It was Jane. I rushed at him.

Cortese heard me in the dark and turned, and I drove my right shoulder into his chest. He grunted and swayed and swatted me across the back, and his flashlight went flying. I stumbled backward, pivoted into a clumsy roundhouse kick, and caught him someplace soft. He made a surprised sound and suddenly his big hands were on my throat. He brought me close and what little breath I had was filled with the stench of him. My hand scrabbled across his face and my thumb found an eye socket, and Cortese squealed and threw me away.

I landed on my shoulder in an explosion of pain, and rolled on my back, wheezing. Cortese's flashlight was on the ground, maybe fifteen feet away, and he picked it up and pinned me in its beam and came closer.

And then the lights in the rafters flickered and came back to life. Cortese looked up at them, and when he did I drove my heel into his crotch. He roared in astonishment and pain and staggered sideways, bent over. I held on to the Beemer and climbed to my feet, gasping, and the Dutch door swung in. I gathered my breath to shout to Jane—to warn her—and let it out in a long sigh when two Berkshire County sheriff's deputies stepped in. My legs began to shake and I slid down the side of the car and sat on the ground.

35

One storm was passing, decamping to the east and dissolving at its trailing edge into icy stars and a crescent moon. And another storm was brewing, with Calliope Farms at its swirling center. I sat in the back of a sheriff's department truck that smelled like old socks, and Jane sat in her Audi, and all around us a carnival had gathered, of big official vehicles, gaudy flashing lights, and bulky uniformed men. The last of my adrenaline was seeping away and I felt vaguely nauseated. I fiddled with my ice pack and my sling, but the pain in my shoulder was relentless.

The two deputies who'd been first on scene were young—no more than twenty-five—and they were sodden despite their rain gear. They'd come into the barn looking irritated and tired, but that had all changed when I told them what was in the car and when Paul Cortese made an incoherent noise and a clumsy lunge for the door.

They'd wrestled Cortese to the ground, and cuffed him, and walked us to their SUVs. I'd seen the Audi on the lawn, and Jane's tense, pale face in its rain-spattered windshield. I'd waved to her but gotten no response. The deputies told me to keep still and keep quiet, and they'd put Cortese in one truck and me in the other.

I'd watched the vehicles arrive in ones and twos: Lenox PD cruisers, another sheriff's 4 x 4, a fire truck from Lee, and the Pittsfield EMS. The

EMS techs climbed into the back of the sheriff's car to look at Cortese, who had apparently lapsed into something like a catatonic state. Afterward, a deputy motioned me out of the truck and the techs had looked at me. They'd flashed lights in my eyes, cleaned the cuts on my face, and rigged a sling and an ice pack for my shoulder. Then the deputy put me back into the truck. No one had questioned me beyond name and address and a few other basics. They were waiting for the boss. I hitched up my sling and rearranged the ice pack again, and finally he arrived.

A caravan of cars and SUVs pulled onto the lawn behind the Pittsfield EMS wagon. They were gray and dark blue and bore the seal of the Massachusetts State Police. A heavyset fiftyish guy got out of the first car and came up the small hill toward the house, and a squad of troopers and crime-scene techs followed. The local cops greeted him deferentially.

He huddled for a while with them and with his own people, and he seemed to do more listening than talking. He was about five-ten, with a big head of wavy gray hair that needed cutting. His face was broad, with drooping features, an unkempt gray mustache, and a day's growth on the jaw. He wore a tan baseball jacket, zipped up, and jeans, and he kept his hands in his pockets as he listened and nodded and occasionally glanced in my direction.

He dispatched one team of troopers and crime-scene guys to the barn and another to the house, and he sent a remaining trooper back down the hill to the cruisers. He stood alone near the farmhouse and looked around at the men and cars and lights until the trooper returned and handed him a large Styrofoam cup. Then he went to the Audi and knocked on the glass.

Jane ran the window down and the man bent his head and offered his hand. They shook and spoke and he proffered the cup. Jane took it and the man climbed into the passenger seat and closed the door. I saw Jane sip at what was in the cup and nod her head, but soon the windshield fogged and I could see only shadows. After forty-five minutes, he came to talk to me.

He climbed into the front passenger seat and brought a smell of pipe tobacco with him. He looked at me through the metal grate. His dark eyes were weary, but even so, and even through the grate, he managed an avuncular twinkle.

"Smart lady," he said. "Very smart. And tough. That was a hell of a blow to go driving in, especially in a wind-up toy like that and on these roads. She must've been plenty worried to do that. She must like you." His voice was deep and intimate, with a distinct Boston accent.

I nodded, and he looked at me silently for a long moment.

"She's a little shaken up—no surprise—and a little tired, maybe, but even with that she's real smart. I like smart people. I'm Barrento, by the way—Louis. I run the detective division in Berkshire County." And then he asked his questions.

There were a lot of them, but none that I didn't expect: who I was; what I did; why I'd come there; what I'd been looking for; how I got into the barn; if I had been in the house; if I had touched anything; who the big crazy guy was; why he was tossing me around like a rag doll; whose car was in the barn; whose body was in the car; what I knew about how it got there. He took me through everything I'd done at Calliope Farms several times, from several angles, and every time I told him nearly all of it, withholding only the actual breaking in and my examination of the red accordion file. He listened and nodded and gave nothing away. And when I thought he was through, he sighed and pulled a piece of paper from his jacket pocket and looked at it.

"I read here you used to be a cop—a sheriff's deputy over in New York—Burr County."

I looked at him and said nothing.

"That's not so far from here—three, four hours maybe. I remember that case from a few years back. I was working out of Springfield then, but I remember it."

He studied my face and shook his head a little. "So you tell me, back when you were a cop, what would you have done in my shoes? What would you have done with an out-of-state private license you found prancing around a crime scene—a murder scene, no less? One who fed you some bullshit story about doors already open and locks already busted? One who claimed to be so worried about a missing guy that—even though his client had fired him—he had to drive all the way up from goddamn New York City to go looking. But who—even with all this worry—couldn't be bothered to pick up the fucking phone and give the local cops a heads-up? I mean, hypothetically, what would you have done?"

Barrento didn't raise his voice and didn't take his eyes off mine. I sighed and ran my hand down my swollen cheek. "Hypothetically, I guess I'd be pissed," I said. "But I'd also think about how long it might've taken me to find the body, if this private license hadn't come along, and how long it might've taken to grab a suspect. If I thought he'd done me a little good, then, hypothetically, I might cut him a break."

Barrento pursed his lips and ran a thumb and forefinger over his bushy mustache. "And if the case was a high-profile one? If you knew the press—the national press—would be all over it, along with every boss and politician in the commonwealth? You still think you'd give the guy some slack?"

"I guess I'd want to be sure that he was a right guy," I said. "But if I was, then—on a high-profile case—I'd be happy not to waste my time on bullshit."

Barrento smiled a little. "Thanks for the advice," he said. He settled himself more deeply in the passenger seat and stroked his mustache and looked out the window for a while. Then he turned to me.

"Go sit with her," he said.

Jane was still holding the white Styrofoam cup when I climbed into the Audi. She looked at me—at my face and my arm in its sling, at my clothes that were sodden and mud-covered—and then she looked away.

"Is it broken?" she asked.

"Dislocated. They can reset it in the ER."

"Otherwise you're . . . okay?"

"I'm okay."

"That's good," she said softly. She was quiet for a while, watching troopers carry things to and from the barn, and then she told me what had happened.

It was a simple story. When she hadn't heard from me for hours, and couldn't raise me on the phone, Jane had grown worried and had driven to Calliope Farms. She'd parked on the road, and even through the rain she'd seen lights in the barn and a car—Cortese's Chrysler—in the turnaround, and her worry had grown larger still. And then she'd seen the lights go out and thought she'd heard . . . something, and she'd dialed 911. The emergency operator had been swamped with calls and skeptical, and it had taken a while for the sheriff's deputies to roll up. When they did they were a minute behind Jane, who had waited as long as she was able and had driven up the hill with no plan in mind beyond honking her horn. She finished telling it and took a deep breath and drank the chilly dregs that were left in her cup.

Cars and trucks pulled in and out, and uniformed men came and went and milled around in the mud, and Jane and I watched them and were silent. Colored lights washed across the car, and Jane's hands and face were tinted blue and white and red. The ice pack was spent and the pain in my shoulder was swelling. My stomach was empty and my eyes were gritty and hot. I closed them and kept very still and breathed very little. Thoughts careened in my head for a while, and slid and staggered, and then they stopped altogether.

Barrento rapped on the glass and I jumped. Jane ran the window down.

"You two can go for tonight. But I want you both at the Lee barracks in the morning, for formal statements." He looked at Jane. "You should be out pretty quick," he said. He looked at me. "You'll be longer."

Jane turned the Audi in a tight circle and headed slowly down the driveway. There were flares at the entrance, and state troopers. There was a van parked by the side of the road, a hundred yards from the signpost. It was white and had a large red number eight on its side and a satellite dish on its roof. There were men near it, with lights and a big video rig that they pointed at us as we drove past. Heavier weather was coming.

The ER at Pittsfield Hospital was clean and pleasant, and its array of vending machines was vast. Jane sipped a Sprite while we waited, and turned the pages of a magazine, and was quiet. I ate a chocolate bar and made phone calls.

My first was to Tom Neary. He listened silently while I told him what I'd found and what had happened afterward, and he sighed heavily when I finished.

"Murder and insider trading," he said. "It's a shitstorm all the way around. Unless there's another war or something, the press will go nuts with this. There are probably cable news guys drinking your health right now. I don't envy what's-his-name—Barrento. You think he's any good?"

"I think he's plenty good. And he's been around the block enough times to be expecting the worst on this thing."

"With something this high profile, he's right to. Everybody north of him on the food chain will be pushing for a fast close. At least he's got hold of someone already." Neary thought for a moment. "Will he and his boys know what to make of Danes's file?"

"They'll figure it out eventually, but it might be a while before they get to it. They've got to make a formal ID of the body first, and autopsy it, and then they've got a mountain of forensics to move."

"But when they do—"

"Then Marcus Hauck will be scrambling a squadron of lawyers or else taking an extended vacation to points south. And all the folks at Pace-Loyette will be working on their résumés."

Neary laughed grimly. "I'm not sure it'll sink them, but if it doesn't they'll be doing some serious housecleaning—which will no doubt include their security services."

"Timing is everything," I said. "I'm a little exposed with this file thing—I told Barrento it was all look-but-don't-touch with Danes's car. So you can't know about the file until Barrento gets around to finding it."

"Are you kidding? I plan to keep a healthy distance from Pace until this thing breaks. I'll gladly take their money afterward—assuming there is an afterward—but I'd rather not get splashed with the first wave of sewage. You think Barrento will jam you up?"

"It seems to me he should have a lot of other things to worry about, but you never know."

"You tell Sachs about this yet?"

"She's my next call."

"It's tough for the kid."

"Billy. His name's Billy."

"Right—Billy. And how are you doing?"

I looked over at the waiting area to where Jane sat with a magazine in her lap, looking at the wall.

"Fine," I said. "I'm fine."

I tried Nina Sachs but got only her machine and left no message. Then the man at the desk called my name. I was in and out in fifteen minutes, with my shoulder reset, re-iced, wrapped, and resting in a new sling. Jane was waiting in the car.

The streets of Lenox were quiet when we drove through town, and almost dry. The small parking lot at the Ravenwood Inn was empty. Jane shut the engine down and sat with her hands on the wheel and looked straight ahead. Her cropped black hair was sculpted around her ear, which was small and intricate. Her lower lip was trembling. Muscles flexed in her forearms as she tightened and loosened her grip on the wheel. The ticking of the engine was loud.

"Jane, I . . ." My throat was tight and I was out of air. I took a deep breath. "I know *thank you* doesn't cover it, and neither does *I'm sorry*—"

Jane cut me off. Her voice was quiet and very steady. "Why are you sorry? It's not you, right? It was that crazy man. It was just work, right?"

"Right."

Jane swallowed hard. "Are you in trouble . . . with the police?"

"I don't know. It depends on what Barrento wants to do, how big a deal he wants to . . ."

I stopped and stared at Jane, who had reached under her seat and come up with the Glock. It was matte black and ugly in her lap. She stared at it as if it had just fallen from the sky.

"We shouldn't leave this here," she said. "We should remember to take it inside."

"Jane, what are you—"

"I don't know why I brought it. I thought you might need it . . . or that I could—" She made a small gasping laugh. "So . . . I brought it along." She turned to me, and her perfect face crumbled and her perfect eyes dissolved in tears.

36

Jane was up before six on Wednesday, and she moved quickly about the room—showering, dressing, packing her bag. I lay in bed, in a half-sleep, and for a while I told myself we were at home and that she was getting ready for work. Then I felt a twinge in my shoulder and the whole of the day before came back to me. I opened my eyes, and Jane was at the end of the bed. She was fully dressed and her bag was on her shoulder. Her car keys were in her hand.

"You all right?" she asked. I nodded. "And you can get to the rent-a-car place okay, and drive with that arm?"

"I'm fine."

"Okay. Then I'm going to give my statement and get back to the city."

I sat up but turned wrong and something like a hot wire ran through my shoulder. Jane saw it in my face.

"Don't," she said. "Rest more." She patted my foot.

I looked at her and nodded. "Drive carefully," I said.

Light was streaming through the big windows, and I heard birds, and a dog bark. In a minute I heard Jane's car start, and turn in the drive, and pull away. I looked at the ceiling and wrapped the covers around me and thought about going back to sleep, but didn't.

I got up and worked my left shoulder in tentative circles. It was sore and bruised and still a little swollen, but it was all there. I checked my face in the mirror. The puffiness had gone down, but there was a cut across the bridge of my nose and bruising around my eyes. I picked up the phone and tried Nina Sachs again. This time I didn't even get her machine.

Lee is next door to Lenox, to the south and east, and the state police barracks there is just off Route 7, in a stolid brick building with white trim, lots of antennae, and, when I pulled up, three TV news vans out front. I went in a side door, and a trooper led me to Barrento's office.

It was small and square, with a window onto Route 7, a beige metal desk, and the smell of old coffee. Barrento wore a wrinkled green shirt and last night's jeans. His baseball jacket was collapsed in a corner, and Barrento seemed like he might soon follow. His beard was heavier and his eyes were ravaged, and he looked years older than when I'd seen him last. He had a telephone propped in his ear, and he pointed at one of the plastic chairs in front of his desk. I sat.

The desk was layered in papers, the only clear spots taken by graduation photos of two boys whose square faces and heavy features were younger, less cautious versions of Barrento's own. Barrento dug with a wooden matchstick at a well-used brown pipe while he listened to the phone, and every now and then he said "Uh-huh."

He hung up and scanned my face, and my arm in its sling. "Well, at least you got a change of clothes," he said. "You see the fourth estate out there?" He stifled a yawn and tossed a thumb at the window. "This place is a fucking sieve. And it'll only get worse when we release the ID. You should figure they'll get hold of your name. I told your friend the same thing when she was in."

I nodded. "You made the ID?" I asked.

"Just between us girls, we matched his prints with the ones he gave for his brokerage license. It's Danes."

"You have a cause of death too?"

"I don't have the report, but the bullet hole I saw in what was left of his chest was a clue."

I thought about that for a while, and Barrento watched me think. "You have a time of death?" I asked.

He shook his head. "Got to wait for the report. It's weeks, though."

"Have you spoken with his ex-wife yet?"

"Early this morning. But enough with your questions, let's do some of mine. You give any thought to what we talked about last night?"

"Some."

"Any parts of your story you want to change?"

I shook my head.

Barrento's laugh was deep. "No? That's a pity. 'Cause I was hoping you could help me account for these."

He pulled open a file drawer and reached in. He came up with a large plastic evidence bag. My waist pack was inside. The tools clanked when he put it down. He reached into the drawer again and came up with two more bags. My flashlight was in one and my cell phone was in the other. They were caked in mud. My shoulder was throbbing and I rubbed it. Barrento chuckled some more and knocked his pipe on the edge of the desk. Fine ash came out, and he whisked it away with the side of his thick hand.

"I was thinking about what you said last night—about not wasting time on bullshit—and I was thinking that it's actually good advice. I mean, I've got more than enough bullshit in my life right now, you know, and it would be great to get rid of some. Like, for example, your bullshit story about how you got into the house and the barn—which by the way was even less convincing once I found your burglar's tools lying around the yard. Then there's the bullshit I'll have to go through if you stick to that story—searching for the nonexistent third party who jimmied those locks. And there's the bullshit any half-bright defense lawyer will sling to take your crappy story and my failure to find this third party and turn it all into reasonable doubt. That's three big piles of crap I'd really like to get rid of." Barrento shook his head regretfully. "You see where I'm headed with this, March?"

"More or less."

Barrento smiled. "And now, would you *more or less* like to change your story?"

I was quiet and Barrento looked at me some more.

"Nobody around here is looking to make their career with a B and E bust, March. I'm doing you a favor."

"Why?"

He shrugged. "Like I said, I don't want to waste my time. And maybe I figure you did me a little good yesterday. And maybe a couple of buddies of mine over in New York State said you were a decent cop back when, and a pretty smart guy."

"You've been busy."

"All night long."

I nodded. "Okay," I said. "I appreciate the break."

"Great. Now you get a chance to show me how much." Barrento's smile was tired and disarming, and his dark eyes were as honest and shiny as a spaniel's. My stomach tightened.

"How?"

"You've been working on Danes longer than me. I thought you could give me some background."

"What kind of background?"

"On his friends, his family, his colleagues, anybody pissed off at him, anybody he was pissed off at—the basic stuff."

I was quiet for a long while, thinking careful thoughts. Barrento watched me, a tiny smile lurking beneath his mustache. "I thought you had a suspect," I said finally.

His smile grew. "I do. But you know how it is. You like to be sure, especially when half the world is watching."

"You're not sure it was Cortese?"

Barrento shrugged. "Probably I'll feel better when I get more forensics back, and when I can talk to the guy."

"He's still out of it?"

"Docs tell me it'll be a while before the drugs kick in and he can say anything sane. By which time he'll have a lawyer. The lab work is coming along, but there's a shitload to process."

"So—for now—you're not sure it was Cortese?"

"Are you?" he said, and poked again at the bowl of his pipe. Somewhere I heard the turning of wheels within wheels.

"I think he wrapped Danes in plastic and packed him in the car."

"Me too," Barrento said. "Especially since we're lifting Cortese's prints from the sheeting and the car and all the crap inside. Though I'll be damned if I can figure out why he did it."

He stuck the pipe in his mouth and tested the draw. Something was amiss, and he dug at it some more with the match.

"What do you think about the shooting part?" he asked.

My stomach got tighter, and I answered carefully. "I didn't see a gun."

Barrento smiled a little. "Neither have we—not yet, anyway."

"Not in the house or in Cortese's car?"

"Nope."

"Which doesn't mean much by itself."

"Not much," Barrento said. He drew on his pipe some more and then he looked at me. "We think he was killed in the dining room. The floors were cleaned in there, but there was blood in the boards." Barrento paused and smiled at me. "But you know all that already, don't you?"

I smiled back and he continued.

"Curtains and a curtain rod were missing from the dining room. We found them in the trunk, with Danes's blood on them." Barrento sighed deeply and put his pipe down. He ran his hands over his mustache. "There was quite a collection of stuff in there—a bottle of red wine, two wine-glasses . . . Did you happen to notice the stain on the dining room table? No? It was red wine. Turns out there was some in the floorboards too, mixed in with the blood, and there was even some on the curtains. We think it spilled when Danes was shot." Barrento's eyes were on me, and they weren't tired now.

"*Two* glasses?" I asked.

He nodded. "You think he and Cortese were having a drink together?"

"Probably not," I said slowly.

"Probably not. There was other odd stuff in the trunk, too—news-papers, magazines, all kinds of catalogs."

I nodded vaguely. I was still thinking about the two glasses, and his next question took me by surprise.

"Danes has a kid, right?"

I looked at him for a moment. "A son."

"He lives with the ex?"

"In Brooklyn."

"That's where he goes to school?"

I nodded. "Where are you going with this?"

Barrento shrugged. "The catalogs we found in the trunk, they were from different private schools—boarding schools—most of them up here in New England. That tell you anything?"

"I don't know," I said, and I said it like I meant it. My shoulder was throbbing again and I was feeling oddly light-headed.

Barrento looked at me and stroked his mustache. He took his time getting to the next question. "You know if Danes was a smoker?"

I shook my head. "He wasn't."

"We didn't think so, and Cortese isn't either—not according to his car ashtrays anyway. But somebody in that house was. We found a dirty ashtray at the bottom of the trunk and lots of cigarette ash. And we found these." Barrento reached into his desk drawer. "There are five of them," he said, and he held up the evidence bag. The cigarette butts were brown and wilted and wet-looking.

He let me look at the bag for a while, and then he called someone on his telephone and a trooper came in and took it away. Barrento leaned back in his chair and folded his hands across his solid middle.

"We've got a lot of evidence to process still," he said. "Prints off the wine bottle and the glasses and the ashtray, for instance, and DNA off the cigarette butts—plenty of stuff. And we've barely touched Cortese's car.

"But I took a quick look last night. Seems like the guy was living in there when he wasn't camping out in kitchen closets. The thing is full of smelly clothes and candy bar wrappers and half-eaten hamburgers. And store receipts. It looks like Cortese saved every goddamn Seven-Eleven sales slip he ever got, and from the stack I saw, it seems like he hit every one between here and Florida in the last few weeks." Barrento leaned forward and opened his top drawer and took out a brown leather tobacco pouch. It was weathered and soft, and the smell of tobacco filled the room when he opened it.

"Be interesting to take a look at the dates on some of those," he said, "once we get a time of death for Danes." We were quiet for a while. Barrento watched me as he packed his pipe. I looked out the window and tried to catch the thoughts that were spinning away from me. The throbbing in my shoulder was worse and the light-headed feeling had become free fall.

"You're not interested in Cortese," I said finally.

Barrento smiled. "I feel good about the forensics," he said. "There's a lot to process, but there was no master criminal working here; forensics will get me where I want to go. The only problem is, they take time." He stuck the pipe in his mouth and tested the draw again. "I figure you've been traipsing around in Danes's life the last few weeks—maybe you have some ideas."

My mind was racing, swirling with all the things I hadn't seen last night, all the pieces I hadn't put together while I'd been thinking about Hauck and reading through the red accordion file. I looked at Barrento and shook my head slowly.

His mouth twitched beneath his mustache, and for the first time a note of impatience crept into his voice. "C'mon, March, what did they teach you over in Burr County? Who's the first person you look at when somebody gets whacked?"

.   .   .

Barrento took my amended statement without comment and walked me to the door. The crowd of press outside had grown larger and more restless.

"You going to give out the ID soon?" I asked.

"Half hour from now. I got some boy genius from the AG's office coming over, and then the fun really starts." Barrento put his hand out and we shook, and he locked his tired eyes on mine. There was no twinkle in them. "You stay in touch with me, March," he said, and he handed me a card. "And if something—anything—occurs to you, you make me your first call."

I got back in my rental car and put the key in the ignition. I looked at Barrento's card and closed my eyes and took a deep breath. I let it out very slowly.

"Goddammit," I said softly.

37

News of Gregory Danes's death beat me back to New York, and so did news of my involvement in the case. There was a camera crew in front of my building when I got home, but they were slow or inattentive and I was inside before they could get out of their van. My voice mail was full.

There were a lot of messages from reporters, including three from Linda Sovitch. She was chatty and intimate and she called me John. She wanted to interview me for *Market Minds*.

There were messages from my family, too—from Lauren and Liz, who wanted to know that I was okay, and from Ned, to tell me that reporters had been calling him, that he didn't like it, and that if I did talk to the press he'd prefer me not to mention any connection to Klein & Sons. It was touching, really.

Mickey Rich had called also. I called him back.

"They're saying on TV that Paulie killed Danes," he said. He sounded very old.

"That's because they feel compelled to say something. Paul's in custody—which is probably a good thing all around—but the police haven't come to any conclusions."

"Is he in bad shape?"

"Physically he seemed quite fit to me, but otherwise he's not good. No matter how this shakes out, he's going to need a lot of help."

"Did Paulie . . . hurt you? I saw something on the news—"

"I'm fine, Mr. Rich. A little scuffed but nothing worse."

Rich sighed and was quiet. "I'm going up there," he said, after a while. "I mean, Joe would want it, and who else has he got if not me?"

He hung up and I went back to deleting messages. While I did I turned on the television to BNN. One of their reporters was standing in front of Pace-Loyette's office building, annoying the guards and harassing anyone going into or out of the lobby. I flicked to an all-news channel, which just then was an all-Danes channel. They ran old clips of him addressing an investor conference, and with Linda Sovitch on *Market Minds,* and more recent, less flattering footage of him walking fast and looking furtive on Park Avenue.

Then the coverage switched gears into a recap of the story so far. I froze when they got to the part about the discovery of his body. Aerial footage of Calliope Farms was followed by a nighttime shot of the driveway and flares and state troopers, and of a gray Audi TT turning onto a road. My face was clearly visible through the window glass, and so was Jane's.

"Shit." My voice echoed in the apartment. I flicked the TV off.

My second-to-last message was from Marcus Hauck. He was quiet, cold, and very brief. "Call me." The last message was from Billy. He spoke in a whisper.

"You said you'd find him and I guess you did, so I should say thanks. Maybe you could call me. I want to know what happened to him is all, and Mom won't tell me or let me go online or even watch TV. The phone is ringing every five seconds, and TV people are outside, and she's all freaked out. She and Nes are screaming at each other about I don't know what. Mom's taking me out to New Jersey in a while, to Grandpa's place. Maybe you could call me there. I just want to know what happened." He left me his grandfather's phone number and hung up.

I took my sling off and worked my shoulder around. It was sore, but less so. I opened some windows and powered up my laptop. Then I sat at my table and spent the next half hour reading again through Danes's phone records and through my own notes. When I was done I pushed my chair back and ran my hands through my hair.

"Shit."

I called Nina Sachs's apartment again, and again got no answer. Then I tried the Jersey number that Billy had left. It was busy and stayed that way for half an hour, and finally I gave up. I tried the I-2 Galeria de Arte in Brooklyn next. The phone rang for a long while before an irritated-sounding woman with a high-pitched voice picked up. She claimed not to know Nina Sachs and told me Ines was out. When I pressed, she suggested I try the gallery in SoHo. I called the SoHo number and someone picked up on the first ring, but whoever it was kept silent and hung up when I asked for Ines. After that the line was busy.

I went to the window and looked out at the street. The news crew was gone. The sun was fading and a wind had picked up. I pulled on my field jacket before I left, and clipped the Glock behind my back.

The I-2 gallery in SoHo was on Greene Street, near Canal. It was smaller than its Brooklyn cousin, a narrow space in a narrow brick building flanked by pricey shoe stores. It had a glass front and a glass door, and all the glass was covered by fabric shades. The door was locked and I pressed the bell. Nothing happened for a while and then a corner of a window shade was pulled back. It was Ines. She looked at me for a long moment and then she went away. I rang again and after minutes of nothing happening I rapped on the glass with my fist. The door buzzed. My pulse quickened and I went in.

The gallery was dim inside, lit only by the gray haze that filtered through the shades in front and by the chrome gooseneck lamp on the big black desk in back. The walls were empty and the bleached wood floors were bare; the ceiling was hung with shadows. The whole place smelled of cigarettes and plaster dust, and the air felt ten degrees colder than out on the street. My footsteps were loud and hollow.

Ines sat behind the desk, at the edge of a black wooden chair. She wore a green jersey dress, and her hair fell around her face. There was a wineglass on the desk, nearly empty, and a bottle of merlot, mostly gone. There was a round glass ashtray beside the bottle, with a cigarette burning in it. And beside the ashtray there was a small chromed semiautomatic.

I took a deep breath.

Ines leaned forward and her face came into the cone of light from the desk lamp. She was gaunt and sallow, and her huge almond eyes were painted with ash. Her straight strong nose was red at the end, and pinched-looking, and the creases on her forehead were dark and deep. And there were three parallel lines—angry red scratches—that ran from the bottom of her left ear to the left corner of her mouth. She looked up at me and made a wry face.

"You do not look well, detective," she said. She was hoarse and tired-sounding.

"You and me both."

"Yes. It has been a difficult few weeks."

"I can imagine."

Ines laughed bitterly. "Can you, detective?" She rested her long fingers on the edge of the desk. She stretched out one and nudged the butt of the gun.

"Where is Nina?" I asked.

"She took Guillermo . . ." Her breath deserted her and she stumbled over his name. "She took him to New Jersey, to her parents' home. It was . . . too much in Brooklyn." She took a hit off her cigarette, and the ember hissed.

"Is she coming back?"

Ines shrugged. Her shoulders were stiff and brittle-looking beneath the jersey. "I do not know her plans, detective."

"What happened to your face?"

Ines shook her head. Her black hair was dull and heavy. "A household accident," she said, and drained her wineglass. She stubbed out her cigarette and lit a fresh one.

"Was Nina part of it?"

She looked at me through a cloud of smoke. "Was Nina part of what?"

I shook my head. "Now is not the time, Ines. I know your taste in wine and your choice of smokes. The cop who's running this case doesn't, but he'll know other things. He'll pull prints off the wine bottle and DNA from the cigarette butts, and it won't take him long. And the first comparisons he's going to make are with you and Nina. So now is not the time to play around. Now we have to think about Billy, and it's a whole different story if Nina knew about this."

Ines sighed and her shoulders sagged. A look that might have been relief rolled across her face like cigarette smoke and vanished. *"Dios mío,"* she whispered. *"He* is all I think of: what will become of him, what he will think of me. He is what this is all about." She made her long fingers into a fist and slammed it on the desk. *"¡Mierda!"*

"Did she know, Ines?"

She shook her head, and her eyes roamed the shadows over my shoulder. "I did not tell her, if that is what you mean; we have never spoken of it.

She did not know what happened—otherwise she would not have hired you. Later on, after you began your work, when you told her about Gregory calling for his phone messages, and that he had suddenly stopped calling, and the date that he stopped—then I think she began to know something. Then I think she remembered that I had been away, and when. I think she knew then what I had done, but she did not *want* to know. You understand?" I let out a deep breath and nodded. "That is why she fired you, I think."

"But you never discussed it with her?"

"When we got the news . . . that his body had been found . . . I tried. But she was so frightened and . . . angry." Ines touched the scratches on her face. "She would not hear it, and she would not let me speak of it."

Ines shook her head and clasped her hands in front of her, as if in prayer.

"But how can I not, detective? When I look at Guillermo—when he asks about his father—how can I not speak of it? It is like a weight on my chest. It squeezes the breath from me and breaks my ribs. How can I bear this thing any longer?" Ines rested her forehead on her clasped hands, and her shoulders shook. Her cigarette fell to the desktop and began to smolder. I reached down and put it in the ashtray. Ines put her hand over the gun.

"How did you know where to find him?" I asked softly.

"We spoke, and he told me where he was," Ines said. She ran her hands over her eyes. "He gave me directions."

"You spoke when he called for Billy?"

She nodded. "He called to leave a message for Guillermo, and I was at home. I picked up the phone." She looked up at me. "How did you know?"

"His phone bill. There isn't much activity on it, but there is a call to Nina's number, made about two weeks after Danes left town. At first I thought it was one of the calls Billy told me about, one of the times his father had left a message. Billy told me those calls had come in the first ten days or so after Danes left, but I thought maybe he'd gotten the dates wrong. Then I checked the bill again, and the length of the call, and I realized Billy wasn't mistaken. Danes called a third time."

A look of disgust crossed Ines's face. "Yes, he called and I picked up the phone and spoke to him."

"About what?"

"About Guillermo . . . about the schools and the custody."

"You were involved in those discussions?"

Her bitter smile returned. "No, detective, those were between Nina and Gregory only. I merely had to live with the consequences, with Nina's upset . . . and Guillermo's. It has been very bad for him, especially in the last months, since his father started again with lawyers."

"Since he reopened the custody suit?"

She nodded. "It was very difficult for Guillermo, very upsetting. And then I heard Gregory's voice on the machine and I just . . . picked it up."

"What happened then?"

Ines lit a fresh cigarette and shivered. "It was terrible. He was angry and mocking and cruel, and he was . . . triumphant. He talked about Guillermo coming to live with him, and sending him away to boarding school, and he thanked me for it . . . for making it possible."

"Thanked you why?"

Ines blew out a cloud of smoke. "He said it was because of me that he would win the custody—that no judge would leave Guillermo in a house-hold with me."

I shook my head. "Being a lesbian is hardly grounds for—"

"That is not what he meant, detective. He meant something else." Ines looked down at her smooth right arm and ran a finger over the fat shiny scar just below her elbow. "It seems like such a small thing now," she said.

"What was he talking about, Ines?"

"It was in Spain, when I was much younger. I was a fool, and I did a foolish thing. I carried a package for a friend, from Istanbul back to Madrid. I was stopped at the airport. It was heroin, and there was over a kilo. I was in prison for almost two years. I had never done anything like it before, and I never have since." Ines poured the rest of the wine into her glass, and took a drink. "Years later, when I came to this country, I made sure that none of that appeared on my immigration forms or came to the attention of the INS."

"Danes found out?"

"When he started again with lawyers, he hired detectives of his own, detectives in Madrid. They found records." She sniffed and wiped her eyes. I thought about the business card I'd found in Danes's desk: FOSTER-ROYCE RESEARCH. "Gregory thanked me for my help, detective, and wished me a good trip back to Spain."

I sighed and ran a hand through my hair. "What did you say?"

"I . . . I pleaded with him . . . for Guillermo's sake. I said we all wanted what was best for Guillermo, and that destroying the home we had made for him could not be for the best. I said if he wanted more participation in

Guillermo's life, we would welcome that. And I asked if we could meet, to work something out. I pleaded with him to meet me, detective."

"And he said yes?"

Ines shook her head. "At first he was angry. He called me filthy names and said how dare I talk to him about what was best for his son. He said all I cared about was not being deported. But I pleaded and . . . I cried, detective, and he enjoyed that. He said if I wanted to waste my breath, why not, and he told me where he was staying."

"And you went up there?"

"A few days later."

"And Nina had no idea?"

"She thought I was visiting the gallery in Kinderhook." Ines sighed deeply. Her gaze fell to the desk and wandered across its surface and came to rest on the gun. It seemed to exert a gravity of its own on her, and her eyes were drawn to it again and again. She placed her hand on it once more.

"Why did you go there, Ines? What did you think would happen?"

Ines started to speak and stopped. She looked up at me, and tears were falling from her almond eyes. "I do not know, detective."

"Did you think that you could talk to him—that he would listen and be convinced?" She shook her head slowly. "You had that with you?" I pointed at the gun.

She slid the gun across the desk until it was in front of her. She looked at it as if it might speak. "Yes," she said.

"Where did you get it?" I stepped closer to the desk.

"It is mine," she said, and she picked up the gun and put it in her lap. "I have owned it for years."

"And you took it with you—why?"

"I . . . I do not know, detective, I—"

"Were you afraid of Danes?"

She nodded vigorously. "I was terrified of him. He was a small man, and full of anger and bitterness and fear. Even before Nina and I became lovers, since the time we were merely friends, he has hated me. I have always been afraid of him."

"And that's why you took the gun?"

Ines looked up at me and made a small and very tired smile. "Is that what you want me to say, detective? Is that what you want to hear—that I did not go there to kill Gregory? That I had the gun with me because I feared for my life?"

I shook my head. "I just want to hear what happened. What happened when you went to see him?"

Ines took another drink. "It was terrible—worse than on the phone. I tried to be very friendly. I brought wine and he opened it and poured glasses for us both. We sat at the table and I talked. I talked again about wanting only what was best for Guillermo, and how Nina and I had made a good home for him. I talked about this being a difficult time for Guillermo, a difficult age, and that he needed all of us to help him. And Gregory nodded and smiled and I thought . . . that he was listening to me. Then he went into the next room and came back with a stack of booklets. They were from different boarding schools, and he laughed and asked if I wanted to help pick the one that Guillermo would go to.

"He called me a *drug addict bitch* and said the drugs must have made me crazy or stupid if I thought he would ever allow his son to be raised by a *spic bull dyke*. And then he told me never to call his son by a *spic* name again—that his name was William or Billy or Bill and not *Guillermo*. And then he asked me if I was going to cry again, because he had really been looking forward to that."

"And then?"

"And then I threw my wine in his face and called him a dickless little weasel. And then he punched me."

"He hit you?"

"In the stomach. I fell down and he stood over me and laughed and . . . that is when I shot."

"Did you think he was going to keep hitting you?"

She shook her head wearily. "I do not know what I thought, detective. I do not know what he would have done." Ines rubbed her eyes and raked a hand through her hair.

"And afterward?"

She shook her head. "Afterward, nothing was real. I walked out of the house and I was . . . surprised. I was surprised that I could still walk, and that my car could start, and that I could drive. It seemed to me that people should stop and stare, or that the police should come, but they did not. I drove all the way to New York—all the way home—and everything was very ordinary and no one noticed me. And then I saw Guillermo and found that I could not breathe.

"He was as he always is, sweet and funny and bright—and difficult—and he spoke to me about his school and his comic books, and he had . . . no idea. He had no idea that everything had changed." Ines pressed her fingers to her eyes, and her shoulders shook. She took a deep breath and let it out slowly.

"No one had any idea. I woke, I ate, I worked. I spoke and people spoke to me. I could even laugh. It all was as before—but of course it was not. There were moments I told myself that it could go on this way, that no one would find him . . . but then I would see Guillermo, walking around, not knowing. . . .

"I try to tell myself that I saved him, detective, but I know it is not so. I know that I have lost him. I know I have destroyed him." She ground the heel of her palm between her breasts, and her voice became choked and desperate. "And the weight is so great, detective . . . I cannot breathe."

Ines put her arms on the desk and her head on her arms. The sun was nearly set and street light could not penetrate the window shades. I stepped closer to the pool of light around the desk and put my hand on her shoulder. It was bony and trembling, and after a while she reached out and placed a cold hand on mine.

We stayed that way for a while and then Ines raised her head and pushed back from the desk and away from me. She took the gun from her lap and held it in both her hands and turned the muzzle inward. My heart began to pound.

"I was scared when Nina hired you—terrified. But a part of me was relieved that someone had come . . . to take all this from me. And now you have, and I thank you for that, detective."

I took a deep, shaky breath. "We have a lot to do, Ines—a lot to do for Billy. And the first thing is to have you talk to a friend of mine. He's a lawyer—the best one I know—and he can help us with this." I was too far away. I took a half step forward and tried not to look at the gun.

Ines smiled grimly. "A lawyer cannot help me, detective. A lawyer cannot make this right with Guillermo or let me look at him again. A lawyer cannot make this . . . stop." She ran a forefinger along the top of the gun barrel. My skin prickled, and sweat rolled down my back. My throat was closing and I had to fight to get words out.

"He can help you to survive it, Ines, and that's what Billy needs. He needs for you to survive this."

She shook her head. "I cannot. I have destroyed his life, detective, and I am too much of a coward to see the aftermath." She stared at the gun some more and I took another half step. I was still too far.

"Billy will need a lot of help—it's true—but he'll need even more without you."

"Nina is there," she said, but there was more hope than certainty in her soft voice.

"We both know that Nina's not so good at help, Ines. Billy needs *you*."

She closed her eyes. "He is the closest I will have to a child, detective," she said softly. She slid her thumbs along the trigger guard and put her right thumb on the trigger. I edged closer. My heart was hammering at my ribs and blood was roaring in my head. I flexed my fingers. My joints felt welded shut. I was too far.

"And you're the closest he has to a parent, Ines. You're all he has of home. Don't take that from him."

Ines brought the gun up and stared into the barrel. Her chest was heaving and her eyes were black and shattered and fixed on something far from the empty room. She squeezed them shut and grimaced, and my body clenched for impact.

"Please, Ines," I whispered. "He's lost too much already."

Her knuckles were white over the pistol grips and her arms were shaking. And then she opened her eyes, and they were filled with tears. Color came back into her fingers, and she lowered the gun and put it on the desk. I put my hand over it and let out an ancient breath.

38

My head rested on the seat back and I watched the traffic crawl south-bound on Park Avenue. The taxi hadn't moved in ten minutes and I thought about getting out and walking and instead I closed my eyes. It was Thursday afternoon, and I was on my way home. Ines Icasa was on her way to Lee, Massachusetts, to give a statement regarding the death of Gregory Danes and to be taken into custody. She was accompanied on her journey by Michael Metz, the best lawyer I knew, and by the best lawyer that he knew who was a member of the Massachusetts bar. They had negotiated Ines's surrender over the course of several long and tense conference calls in which I had participated, along with Louis Barrento, a man named Graham from the attorney general's office, and a few dozen other people whose names I never got. The first of those calls had taken place on Wednesday evening, and the last one had ended an hour ago. No one knew how it would turn out for Ines, but her lawyers were cautiously optimistic. Ines herself had moved for the moment beyond hope or worry into realms of deep exhaustion.

I'd seen her last in a well-appointed conference room in midtown. The drapes had been pulled and she had been asleep on the sofa when I'd come in. She was disoriented when she woke, and scared, and she sat up quickly. Her dark eyes were darting and huge in her face.

"I didn't mean to disturb you," I said.

Her eyes settled on me. She ran her hands over her face and through her hair. "No, I must get up. Nina is coming. She is bringing my clothes." Her voice was hoarse and low and she cleared her throat. "She wanted to bring Guillermo, but I told her no, not now. The lawyers say that in a few days I will probably be able to return home, and when I do, then we will talk." She yawned deeply. "I am told there is a shower here. I need a shower." She looked at me. "You have come to say good-bye?"

"Only for a day. I'll be in Lee tomorrow, for statements."

"I will be glad to see you," she said. She perched at the edge of the sofa and stretched her arms in front of her and rubbed her hands on her thighs. She was pale and drained and unprepared for what would come, and I suddenly wished I had a blanket to put around her. But I didn't.

"I'll be glad to see you too," I said.

Ines smiled absently and rubbed her eyes. She pointed to the drapes on the big windows. "Could I trouble you to open those, detective?" I did, and a brilliant spring day rushed in at us. The sky and the river were impossible shades of blue, and the office towers were shining and sharper than etchings. The thin clouds were like spun-sugar ribbons in the sky. Ines drew a breath and blinked against the light. After a minute she came to the window and stood near me and looked out. When she spoke, her voice was very soft.

"This is a beautiful city, detective," she said, and I had agreed.

I'd run into Nina Sachs downstairs. She wore black and carried an overnight bag, and her auburn hair was bound in a tight queue. The skin on her cheeks was veined and blotchy, and her arms and legs were rigid with anger. She moved quickly across the lobby and stopped in her tracks when she saw me coming.

"You proud of yourself?" she said when I came up to her. Her voice was a hiss. "You happy with what you've done to me?"

"I don't think anyone is happy with this," I said. "Ines and Billy and Gregory least of all."

"Don't!" she shouted, and people looked at us. "Don't you fucking talk to me about them—don't even say their names. Jesus Christ, if I had a time machine, I'd take it back to the day I met you and throw your ass out the door."

"How about using it to stop Ines from going to Lenox?"

"You think this is a joke, you prick?"

My shoulder was sore and my head ached, and it had been a day since I'd slept or changed my clothes. My eyes were full of grit and my stomach was full of too much coffee, and I was full to bursting with Nina Sachs. I almost told her so, but I didn't. "I think this is the least funny thing I've ever heard of," I said quietly.

"You got that right, asshole," she said.

"How is Billy?"

The red patches on Nina's face grew darker. "How the fuck do you think he is? He's a disaster, thanks to you."

I took a deep breath. "Tell him if he'd like to talk—"

"To *you*? Why, you want to make sure his head is completely screwed up? Well, rest easy. That one's covered."

"He's going to need help to get through this, Nina. He—"

"My God, you've got nerve!" Heads again turned in the lobby, and the security guards eyed us anxiously. "You ignore my orders, betray my confidences, open up my life to the police and the fucking press, and then—while I'm standing in the wreckage—you have the gall to lecture me about how to handle my kid.

"Well, how I handle him is none of your goddamn business, March. You've done enough to me and my family—more than enough. Just stay the hell away from him. Stay away from all of us." Her heels had been like gunshots as she walked away. Another satisfied customer.

It was nearly four when I got home. There were no news crews, but there was a shiny black Porsche Carrera parked in front of my building. Valentin Gromyko climbed out to meet me. He was immaculate in gray.

"You looked better on television," he said. There was some irony in his voice but no trace of it in his frosty eyes.

"I get that all the time," I said. I yawned and massaged my shoulder.

Gromyko looked at the cuts on my face. "A miscalculation?" he asked.

"That and distraction."

"A dangerous mix, especially for someone who minds so much of other people's business. I hope it is not a habit, or I may never receive my payment."

"Thanks for the concern. But if you're here to collect, I should tell you that the Commonwealth of Massachusetts has my dance card booked for the next few days."

Gromyko shook his head. "I am not here to ask anything, but simply to remind you of the premium that I place on discretion. It is something you should keep in mind if you find yourself talking to the press or to the authorities. You should make no mention of Gilpin . . . or of me."

I laughed. "My brother gave me similar advice."

"A sensible man."

"Terminally. But don't worry. I have nothing to say to the press and no reason to mention Gilpin or you to the police."

Gromyko nodded. "Then I will leave you to your rest," he said. He turned toward his car and turned back when I spoke.

"How is Gilpin doing?" I asked.

Gromyko gave me a long speculative look. "Sad," he said finally. "And angry. And guilty—though I doubt he knows it, or knows why. He is drinking heavily, and it will be some time before he is of any use." He looked at me some more and shrugged. "Families are complex," he said, and he got into his shiny car and drove away.

I went upstairs and opened my windows wide and let the day in. I drank from a carton of orange juice and turned the pages of one of Jane's travel magazines while I listened to my messages. There were four of them. The first three were from Marcus Hauck, and each was more urgent than the one before.

"Mr. March, please call. I'd like to discuss your recent trip to the Berkshires and what you discovered there. I will of course compensate you for your time and expertise.

"Mr. March, please call as soon as possible. I wish to engage your services on an immediate basis, and I will wire a retainer to whatever account you name by close of business today. Please call me.

"March, it is imperative that I speak to you regarding Gregory, and what, if anything, you might have seen among his personal effects. Call me. I assure you, I will make it worth your while."

I shook my head. The stakes were very high for Hauck, and I wondered how desperate he was, and how stupid and reckless he would get. He was already desperate enough to call me and stupid enough to leave messages. But would he be reckless enough to send Pflug on a hunting expedition up north—a mission, perhaps, to creep the evidence lockup at the Lee barracks? I certainly hoped so. Because after our conversations last night, Louis Barrento would be waiting, and the red accordion file was already on its way to the Feds. I saved all three messages.

The last call was from Jane. There was a lot of noise in the background, and her voice was tired and sometimes lost in the din, but I got the message.

"The buyer's board met this morning and approved the deal, and we signed everything before noon. So I'm done. And I'm done with these guys for good; they decided not to make an offer to keep me around. Apparently some of their board members saw me on TV yesterday—that clip of us driving from the farm—and had second thoughts. Talk about a silver lining." There was a pause, and for a long minute I heard nothing but distorted announcements and Jane's breathing.

"I can't do this, John. I thought I could, but I was wrong. I tried to keep things at arm's length—tell myself you were like Nick Charles or something, and your work was clever and glamorous, and somehow separate from you. But that's bullshit, and I can't pretend otherwise.

"There's nothing amusing about being followed. There's nothing witty about beatings and guns and emergency rooms. There's nothing funny about getting shot. I don't know why you want that in your life, John, but I know I don't.

"Maybe it would be different, easier, if I knew what you were looking for from this—from us. Or maybe there's no mystery to it. Maybe you're not looking for anything at all. Maybe your life is already just the way you want it, and I—" A garbled announcement went off somewhere near Jane, followed by a storm of static. When her voice returned it was clear and sad and full of conclusion.

"They're calling my flight again. I'm sorry."

I drank my orange juice and looked at my watch and played the message through twice more. It was hours since she'd left it, hours since her plane had pulled back from the gate and sped down the tarmac and climbed into the air, hours since it had wheeled above Jamaica Bay and found its heading and dwindled over some horizon. I looked out the window and up at the sky. I don't know what I expected to see, so many hours later, besides impossible blue and spun-sugar clouds and no sign at all of her passage.

ALSO BY PETER SPIEGELMAN

BLACK MAPS

John March walked away from his family's merchant bank for the life of a rural deputy sheriff—a life that would explode in personal tragedy and professional disaster. Three years later, March is back in New York City, working as a private investigator and still running from his grief and guilt. When he takes the case of Rick Pierro, a wealthy investment banker threatened by blackmail, March is swiftly drawn into a web of Wall Street insiders and outcasts, and back to a world he thought he'd left behind. The more he learns about Pierro's connections to a notorious international bank that made billions in blood money, the darker the terrain becomes. Soon March's own life is in danger, as he follows a trail of blood and shattered lives to a ruthless and depraved extortionist.

Crime Fiction/1-4000-3359-4

VINTAGE CRIME/BLACK LIZARD
Available at your local bookstore, or call toll-free to order:
1-800-793-2665 (credit cards only).